PRAISE FOR *THE LAST HOUSEWIFE*

"A truly terrifying novel."

—*Cosmopolitan*

"I barely breathed through most of this horrifyingly engrossing story, so consider yourself warned."

—*Good Housekeeping*

"Deliciously unputdownable."

—*Washington Post*

"A story that needs to be told—about misogyny, sexual violence, and human trafficking, and how innocent trust can lead to abusive seduction… This explosive cautionary tale of a 'podcast meets sex cult meets murder' will captivate fans of twisted psychological suspense."

—*Library Journal*, STARRED review

"Strap in for a terrifying tale of revenge."

—*Seattle Times*

"A noir masterpiece."

—*Southern Review of Fiction*

"As an exploration of misogyny and violence, this story hits with relevance and a timely anger."

—*New York Journal of Books*

"A dark, twisted tale of feminism and patriarchy, Ashley Winstead has given us a gripping story about a cult and the ways in which women became psychologically bound, while at the same time exploring themes of power and redemption. Timely and terrifying, *The Last Housewife* will haunt your dreams and change the way you view the world."

—Julie Clark, *New York Times* bestselling author
of *The Last Flight* and *The Lies I Tell*

"It's not every day I finish a novel and decide right then and there that the author is now an auto-buy. While I was anticipating a great story from Winstead, I wasn't expecting to inhale her new book in one breathless read. *The Last Housewife* is a propulsive, unputdownable thriller with a dark, beating heart. It chilled me to the bone, and I'm still recovering. Ashley Winstead, I bow down."

—Jennifer Hillier, author of the bestselling *Little Secrets*

"A stunning, disturbing thriller that will have your mind and heart racing. *The Last Housewife* is a clever, twisty, unnerving ride through feminism, patriarchy, and power, and it had me gasping for air."

—Samantha Downing, international bestselling
author of *For Your Own Good*

"Provocative and downright terrifying, *The Last Housewife* feels ripped from the headlines as it explores the dark world of a violent, misogynist cult in a New York college town. The story unfolds through the eyes of Shay Evans, who returns to avenge the deaths of two college friends and save the women who are still in danger. Winstead deftly tackles the complicated issues of gender, coercion, and agency while crafting an edge-of-your-seat, action-packed thriller!"

—Wendy Walker, international bestselling author
of *All Is Not Forgotten* and *Don't Look for Me*

"Ashley Winstead takes her reader into the heart of darkness—and brilliantly reveals the tender, human part hidden in those shadows.

Propulsive, smart, and chilling, *The Last Housewife* confirms what *In My Dreams I Hold a Knife* promised: no one writes thrillers like Ashley Winstead."

—Alison Wisdom, author of *The Burning Season*

"The total package—fearless, disruptive, and gripping. Ashley Winstead's talent is astounding. One of the best books I've read this year."

—Eliza Jane Brazier, author of *Good Rich People*

"Only fifty shades of grey? Please. Ashley Winstead's *The Last Housewife* is a Technicolor rainbow, provocative and unflinching in its brilliant portrayal of female desire, male violence, and the unsettling link between them. A disturbingly sexy thrill ride that does more than 'twist'—it explodes off the page, confronting dark truths about women in the patriarchy and forging weapons of resistance from the flames. You don't read *The Last Housewife*. You face it down."

—Amy Gentry, bestselling author of *Good as Gone*, *Last Woman Standing*, and *Bad Habits*

"*The Last Housewife* is a seductive, provocative work of literature, steeped in a mystery, that kept me turning page after page. The story touches on the loyalty of friendship, the determination to uncover truths no matter how difficult, and the power of a woman in the face of ever present danger and with all the decks stacked against her. I cannot wait for what Ashley Winstead brings us next."

—Yasmin Angoe, bestselling author of the critically acclaimed *Her Name Is Knight*

PRAISE FOR *IN MY DREAMS I HOLD A KNIFE*

"Deeply drawn characters and masterful storytelling come together to create an addictive and riveting psychological thriller. Put this one at the very top of your 2021 reading list."

—Liv Constantine, international bestselling author of *The Last Mrs. Parrish*

"Tense, twisty, and packed with shocks, Ashley Winstead's assured debut dares to ask how much we can trust those we know best—including ourselves. A terrific read!"

—Riley Sager, *New York Times* bestselling author of *Home Before Dark*

"Nostalgic and sinister, *In My Dreams I Hold a Knife* whisks the reader back to college. Glory days, unbreakable friendships, all-night parties, and a belief that the best in life is ahead of you. But ten years after the murder of one of the East House Seven, the unbreakable bonds may be hiding fractured secrets of a group bound not by loyalty but by fear. Twisty and compulsively readable, *In My Dreams I Hold a Knife* will have you turning pages late into the night, not just to figure out who murdered beloved Heather Shelby, but to see whether friendships forged under fire can ever be resurrected again."

—Julie Clark, *New York Times* bestselling author of *The Last Flight*

"Fans of *The Secret History*, Ruth Ware, and Andrea Bartz will devour this dark academic thriller with an addictive locked-room mystery at its core. Ten years after an unsolved campus murder, the victim's best friends reunite, knowing one might be a monster—but is anyone innocent? Over the course of a single shocking night, Ashley Winstead peels back lie after lie, exposing the poisoned roots of ambition, friendship, and belonging itself. An astonishingly sure-footed debut, *In My Dreams I Hold a Knife* is the definition of compulsive reading. The last page will give you nightmares."

—Amy Gentry, bestselling author of *Good as Gone,*
Last Woman Standing, and *Bad Habits*

"Beautiful writing, juicy secrets, complex female characters, and drumbeat suspense—what more could you want from a debut thriller? I'm Ashley Winstead's new biggest fan. If you liked Marisha Pessl's *Neverworld Wake* or Laurie Elizabeth Flynn's *The Girls Are All So Nice Here*, trust me—you will love this."

—Andrea Bartz, bestselling author of *The Lost Night* and *The Herd*

"An unsolved murder, dark secrets, and dysfunctional college days, all wrapped up in a twisty plot that will keep you flipping pages."

—Darby Kane, #1 international bestselling author of *Pretty Little Wife*

"With its compelling puzzle-box structure and delightfully ruthless cast of characters, this twisty dark academia thriller will have you flipping pages like you're pulling an all-nighter to cram for a final. *In My Dreams I Hold a Knife* is required reading for fans of Donna Tartt's *The Secret History* and Amy Gentry's *Bad Habits.*"

—Layne Fargo, author of *They Never Learn*

"Looking for an eerie campus setting? This chilling suspense novel has murder, friendship, and defiance when six people return to their college reunion a decade after one of their close friends was murdered."

—*Parade Magazine*

"[A] captivating debut… Winstead does an expert job keeping the reader guessing whodunit. Suspense fans will eagerly await her next."

—*Publishers Weekly*

"A twisty, dark puzzle... Fans of books such as *The Girl on the Train* and *Gone Girl* will find this book captivating, as will anyone who enjoys being led down a winding, frightening path. Highly recommended."

—*New York Journal of Books*

"Packed with intrigue, scandal, and enough twists and turns to match Donna Tartt's *The Secret History*, this is a solid psychological-thriller debut."

—*Booklist*

"Ashley Winstead's mordant debut novel is the latest entry in the budding subgenre of 'dark academia,' where the crime narrative takes place on a college campus... At its heart, Winstead's novel examines what it means to covet the lives of others, no matter the cost."

—*New York Times*

THE
LAST
HOUSEWIFE

a novel

ASHLEY WINSTEAD

sourcebooks landmark

Published by Sourcebooks Landmark, an imprint of Sourcebooks
P.O. Box 4410, Naperville, Illinois 60567–4410
(630) 961-3900
sourcebooks.com

The Library of Congress has cataloged the hardcover edition as follows:

Names: Winstead, Ashley, author.
Title: The last housewife : a novel / Ashley Winstead.
Description: Naperville, Illinois : Sourcebooks Landmark, [2022]
Identifiers: LCCN 2022002448 (print) | LCCN 2022002449 (ebook) |
  (hardcover) | (epub)
Subjects: LCGFT: Novels.
Classification: LCC PS3623.I6646 L37 2022 (print) | LCC PS3623.I6646
  (ebook) | DDC 813/.6--dc23
LC record available at https://lccn.loc.gov/2022002448
LC ebook record available at https://lccn.loc.gov/2022002449

Printed and bound in the United States of America.
WOZ 10 9 8 7 6 5 4 3 2 1

In the words of Patricia Lockwood: This is for every woman who isn't interested in heaven unless her anger gets to go there too.

Content warning: Suicide, rape, physical violence, sexual violence, trauma, self-harm, misogyny, gender essentialism, drug use.

PART ONE
Scheherazade, you careful actress

These are the stories I tell you to save my life.

I am naturally smooth and sun-streaked and fat-lipped in the exact way you like. (Picture me like this, dear husband, as I speak to you.)

You could have any of us. You could have so many, one right after the other. You're hardwired for it; it's the most natural thing for a man like you to take us, to plow through us, to discard. I am lucky you have chosen to keep me.

You ensure we are more than fed and sheltered, that we are rich and careless, and I am grateful. When you thrust, you reach a place deep inside me I could never reach myself.

In your arms I am safe and comfortable.

In your arms I am a good daughter and a good wife. Who has never cheated, never stolen, never offered herself to the god of sin for a single lap of pleasure. Who has never wanted something sick and troubling, who has never held her hands up to the light, watching them fill with dark, hot blood, thrill zipping her spine. Who would? Can you imagine?

These are the stories I tell you to stave off the night you will finally look at me from across the room, see the woman underneath the fiction—weaving, weaving madly—and lop off her head.

CHAPTER ONE

From a young age I could feel them watching. Could feel the weight of their eyes and their hunger pressing over my skin like the skimming fingers of a lover, or an appraiser, dragging a hand down the bones of a rare find. Like most women, I grew up with the looking, grew into it. So that even today, alone in the backyard, I can still feel those phantom eyes and shape my body to the audience. Carrying myself in ways that will please them, stretching out gracefully by the pool, back arched, eyes closed against the sun like a woman in a movie, an icon of mystery and elegance, as delicate and unknowable as Keats's maiden on the Grecian urn.

Always, before, it seemed obvious they were looking: on the street, in the grocery store, staring up from tables at restaurants. But lately, finding myself thirty and unexpectedly alone most of the time, I had begun to face certain facts. To wonder if the eyes of those men hadn't simply burned me deep enough when I was young, so the scars were still sparking years later, like a bad burn from the oven that feels alive for days. Or maybe I'd snatched their eyes, a self-protective measure, buried them deep beneath my skin, and now I was watching myself. As a feminist culture writer—at least, a former one—these were possibilities I knew to consider.

Truthfully, I wasn't doing much considering these days. I'd quit my job writing for *The Slice* six months ago, trading in thousand-word essays with titles like "Why booty shorts and baby talk are fall's surprising feminist trends" for the chance to write my first novel. I'd been waiting my entire life to write the book—my alleged passion project—yet ever since I'd had the time and means to actually do it, I'd found myself without the aforementioned passion. Without any words at all, you might say. The trouble was the ending: I couldn't fathom it, and without that, the words wouldn't flow.

So instead of writing, I'd sunk slowly into the daily rhythms familiar to the other wives in our new Highland Park neighborhood: a gluten-free breakfast, followed by yoga or Pilates, then lunch with the girls, shopping (in person or online), dinner with the husband upon his return from work, wine and sex, maybe. But always, always, a grand finale of quiet contemplation when the lights went out, wondering how the days of one's newly useless life could dissipate so quickly, like grains of sand through an hourglass. How in a twist of irony one could become a piece of art rather than an artist.

Today I was a Hockney painting, awash in still, blue boredom, the pool in the backyard calm as a glass of water. The house behind me—ours, I suppose—massive and angular in the California style so popular here in Dallas, dramatic staircases bending away from the back balcony at harsh angles, like the house was a person on two bent knees, begging to be loved. My husband, Cal, said something about it reminded him of me. He thought it would make me happy.

You look happy, I reminded myself. *Especially from far away.* I

4

accentuated the point by smoothing sunshine-yellow polish over my toenails, chin resting on my knee like a child. I decided now was as good a time as any to indulge in my favorite entertainment these last six months.

Regrettably—but perhaps also predictably—I, like every other woman my age, had become addicted to true-crime podcasts. The attraction was obvious: a morbid fascination with our own mortality. But for me, there was also this: the host of *Transgressions*, my favorite podcast, was none other than Jamie Knight, my childhood friend. It had been years since I'd spoken to Jamie, and although I knew he'd become a journalist—there was never anything else for him—it had been such a surprise to see his name in the podcast description. Such an unexpected eruption of feeling when I pressed Play and heard his voice in my ears, warm and crackling. It had touched something in me deeper than nostalgia, and while I couldn't quite name the feeling, I knew enough about it to keep my interest in *Transgressions* a secret from the other wives and from Cal.

I dabbed polish on my pinkie toe and pressed Play on the latest episode, newly arrived this morning. Jamie's voice curled into my ears, the hills and valleys of his inflections as familiar as a map of home. "Welcome back to *Transgressions*, friends. I'm your host, Jamie Knight." A memory of him flashed in my mind: seventeen and newly a man, scruff shadowing his jaw, grinning at me cheekily from the driver's seat as he drove me home from school.

"This week's murder—" Jamie's voice caught, and immediately, I sat straighter. He cleared his throat. "Hits a little close to home. Actually, that's why I'm telling you about it at all. Because *technically*, the cops haven't decided whether to rule this death a homicide or suicide. I have my suspicions, and we'll get to those, but let's start with the facts. Two weeks ago, thirty-year-old Laurel Hargrove was found hanging from a tree on the edge of the De Young Performing Arts Center on the Whitney College campus. It was her alma mater."

One minute, I was pressing the nail brush like a fan against my toe, spreading sunshine over the cuticle; the next, the bottle slipped from my hand into the pool, golden yellow snaking like spilled blood through the water.

Laurel Hargrove. Whitney College. It couldn't be. Laurel Hargrove was my best friend from college. It had been eight years since I'd talked to her, but back then, we'd sworn to run as far as possible from Whitney, from Westchester, from the entire state of New York.

And I'd done it. I'd worked hard to shut the door on the past, to keep it locked, fast and tight. *Don't let it in*, I warned myself, the instinct knee-jerk. All of my calm, blue boredom, my luxurious ennui, was replaced in an instant by visceral fear, my teeth sinking into my kneecap as if it were a leather bit to quell a scream.

"Laurel's death has all the markings of a suicide," Jamie said, his words coming faster now. "According to the police report—which I'm admittedly not supposed to have—she was hung by a rope, the kind anyone can buy at a hardware store. The furrow the rope created in her neck slanted vertical, breaking her hyoid bone and tearing her cartilage. Although some doctors have claimed injuries like Laurel's *can* occur with strangulation—you'll remember the media circus around Jeffrey Epstein's death—most agree these types of injuries occur more often in suicidal hangings."

I'd sworn to protect Laurel, years ago. How many things could you fail at in one lifetime? I felt as though I'd plunged into the pool after the nail polish, and now I was suspended underwater, pressure crushing me from every angle.

Jamie Knight, of all people, kept reciting the cold facts of Laurel's death, each detail so clinical, so...*familiar.*

I shot to my feet, pressing my hands to my mouth. Laurel's death was the twin of Clementine's, our best friend from college whose blood we would never wash from our hands. First Clem, now Laurel. Two hangings, both on campus, eight years apart.

It became hard to breathe. But even in the thick of shock, I had a sudden burst, a picture of what I must look like to anyone observing. Scene: *Beautiful Woman in the Throes of Grief.* Or: *A Portrait of Panic, All in Blue.*

"The Performing Arts Center meant something to Laurel," Jamie continued, telling me what I already knew. "According to the Westchester County police interview with her mother, Laurel was a theater nut and concentrated on costuming in college. Her mom said the Performing Arts Center was Laurel's favorite place on campus. As an undergrad, she tried to live as close as possible so she could save time going back and forth from rehearsals."

Yes, we'd worked hard to live in Rothschild. Laurel was a shy girl who worshipped theater, who lived to create costumes for Whitney's drama department. And we did everything for her because Clem and I loved her, and because to know Laurel was to want to protect her. In order to live in Rothschild's four-person suites, we'd needed to add someone to our three-person crew. We went searching, found a girl, and that was the beginning of the end. The consequences of those simple decisions—*make Laurel happy, find a fourth, give the girl a chance*—would reverberate forever.

"Putting these pieces together paints a picture of a woman who took her own life in a place that was meaningful to her," Jamie said. "In fact, Laurel's mother told the police that college was the last time she could remember Laurel being happy. So why discuss Laurel Hargrove's suicide on a podcast about unsolved murders?"

I bent down and snatched my phone, wishing I could talk back to him, yell across the distance. *Why* are *you, Jamie? Clem committed suicide, and it was so clearly, so irrevocably our fault. And now Laurel. What does it mean? What are you saying?*

"One detail in the police report caught my attention," Jamie said, answering me. "And yes, I'm going to get in trouble for telling you this. But Laurel was discovered with lacerations all over her hands and arms, made roughly around the time of her death. None of them life-threatening, but cuts everywhere, fourteen in all. There aren't any pictures of her included in the police record—which is strange, by the way. But what the responding officer did note is that the cuts were thin, like from a razor blade. And they appeared in places you would expect if someone was defending herself. There's actually a question in the police report, written in the officer's notes, which he or somebody else later tried to scratch out. He wrote: 'Defensive wounds? But why, if suicide?' Why, indeed."

Thin cuts, like from a razor blade. This was too much. I rushed across the grass, blades bright and stiff under my feet despite the August swelter. Clutching the phone to my chest, I caught my reflection in the glass of the back door—wild-eyed, shoulders hunched—before I flung it open and slipped inside.

The frigid air-conditioning sucked the summer heat from my skin. I'd come inside to feel safe, contained. But one glance at the sweeping white ceilings, the gleaming kitchen, the sharp, modern furniture— all of it, my choices—and I felt suddenly wrong. Like I'd entered not a home but a museum, a mausoleum. A cold, beautiful place where things were laid to rest.

"One more thing," said Jamie, from the center of my chest. "I told you Laurel Hargrove's death hits close to home. Here's why. Years ago, I met her."

I jerked the phone away, studying the screen as if it were Jamie himself standing in front of me.

"When I was younger, I was friends with a girl who went to Whitney at the same time that I went to Columbia. The schools are an hour apart, so we'd see each other from time to time, usually after I'd begged her enough times to come visit. She and I had a...complicated relationship, to say the least. And she was friends with Laurel."

Me. Jamie Knight was talking about me.

CHAPTER TWO

"This is the part I can't shake." Jamie paused. "The same day I met Laurel Hargrove, I met another girl who would end up committing suicide— only she died much sooner, by the end of our senior year." His voice caught again. "Clementine Jones was her name."

Of course he remembered Clem. There was no way he'd forget, given the circumstances.

"The truth is," Jamie continued, "meeting them went poorly. Have you ever had an encounter that went so wrong you lay awake at night reliving it? Months later, when I heard Clementine committed suicide, I couldn't get in touch with my friend or get any details from the news. It was hushed up quickly, which at the time seemed reasonable. It's tragic, right? Someone that young, on the cusp of graduating and starting her life. About to get free."

Get free. It was like Jamie was speaking to me in code. I thought of how he'd met Clem and Laurel—what he'd witnessed—and pressed a hand over my eyes, as if not looking could block the memories.

How much about us had Jamie guessed?

"Now, this was years ago," he said, "but I still remember Clementine Jones hung herself. That stuck with me. Left an impression. So when I realized I'd met Laurel—that she'd been there the same day I'd met Clementine—I thought: what are the odds two of the three girls I've ever met from Whitney both hung themselves? I went digging into Clementine's death, looking for details. I couldn't find much—just one old, flimsy police record that said her body was found on campus. But— and here's where it gets stranger—not in her dorm. She was found in the Cargill Sports Center, which is Whitney's big athletic center. In other words, this girl was found, just like Laurel, in an eerily public place."

They'd found Clem hanging in the women's showers, actually. Fully clothed, her chin bent to her chest, fragile and limp as a broken dandelion. A delicateness in death she would have hated in life. Clem had once been the star of the Whitney women's soccer team, and Cargill had been a home to her as much as the Performing Arts Center had been to Laurel. I'd always thought she'd done it there because it was the last place left where she felt safe.

"What we have, dear listeners, is a pattern. Now, I tried to find my old friend, the one who knew Clementine and Laurel back then, to see what she could tell me. But this friend has dropped off the face of the planet."

He'd tried to find me. Just for his show, but still. And it was true: I'd gotten new contact info after college, my articles were up on *The Slice* under a pen name, and my work email was no longer active. I had no social media, and I was Shay Deroy now, not Shay Evans. I'd bet anything Jamie had reached out to my mother—which meant she must have shielded me, respected my wish for privacy. It was entirely unlike her.

I'd run after college. I hadn't looked back. And *still* this had found me. I'd pressed Play on Jamie's episode like Cleopatra sliding the lid off the woven basket, unaware of the coiled asp inside.

"Two friends," Jamie said, "who died in disturbingly similar ways. It could be a coincidence, I grant you. Suicides are more common than people think, especially among college students. And maybe the fact that Laurel and Clementine knew each other makes it even more likely Laurel's death was a suicide. A kind of contagion effect, but in super slow motion. I don't know... I just have a hunch the deaths are connected in a way I can't see."

He was putting pieces together, but there was still so much Jamie didn't know. Case in point: a small, painful detail no one knew except the people who'd found Clem that day, and those of us close enough to her to hear the details of her death. Remembering made my skin flush, despite the air-conditioning, a sensation I recognized as the beginnings of panic.

Carved into Clem's forearm, they'd found thin, bloody letters, spelling out *IM SORRY*. They'd never found the weapon, but there were small cuts on the fingers of her right hand, in the places where she would have held a razor or a knife. It was clear she'd carved the words herself.

Meaning it was obviously a suicide. Right? Eight years ago, when I saw what Clem had done, I'd accepted the truth immediately— recognized that it made a deep, awful kind of sense. It had been powerful enough to break through the fog of my mind, like a lifeline cast into the sea of my disordered thinking. It had shaken me, made me see sharp and clear again. In the worst irony, Clem's death had given me back my life.

But now Laurel was dead the same way, in the same pattern. With razor-blade marks all over her arms and her hands, just no words.

Jamie's voice returned to the kitchen, warm against the cold. "The last thing I'll say before we take an ad break is that, in the absence of information about Laurel and Clementine—like I said, the police reports are thin, and neither death received much media attention—I decided to widen my search and look at other women's deaths in the Hudson Valley area since Clementine died. You know I'm always searching for patterns, and I can be persistent. What I found was alarming. There has been a high—and I mean *unusually* high—number of missing persons reports for women aged eighteen to thirty-five in the last eight years."

I gripped the phone so hard I thought, for a moment, I might shatter it.

"Why is there an eleven percent higher chance a woman will go missing in this region than in any other place in America? Eleven percent might not seem big, but it is. Statistically, the area's an anomaly. Where are these women disappearing to, and why is no one paying attention? We're talking about an unsolved mystery right in my own backyard, and I had no idea until now.

"Research shows the only high-profile person to reference the disappearances is Governor Alec Barry, who vowed to investigate two years ago in his State of the State address. But his investigation doesn't seem to have amounted to much. When our producers talked to some of the women's families, most said they'd given them up as runaways—or suicides.

"So here's my transgression of the day, and it comes in the form of a question. Laurel and Clementine fall into the same age group, and their 'suicides'—that's in air quotes, by the way—essentially bookend the years we've seen these other women go missing. According to her file, Clementine's parents called from their home in Wisconsin a few months before she died, trying to file a missing person's report, but the police dismissed it after they confirmed she was attending classes. And Laurel's mother told the police it had been years since she spoke to her daughter. Missing, then dead; missing, then dead. Could there be a connection between Laurel's and Clementine's deaths and these other women?"

It felt again like Jamie Knight was sending a private message to me, hidden in a podcast episode.

And then it was no longer private.

"If *anyone* out there has information, big or small, email my producers." Another pause, longer this time. "And if my friend from long ago ever hears this, the one who went dark…call me. Please. My number's still the same."

The next moment, Jamie's voice was replaced by a cheerful woman recommending a brand of rosé guaranteed to slim your waistline. I clicked out of the episode.

Standing frozen in my bikini, surrounded by the gleaming white kitchen, I knew I was the wrong kind of picture. An aberration in this home, this monument I'd built to moving on. I could feel its displeasure. It wanted me calm and docile, and in my panic I was disobeying.

Don't think like that, I told myself. *Not everything is sinister. Not everyone has bad intentions.*

But I fled the kitchen anyway, sprinting upstairs to the master bedroom, straight to my walk-in closet, shutting the door to make the space tight and secure. I ripped off my bathing suit and pulled on stretchy pants and a sweatshirt, wrapping myself in comfort, cover. These renegade thoughts were popping up more frequently, whenever Cal went away on his work trips. In his absence, my mind churned, twisting my life into a more disquieting picture. The house didn't want me *docile*. That was ridiculous. I needed to stay calm and think.

My phone buzzed from where it lay on the floor, Cal's face suddenly grinning up at me. I jumped, heart pounding. One hand pressed to my chest, I waited until the call died, then peered at the text flashing on the screen: You went to Houndstooth without me! Such a betrayal...

A stupid joke, so divorced from the news of Laurel's death that I almost laughed at the sheer incongruity—except for the image that flashed in my head: Cal sitting in his hotel room, at his laptop, poring over our credit-card charges. Checking my spending like I was a child. Knowing where I'd gotten my coffee this morning, from hundreds of miles away.

But he was only being responsible. Keeping the life we shared in order was a form of intimacy, wasn't it? Plenty of the Highland Park husbands managed their household finances. I forced myself to leave the closet, heading back downstairs, but the slap of my feet against the steps wasn't enough to drown out Jamie's voice, Laurel's death, Clem's memory. The ghosts had been unleashed, and now I couldn't stop seeing my life through their eyes, couldn't escape the suspicion that if they saw me here, in this cold, empty house, they'd shake me by the shoulders.

Cal and I had gotten married a year ago, and everything had been fine until I'd quit my job six months ago. Then the balance of power had shifted. Cal would refuse to admit there was even such a thing as a balance of power between us. According to him, that wasn't how good marriages worked. And maybe he was right, maybe I was too sensitive because of how I'd grown up, watching my mom contort herself to keep men around, or too paranoid because of what happened in college. Because every time *I* saw two people, I saw a scale, tipping this way and that. And the scale had been tipped toward Cal for a long time. Oh, he would deny it, but now *he* held the purse strings; now every big decision was ultimately his. It had been six months of checked charges, of attending fancy Highland Park parties on his arm, of insipid gossip and aching loneliness, of staring at the blinking cursor on my laptop's blank screen.

Six months, and here was the truth: I wasn't a writer. I'd turned into a housewife.

What would Laurel have said to that? Dear god, *Clem*?

I looked up and caught my reflection in the window above the sink. Raised fingers to my cheeks. I was crying, gentle tears tracking down my face. I hadn't even felt it start. I'd trained myself to do this, years ago. To cry effortlessly, elegantly, like a silent movie actress. But now that I was older, the tears had a habit of creeping up on me, arriving when I least expected. Maybe I'd performed for so long I wasn't capable of recognizing my real feelings. Were there even such things, or was everyone always reacting in ways we understood we were supposed to? When did the performance ever end?

Mentally, I slapped myself, and bit my tongue as punishment. It ended when you were dead, for fuck's sake. When your body was found hanging from a tree or a showerhead in the place you loved most, the place you used to sit for hours reading scripts, or where you were a star, your body flying strong and triumphant across the grass. It ended when you killed yourself, or when somebody killed you, and all your chances to wake and breathe and cry were stolen from you forever. When everyone who was supposed to love you brushed your death aside, and the only one who cared to look deeper was a stranger. A true-crime podcast host.

But I cared. That was the truth I couldn't shake, the one that followed me no matter where I hid, staring back from every mirror, screen, and window. I'd sequestered myself in a safe, faraway place, and still the past had found me.

Now I had a choice.

I could almost see myself making the decision, as if I were floating outside my own body. I would not let Laurel and Clem disappear into the fog of forgotten people. I'd told Laurel I would protect her, and instead I'd run. I'd promised Clem I would stick by her, yet I'd chosen wrong when it counted. I'd failed too many women.

I would not leave this to Jamie Knight, even if he was more qualified. I would go back to New York, and I would find out what happened to Laurel. I would trace the contours of her life since I couldn't hold her hands. I would pick up her memory and cradle it. I would whisper my apologies; I would kneel on my hands and my knees in the place where she'd died and I would repent. If it was true someone had hurt her—if someone had killed her—then I would find out who and I would protect her, years too late, the only way I could.

I clutched my phone and sprinted back upstairs, through the master bedroom to the walk-in closet, where my suitcase stood tucked and waiting in the corner.

CHAPTER THREE

When I arrived in New York at eighteen, I understood for the first time that there are some places in this world with *presence*. Watching the landscape change through the window on the train up from the city, I saw the gulf between where I was coming from—a strip-mall suburb in East Texas—and the Hudson Valley, where the wide, open sky didn't just exist but confronted you. Where the dark Catskills rising in the distance made you feel small and the unrelenting river had a heartbeat, a voice that whispered you might be here now, but it had been here long before and would be long after.

Whitney was only a short train ride up from New York City, but that first time, it felt like entering a new world, one in which my life would truly begin. The day was full of firsts: my first plane ride, first train ride, hell, first time setting foot outside the great state of Texas. Unlike Heller, a Reagan-era boom town whose history was charted only by the slow evolution of fast-food signs, the towns that made up the Hudson Valley were suffused with a past so rich it was nearly tangible. The towns held the former homes or headquarters of George Washington and FDR, Vanderbilts and Rockefellers, sites from the American Revolutionary War. And they thrummed with green beauty—so much that they'd given rise, I'd read, to the first true school of American painters. This, I'd thought, was where the kind of life that made history books happened.

Now, after eight years away, my awareness was finer-tuned. I understood what made the Hudson Valley beautiful, what kept the history pristine, towns quaint, land wild: money. Old money and new. Families with far-reaching Dutch heritages, New York City financiers and real estate tycoons, renowned artists, Hollywood actors—all of them had homes here, lives here. Often second lives, hidden chapters that could unfold in the dark, in a place fewer people were watching.

I drove my rental car down a residential street lined with trees and dappled with sunshine, stifling a yawn. Cross-country flights were exhausting. At this point, I couldn't remember what I'd packed yesterday. I'd moved through my closet in a fugue state, pulling clothes off hangers and stuffing them in my suitcase. It had seemed critical to pack quickly, to purchase a seat on the next available flight and push myself out the door before Cal called or anything else intervened to change my mind.

Speaking of. I glanced at my phone, to the text I'd sent Cal and his response.

> **Me:** Hey, decided to go to New York for a few days. Wanted to see if my old stomping grounds inspired me. See you when we're both back.
>
> **Calvin:** You should have told me! Could've had my assistant book your travel. Hope you solve your writer's block. Call you later.

I'd bought myself a week, max, before Cal was back from his trip to some hedge fund they were looking to buy in Silicon Valley. Given the timeline, I'd have to work fast. I glanced at the bag from the airport gift shop that held my slapdash supplies: a laughably bright-purple notebook from the Lisa Frank line, all they'd had left; a slim packet of pens, thankfully normal; and a portable cell-phone charger. I assumed this was the full battery of things I'd need for an investigation. Jamie Knight would probably shake his head at me.

According to my phone, cutting through this neighborhood was the shortest route to the River Estate, a swanky hotel I'd only dreamed of staying in when I was an undergrad. But I had a whole new lifestyle now, thanks to Cal's money.

Your money, I corrected, but only out of habit.

Most of the houses were large and set back from the road, hidden behind walls of trees. But up ahead, one of the mansions revealed itself, the first to forgo a privacy gate. I felt my foot lift off the gas, and the car slowed to a stop.

It was the architecture that haunted me. A particular style of Tudor I hadn't found anywhere else. The roof climbing into vaunted triangles, sharp as knifepoints, stabbing the air. The stone facade covered with a lattice of brown bars, fitting around the house like a cage. The shades in the windows drawn tight, so no one could see in or out. The lawn so wide, so far to run; the bushes so neat, so full of hidden thorns to snag your stockings, to slow you, to hold you down until that dark shadow towered over you and you were reclaimed.

Cold fear washed through me. I jammed the gas and raced away.

An hour later, after checking in to the hotel—still as glamorous as I remembered—and carefully reapplying my makeup, I pulled up to the

Yonkers police station. The muscles in my stomach tightened in anticipation. In my lifetime, I'd visited this station more times than I would've
liked, and far less than I should have.

Inside was nicer than it used to be: fresh paint on the walls, friendly
posters of police officers shaking people's hands, directional signs in
slender sans serif spelling out *Booking, Restrooms, Front Desk.*

I approached the front desk, and a woman only a few years older
than me swiveled in her seat. "How can I help you?"

I tucked a piece of hair behind my ear. "I'd like to speak to someone
about Laurel Hargrove's death."

Immediately, her eyes narrowed. "Let me guess. You listened to the
podcast."

Jamie's podcast? "Well, yes, but—"

"We're running an investigation," she snapped. "Not catering to the
whims of bored amateur sleuths."

I gave her a pointed look. "I know Laurel. I was one of her roommates in college. I'd like to speak to whoever's in charge of her investigation. I know information that might help."

She studied me. This is why I'd redone my makeup. I knew the difference a polished facade could make. I flashed her a beauty queen's smile.

"Hold on," she sighed, turning and picking up the phone. A second
later she was saying something in a low voice, then nodding at a closed
door to my left. "Chief'll be right with you."

The chief of police? That was unusual, wasn't it, for a chief to handle
something like this? Before I had too long to think, the door swung
open and a familiar face frowned at me, nothing changed in eight long
years besides some extra lines around his eyes.

"You the friend of Hargrove?"

I waited for some sign of recognition—a light in his eyes, a head nod,
something—but there was nothing on his face but gruff annoyance.

I adjusted my purse strap. "Yes. You're in charge of her case?"

He made a beckoning gesture. "Follow me."

I studied his back as we walked deeper into the station, past an open floor full of desks. So, Detective Adam Dorsey was the chief of police now. Not only that, but he was handling Laurel's case. What were the odds the same man who'd been in charge of her case freshman year would be the one investigating her death more than a decade later? Yonkers wasn't *that* small.

The chief gestured for me to enter a corner office. I perched on the edge of a chair and waited for him to drop himself, with a heavy sigh, on the other side of the desk.

"Okay then." He steepled his fingers. "Name? Relationship? Let's hear it."

Dorsey had already been graying a decade ago, the first time we sat before him. He was a tall man with broad shoulders that strained his crisply ironed shirt, and serious bulk in his stomach, barely leashed in by his belt. His lashes were stubby, but the eyes beneath were sharp. The disbelieving way he squinted at me stirred déjà vu.

I couldn't believe they'd given him more responsibility, made him the one in charge. How did men like him keep climbing?

"I'm Shay Deroy." I wiped damp palms against my knees, but my voice betrayed nothing. "Like I told the woman at the front desk, I was Laurel Hargrove's roommate at Whitney. We attended together from 2010 to 2014. I knew her very well. Probably better than anyone."

"I see." Chief Dorsey picked up a pen and held it poised over a legal pad. "So, you spoke with her often, then?"

"No, I—" I felt my cheeks flush. "We actually hadn't talked since graduation."

He looked up. "Since 2014? You hadn't spoken to her in *eight* years?"

"Yes, but—"

"Well. Shit. At least if you'd said anything different, I would've known you were lying. Laurel Hargrove didn't even own a landline."

Didn't own a—"What?"

"You said you had information?"

I sat up straighter, remembering how I'd been on alert just like this, in this same station, in front of this same man, years before. "I can tell you what kind of person Laurel was, who she used to spend time with, what…"

On reflex, I stopped before saying, *what happened to us in college.* But I'd come here to do what Laurel needed of me, so I took a deep breath. "What we did back then." That was probably truer, anyway. "I'd like to know where you are with her case."

"Lady, first of all, I don't have to tell you nothing." Chief Dorsey settled back in his seat. "Second, I don't care what a thirty-year-old woman got up to in college. Unless you have more updated intel, I'm afraid I'm going to have to ask you to skedaddle."

"Shouldn't you hear what I have to say?" My voice was steely. I was no longer a scared eighteen-year-old girl. "Isn't everything pertinent in a murder case?"

The chief slapped down his pen. "A *murder* case? See, I *knew* you were one of those podcast people. You crazies have been lighting up our call board for a damn twenty-four hours. If I ever catch that bottle-necked prick who stole our report, I'm going to skin him alive. Vultures, all of you."

This was the Adam Dorsey I remembered.

"Sir, I'm not a 'podcast person.' I'm here with information about Laurel to help you with her murder case. Are you actually turning me down?"

"Her *murder.*" Chief Dorsey practically spit the word. "It's a goddamn suicide, like we've told every one of you. We made the official ruling

23

this morning. After considering the full evidence, it was cut and dry. A depressed woman hung herself. The end."

"You made the ruling?" I blinked at him. "What about the cuts all over her arms?"

"You ever climbed a tree and tied a noose to hang yourself? The cuts were from that. Just because some moron with a microphone says he has questions doesn't change a thing about the facts of the case."

"Why did you even talk to me, then? Why bring me to your office?"

Dorsey's eyes gleamed. "You're the first crazy to show up in person. I wanted the chance to tear you a new one. So here it is: You're a disgrace with no respect for the law. You should be ashamed of yourself."

The familiar words were a trigger. I shot from the chair. "You don't even remember me, do you? Or that Laurel sat in front of you when she was eighteen and cried her heart out, and you did nothing to help her. Do you remember you left us to fend for ourselves?"

Dorsey's face was bright-red now; his stubby lashes blinked quickly. "I read Laurel's file, so yes, I'm aware I was her intake officer. But no, I don't happen to remember her. Do you know how many sobbing women cycle through this place?" The chief stood and gripped the edge of his desk, forearms flexing. "Telling their pitiful stories, reeking of booze. *Oh, he hurt me. Oh, he kissed me when I didn't want him to.* Meanwhile they're standing there in a dress that barely covers their ass, after spending all night pounding beers and flirting and doing God knows what else. And they have the nerve to ask why it keeps happening to them."

"You're the disgrace," I said, mouth moving ahead of my brain. "You're the one who should be ashamed."

He thrust a finger in my face. "Get out of my office, and tell your psycho friends to stop wasting their lives on internet conspiracies and start contributing to society. Or you can all rot."

I practically tripped in my haste to leave, wrenching open the chief's door and storming out. I could feel the eyes of the officers at their desks following me until I disappeared into the lobby.

"Thanks for nothing," I said to the woman at the desk and strode out of the station, chest heaving.

What a disaster. Why had I thought going to the police was the right answer, when they hadn't helped before? It was like the years I'd spent away, safely nestled in Cal's blue-blood crowd, had erased those lessons.

And Adam Dorsey—that motherfucker. I pulled at the driver's door, cursing when it wouldn't yield, stabbing the key fob until it finally unlocked and I could throw myself in.

He was every inch as terrible, as condescending, as he'd been when we were freshmen. Except now he had so much more power. Whatever nascent, half-formed fantasy I'd conjured about partnering with the police—my vision of coming here and sharing information, of helping them dig into my friend's life until we found answers—was a crock of shit. Dorsey had shut me down as summarily as he had in college. I was on my own.

I peeled out of the parking lot and sped onto the street, foot heavy on the gas, no idea where I was going but going there fast.

The streets were familiar, even if the stores had changed. I found myself almost unconsciously taking turns, like I was pulled by a magnet. I only realized where I was heading when the streets turned wider, the urban sprawl surrounding the police station relaxing into residential homes, pine trees lining the road, dense branches forming an awning over the asphalt.

I was going back to school.

And there it was, the long, perfectly groomed hedge and large silver letters announcing Whitney College. Behind it, a swell of trees, vivid green lawns, and muted brick buildings, a campus that looked more like a summer camp, or another tony suburb. I turned in, driving down a street I'd traveled a million times, half in waking life, half in dreams.

I passed the science center, the faculty house, then Davis, the large, sprawling dining hall. There was no looking at Davis and not remembering going to their cheesy themed dinners with Laurel and Clem, or studying together in the lounge until ungodly late hours. Their famous weekend brunches, heaven for a kid like me who'd grown up worrying about her next meal. Clem's plate stacked unapologetically high with waffles—soccer carbo-loading. Laurel downing thimble after thimble of espresso, a habit that had started as a way to impress the other theater students, then morphed into an addiction.

Today there were students everywhere: crossing the lawns, jogging down the side of the road, trickling in and out of Davis. It hadn't occurred to me they'd be back already, but of course—it was nearly Labor Day. If I remembered right, school would've started about a week ago. They'd had a death on campus before fall semester even began, but you couldn't tell by the way the students buzzed around, calling to each other and laughing.

They hadn't changed much since my time. Kids with brightly dyed hair, septum piercings, undercuts and side shaves; others with long, scraggly hair, defiant acne, thrift-store clothing. The campus was a sea of black, rainbow-flag shirts the lone exception.

Whitney: the most progressive school in America, according to the *Fiske Guide to Colleges*. How we'd groaned, Laurel and I, whenever someone said, "Whitney—that's the school for commies and lesbos, right?" Clem had loved it, would always say, "Damn straight." And the truth was, Laurel and I had liked the school's reputation, too, no matter how much we complained.

We'd made our choice, after all, had come here for a reason. For me, it had been an act of defiance, of self-naming, and so no matter how hard I rolled my eyes, inside I cherished what attending meant about me. The reputation was a shield, a suit of armor I was determined to grow into. We'd marched in the quad for equal pay, signed petitions, and watched ads from the fifties in our history of gender class, snickering at the women vacuuming in black and white, those poor, blind fools.

None of it had saved us.

Laurel had died a week before school started. That meant campus had been much quieter that day, and the next when her body was found. I was suddenly desperate to talk to the person who'd found her, to know exactly what they'd seen. But without help from the police, I had no idea where to start.

Up ahead on the left rose KPR, the three largest, newest dorms—at least when we went here. I counted as I passed: Kimball, Penfield… and Rothschild. Where we'd lived junior and senior years, at least on paper.

Rothschild's redbrick walls, long, slender white columns, and tall windows were unchanged. If anything was different, it was me. Where once I'd coveted this place, looked at it with longing, now it looked painfully ordinary. Nowhere close to my Highland Park house, beautiful and begging on its knees.

I dragged my eyes away, knowing the Performing Arts Center came next. I turned right, sliding into the parking lot across the street, near Lynd House. The simple tug of my hand, leading me to the right place— more muscle memory than anything—filled me with a sudden swell of profound, almost desperate gratitude.

I parked and pulled my keys from the ignition. They hadn't changed it, then. Hadn't moved the buildings like chess pieces or torn down the places I remembered. Part of me had feared it, after eight years away: coming back to find campus unrecognizable. To find all that was left of my life with Laurel and Clem were the memories inside my head—such an unreliable place to store such precious things. But the campus I remembered was still here, which confirmed what happened had been real. No one could say otherwise. No one could take that away from me.

I gripped the steering wheel. And this time, I felt it when I started to cry.

CHAPTER FOUR

I met Laurel Hargrove twelve years ago, a few weeks after the start of freshman year. I'd lived on the other side of campus then, in McClellan, and classes had just started. Those classes brought temporary friends, girls who invited me to come with them to parties so they didn't have to go alone. Some of the parties were in Sussman Woods, some in Pinehall, but the best were off campus, in the houses students shared by the half dozen, all crammed in, or else in ones their rich parents had bought them, letting them live alone like young millionaires.

That Saturday's party had been at one of the crammed houses. When I arrived with a group of girls from art history, we were introduced to at least five guys who lived there, all of them varying degrees of Whitney-unkempt-intellectual, none of them interesting enough to make me want to break away. The party turned into a rager, and everyone I came with got too drunk on cheap beer. We sang to Arcade Fire, tripped over tables, broke bottles out on the back patio where the smokers held court. And at the end of the night, we all stumbled home, holding on to each other.

When I woke the next morning in my single dorm, mouth full of cotton, I'd groped for my phone, then tore through my room—twice—before admitting I'd left it at the party and would have to go back. Even at eighteen, I knew the last thing you wanted to do with a party was look it square in the face in the light of day.

A shirtless guy, hair past his shoulders, answered the door, shrugging when I asked if I could look around. He quickly slumped back upstairs, and I was on my own. The house was trashed but eerily quiet, like a battleground in the aftermath of combat, all the boys who lived there either outside or out cold. I'd just found my phone wedged into a couch cushion—miracle of miracles—when I heard it: a single, heart-rending sob.

I froze. There it was again, the sound of pain raked with fear. Goose bumps crawled up my arms. The crying sounded like it was coming from underneath the floorboards. I crept through the house until I found a set of recessed stairs in the corner of the kitchen.

It was pitch-black wherever the stairs led. In Texas, we didn't have many basements, so the mere presence of this subterranean layer struck me immediately as sinister.

I called softly into the darkness. "Hello?"

The sobbing stopped. It had definitely come from down there. And I couldn't, god help me, leave without checking, even though I knew this was how girls died in horror movies. Against my better judgment, I climbed down the stairs, gripping an unfinished wooden rail I was sure would give me splinters.

I stepped off the staircase, eyes adjusting to the darkness. The moment my vision sharpened, I saw her.

She was so pale she practically glowed. Her hair was blond and stringy, falling past her shoulders. She wore nothing but a spaghetti-strap shirt, and her bottom half was naked. She crouched over a futon, trying to cover herself with her hands, her eyes huge and dilated. A sound came out, escaping her involuntarily, something between a sob and a hiccup.

I stopped midstep. "What happened?" Strange, I would think later, that I didn't introduce myself, ask her name first, something humanizing. But some part of me recognized the scene—*woman in danger*—and my instincts kicked in: *First, identify the threat.*

She tried to take a deep breath, but it turned into a ragged noise in her throat. "He," it sounded like. Her hands were still crossed over her lower half. I couldn't tell the color of her eyes—they were too bloodshot, the foggy circles of mascara underneath too distracting.

"He? Who?"

"We came down here to do shots." Her tone had turned pleading, like there was something she needed me to understand. "He said he could show me a trick where he lit his mouth on fire, but only with the amaretto. It was fine for a while, funny, but then I felt sick. And the ground…"

She squeezed her eyes shut. My heart beat fast enough to match her pulse, which I could see, jumping in her throat.

"It tilted. I lay down right here"—she looked at the futon—"and I think I fell asleep. The next thing I knew—" She stopped. The next thing was something she didn't want to say.

I scanned the room. Just as messy as upstairs. A flat-screen TV and a video game console. And there, in the corner near a mini-fridge, a slip of light-blue skirt, tangled with panties. I snatched the pile and handed it to the girl. Her fingers curled around the fabric.

"I'll turn around," I said quickly. With my back to her, I could hear her moving, soft and slow, like she was still reorienting herself to her body.

Her voice was quiet. "I woke up, and he was on top of me. There was this second where I was confused. He was weighing me down, fumbling, and I didn't understand. That's why I didn't move at first. I didn't realize."

I started to turn around, but she said, "Don't. Please."

I bit my tongue and nodded.

"I begged him to get off. But he just kept shushing me." There was that sound again, like a sob she'd tried and failed to stop. "When he finished, he sat there and drank a beer."

I closed my eyes.

"I was too scared to say anything. I was afraid he'd do it again, and I still felt so dizzy. My legs were too heavy to move."

Now I recognized her tone. She was justifying. Explaining why she hadn't run or yelled, how the fear and alcohol had combined to make her paralyzed and docile. She was already anticipating the arguments against her. I wanted to turn around and tell her she didn't have to do that, that I understood.

"I felt like my heart was going to pound out of my chest," she said.

"Then what happened?"

"He left, and at some point, I think I passed out again."

This time, I turned around. "Did you just wake up?"

The girl nodded, rubbing her eyes. Now that she was dressed, I saw that her top and skirt matched perfectly, pretty sky blue, like a little set you would sew for a doll. "I can't make myself go upstairs." A desperate note sank her voice. "I'd rather die than see him again."

I thought of the things I'd wanted someone to say to me. "You don't have to do anything you don't want to. But I do want to get you out of here." A beat. "What's your name?"

She crossed her arms over her chest like she was cold, despite the humid basement, and whispered, "Laurel."

"Laurel, I'm Shay. Trust me, I understand what you're feeling. Will you tell me the guy's name?"

"Andrew," she said quietly. "I don't know his last name. I'm sorry. But he lives here."

I nodded. "Good. What do you think about talking to the police? I can come with you." I gestured to the stairs. "I was just upstairs, and it's empty. If you say yes, I'll go first, and we can slip out the front door and go straight to the station."

She looked at me with hope and fear. "Okay," she whispered.

I blinked in surprise, then held out my hand. Laurel stepped forward and took it. Her skin was paper thin. I would always remember that about her, how the skin of her hands was so fragile, you couldn't help rubbing it with your thumb.

I tugged her up the stairs, moving slowly, listening. But there was nothing, so we proceeded out of the darkness, creeping across the house, closing in on the front door.

Then the thunderous sound of footsteps down the staircase made us jerk to a halt. I threw myself in front of Laurel, who shrank behind me.

But it was just another girl. Short and stocky, with close-cropped pink hair and a silver nose ring. "Hey," she boomed. "Fellow walk-of-shamers. Excellent." She waved at the door. "Going back to Whitney, right?"

I could feel Laurel shaking by the brush of her hair against my shoulders.

"Yes... I mean, no," I stammered. "We're not going there."

The girl frowned. "Is something wrong?"

"No, nothing." I tugged Laurel out the door. The early September sun was still high and hot, so I squinted, shielding my eyes.

To my surprise, the pink-haired girl raced after us. "Wait," she called, but Laurel and I kept going. I could feel Laurel's nerves wrapping around me like a staticky blanket.

"Did something happen?"

I stilled, then turned. "Do you know something?"

She shook her head, but the way she looked at Laurel… It was recognition. "I've seen that look before. Did someone hurt you?"

My hackles rose. I expected Laurel to deny it, shut down this invasive stranger and run away, but instead she exhaled and said, "Andrew. He…wouldn't stop."

The girl's reaction was instantaneous: her cheeks flamed, and her eyes flew wide. "That fucker… I *know* him." She turned for the house. "I'll *kill* him."

"Wait," Laurel pleaded. "Please. I don't want to see him."

"We're going to the police," I said in a low voice, eyes tracking to the house. We'd left, but we hadn't made it far. I was painfully aware of who might overhear us.

The girl's eyes searched me, then Laurel. There was a quality to her expressions, a rare kind of openness. "Can I come? I don't have to go in with you. Just want to walk you there."

It was the last thing I'd expected. I turned to Laurel.

"Okay," she said softly, surprising me again.

So then it was the three of us, Dorothy and her menagerie, walking the yellow brick road. The pink-haired girl introduced herself as Clementine Jones, Clem for short. She did most of the talking, which was a favor. Laurel was bone-tired, still in shock. I could tell every time she re-woke to her body because she gave a little start. We walked and walked through neighborhoods, and all the while Clem rattled on, telling us about growing up in Wisconsin with a big family, being a soccer fanatic in high school and here at Whitney, where she played striker. She was telling us about her strange roommates, one of whom was obsessed with anime, when we arrived at the station.

"It'll be okay," I said to Laurel, when she froze. "I'm not going anywhere."

"And I'll be right out here." Clem pointed to a bench.

"Come with me," Laurel said. "I need you both to make me do it."

Clem and I looked at each other.

"Of course," she said.

I think that was the moment I decided to love her.

We waited our turn to talk to the woman behind the counter, who was gray-haired and old enough to be our grandmother. "Yes?" she asked without looking up.

"We're... I'm here..." Laurel's voice faltered. She looked down at her hands, her fingers twisting.

"Laurel was hurt by a boy named Andrew at a party," Clem said, looking at the woman expectantly. "We have his address. We can take you there."

"She was raped," I clarified. The word reverberated in the lobby, but I pressed on. "We need to file a police report. Press charges. Whatever the protocol is."

The older woman pushed a clipboard at Laurel, then pointed to the chairs. "Fill this out, then you'll wait to speak with a detective."

From the paperwork, I learned Laurel's last name was Hargrove, that she was from South Bend, Indiana, and that she had only a mother left, like me. Then we waited. And waited.

Finally, the receptionist led us through the door into the heart of the station, a massive open room full of desks, and dropped us off at one with a placard that read Detective Adam Dorsey. Officers milled around, and for some reason, even though we were here for help, they put me on edge. I tracked their movements out of the corner of my eye as we waited. It was only the circumstances, I told myself.

Detective Dorsey rushed to us, obviously in a hurry, and perched on the edge of his desk. He leaned close to Laurel, eyeing her. She leaned back. Then Dorsey studied Clem and me, lingering on Clem's pink hair. "So. You want to report a rape?"

35

ASHLEY WINSTEAD

His casual bluntness was startling. Clem adjusted in her seat. "Laurel was at a party—"

"I want to hear it from the girl," the detective said. "Not her friends."

It was an odd way to talk about Laurel, who was sitting right there, but she gathered her breath and told the detective every detail. He kept interrupting to ask terse questions: Had she thought Andrew was attractive, had she been interested in him? To which Laurel replied, red-faced, yes, but obviously only at first. Had Laurel intended to have sex with him, and if so, had she hinted at the possibility? To which Laurel grew even more red-faced and said no, she hadn't been planning to have sex with him. Because she was a virgin, and a party wasn't how she'd imagined her first time.

The detective breezed on from that, but I could tell Clem and I were thinking the same thing: If Laurel had kept her virginity until college, that meant she'd been precious about it. She'd probably planned on romance and maybe even love for her first time. Instead, she'd been raped. Yet another blow.

At the end of a long line of questions, Detective Dorsey sighed.

I bit. "What?"

He gestured at his legal pad, where he'd scribbled notes. "There's not much to go on."

"What do you mean?" Clem asked. "She just told you every detail. You have his name and address. Go arrest him."

"There were no witnesses to the alleged assault," Dorsey said. "No one to confirm Ms. Hargrove's accusation."

"How many times are there witnesses to a rape?" I asked. "Seems rare."

The detective narrowed his eyes at me, then turned back to Laurel. "You can go to the hospital and get a kit done, but I'm warning you, it's invasive as hell. Some girls say it's like being raped all over again.

36

And you've waited an awfully long time. Would've been better if you'd reported this last night, while it was fresh."

Laurel closed her eyes.

"The truth is, and I'm sorry to have to say this, but you didn't yell at the guy, according to your own story. You let him sit there and drink a beer. You didn't run… You fell back asleep. I bet this Andrew kid would be shocked to know you think he raped you."

My spine zipped straight. Laurel's eyes were still closed, but she was crying.

"She said no," Clem spit out. "Of course he knew."

Detective Dorsey stood up. "If you want my advice—because I'd hate to see you go to court and have an emotional experience, just to lose—if you lay out the details to an objective audience, they're going to have a hard time convicting. We're talking about a boy's life hanging in the balance."

"You've got to be kidding," I said. An old anger unleashed itself. "You're telling Laurel to ignore what happened?"

"Watch your tone," the detective snapped. "What I'm telling Ms. Hargrove is that the details of her story don't make a strong case. She should take it as a lesson—"

"A *lesson*?" This time, I raised my voice.

I could feel the eyes of the other officers turn to us. I kept my gaze locked on the knot of Dorsey's red tie.

A flush crept down his neck. "Consider this a lesson in being an adult. If you go to a boy's house dressed like an invitation, take shots and flirt with him all night, give every indication of wanting to sleep with him, what do you think he's going to do? Ms. Hargrove can't go crying wolf over every sexual encounter she regrets, or else cops would spend all our time chasing hungover college kids after a bad lay."

"I can't believe how unprofessional you're being." Clem stood and pulled Laurel with her. "We want to talk to your boss."

Detective Dorsey waved a hand. "Oh yeah? You seeing a lot of sympathy here for a bunch of spoiled Whitney girls who got their first knock and want to make a federal case of it?"

We looked around. Farthest from us, the officers were going about their business. But closer, they looked back with steely expressions. They were all men, I realized. We were the only women in the room.

My anger died in a sudden gust of fear.

"Come on, Laurel," I said quietly, pulling her away from the desk. "We'll figure out another way."

We left as fast as we could, the three of us power walking out of the station, back into the tree-lined neighborhood. Laurel was still crying, but it didn't slow her. I touched a hand to her shoulder and said, "It's going to be okay," because there was nothing else to do.

Out of nowhere, Clem took off in a burst of speed.

"Hey!" I shouted. "Where are you going?"

She didn't answer. Laurel and I stared at each other for a moment, then Laurel took off, too. I couldn't let them leave me, so I started running after them, and then we were three wild girls streaking down a shaded street, chasing something or being chased, impossible to tell.

Clem was so blazing fast we couldn't keep pace with her for long, but it felt good to run. To make my feet pound and my lungs burn. Eventually, Laurel and I dropped to a jog, limping after Clem.

We were too far behind to stop her when we realized she was going back to the house. By the time we caught up, she'd picked up a thick branch from someone's yard and was pounding it against the living room window, making startling, insistent *thwacks*.

"What are you *doing*?" Laurel shouted, struggling to get her breath back.

"If the cops aren't going to do shit, I'll do it myself," Clem yelled, swinging the branch at the window, where it hit with a sharp clap.

"*Stop*," I hissed. "They'll come out." There were more cars in the driveway than when we'd left. The boys were definitely home.

Clem turned to us, chest heaving, face red and sweaty. "I'm not scared of them." She swung the branch again. "Andrew, you *rapist*! Come face us!" She beat at the glass, and suddenly, it cracked—only a hairline, but it was all she needed. Clem smashed the branch like a pole against the window until it shattered.

Laurel pressed her face into my shoulder. "Oh my god, they're going to call the cops. They're going to come outside, they're going to see me—"

"*Assholes!*" Clem moved to front door, kicking it. "You think you can get away with it?"

A face appeared at the second-floor window. It was a boy's, pale and stricken. He and I locked eyes—and as soon as we did, he jerked away, the curtains rustling in his wake.

"Make her stop," Laurel pleaded, but her voice had grown soft. Together, we stood and watched Clem, a tidal wave of anger lashing out against the still and silent house.

I thought of the way Laurel had looked in the basement, like a cornered animal, vibrating with shame. I thought of the detective's narrowed eyes when we talked back. The surprise on the boy's face when he looked through the window. I remembered the sight of a school going up in flames, brilliant against the night sky, blazing hotter than the stars, and the faces of all those adults afterward, wary for the first time. All that fear, transferred back where it belonged.

I remembered it and let Clem rage.

I may have even smiled.

So which was worse: the way I'd met Laurel, or the way we were saying goodbye?

I dodged cars to cross the street and entered the thicket of trees surrounding the Performing Arts Center, the angular glass building hidden somewhere among them. How would I know the right tree where Laurel had been found?

It turned out I didn't have to wonder. At the edge of the thicket, with the Performing Arts Center towering in the background, a white cross leaned against the trunk of an old, bent tree, its branches creeping low to the ground. A teddy bear and two bouquets of flowers rested on the grass.

Maybe the students hadn't brushed Laurel aside, after all.

I walked to the tree and studied it, running a hand over the trunk, letting the rough, coarse bark snag my skin. This was where she'd stood. Where she'd made a hard decision all alone, without Clem or me to stop her.

Or maybe this was where she'd fought for her life, and lost.

I pressed my forehead to the tree, hard enough so the wood bit, and imagined climbing it, whether the bark would be rough enough to slice me. *Come back, Laurel. Tell me what happened.*

"Excuse me?" came a voice.

I startled back. Behind me stood a girl with strawberry-blond hair, dressed in a forest-green Whitney College hoodie. She looked so young to be a college student.

She thrust a pamphlet at me. *Suicide Prevention Hotline*, it said.

Her voice was soaked in reassurance. "No matter what you're feeling, I promise it gets better."

I stared at her until she staggered back. "No," I said. "It doesn't."

On the way back to the car, I pulled my phone out of my purse and tried to recall a number I hadn't used in a decade. But it turned out there was no need to worry; it came back to me quickly, as if it had been floating just beneath the surface, waiting.

CHAPTER FIVE

Jamie answered warily—then, after a long beat of silence, his voice softened into something lighter, almost hopeful. "Shay?"

The fact that Jamie Knight was on the other end of the line—real, flesh-and-blood Jamie—only truly hit me the moment it became clear I could no longer simply listen to him. That unlike with the podcast, this time I would have to talk back.

"Yes," I said finally.

"It actually worked," he breathed.

At least I was used to the sound of his voice in my ear. "I heard your podcast."

"You're calling about Laurel's murder."

"Her suicide, according to the police."

"You were friends with her. You were with her the last day I saw you."

"We were best friends."

"I'm so sorry, Shay."

"I know. Thank you."

There was another stretch of silence, then he said, "I have so many questions, but... Where are you right now?"

I dug my thumbnail into the steering wheel. "Sitting in a parking lot at Whitney."

He whistled, the sound low and sharp in my ear. "Perfect. Stay in town. I'm on my way."

"Wait... What do you mean?"

"I'll take the train from the city and meet you tonight."

"I'm investigating her death, Jamie." The statement was blunt, and nothing more than bravado, since I'd had zero luck so far. But still, I felt the urge to stake my claim.

"That's great," he said. "We can do it together."

"I know you're the journalist, but I'm not going to follow your lead."

"When have you ever?" Jamie made a noise of amusement. "Look, you can call the shots, as long as you're okay with me covering the story for the podcast."

"Not to be glib, but aren't there more exciting dead women to cover? Women who were definitely murdered?"

He was silent for a moment. "I think your friend *was* killed, Shay, and the police are withholding information or incompetent. I want to know the truth. I have copies of the police files, you know."

I did know. It was why I'd called, after all.

"All right," I agreed. "Meet me for drinks at the River Estate. That's where I'm staying."

Jamie whistled again. "Look at you. Shay Evans, all grown up and fancy."

I chose not to correct him.

I was already seated at a table in the hotel's candlelit restaurant when Jamie walked in. I told my body to stand, but my legs were weak and disobeyed.

I'd known Jamie since we were five years old, so I'd seen him through every phase: when he was the smallest boy in class, skinny-elbowed and bespectacled; then gawky and acne-prone; then tall and deep-voiced, unsure what to do with his long limbs. The last I'd seen Jamie was senior year of college, when there'd been only a glimmer of the man who walked toward me now.

He was beautiful and didn't seem to notice. He didn't register the eyes that flitted to him in the restaurant, seemed unaware of the head tilts. That kind of ignorance was a luxury I'd never had, but never mind. Growing up, people had sometimes asked if Jamie and I were brother and sister. He had hair as midnight black as mine, though his was longish over his forehead and styled with some sort of product now, a new trick. He'd grown a beard, a week or two beyond a five-o'clock shadow, and wore dark jeans and one of those well-tailored hoodies that somehow manage to look urbane. But the best part about Jamie had always been his eyes: bright and dancing, even from far away.

It was rare to see an old friend. I drank him in until he stood in front of my table, and my body finally rose.

"I can't believe it's really you," he said. I hugged him quickly, then slid back into my chair. Jamie slung his duffel on the floor and took the seat across from mine. We studied each other from opposite sides of the table.

"It's good to see you," I offered.

His grin grew wider. His was not a face for podcasts.

"What?"

"I've been trying to make contact with you for years. I was *this* close

43

to begging your mom on my knees to give me your number. I even talked to the old crew from Heller High."

"Painful."

"Then I actually pleaded *in public* for you to contact me. So yeah, it's pretty fucking great to see you, too. I feel like I conjured you."

"I'm sorry it's been a while."

Our waitress slid up to the table, flipping her hair and flashing a smile that lingered a second or two longer in Jamie's direction. I recognized the move from my own restaurant days. "What can I bring you?"

Jamie smiled. "Whiskey, please. Neat."

"Look who evolved beyond Shiner." I looked at the waitress. "A glass of Sancerre, please."

Jamie said nothing until the waitress took off. Then he burst.

"Tell me everything. What do you do? Where do you live? What's your life like? I've missed you."

He was smiling, earnest, but that only made me more nervous. I picked up my napkin and twisted it. Immediately, his eyes dropped to my hands, and his smile faded.

"You're married."

I dropped the napkin and twisted my ring. "I am."

"Well, congratulations. Tell me about him."

At that moment, my phone lit up in the corner of the table: *Calvin Deroy calling*. I clicked the screen black, heart thumping.

He raised an eyebrow. "Speak of the devil?"

"His name is Cal. We live in Dallas. I used to write for *The Slice*, but lately..." *Lately, nothing.* I felt the words die.

Jamie tilted his head. "I never thought you'd end up back in Texas."

Jamie had been my best friend growing up, but even so, there was so much I'd kept from him. I'd wanted one person to keep looking at me the way he always had. I cleared my throat. "Maybe we should talk about the case."

"Okay." He said it slowly, dragging a hand through his hair. "I'm doing great, by the way. Bought an apartment in Brooklyn, the podcast numbers are high, my parents are retired and loving it. They ask about you."

"Shit. I'm sorry, Jamie. Of course I want to know how you've been."

"It's fine." He bent to his bag and unzipped it. "We can get straight to business."

He pulled out a file and cracked it open on the table. Inside were papers, each with the seal of the Westchester County Police Department.

The waitress came back and slid our drinks across the table. Jamie casually flipped the file closed, and we both remained silent until she left.

"Laurel's police report," I breathed, once she was gone. "How'd you get it?"

"Ah, you know. Those municipal data systems: famously impenetrable. I've got someone talented on my team. I asked, he delivered." He gave me a faint smile, straightening the papers. "How do you think I get so many scoops?"

"What you said in the episode..." I pointed at the report. "That Laurel was found almost exactly like Clem, both on campus. It doesn't make any sense. Laurel was thirty years old. Why would she go back to college to kill herself? She had a lot of reasons to stay away."

Jamie's eyes narrowed, and I could feel his scrutiny travel over me. This must be his reporter face. "You think Laurel was killed, too?"

"I don't know. Yes? The similarities between her and Clem are too strange to be a coincidence." *Unless it was guilt*, my mind whispered.

Jamie's grip on the papers tightened. "Shay." He said it urgently enough that I met his eyes. "Who would do this?"

My throat went dry. "I don't know."

He held my gaze, and an uncomfortable flush spread down my neck. His eyes were an arresting mix of green and brown. Worse, they were knowing.

"That man," he said. "The one from that day in the city. This has nothing to do with him, does it?"

I was already shaking my head, all my instincts firing: *Turn around. Run. Don't let it in.*

But I was here to do what Laurel and Clem needed. To be brave.

"I don't know," I admitted. "But I need to find out."

Jamie picked up his drink and stared into it. "That day, when I saw you—when I met Laurel and Clem—I didn't know what to think. I was scared, Shay. That's part of why I've been trying to track you down. I was tempted to use my guy, but I didn't want to violate your privacy—"

"What does the file say?" I interrupted. "Are there any details you left out that could help us?"

For a second, all Jamie did was look at me. Then he slugged down his drink and dropped the empty glass on the table. "Yeah. Interviews." He wiped his mouth with the back of his hand. "I mentioned in the episode Laurel's file is missing pictures—"

"And that's unusual?"

"Very. Every police report I've ever seen with a body involved pictures. Photos of the crime scene, the body when it was found, possible evidence. But Laurel's... Zilch."

"What about Clem's?"

His eyes softened. "It's a slim file, but there is one picture. I'm sorry, Shay. I wish I could've been there for you back when—"

"Did it show the words carved into her arm?"

Jamie frowned. "What?"

"When they found Clem, she had 'I'm sorry' carved into her arm.

Razor-thin cuts. They thought she'd done it herself because there were cuts on her fingers. It wasn't in the police report?"

"No." He hunched forward. "Razor-thin cuts. That's another similarity."

"I know." I nodded at the file. "So who'd they interview in Laurel's case?"

Jamie pushed the papers toward me. "Only four people. The girl who found her—a college kid, sophomore who was up early for swim practice. Then Laurel's former employer."

"Former?"

"Yeah. Apparently, she hadn't held a job in five or six years."

That didn't sound a thing like Laurel, who'd been perpetually busy, always wrapped up in making costumes for one play or another. "How's that even financially feasible?"

"I have no idea," he said. "And the cops did zero digging. The employer's a local caterer."

"Caterer?" Laurel working at a theater, I could picture. Even...I don't know, a tailor. But catering? Food had never been one of her interests.

"Then they interviewed her landlord, who's also her neighbor...lives in the apartment above her. And her mom."

"Oh." I'd never met Laurel's mother, though I'd heard plenty about her. "Is she in town?"

Jamie shook his head and pointed at the police report. "Nope. They talked to her by phone. She's out in the Midwest, still in the same town where Laurel grew up."

"South Bend," I murmured, and Jamie nodded.

"So where do we start?" I asked.

"We do our own interviews, retrace the cops' steps. First, I bet they were sloppy, and second, you were Laurel's friend, so you might see things they didn't. We can start with any of them."

"I'll call her mom tomorrow," I said. "From what I've heard, she can be hard to get ahold of. Might as well start trying. And I want to talk to Laurel's landlord. Ask about her habits, how she could afford rent without a job." I didn't say it, but what I really wanted was to walk into her apartment, into the private heart of her. It felt like the closest I could come to seeing her again.

Jamie nodded. "Pick me up tomorrow morning at nine. I'm at the Motel 6 in Yonkers."

I blinked. "Really?"

"Nothing but the best for Stitcher's third-highest-rated true-crime podcast." He stood up, dropped two twenties on the table, and pointed at the police files, still splayed out in front of me. "I made these copies for you. Do you mind trying her mom when I'm around? I'd like the audio for the episode."

"No problem." I watched him prepare to go with a dense ball in the pit of my stomach. I didn't want to open up to Jamie about my life, but I also didn't want him to leave. I wished he would just sit across the candlelit table and let me look at him. Let me catalog his changes; convince myself there were none too many. Just exist in the same space again, breathe the same air.

I've always had such strange desires.

Jamie gave me an imaginary tip of the hat. "Night, partner. See you bright and early."

———

The next morning, I slid the rental car into what passed for a valet circle in front of the Motel 6, texted Jamie, and waited. It was a bright, sunny day, but the heat was dialed down a notch, a small promise of the coming fall. I'd tossed and turned all night in the down-stuffed hotel bed, unable to exorcise thoughts of Jamie or Laurel. Now I was bone-tired. I pressed fingers into the delicate skin under my eyes. Puffy. Great.

Before I had much time to wallow in vanity, Jamie strode out of the sliding glass doors in dark sunglasses, holding two large coffees. My heart gave a little lift before I stretched over the passenger seat and popped the door for him.

"Morning." He dropped inside and held out a cup. "You still drink this, right?"

I took it gratefully, the cup hot against my fingers. "Inhale it, more like."

Jamie yanked the door closed. "That's the Shay I remember."

I took a sip and almost spit it out. It was sweet and milky.

"What?" Jamie frowned. "Two sugars, fill the milk a quarter way, right?"

It was my old coffee order, the one Cal thought was gross and childish, though the latter was only subtext. I'd been practicing mature asceticism by drinking it black, so the sweet sip was a shock to the tongue. It turned out I still liked it this way.

I fit the coffee cup into the drink holder and threw the car into drive, pulling away from the motel. "I have no idea how you can remember the way I like my coffee. Don't you need that mental real estate for something more important?"

Jamie shrugged. He wore all black today—slim-fitting jeans and a well-tailored shirt I could tell cost money. He'd shed Texas so well. "I remember everything about you," he said casually, leaning back and propping his feet on the dash. "Probably because we knew each other during a formative time. Imprints on the brain, you know?"

I kept my eyes trained on the road. "Half a pack of sugar, splash of milk. Any more than that and you'll toss it."

He laughed. "Guilty."

I smiled at the upcoming streetlight. I'd forgotten what it felt like to have a friend.

Laurel's neighborhood in Bronxville was one of the less manicured ones: small houses, fewer trees, more long-grassed lawns, the occasional loose trash rolling like tumbleweeds.

We pulled up in front of her duplex, a modest two-story home, painted a light olive green that might have been fashionable a few decades ago. It was dated, but I could imagine Laurel here. She wasn't one of those Whitney students who came from money, and she never strove for it, either. It just didn't seem to interest her, not the way art did, especially theater. I could picture her being happy in a place like this.

There was an old, beat-up car in the driveway. I parked and followed Jamie up an exterior staircase to the door on the second floor. He rapped a few times, and there was scuffling from inside, a dog's bark, then the door opened.

"Hi," Jamie said brightly. "Ms. Morgan? It's Jamie Knight. I called you earlier to see if we could ask a few questions about your former tenant Laurel Hargrove."

The woman was in her sixties, with short, ash-blond hair and thick bifocals. She was wearing a light-pink house robe, so I was afraid she'd turn us away. But she nodded. "The podcast guy?"

Jamie tucked his hair behind his ears. "Yes. And this is my partner, Shay—" He turned to me, a question in his eyes.

"Deroy," I supplied.

The woman blinked at us. "Are you sure you're not TV actors or something?" She studied me. "You look familiar."

Jamie and I glanced at each other. "Shay was one of Laurel's friends from college," he said.

Linda snapped her fingers, then shooed the small dog that whined at her feet. "I must've seen you from Laurel's pictures." She stepped away for a second, out of sight, returning with a key. "You probably want to look through it, right? Her mom promised she'd get it packed up, but so far no movers have shown up." The woman squinted. "I'm not trying to be insensitive, you know, but I've got to get another renter in there soon."

"That makes sense," I assured her. "We can help with whatever you need."

Jamie gave me an approving nod, like I'd said it to butter up the witness.

"Follow me," she said. "And you can call me Linda. Are you going to record me?"

"Only if you consent." Jamie pulled a piece of paper out of his jacket and handed it to her. "Otherwise, we'll keep our conversation private."

She nodded, and we followed her down the stairs to Laurel's front door, which she cracked open with a twist of the key.

The first thing that struck me was the smell. It was a woodsy, almost patchouli scent, and it was Laurel's signature. She'd always said it made sense to deliver on what her name promised. The scent was faint, just barely there, but so familiar and distinctly Laurel that my throat seized. A thousand memories of her gelled into a sense of presence, almost like she was here.

The space was small and tidy, very spare. Laurel had always been neat, but this was a step beyond—almost unlived-in. She'd loved nesting, but here, there were only a few pieces of furniture—a couch, small dining table, the hint of a bed in the back room.

Linda sighed. "You know, I already told the police this, but Laurel was rarely here."

"Hold on," Jamie said, pulling out his phone. "Let me start recording."

I moved to touch the single coaster on her small coffee table, which sat facing one of those boxy, old-time televisions. "How often did you see her?"

"The first two years, she was here all the time. Heard or saw her every day, like you'd expect. I liked her, and we got friendly. She was a sweet girl. But then at some point—I can't remember exactly—I realized I hadn't seen her in a while." Linda shifted uncomfortably. "I tried calling, but she didn't answer. I got worried, so I let myself in here, but nothing seemed amiss. And the rent checks kept coming. I figured maybe she was traveling. And then a few months later, she just showed up, out of the blue. I asked her where she'd been, if everything was okay, but she brushed me off."

I frowned, stepping into the kitchen. Neither the brushing off nor the large chunks of time away sounded like Laurel, who was a homebody. But when I yanked open the drawers, there was only the bare minimum of cutlery and utensils, a few lonely pieces rattling around.

Linda crossed her arms over her chest. "Then she disappeared again. And that's how it was from then on. Months and months would go by without seeing her, and then she'd show up, spend the night, and leave again. But the checks kept coming."

"Wait." I turned from Laurel's cupboard, which held only a box of cereal. "Exactly how long did Laurel live here?"

Linda tapped her foot. "I looked this up for the police. Eight years, give or take. Some people would say she made the best kind of tenant. Never here, never a nuisance. But I kind of missed having her around. Like I said, we were friendly in the beginning."

Eight years? But that meant Laurel had never left New York after we graduated, despite our promises. I'd thought she was heading back to Indiana with her mother, where she was going to figure out if she wanted to get her MFA or find work with a theater group. What made her stay?

"Linda, you said Laurel's checks kept coming." Jamie ran a finger over the arm of Laurel's worn couch. "Is there any way you could share her account information with us? I know it's a lot to ask, but tracing money can be a good way to understand someone's life."

Linda bit her lip. "The cops didn't ask for that. Are you sure it's legal?"

Jamie gave a noncommittal shrug, but I could see him discreetly press the stop button on his phone. "Strange the cops didn't ask for it. I'll be frank with you, Linda. We don't think Laurel killed herself. We think someone killed her."

Linda's hand flew to her chest, and she pulled her robe tighter. "The police said suicide." Her eyes dropped to the floor.

I stepped closer. "What is it?"

"It's just—" She took a deep breath. "Laurel was a nice girl. But she was also a little...off."

"Off how?" I shot Jamie a look.

Linda walked through the hall into the bedroom, and Jamie and I followed. "Sometimes I'd find her in the backyard, just standing there, staring at nothing." She pointed through the sliding glass doors at the back of Laurel's bedroom. They looked out into a small backyard, with a single tree and a tall fence. "When I tried talking to her, she wouldn't say a word. Didn't even register my presence. Like she was catatonic or something."

I stared into the yard. Laurel had done that once before in college, when she was very sad. It had taken a few days to shake her out of it.

"Other times I'd just hear her sobbing." Linda shifted her gaze to Laurel's bed. It was a full, not much larger than the twins we'd suffered through in college, and draped with a faded floral comforter. I walked to her bedside table and pulled open the drawer.

"My bedroom is right above," Linda continued. "And one time she woke me up in the middle of the night crying. The sound just floated through the ceiling." She pulled her arms tighter over her chest. "She kept going and going through the morning and wouldn't answer when I knocked on the door, so eventually I left. She was gone when I came back."

I frowned. Linda was painting a picture of a deeply depressed Laurel. Were Jamie and I wrong? *Had* she killed herself? I rooted through her bedside drawer, finding a matchbox, a notepad with torn-out pages, and a ballpoint pen with dried ink around the nub.

"She used to have pictures up," Linda said. "Lots. Friends and family, she said."

I dug into the drawer and hit something sharp, pulling out an empty silver picture frame. I dug deeper and found the last thing—a worn photograph that looked like it had been bent a thousand times over.

Linda looked over my shoulder. "See! I knew I recognized you."

It was a picture of Clem, Laurel, and me, from junior year of college, standing in front of Rothschild. Clem wore a Whitney soccer jersey and bright-purple hair—she'd gotten into the habit of dying it a different color every few months. Laurel and I looked like polar opposites, her blond next to my dark, but we wore matching grins.

There'd been someone else standing in front of Rothschild that day. I unfolded the last quarter of the picture and sucked in a breath. Rachel, our fourth roommate, with her arm slung around Laurel's shoulders. But you couldn't see Rachel's face, see how much she and Laurel looked alike, or the flat, dead smile she was giving the camera. Because Laurel had destroyed her with thick slashes of pen, turning her face into a dark, inky miasma.

"Jesus. Who's that?" Jamie asked.

I handed him the picture. "Rachel Rockwell. She was our roommate junior and senior years."

He gave me a sharp look. "You had another roommate? You never mentioned her."

"She was..." I thought back to Linda's word from earlier. "Off."

Off was only the tip of the iceberg, but Rachel was a part of the past I refused to revive. Even saying her name out loud felt like invoking a curse, like calling Bloody Mary three times in the mirror. I understood Laurel's impulse to erase her.

I was saved from explaining when Jamie turned over the picture and stilled. "Look."

Words crawled across the back in unfamiliar writing: *Tongue-Cut Sparrow*.

Jamie looked up. "Either of you know what this means?"

"No idea," Linda said. "Never heard of it."

I frowned. "Me neither. Can we keep the picture?"

Linda glanced at Rachel's scratched-out face. "You'd be doing me a favor." She rubbed a hand over her eyes. "I'll get you those accounts Laurel used to pay her rent."

Jamie paused on the way to Laurel's closet. "Accounts, as in plural?"

"She paid with a personal account for years," Linda said. "Then, one month, her rent started coming from a new one. Some corporate-sounding place. Dominatrix...no, that's ridiculous. *Dominus* Holdings, that's it. Figured it was coming from wherever she worked, though that's still a little odd."

Jamie caught my eye. Laurel hadn't held a job in years, at least according to the police. Where was the money coming from?

"Before you leave," Linda said, "I'll go upstairs and write them down for you."

"Thank you." Jamie slid open the closet to reveal a sparse collection of jeans and T-shirts, hanging neatly. "We appreciate it."

I looked under the bed, the pillows, even swept my hand under the mattress, looking for anything Laurel might've hidden. Nothing; but then again, Laurel was an only child, like me. She'd never learned to put things in hiding places. One thing did strike me: "Where's her sewing machine?" She was never without one.

Linda looked dumbfounded. "I didn't know she sewed."

I felt a hollowness in the pit of my stomach. It was like Linda and I had known two different people. "I think I'm done," I told Jamie. Coming to Laurel's place had turned out to be chilling, not comforting.

"Wait a sec." He reached above his head into the high, empty shelf in Laurel's closet. When he pulled his hand back, it was covered in dust, but he held another photograph. He looked at it and his face paled.

"What?"

Wordlessly, Jamie handed me the picture.

It was another from college, but earlier: sophomore year, when the three of us were nothing but happy. Younger, smaller versions of Clem, Laurel, and me backstage, after one of Laurel's plays. Clem was blue-haired. Laurel was beaming with pride.

My entire face was scratched out with vicious, cutting marks.

CHAPTER SIX

That night I dreamed Laurel bent over me in bed, pressed a hand to my mouth, and whispered, *Shh.*

"You're all right," I said against her fingers, and she nodded.

I'm not dead, she whispered. *Only hiding where the light doesn't reach.* I sat up and her hand fell away. She looked just like she did sophomore year, when she was strong and happy.

"Hiding from him?" I asked, and she nodded.

For the first time, it made sense. Laurel wasn't dead; Laurel didn't hate me. She was waiting. I was so relieved.

Don't let him find me, she breathed and shifted into the girl she'd been when I found her in the basement freshman year, stringy-haired and sucked by horror.

"Laurel." I reached for her, but she slipped away. The ground opened, tugging her into the dark.

I'm waiting, she echoed, disappearing inch by inch. *Come find me.*

"Stop!" I yelled, lunging.

Shay, she whispered. *What did you know, and when did you know it?* The ground swallowed her whole.

I woke the next morning to a spot of blood on my pillow from where I'd bitten deep into my tongue.

I let Jamie drive this time. He walked out of the motel in another all-black outfit, holding an orange soda and a root beer, the kind I'd liked when I was a kid. When I slid out of the driver's seat, he handed me the root beer and got in without a word. He'd been cautious with me since yesterday, when he'd asked why Laurel might do that to my picture, and I'd snapped *I don't know.*

We were on two missions today: first, talk to Laurel's former employer, the head of a catering company called Hudson Delights, which was up in Beacon, an hour away. Jamie had set up the interview last night, presumably after I'd fled back to my hotel room. Second, we were going to track down the college student who'd discovered her body. I'd called Laurel's mom three times in the last twenty-four hours with no luck; the last time, the call went straight to voicemail. I remembered Laurel telling me her mom was moody and unpredictable. She suffered from depression, Laurel had said, and it had gotten a whole lot worse after Laurel's father passed away when she was fifteen. Sometimes Laurel didn't hear from her mom for weeks at a time. I wondered at my chances of getting through to her.

It would be a long ride up to Beacon, and by the set of Jamie's mouth, I could tell he was determined not to provoke me. I sighed. I'd been nothing but prickly and withholding since we'd reunited. He probably regretted finding me after all.

My phone rang; I pulled it out to find Cal calling yet again. I knew

I needed to talk to him—texts wouldn't suffice—but the truth was, I was dreading it. Cal was due back from his work trip soon, and he'd ask when I was coming home. I clicked it silent and caught Jamie watching me out of the corner of his eye.

"Cal works at a hedge fund." I offered it like an olive branch. "He loves numbers. And making money, obviously."

Jamie cracked a grin. "You always loved numbers, too."

"I liked words more."

"You were the smartest person in school," he said. "You could do both."

If that was true, Jamie was the only person who'd noticed.

"Even if they did take valedictorian away from you for some mysterious reason…" He lifted his eyebrows suggestively.

"Stop being such a reporter," I said. "Just thank me for handing you the title."

He shrugged. "You can have it back. I'd much rather know the scandal."

I looked out the window, and after a second, he changed tack. "So, how'd you meet this money-hungry hedge funder from Dallas?"

I rolled my eyes. "Covering an event for *The Slice*. The Cowboys were hosting a fundraiser for breast cancer research. I thought it might be a nice angle, you know, football players wearing pink and doing something nice for women. Cal was one of the attendees. He made the biggest donation out of anyone." I didn't mention that philanthropy was a competitive sport in Highland Park, a way for old Dallas families to flaunt their wealth. And Cal liked winning.

"Ah. So you got swept off your feet by a big shot. Makes sense."

"Why?"

"Remember how obsessed you were with Anderson Thomas in high school? That's your type. The prom king."

My mouth went dry. I quickly changed the subject. "Cal and I got married a year ago. It was a small wedding."

He shot me a look, mouth quirking. "I bet your mom was thrilled you married a rich guy."

I huffed a laugh. "Marrying Cal's about the only thing I've ever done right."

"Yeah, well, she was always desperate for you to not end up like her."

My smile faded. "I barely talk to her these days."

"Yeah, I know." He glanced at me in the rearview. "Trust me, she told me."

Hudson Delights was a small, old-timey building on a picturesque postcard street in downtown Beacon. How in the world Laurel had found this place, and what brought her here, miles outside the town she lived in, to a job outside her interests, I could not guess.

Clarissa Barker, the owner, was only a decade or so older than us, or so I'd read on the internet. In person, she looked considerably older. Her face was lined, skin rough, nose red and bulbous. She telegraphed hard living.

But her kitchen was large and clean. I looked around, trying to imagine Laurel here. In college, she couldn't even get a grilled cheese right. Maybe she'd stuck to serving.

"Ms. Barker?" Jamie wore what I was beginning to understand was his approachable reporter face, all gentle affability. I needed to work on my own.

Clarissa glanced up but didn't stop mixing, arm muscles flexing. "I have to do this for two more minutes or the batter's ruined."

"That's okay," I said, trying on affable. "We can wait."

She shook her head. "Go ahead and ask me your questions. I've got an event tonight, so I'm on deadline."

"Right." Jamie pulled out his phone. "Do you mind if I record you to use in the podcast?"

She managed to shrug while swirling. "Fine by me. My daughter loves listening to those things. Maybe she'll get a kick out of it."

"Great," Jamie said. "We were—"

"You can start by quoting me on this," Clarissa interrupted, wiping her brow. "I always knew I'd be answering questions about that girl one day."

I leaned over the stainless steel table. "You mean Laurel?"

"Yep. I figured it was only a matter of time before someone showed up on my doorstep."

"Can you tell us what you remember about her?"

"Before you do," Jamie said, "do you know anything about a company called Dominus Holdings? Is it connected to Hudson Delights in any way?"

Clarissa huffed a laugh, flashing yellowed teeth. "You think I got money for a *holding*? Nah. These days, I'm barely keeping my head above water. Never heard of it. Weird name."

Jamie nodded. "Okay. Thanks. Tell us about Laurel."

Clarissa stopped mixing, dropping the spatula with a clatter. "I hired Laurel about seven, eight years ago, something like that. She was a freshie, right out of college. Whitney, I think. I remember because she still had that glow on her, that 'I just spent four years living on campus' shine. With all those brick mansions and ivy trellises, soaking in money, you know? She knew nothing about catering, but she seemed desperate for the job, and I figured I could use some of that college polish to class up the joint. Plus, she was pretty—a little frail, but pretty. Which is something." Clarissa cast me a knowing look. "I'm sure I don't have to tell you."

"Shay went to Whitney, too, on a beauty pageant scholarship." Jamie flashed me a grin. "You're looking at Miss Texas 2009."

You have no idea what it was like, I wanted to say. But that would only invite questions: *So, what was it like?* And Jamie had been the one who'd told me not to do it in the first place. He was being generous now, acting like he thought the pageants were something positive—an accomplishment, not an embarrassment.

"Good for you. Use what God gave you, I always say." Clarissa raised an eyebrow. "I bet you didn't tell your Whitney friends you were a beauty queen, though. I know the kinds of girls who go to that school. They'd eat you alive."

I crossed my arms. "You said Laurel was desperate for the job. Why?"

Clarissa shrugged, moving to the large stainless-steel sink to wash her hands. "Don't know. She practically begged me to hire her, said she'd do anything. At the time I figured she wanted to run her own catering firm one day and thought my shop would be a leg up. Back then, we were one of the most popular caterers in the area. Had some exclusive contracts." She wiped her hands on a dish towel. "I was living high on the hog."

"How long did Laurel work for you?" Jamie asked.

Clarissa pulled the batter out of the mixing bowl and began kneading it with strong, sure hands. I dropped my eyes, her movements triggering a flood of memories: a bright flash of molten shame, a twinge of arousal.

Once, I'd kneaded dough naked on my hands and knees, and I'd liked it.

"I got a good year out of her." Clarissa's voice broke the spell, and I swallowed hard. "Then she started missing work. She'd lie, tell me she was sick, and then people would see her out around town. She started getting off-balance."

"What do you mean?" Jamie asked. I was grateful he was doing the talking.

Clarissa shaped the dough. "Moody. Irritable. Erratic. When you're a waiter, you have to be charming. Hell, at least *nice* to your customers. I started cutting her shifts because she'd come in with bags under her eyes, all angry and sullen, and she'd back-talk the clients. I was starting to think she was on drugs, to be honest. They find any drugs in her system?"

None of this sounded remotely like sweet, accommodating Laurel. But maybe Clem's death had broken something in both of us.

"None we know of," Jamie said. "How'd she quit?"

Clarissa huffed, pulling open the oven and shoving her baking tray inside. "One day she completely lost her shit. We were out working an event. It was important, maybe our most important one, for one of our exclusive clients. And she just blew up, out of nowhere, over nothing, and stormed out. I never saw her again. It's real sad how she ended up, but like I said, you could see trouble coming."

"That was how many years ago?" Jamie asked.

Clarissa squinted. "Five or six, thereabouts. It's been a while, but you don't forget a meltdown like that."

Jamie and I glanced at each other. The timing roughly matched when Laurel's landlord said she'd started disappearing.

What kind of trouble had she gotten into?

Clarissa rested her hands on her hips. "Not to rush you out, but I need to move to savories if I'm going to be ready. We're doing an anniversary party in Poughkeepsie."

"We appreciate your time." Jamie checked his phone. "If you think of anything else—"

"Wait," I said. "Do the words 'Tongue-Cut Sparrow' mean anything to you?"

Clarissa froze in the middle of untying her apron. "You know that place?"

"It's a place?" I took a deep breath. Instinct told me to play it easy.

Clarissa's eyes darted to the door, and the fine hairs on my arms lifted. "I don't know for sure, but when you've lived here long enough, you catch whispers." She glanced down at Jamie's phone. "Would you mind turning that off?"

He stopped recording and leaned over the table. "What have you heard, Ms. Barker? I promise, anything you say is safe with us."

"I told my daughter not to go near it," she said. "The Hudson Mansion, up the river... You know, the hoity-toity hotel?"

"I've never heard of it," I confessed.

"Yeah, well, it's real old money. Those kinds of people don't *want* you to hear about them, trust me. I brush up against those circles sometimes in my line of work. And it's not just fancy airs and nice things. They're a different species."

"We'll look up the Mansion," Jamie assured her. "What's the relationship to Tongue-Cut Sparrow?"

Clarissa's voice lowered. "During the day, the Mansion's all blue bloods and high teas. But I've heard it runs a seedy club at night. Not trashy—the other kind."

"What do you mean?" I asked.

She looked me up and down. "The kind where on the outside, they're wearing blazers. But on the inside, they're wolves." She cleared her throat. "We were actually working a job at the Mansion the day Laurel flipped her shit."

Jamie canted his head in my direction, and I buried the urge to grab his arm. I could feel it. This was important.

"Ms. Barker," Jamie said, much calmer than I felt, "I know you need to get to work. But could you spare one more minute and tell us exactly what you remember about the day Laurel quit?"

Clarissa's eyes moved between us. They were bloodshot, like she wasn't used to sleep. "It's been years now. And I'm not going to lie to you. I've struggled with…getting some habits under control. So there might be holes. Maybe there's even a few things I made up, I don't know. I'll give you what I remember, but I'm trying to be honest about what it's worth."

"Anything you can tell us is worth a lot," I said quietly. "To the investigation, and to me."

She sighed. "The Hudson Mansion used to be one of our exclusive contracts—lucrative, because they wanted everything top-notch. The trade-off is you've got to be on your best behavior, which is what I tell my waiters. The day Laurel quit was the first event we'd done at the Mansion since she started. Even during setup, I noticed she kept going missing. Trust me, I get it, it's a fancy place, and maybe she wanted to poke around, bump into a rich guy. Wouldn't be the first. But she had a job to do. So I warned her in no uncertain terms, stay put. The event starts. The room's stuffed wall to wall with billionaires, and at some point, I realize there's no one serving the hors d'oeuvres. I swear to god, there she was, gone again.

"When she crept back, I confronted her. Tried to make it discreet, because obviously I didn't want to scare off the clients. But she started yelling, defending herself, saying I didn't understand, I wasn't her mother—strange stuff. Then in the middle of a sentence, I kid you not, she stops and goes white as a ghost. I turned around and tried to figure out what she'd seen, but all I could see was a bunch of people in black tie, drinking champagne. Next thing I knew, Laurel's quitting and high-tailing it out of there. No one's ever quit in the middle of a job like that. I had to fill in for the rest of the day. That's the long and short."

"Did you recognize anyone at the party?" Jamie asked.

Clarissa snorted. "Not exactly my crowd."

"Okay. Well, thanks again, Ms. Barker." Jamie nodded subtly to the door, with a look that said *We have a lot to talk about.*

"I hope you find whatever you're looking for," Clarissa said. She was looking directly at me.

"Thanks," I said faintly, because I was already a million miles away, trying to imagine what had scared Laurel so bad she'd quit her job on the spot, never to be seen again.

Jamie and I fell into a pensive silence as we waited outside Cleary Hall. Edie Marlow, the Whitney girl who'd found Laurel's body, was due out of her sociology class at 4:15 p.m. We'd catch her in a public place.

"Okay. So this glorified country club hosts a seedy underground called Tongue-Cut Sparrow at night," Jamie said, leaning against a tree. "Laurel was interested in it for some reason. We know that from the note scrawled on the back of that photograph. But then she runs *out* of the Mansion during a gig. Why?"

"Why even start at the catering firm in the first place?" I asked. "Clarissa said she was desperate to work there. Laurel couldn't have cared less about cooking. She—"

My phone buzzed; I looked down to see a text from Cal: Shay, call me back already.

The next second, his face flashed on the screen. A pang of reflexive guilt made me accept. "Hi, Cal."

"Hallelujah, you answered." His voice was wry, but deep and gravelly. He was a big man; he'd fit in among the football players at the charity event the first night we'd met. "What's going on?"

"Nothing." I turned my back so Jamie couldn't hear.

"Mary Ellen says you texted her you weren't coming back in time for her Labor Day party. I thought we were planning to go. You know I'm home in a few days, right?"

"I know, but I'm finally writing," I lied. "Being back's been inspiring."

His voice softened. "Look, I'm glad your block's gone. But I've been away for almost three weeks. You'll be home when I get back, right? I told Eddie Dillard we'd have dinner with him and his wife before the holiday. Can't do it without you."

Of course Cal could do it without me. All it would take was making sure there was food and wine on the table. He meant he didn't want to, because hosting was one of my jobs.

A flood of students poured out of Cleary Hall. In the crowd, I spotted the dark, fashionable bob of Edie Marlow, whose social media I'd studied so I could pick her out.

"Of course," I said quickly. "Sorry, I have to go." I hung up over his protests, shoving away the creeping knowledge that I was being a bad wife. I'd make it up to him later.

I glanced at Jamie, trying not to notice the way he looked at me—like he was a little embarrassed for me—and waved him on. "That's her. Let's go."

We fell into stride with Edie, a beautiful girl, slender and doe-eyed. She gave the slightest start.

"Edie Marlow?" I tried to smile soothingly. "Sorry to bother you, but my friend and I were hoping we could ask a few questions about Laurel Hargrove. You're the one who found her, right?"

A shadow passed over Edie's face. "Yes," she said, adjusting the straps of her book bag. She didn't slow down.

"I'm Jamie Knight." Jamie held out his hand and smiled warmly.

Edie's eyes widened as she took stock of him. "From *Transgressions*?"

"Yep." He withdrew his hand gently from her grip.

"My friends and I listen to you all the time." Her cheeks pinked.

"And you did that episode on Laurel, so of course everyone at school listened…"

"Great," he said smoothly. "Then you already know I'm looking into her case."

We were coming up to the Performing Arts Center. Edie spotted it, froze, then did an about-face, pivoting left. We scrambled to follow.

"Sorry," she mumbled. "I don't like walking past it anymore."

"Edie," I said, "I know this isn't something you want to remember, but can you tell us about finding Laurel? It would really help us. And her, hopefully."

She stopped in her tracks. Her eyes darted to Jamie. He seemed to be the winning factor, because she nodded. We settled down on a bench, Edie in the middle. All around us, students streamed by.

"Like I told the cops," she said, twisting a ring, "I was on my way from Penfield—that's where I live—to Cargill for swim practice. We meet super early, when the sun's just coming out. I was passing by the theater when I saw her"—her voice thickened—"hanging from the tree. I didn't think it was a person at first. I thought it was, like, a banner or something. But when I got closer, I saw."

"What did you see?" Jamie asked.

She cleared her throat. "She was wearing a blue dress, kind of old-fashioned."

Laurel could have made it herself.

"Light-blond hair, pale skin. Her head was…facing down…but I could tell she was pretty." Edie bit her lip.

"It's okay," I said, resisting the urge to pat her.

Her voice grew smaller. "I'd never seen a dead body before."

I gave up resisting and patted her shoulder. "I'm sorry. I know this is strange and painful, but these details are very helpful. There were cuts, right?"

She nodded. "On her arms and hands. Thin cuts, but they still looked terrible. Bright red and angry."

Fresh, then. "This is going to sound weird," I said, "but did they spell out any words?"

Edie frowned. "Words? No."

"Okay. It was worth a—"

"But there was that symbol on her arm."

I froze. On the other side of Edie, Jamie leaned closer. "There was no mention of a symbol in the police report."

"What did it look like?" I asked.

Edie looked between us. "I told the officer who interviewed me." She lifted her right arm and pointed to the soft flesh underneath. "It was right here. I could see it because her arm was twisted. It was the size of a quarter."

"A tattoo?"

She shook her head. "Like a birthmark, or a scar. It was a triangle." Edie drew the shape in the air. "With four little lines branching down from it, and a horizontal line at the bottom. Kind of looked like a frat house, like you see in movies. Whitney doesn't have a Greek system."

I tried to envision what she was describing. "Like a…temple?"

She brightened. "Or maybe a jail? It was hard to tell."

Jamie's eyes met mine over Edie's head. Laurel had a symbol hidden on the underside of her arm, and the police hadn't mentioned it in their report. Why?

"I record my lectures, so I don't have paper on me," Edie said. "But if you have some, I could draw it."

I hesitated for only a second before swallowing my pride and reaching into my purse, pulling out the bright-purple Lisa Frank notebook.

Half an hour later, Jamie pulled up to the valet at the River Estate, threw the car into park, and hopped out. A valet rushed up and Jamie tossed him the keys, along with a quick "Shay Deroy." He turned to me. "Is there somewhere private we can keep talking?"

The air grew charged. The awareness tickled the soft hairs of my arms into standing.

"You can come to my room, if you want." I kept my eyes straight ahead, on the River Estate's stone entranceway.

"Okay," he said lightly. "That'll work."

He was so impressed with my room that I expected to feel embarrassed. But to my surprise, I felt nothing but pleasure at his reaction. I suspected some part of me had always longed to show off to him, to confirm his high estimation of me.

"Not to pry," he said as he slid onto the plush couch in the sitting room, "but this can't be writing-for-*The-Slice* money, or I'm in the wrong kind of journalism."

"It's Cal's money," I said, the pleasure fading.

"Shit. Where do I find one of those hedge funders of my very own?" He read my face and cleared his throat. "Anyway." He patted the couch. "Do you want to talk?"

I sat gingerly on the opposite end. The curtains on the floor-to-ceiling windows were pulled back, revealing the dark Hudson River, the green, tree-lined shore, and the rising mountains in the distance. All of it was lit by a slowly dying sun.

"We have to go to the Hudson Mansion," I said. "Find Tongue-Cut Sparrow."

He nodded. "That's what I was going to say. Any luck with our last interview?"

"No." I drew my feet up on the couch. "I left Laurel's mom half a dozen voicemails, but I haven't heard anything."

"You'd think she'd want to connect with one of her daughter's friends."

I watched the river, little waves eddying, lapping at each other. "We know so much more than we did just two days ago. The fact that Laurel started acting erratically five or six years ago, quitting her job and disappearing from her apartment for months at a time. That she was interested in Tongue-Cut Sparrow. That she had a strange symbol on her arm—"

"That the cops are clearly withholding information," Jamie added.

"I just wish I knew how it all fit together."

We fell into silence. Jamie's eyes roamed to my bed, which was large and white and perfectly made, the comforter turned down invitingly.

I felt a flush of heat.

"Shay." His voice was deep when he turned and caught my eyes. My heart sped up. "Would you let me interview you for the podcast?"

I blinked. "What?"

"You're an important witness." His expression was earnest. "You knew Laurel so well. Maybe some helpful details will surface."

I tensed. Jamie was asking me to do the exact thing I'd avoided. Open doors I'd locked.

"It might help her," he said softly, and my heart squeezed.

You're here to be brave, I reminded myself. *Kick down the door, like Clem.*

"Okay," I whispered. "What exactly do you want to know?"

"Tell me where things went wrong, back in college."

"You want the whole story?"

Jamie laid his phone on the couch between us and pressed a button. Red bars raced across the screen, searching for sound.

"Yes," he said, and the bars jumped. "Tell me everything. From the beginning."

71

CHAPTER SEVEN

Transgressions Episode 705, interview transcript: Shay Deroy, Sept. 1, 2022 (unabridged)

SHAY DEROY: I'm not used to... It feels like there's a physical block in my throat, keeping the words down.

JAMIE KNIGHT: Try starting with something that feels safe.

SHAY: I guess I'll start with the fact that we were best friends. Maybe it was because we'd met under such hard circumstances. I think I told you what happened to Laurel at the start of freshman year...

JAMIE: You told me something happened to a friend of yours one weekend when you came to visit, but I didn't know the friend was Laurel. I never forgot what you said, though. How mad it made me. And scared.

SHAY: Why scared?

JAMIE: For you. The things you had to face that I never had to worry about.

SHAY: Well, I'm going to tell your listeners what happened, because too many people wanted us to shut up back then, and now Laurel's dead, without ever getting justice. She was raped, freshman year, at a party. The guy's name was Andrew Sch—

JAMIE: Don't say it, for libel purposes. Sorry.

SHAY: Oh. Okay. Well, he never paid for what he did. He went on to have two more great years at college. Probably raped more girls, too. Andrew, if you're out there, fuck you with all my heart.

(*Silence.*)

Sorry. I guess that wasn't a safe subject after all.

JAMIE: You were saying going through that experience made you, Laurel, and Clem really close.

SHAY: We were like sisters. I can't remember being apart for anything, except for class sometimes. Even then, we tried to take the same ones. I've never been that close to anyone, even you and Clara growing up.

It was funny, because the three of us were so different. I doubt I would've been friends with them if we hadn't been thrust together. Clem was a radical. Loudmouthed, sometimes abrasive, but so confident, and so knowledgeable about politics and history. She was kind of a genius. If you got her drunk, she could go a full hour without taking a breath about the demise of labor unions and the mistakes of the counterculture movement, like she was a host on *The Young Turks*. You could tell it was stuff she'd just taught herself. She was the perfect Whitney student in every way. Ironic, because she came from a huge family in the Midwest, like, seven siblings or something, and they were all religious conservatives. Her parents did not understand her. I used to picture her as this alien creature they adopted. From the stories she told, it seemed like her dad was even a little afraid of her. Which was kind of fair. Clem could be intense. But if you dug down, she was the most loyal friend.

Laurel was the opposite. Just as kind, but deathly shy and soft-spoken. She liked being behind the scenes as much as Clem liked being in the spotlight. You already know Laurel loved working in the theater. She was the epitome of a theater kid, and also an amazing seamstress, which sounds old-fashioned but was kind of cool, actually. She even used to make us clothes. Every holiday and birthday, Clem and I would get a Laurel original. She'd make us these wild things—shirts with fairy wings attached, long, droopy hats, like she was daring us to wear them. You should've seen the look on her face when we did. Incredulous, like a kid.

But the most important thing to know about Laurel, I think, is that even when she was happy, she was sad. It was a constant undercurrent. It wasn't just because of what happened freshman year. It was her dad. They'd been really close until he died in a car accident on his way to pick her up from band practice when she was fifteen. His death sent her mom into a tailspin, and Laurel felt like she had to take care of her. It's weird to say, but I think going away to college was a reprieve, because she didn't have to be the adult anymore.

I remember this one time, she brought us backstage after hours. She wanted to show us the costumes she was working on for an adaptation of *A Doll's House*. You remember that play.

JAMIE: Ibsen. We had to read it in high school. I hated it.

SHAY: Well, we were the only people in the theater, and we brought beer, so we were being silly. We got the idea to try on Laurel's costumes. I dressed up in this three-piece suit—one of the characters was a rich man—

JAMIE: (*laughing*) You dressed up in a three-piece?

SHAY: I couldn't stop staring at myself. I tucked my hair and I swear, I looked like a man. I remember getting goose bumps, imagining walking outside, no one watching me or making comments. I could be invisible. I could even walk around at night. Imagine not being scared all the time. You could travel the world in a three-piece suit.

JAMIE: Are you really scared all the time?

SHAY: I'll say this: when I'm outside, there's always a hum in the back of my mind. A little thread of anticipation. I think most girls are the same.

(*Throat clearing.*)

You know, I can't believe I'm telling you all of this.

(*Rustling.*)

Anyway. Laurel tried on men's clothes, too. A sweater with elbow patches and slacks. And then she started crying. When we asked what was wrong, she said she looked like her dad. We tried to comfort her, told her to take off the clothes, but she said no. She wanted to remember him, even if it meant feeling sad. That was just the way she was. She really missed him.

JAMIE: Was it hard being friends with someone that sad? Seems like a lot for a college student to handle.

SHAY: Sometimes, yes. But most of the time, we were happy and carefree. We stuck to each other. Became roommates, ate every meal together, studied together. If we went to a party, we hung out together, left together. At the time, it didn't seem weird. Looking back, it was probably a little codependent. But it was important to Clem and me to make Laurel happy. I think ever since the day we met her, we were trying to shield her. Take care of her, make something up to her. It was this shared mission.

(*Laughter.*)

I used to tuck her into bed, sometimes. I'd lie on the floor and tell her stories until she fell asleep.

JAMIE: That's very maternal of you.

SHAY: Yeah... Who knows where I learned it. It's funny, what you have hidden inside.

(*Silence.*)

Sophomore year, we had to choose which dorm we wanted to live in the following year. Laurel wanted Rothschild because it was closest to the Performing Arts Center, and she could stay late at rehearsals without being scared to walk home. Of course Clem and I said yes to that. The problem was, Rothschild only offered four-person suites. Our other friends all had plans. So we needed to find a fourth person to live with, someone who wasn't already attached. It was surprisingly hard.

JAMIE: You found Rachel Rockwell.

SHAY: Yes. She was in one of Laurel's classes, I forget which. Laurel told us Rachel was shy and didn't talk much. Didn't seem to have many friends. Laurel felt bad for her. Plus, she figured it would be nice to have a quiet roommate. So Clem and I agreed to meet her.

JAMIE: What was she like?

SHAY: The first thing we noticed was the most obvious: she was Laurel's doppelgänger. It was creepy how much they looked alike. I used to wonder if that's why Laurel had this weird sympathy for her, because it was like rooting for herself. As for Rachel's personality... She wasn't shy. Clem and I knew that off the bat, that Laurel had misread it. Rachel was... Look, there's no delicate way to say this. She was so cold and flat she didn't seem human. She was withdrawn, yes, and she didn't talk much, but that wasn't because she was *timid*. It was because she was fundamentally uninterested in other people, except for... you know, occasionally.

JAMIE: What do you mean?

SHAY: It's hard to describe. Have you ever met a person who seems completely out of reach, like you can't connect to them, and you feel like they're looking back at you...I don't know, like the way a shark watches a seal on the surface of the water. Calculating. Removed. Rachel unnerved me.

But she was our only option. Clem and I figured maybe there *was* something wrong with her, but it wasn't like we had to spend much time with her. She was just a ticket into Rothschild, to make Laurel happy. So we agreed. Junior year, we all moved in together.

At first, things were okay. Rachel kept to herself. I've never met anyone who spent so much time alone, but that was the way she liked it. She never wanted to do anything we invited her to. The only time she would engage was when one of us was sad. Or hurt. Then she was interested. Whenever Laurel cried, you couldn't get Rachel to leave her alone. She asked a million questions, and most of them were strange. Pointed, like she was trying to figure out the best way to poke your wound. It wasn't just emotional—physical, too. This one time, Clem cut her finger in the kitchen, and I swear to god, Rachel could smell it. She came out of her room and hovered. Didn't want to help get a Band-Aid or anything, just wanted to look.

JAMIE: Do you know if she was ever...I don't know, diagnosed with something?

SHAY: No idea. Clem and I wanted nothing to do with her after a month, but Laurel still felt sorry for her. She kept trying to get her to open up. But Rachel was super evasive. It was kind of a running joke between Clem and me, how dodgy she was.

Then one day, out of the blue, Rachel came home from class and announced her dad was in town and wanted to meet us. We were in the middle of watching a movie, and she just walked in front of the TV and started talking. Par for the course, really. She never cared what other people were doing if there was something she wanted.

JAMIE: Didn't you think it was weird she wanted you to meet her dad?

SHAY: We thought it was super weird. But Laurel convinced us to go. She kept saying...

(*Rustling.*)

JAMIE: Shay?

SHAY: She kept promising us we wouldn't regret being kind.
(*Silence.*)

Excuse me—

JAMIE: Wait. Shay. I'm putting the pieces together. Was Rachel's dad the man I saw in the city?

(*Creaking. Sounds of movement.*)

SHAY: I don't... I don't want to do this anymore. I'm sorry. I can't—

End of transcript.

I sprang from the couch, panic washing through me. I didn't want to remember him. I didn't want to remember what we'd done, who I'd been. Why was I doing this to myself?

Jamie had inched closer throughout the interview, as if drawn in by my words; now, he leapt to his feet.

"Shay." He stood behind me, and his hand found my shoulder.

Outside, night had fallen. Small lights near the shore revealed glimpses of the river, moving steadily in the dark.

"I'm sorry." I kept my face turned because I didn't want Jamie to see it. My eyes stung. For all I knew, I'd start crying in front of him. "I just—"

He moved around me until we faced each other, then took my hands. I still couldn't look at his eyes, so I looked at his fingers: long and elegant. "Hey. Don't worry. In your own time, okay?" His voice was so gentle.

He didn't know yet that I didn't deserve it.

CHAPTER EIGHT

The Hudson Mansion was far downriver, in a place with no lights. At night you could sense the surrounding trees by the quiet whisper of leaves moving in the wind, sense the river by the pinprick alertness of your body, alive to the presence of something deep and dangerous nearby. Twenty minutes of driving with nothing but velvet night through the windshield, and then the Mansion loomed ahead of us, sprawled atop a steep hill.

It was tall and turreted, stone-walled and beautiful. A place for people with money, that was clear. A lifetime without any had honed my ability to pick up on the tell: a cold, slippery unwelcome. There was something unsettling about the estate, too. Perhaps its domineering bulk.

I swallowed down unease as Jamie and I walked across the gravel parking lot. It was too quiet. The Mansion was a hotel and social club, it turned out, with a storied history of hosting old Hollywood stars and foreign dignitaries. Supposedly, it was home to Tongue-Cut Sparrow, though Jamie hadn't been able to find any official record of it. All that, yet the hum coming from inside was so low it barely competed with the crickets.

"I don't think this is the kind of thing where we can go to reception and ask them to point us to the Sparrow." Jamie adjusted his jacket as we walked. He wore a dark suit tonight, perfectly tailored, and moved with a new gait—a careless elegance, like he belonged in any room. "I think we're going to have to take a different tack."

"Like what?" I hadn't shared Jamie's packing foresight, so I'd had to shop and wore a black dress and spiked heels I'd paid full price for at a boutique near campus.

Jamie spoke in a low voice as two doormen pulled open the Mansion's thick doors, revealing an opulent stone-and-cream lobby. "We play the game. I'll be a man with too much money and a dark appetite, and you'll be a woman who's hollow inside and willing to be eaten. Eventually, someone will point us in the right direction."

I froze in the doorway, chill mixing with the faintest twinge of heat. Maybe I was more legible to Jamie than I'd realized.

But he only strode ahead, in the direction of the lobby bar. I hurried to catch up.

An hour later, we'd struck out. No one we'd talked to knew Tongue-Cut Sparrow, and covertly exploring on foot had turned up zero leads.

"Maybe it doesn't exist," Jamie said, leaning against the lobby wall and folding his arms, his well-fitted suit bunching over his shoulders. He ran a hand over his face; the movement opened the collar of his white shirt, revealing another inch of skin at his throat. "If it did, the bartender would've known. He'd direct people there all the time, right? Either he's lying, or the Sparrow's a rumor."

"I don't know." I lowered myself into a chair. "Maybe they want the front of house to be on the up-and-up. Less conspicuous, if the Sparrow's really supposed to be secret." I scanned the room. "Maybe we need to find someone who's so unimportant they're invisible. Someone no one thinks to keep secrets from."

My eyes lit on a young man dressed like a busboy, carrying a pitcher of water with lemon slices to a faraway table. He must have felt my attention, because he looked up and we locked eyes. He glanced down, shyly, then back up.

"Excuse me," I said to Jamie.

When I got to the table, he was replacing the empty water pitcher with exaggerated slowness. I stepped next to him, felt his eyes slide in my direction, and picked up a glass.

He tipped the pitcher, pouring me water.

"Hello," I said.

He swallowed. He looked no older than twenty. "Good evening, Ms...."

"Abrams," I lied.

"Is there something I can do for you?" My glass was full. The young man straightened the pitcher and held it to his chest, his nervousness plain.

If only it was always like this. If beauty was purely a power and not a target, a vulnerability that could draw the wolves and put you at their mercy.

"I was wondering." I bit my lip. "I've heard about...a place, here at the Mansion. Where you can have a different kind of fun. A more private, adult kind."

The young man had a wide, guileless face. When his Adam's apple bobbed, I knew.

"My friend told me about it," I pressed. I was barely speaking above a whisper, but his eyes darted around the lobby. "I think it's called the Sparrow..."

"Tongue-Cut Sparrow," he said, eyes on my water.

It did exist. I put a hand on his shoulder and spooked him; he nearly jumped backward. "Will you tell me how to get there?"

He looked at me for so long I worried I'd pushed my luck. But finally he said in the softest voice, "Are you sure you want to go?"

"Yes. Very much."

He nodded toward the bank of elevators. "Take those to the basement, turn left, and knock three times on the door at the end of the hall."

Victory. I felt a frisson of thrill.

He straightened and started to turn away, then glanced back. There was something like disappointment, or pity, in his eyes. "Stay safe," he murmured and walked away.

I turned and, from across the lobby, caught Jamie's waiting eyes.

———

When the elevator doors rolled open, we stared into a long, dark, empty hallway.

"I feel like Alice, falling down the rabbit hole," Jamie said.

I pointed to the left. "This way."

We walked silently. The farther from the elevators we got, the more the hallway changed. At first, there'd been dark wallpaper, and dim lights overhead. But eventually the wallpaper gave way to rough stone walls, the overhead bulbs to candles dripping wax from sconces on the wall. And suddenly, I heard it: an insistent thumping, running through the floor.

"Look." Jamie pointed. A single black door, far in the distance.

When we got there, I knocked three times, heart pounding, and glanced at Jamie. He looked resolute. *Be a professional,* I told myself. *Like him.*

After a minute, still no answer. Jamie tried, striking the door with three heavy blows.

A rectangular sliver in the door slid open, and the insistent thumping from inside grew louder. A pair of dark eyes gleamed back at us.

Jamie straightened. "Tongue-Cut Sparrow?"

"What do you want?" The voice was gruff.

"To come in," I said.

The eyes slid to me, then back to Jamie. Jamie started to say something, but the voice cut him off. "You're not members."

There were *memberships*? What was this place?

"Potential members," Jamie insisted. "How much to come in for one night?"

The eyes narrowed. After a moment: "A thousand each for a flyby. And you follow all the rules."

Jamie laughed incredulously, turning to me, but I kept my eyes on the door. "Deal."

It swung open, and music rushed out. A remarkably broad man in a pin-striped suit scowled at us. Behind him was a dark wall with a brilliant painting of a sparrow in flight, crying out at the sight of a jewel-handled knife.

I unzipped my purse and handed the man my credit card. I'd hear from Cal about this, no question. Who knew how this would be listed on the monthly bill? But right now, I didn't care.

"You give me everything," the man said, pointing at my purse. "Cell phones, wallets. You can't take anything but cash. No recordings. No outside contact."

Jamie and I looked at each other.

"Once you get inside, bathrooms are around the corner. You can change there."

Change? I didn't dare reveal my ignorance, so I simply nodded and gave the man everything I was holding. Jamie emptied his pockets. To my surprise, the man patted us down, hands moving briskly over my body.

"Fine," he said when he was through. He held out his palm. In the center rested two tiny, midnight-blue pills. "Last thing."

I froze.

"What are those?" Jamie demanded.

The giant man didn't blink. "They're the rule."

Jamie looked at me. "I don't know..."

I didn't want to lose control. Step inside weaponless and vulnerable, a soft thing, easy to tear. The music seemed to grow louder, more sinister and disorienting. That was panic seeping in. This was everything I'd spent years avoiding, the exact sort of situation I'd sworn never to expose myself to again. But...

Laurel was here, I told myself. *Odds are, she stood in this very spot and took a pill just like this one, and you need to know why. Do it for her. What other choice do you have?*

What other choice *did* I have? I reached for the pill and swallowed.

For Laurel.

We stepped through the door in the wall and entered a perverse underground fairyland. It was a vast cave, the rocky ceilings high as a cathedral, stalactites reaching down like grasping fingers, stone pillars creating a maze of rooms. Was this why the Mansion was built atop a hill? We had to be deep inside it now. Through the door, the volume was overwhelming; I could feel the bass in my bones, trying to wrest control over my heartbeat. I couldn't imagine what it took to keep this sound from leaking out into the Mansion's grounds.

Hot baths dotted the cave, their turquoise waters lit like jewels. Candles lined the pathways, as if each pool were an altar. There were people everywhere, more men than women, some of them dancing close, kissing against walls, some pressing into each other in the baths. Most were naked, the rest in nothing but panties or tight, clinging boxers. I nearly choked.

Jamie pulled me close enough to hear over the music. "I think I know why we're supposed to change."

I knew I should protest, maybe even leave, climb my way out of the Mansion. But the panic from earlier was leaking out of me. In its place, a night-blooming flower unfurled its petals, spreading a warm, easy nectar that made my limbs languid.

I leaned even closer to Jamie. "I think the pill was ecstasy. Or some sort of relaxant."

He nodded. "I'm feeling it, too. Are you sure you want to keep going?"

I nodded. "Laurel came here. I'm sure of it." I was Alice, and Laurel was my rabbit. I would chase her into any wonderland, no matter how dark. I pushed Jamie's chest. "Get changed."

I said nothing when he emerged from the bathroom in slim black boxers, but I didn't look away from his stomach, muscles taut as he walked, or the sharp, elegant lines of his clavicle, bones slashing into his broad shoulders like brushstrokes. The night-blooming flower's magic was strong, lending me boldness. It told me there was no reason to be shy, so I leaned against the bar and watched him.

But when Jamie drew close, his eyes cut away, like he was embarrassed to see me in a bra and panties, or too honorable to look. "Where should we start?" he asked.

A stranger walked up to the bar beside me and, unlike Jamie, gave me a close look. He was older, with a thick middle and an even thicker mane of salt-and-pepper hair. "I've never seen you before," he said, eyes lingering on my chest. "What's your poison?"

"I'm not drinking." Not when a mysterious pill was snaking through my body.

"You with him?" The man nodded at Jamie. "Because I don't do doubles."

"No. But—"

He took a step closer. "Then let's talk. I'm a giver, not a taker. Just tell me what you'd like done, and what it'll cost me." He spoke the words with the unhurried cadence of someone uttering something perfectly normal.

What would have been alarm before the midnight pill was now only a muted spark of curiosity. "What I'd like done?"

Beside me, Jamie stiffened.

The man's smile was easy. "Of course. I'll do anything. Name your price."

I looked around the cave cathedral, at the close-pressed bodies on the dance floor and in the baths, all that flesh lit by flickering candlelight. Tongue-Cut Sparrow was a marketplace.

I turned back to the man and placed a hand on Jamie's arm. "Actually, I am with him."

"Right." I could hear the dismissal in his voice as he turned back to the bar. "Whatever you say, vanilla."

I leaned in. "Have you been coming here long?"

His eyes narrowed. "Why?"

"I'm pretty sure there was a woman who used to come here, shorter than me, about five six, with light-blond hair and dark eyes. Pretty, real pale and soft-spoken. Her name was Laurel Hargrove. Is there any chance you remember someone like her?"

"Honey." The man's voice dripped with condescension. "There's no chance I'd remember a single girl. And we don't use names here."

The bartender slid a drink in front of the man, even though in all the time he'd been at the bar, he hadn't ordered one. "Some advice, because you're obviously new: Don't ask questions. You won't like what happens."

Jamie tensed. I tightened my grip on his arm until the man slipped away into a dark corner. Jamie glanced at the bartender. "Come on. Somewhere more private."

I followed him across the dance floor, the sea of writhing bodies opening and surrounding us. Limbs brushed me—strong legs and soft arms and round breasts—trailing pleasure over my skin. The dark, charming voice that lived inside my head whispered, *It feels good, doesn't it? Open yourself. Take it.* Jamie laced his fingers through mine, and I closed my eyes, getting lost, letting the bass take control of my heartbeat.

But Jamie tugged me forward, forcing me to put one foot in front of the other.

We broke free of the dance floor, and cool, musty air kissed my skin. Jamie didn't let go of my hand until we'd made it to one of the baths in the corner. He sank into the turquoise water and let it swallow him whole, reemerging with rivulets running down his face. I slipped in after him. The water was intoxicatingly warm, like silk against my skin. I'd hoped it would calm me, wash away the sensations, but it only made them worse.

I groaned, closing my eyes, and leaned my head against the edge of the bath. "Jamie, I can't think straight."

I heard rustling and opened my eyes to find him moving closer, away from a man who'd slipped into the tub after us. Jamie sank down so we were eye level and drew so close it must've looked, from far away, like we were embracing.

"Is this okay?" He spoke in a low voice. "For privacy."

I nodded, and he placed his arms on either side of me, like a cage. *You like cages,* the dark voice whispered. *You're always walking into them.*

"The pill," I said. "It's seriously messing me up."

"I know." Jamie's pupils were dilated. "Me too. We have to push past it. Find the sane voice in the fog."

"I don't think I have one," I said, and he smiled like I was joking.

"Here's what we know." He was whispering, so I leaned closer. "This place is extremely secretive. Intense security. Caters to members, mostly, but not impossible to get inside if you have enough money. The guy at the bar was excited you were new, so they must get mostly regulars. And obviously, people are buying and selling sex."

I looked around. "Rich men are buying sex," I clarified. "The men are older than the women by a few decades, on average. And they outnumber them by a lot."

Jamie combed fingers through his wet hair. "Why was this place on Laurel's radar?" He focused on me. "Do you think she needed money?"

Laurel had been desperate enough to beg for a catering job. "Maybe. But—" Being this close to Jamie was distracting. My body was urging me to move even closer, though that was ridiculous because I was married, and Jamie was my friend, and the heat in my blood was only the effect of the pill. Still...I reached up and brushed an errant strand of wet hair off his forehead.

His eyes fluttered closed.

"I can't imagine Laurel letting a stranger touch her," I said. But that wasn't right, was it? Because everything had changed junior year. We'd each discovered such startling proclivities, unknown capacities, our insides dark and bottomless as the deepest caves.

Maybe that was the answer. Maybe Laurel had been broken by what happened in college, and broke, so she'd turned to this. After all, selling yourself to a man for a night was nothing compared to what we'd done.

"You two are new."

The voice was honeyed. Jamie and I turned to find a beautiful dark-haired woman smiling at us, the water brushing the undersides of her full breasts.

"And gorgeous." The woman drew closer. "Look at the two of you, alone in your corner. Can I join?"

Jamie glanced at me. A source, if handled right.

"Sure," I said. "What's your—" Too late, I remembered the man's admonishment.

She smiled knowingly. "Are you buying or selling? Together, or separate?" She eyed my wedding ring. "Forgive the bluntness. I like to do business up front."

"Buying," Jamie said and withdrew his arms to let the woman closer. "And we're a package deal."

"I was hoping." She traced her thumb down Jamie's face, then turned to me, laid her palm against my jaw. Her skin was wet and silky; she smelled of clean minerals, like the water. "So. What do you like?"

Jamie swallowed. I hadn't been able to look away from him ever since the woman's soft hands had found our faces, drawing us together, pressing warm heat.

She moved her thumb down Jamie's neck, skimming his shoulders. "What are you offering?" he asked.

She smiled. Her voice lowered conspiratorially. "I'll do anything. Electro, dom-sub, bondage, humiliation." The words rolled off her tongue. "There aren't many like me."

"Humiliation," I said, snagging on the word. "What's that?"

"Exactly what it sounds like." She leaned in so close her lips brushed my ear. I found Jamie's eyes over her shoulder, and my pulse jumped. "I can degrade you, if you want." Her whispered voice curled inside me. "I'll tell you what a slut you are. What a cunt, a liar, a fraud who doesn't deserve anything you have." The tip of her tongue licked the shell of my ear. "Pathetic bitch."

Every nerve in my body was on fire; every hair on my arms raised. The words—and the memories they raised—scythed a path through the fog of the drug. Suddenly I had a terrible hunch about why Laurel might've come here.

The woman pulled back and grinned. "I can tell you like that." She winked. "Don't worry, hon. Your kinks aren't your values. It's supposed to be liberating."

My voice was hoarse. "How long have you been coming here?"

"You're not asking my age, because that would be—"

"No. It's just... We're new. It would be nice to find someone with experience."

"In that case, one more year and I get my service medal."

She was joking, but I couldn't help being sidetracked. There was no way this woman was older than midtwenties. When had she started?

No. Focus. I was here for a different girl. "Do you know other women who liked humiliation? Maybe one who started coming around five or six years ago?"

She blinked at my intensity.

"We know it's a long shot," Jamie said, faithfully following my lead. "But you said there aren't many who do it all, like you. Do you remember another woman who maybe—" He shot me a look, asking a silent question, and I felt my cheeks flame in response. "Liked it kind of rough?"

"Five six, blond, pale, pretty," I added. "Midtwenties."

The grin faded from the woman's face. "Are you saying you want someone else?"

"No," I said. "We're looking for her. Please. She would have wanted humiliation exclusively." If Jamie could read between the lines, he'd know that was an admission. But I didn't have the luxury of hiding because I was ashamed. Not if this woman could tell me something about Laurel.

Her eyes softened. "Don't tell me it's another missing girl."

"Did you know any of them?" Jamie was excited. "The missing women?"

She stiffened. "You're not a reporter, are you?"

"We're just looking for a friend," I said.

She met my eyes. "If she's a friend…then, yes. I knew some girls who came through here, then disappeared. Months, sometimes years later, I'd see their faces on posters. But never on the news."

Jamie opened his mouth to ask another question, but she cut him off. "There've been a few girls like yours. The masochists. There might have been one who matched your description, a few years back. I only remember because there aren't many women who are regulars here— plenty of men, but not us. And she was here every goddamn night. Blond, pale, looked fresh as a bunny, like she'd just come out of boarding school, somewhere the students wear those plaid skirts and knee socks, you know? A perfect little girl. The daddies loved her. Every night, she was looking for someone to hurt her better than the night before."

My heart was in my throat. "Did she find someone?"

The woman's eyes were sad. "She stopped coming, didn't she?"

I flew across the gravel, wet hair plastered to my face. Jamie rushed after me. "Shay, slow down." He eyed the valet and lowered his voice. "We don't know if that woman was even talking about Laurel. It could've been anyone."

The valet rushed off to find my rental. I looked back at the Mansion, dimly lit, sprawling and opulent and stone-faced. No hint of what was happening underground, the sex and drugs and missing women. And Laurel—ghostly Laurel and her search for pain.

I felt too hot, like I was burning from the inside out. It had to be the pill.

The car pulled up and Jamie took the wheel. We drove in silence until I remembered it had been hours since I checked my phone. I clicked the screen: two missed calls, both from an Indiana number. It was Laurel's mom.

"Pull over," I said.

Obediently, Jamie pulled to the side of the road and cut the engine, casting us into velvety darkness. I rolled the window down, needing air on my face, and dialed.

Please pick up.

"Hello?" The voice was ragged.

"Mrs. Hargrove?" I took a deep breath. "It's Shay Evans, Laurel's friend from college, returning your call."

"Laurel's friend." Mrs. Hargrove's words were slurred. I could tell immediately she was drunk.

"Yes, ma'am," I said, eighteen again. "I'm so sorry for your loss. I wanted to talk to you because I loved Laurel, and I'm worried the police aren't investigating her death properly. I was hoping—"

There was a crashing noise, and a sharp crack across the line.

"Mrs. Hargrove? Are you all right? Did you fall?"

"You want to hash out all the gory details." Laurel's mom sounded breathless. "Did you know I hadn't talked to her in years?"

I looked through the window at the night sky. The stars were so vivid that I thought, for a second, they'd crept closer. Maybe Laurel had done it, like a sign.

"I'm sorry, Mrs. Hargrove."

Jamie caught my eye and mouthed *Speaker?* I pressed the button, and Mrs. Hargrove's voice filled the car. "I was worried about her. That's why she stopped talking to me, because she said I was nagging. I was either too distant or too close. I could never win, no matter what I did. She told you her daddy died in high school?"

"Yes," I said quietly.

"Then you probably know I went off the deep end and left Laurel to fend for herself. I'm sure that's why you're calling. It's okay. I deserve whatever you've got."

"I'm not calling to blame you for anything, Mrs. Hargrove."

"I'm the reason Laurel started down this path. It's my fault."

She wasn't making any sense. "What path?"

"I should've stopped her."

"From what?"

"That thing she used to do...cutting herself up. She blamed herself."

Jamie's eyebrows shot up.

Laurel had never said anything about hurting herself. I'd thought we told each other everything.

"I didn't do a good job when she was a teenager, so I tried to be better when she was in college. But she cut me off for a whole damn year, no contact, and then her friend died, and she reached out, and I tried to be there for her, I really did." Mrs. Hargrove paused. "The stories Laurel used to tell about her, always *Clem this, Clem that*, like she was a superhero. Used to make me laugh. I tried to make sure Laurel was okay after she passed."

I found I couldn't speak.

Mrs. Hargrove's voice lost its brightness. "I could tell she was getting depressed again. The signs were there. Did you see it, too?"

I cleared my throat. "Laurel and I hadn't really talked in a while."

"Well, then you know how she was. Instead of letting me help her, she cut me off again, and that was the last time I heard from her." Mrs. Hargrove's voice grew raspy. "I should've flown out there, made her see me in person."

"What if Laurel didn't kill herself? What if someone hurt her? I really think—"

To my surprise, she laughed. "I used to do that, too. Look for any excuse so I didn't have to look at myself."

"But—"

"I'm going to bed now," Mrs. Hargrove said. "You got my confession, and I'm tired. You remember her, okay? Remember how sweet she was. What a sweet girl, and a sweet friend. A darling daughter. She deserved better."

"Yes, ma'am."

The line went dead.

We drove in silence, Laurel's mother's words filling the car so there wasn't room for anything else. I stared at the stars the whole way, thinking about what she'd said about her daughter's bottomless pain. What the dark-haired woman in Tongue-Cut Sparrow had said about a woman who may or may not have been Laurel, doing her best to chase it.

When Jamie finally pulled into a spot in front of his motel, he turned and gripped my shoulder. The drugs were still alive inside me. His touch radiated through my skin.

"Do you think I got it wrong?" His voice was strangled, eyes no longer dilated but bloodshot. "Do you think I got it in my head that Laurel was murdered, and convinced you to drop your life and come out here, and it was suicide all along? You heard her mom."

"I don't think we're wrong."

"But it makes sense. Suicide fits her emotional state and history of self-harm."

"What about the fact that she hadn't held a job in years, and her strange living habits, disappearing months on end?"

"Sounds like depression to me."

"What about Tongue-Cut Sparrow? A secret sex club... Come on."

"We didn't find anything solid. Even if Laurel ended up there, there's no real connection we can track."

"But the symbol on her arm—what's that about?"

"It could've been anything. A random catering burn Edie assigned meaning to in a moment of shock."

"You're wrong. Laurel wouldn't have killed herself." I'd *known* her. That had to be true, because at this point, I had so little left of her to hold on to. I laid my hand over Jamie's. "Let me tell you the next part of my story. What I couldn't say yesterday."

He frowned. "Now?"

"Yes, right now. Let me tell you, and then you'll understand."

"Look, it's not that I don't want to hear, but you shouldn't agree to an interview when you're intoxicated."

"It's the only way I'll do it." As soon as I said it, I knew it was true. It was now, while the pill from Tongue-Cut Sparrow dulled my shame, or never.

Jamie stared at me for a long time. Finally, he shoved the car door open. "Fine. Then steel yourself for the majesty of the Motel 6."

CHAPTER NINE

Transgressions *Episode 705, interview transcript: Shay Deroy, Sept. 3, 2022 (unabridged)*

SHAY DEROY: His name was Don Rockwell.

(*Silence.*)

    I can't describe how it feels just to say that. I'm sweating, my heart's pounding. It feels like somehow I've alerted him, like he can sense me now, wherever he is.

JAMIE KNIGHT: You're safe here.

SHAY: You can't promise that. But I'm going to do the best I can to tell you what happened anyway. I might not get everything right. If you asked Laurel, you might get a different story. I'm saying this to be honest.

JAMIE: I understand your memory's not perfect. Just tell me what you remember, in as much detail as possible.

SHAY: Okay.

(*Exhale static.*)

His name was Don Rockwell, and he was Rachel's father, and we had no idea what he'd be like. Clem and I thought probably like Rachel, right? Cold and strange. We didn't know anything about her mom, or if she had any siblings. Just that her dad was in town and he wanted to take us to dinner at March on the Park.

JAMIE: Wait, the Michelin-star restaurant in the city? With the waiting list?

SHAY: We were just as surprised. The Rockwells had money, clearly. Which you'd never guess from Rachel.

JAMIE: Tell me about Don.

SHAY: He sent a car for us. We got all dressed up, which for Laurel and me meant dresses and for Clem meant her best button-down. Rachel wore flip-flops, and I remember wondering if she just didn't care, or if that was some big fuck-you. When we got to March, the host brought us up to a private room at the top of the restaurant, with windows overlooking Central Park. I'd never been anywhere like it. It was so nice it made me feel sick, like someone was going to recognize I didn't belong and make me leave. I can still feel the butterflies in my stomach, just talking about it. Or maybe that's the pill.

JAMIE: Maybe don't mention the pill.

SHAY: Oh. Sorry.

JAMIE: It's okay. We can edit it out. What was Don like?

SHAY: He was waiting for us in the room. When we walked in, and I saw him sitting in the center of the table, at the top of the world, looking out over Central Park, I thought he was the most beautiful man I'd ever seen. And then immediately I felt guilty, because he was Rachel's father. But he looked nothing like her. He was tall, and so...solid. His shoulders were so broad they spanned the width of the chair. He was wearing a suit, a dark one, and he was just...powerful. Sophisticated. Commanding. I don't know how else to describe him. He rose to shake our hands, and his handshake was so firm. We met eyes, and I just... Did you ever watch the show *Mad Men*?

JAMIE: Who hasn't?

SHAY: He looked like Don Draper.

JAMIE: Right. I can see how that would make an impression.

SHAY: I had no idea how Rachel had come from a man like that. I felt sorry for him, actually, that he had such a strange, antisocial daughter. He and Rachel didn't hug or even touch. I remember that, because I thought it was strange he was more affectionate with us than with her. But then I realized it must be because he knew how she was, and he was being respectful. I was fascinated by that. A good father.

He said something like, "Since you're Rachel's friends, I'd like you to be my friends, too. Why don't you call me Don?"

I'd had adults ask a lot of things of me, but I'd never had one want to be my friend, like we were equals. It felt glamorous. And he ordered everything on the menu. I'm serious. We had three servers all to ourselves, and he ordered oysters and steaks and raw fish, all these things I'd never tried. He gave Clem a hard time for being vegan, joked it was unnatural, but he ordered every vegetable on the menu just for her. And so much wine, bottle after bottle. He knew a lot about it. I mean, he could have said anything and it would have sounded right to me, because I knew nothing about wine. But he was very self-assured. Worldly. And he kept pouring and pouring. That night was the farthest I'd ever felt from Heller, Texas. I was a junior at Whitney, so I'd been in New York for years, but it was the first time I felt like a real city girl.

JAMIE: Sounds opulent.

SHAY: Don was so charming. He wanted to know everything about us: our majors, where we came from, what we wanted to do after college, what we did and didn't like about Whitney. He said Rachel gushed about us, so he knew he had to meet us. That raised all of our eyebrows, and then obviously made me feel guilty that we'd been bad-mouthing her while she'd been saying nice things about us.

Then Don said something unexpected. He told us that ever since Rachel started at Whitney, they'd been talking about what it was like to be a young woman on a college campus in this day and age. How her professors treated her, what they taught, how the other students acted, the resources the school provided. He said he'd grown concerned something was lacking, and that was another reason he'd wanted to meet us.

Clem said, "Really? Like what?" Her tone was skeptical. From time to time, we met people, usually men, who dragged Whitney for being too liberal or too feminist or too...female, I guess. Clem had no patience for it. I remember her eyeing her plate, and I'm sure she was thinking, great, if Rachel's dad turns out to be a tool, I'm going to have to stop eating this forty-dollar vegetable lasagna. I was too busy being surprised Rachel had conversations of substance with anyone.

But Don said, "I'm worried they're not empowering women the way they should."

That hooked us. He could tell, because he said, "The college claims it's progressive, which is great, but are they actually teaching you to own your power as *women*? From everything I can gather, the college's brand of feminism is to teach young women how to ape men. Rachel took this business class, and all the things her professor taught them made a good leader were essentially male CEO stereotypes: you're supposed to be loud, dominant, ruthless. I was saying to Rachel, 'Are you really supposed to deny who you are to be considered successful?' And that's just one example. I think it's a shame. You're the ones who have the opportunity to course correct after all these years, and they're only indoctrinating you into thinking you need to be something that doesn't come naturally. That's a recipe for self-loathing if I've ever heard one. Rachel sure feels it."

Clem, Laurel, and I looked at each other, totally surprised. We'd been talking about the exact same thing in our suite a week or so back, how it felt like the rules for who we could be, and what we could enjoy as feminist women, were so rigid and fiercely monitored. Laurel had this theater professor who kept telling her she had to speak up in class, even though she was the costume person and shy. One day the professor told Laurel that she was setting women back a hundred years by being so meek. Clem's soccer coach made fun of her for reading a romance novel she saw in her duffel bag and said something like, "What's that fluff? I thought Whitney was for smart girls." And I'd always known, since the day I showed up on campus, that I couldn't tell anyone at Whitney I'd been in pageants. There were so many things you weren't allowed to do if you wanted to be the right kind of girl. Being a woman at Whitney came with as many rules as being a woman in East Texas.

But it was surreal to hear Don say these things. No man had ever talked like that to me.

So I said, "I completely agree with you." And I could tell that made him happy.

He said, "Well, I wanted to meet you to see Rachel's influences. And to check up on you, of course. I've come to care about you, you know, vicariously through Rachel. I can tell you're good girls."

That made Laurel blush.

Don said, "At the risk of sounding like a pretentious asshole—or worse, like one of your professors—I've done a lot of research on self-actualization. I've been trying to figure out why people in the past seemed so much more connected to the world and at peace with themselves, unlike all this modern angst and alienation. And I'll tell you something: Aristotle was every bit the genius they say he was. He wrote extensively about men and women— what they needed to be happy, how they were alike and different. And he *celebrated* those differences. It's a shame how far adrift we've come from all that wealth of knowledge, under the guise of progress."

Our professors had taught us about false progress, so the concept was familiar. We all nodded, and Don could tell we were on the same page, because he started pouring more wine and changed the subject to how Greeks in Aristotle's time used to make it.

But for the rest of the night, every so often when someone was talking, he'd catch my eye across the table and smile. It was like we were sharing a secret. Like we were the adults in the room, on the same level, and Clem and Laurel and Rachel were the kids. It was thrilling. I started to think I'd done something right, to get his attention. When it was time to go home, he helped me put my coat on, slipping it over my shoulders. We got close, and I...

(*Silence.*)

JAMIE: What?

SHAY: Well... I could smell him. Spices and wood. It hit me like lightning. The feeling was intense. I was attracted to him, even though he was my roommate's father. It's embarrassing to say out loud.

JAMIE: It's just you and me.

SHAY: On the ride home, even Clem said how insightful he was, how rare that was for a man. We realized Don had talked about everything under the sun except himself, not once. Laurel said he reminded her of her dad, who was always more interested in other people, a real selfless man. That was the highest compliment Laurel could give anyone. I remember sitting there in the car and feeling... jealous, I guess. I could tell how much she liked Don, but I didn't want her to bond with him.

We talked about him a lot after that night. I couldn't stop thinking about him. It was this strange obsession. He pulled at me like a magnet. I... Jamie...

JAMIE: Yes?

SHAY: I'm going to tell you something that might make you uncomfortable. But I want to tell the truth about the impression Don made on me. So you understand everything else.

JAMIE: Right now, don't think of me as your friend. Think of me as a journalist. I want to hear the truth.

SHAY: Okay. After that night at the restaurant, I started... fantasizing about him. I daydreamed about seeing him again, and what would happen. I'd never touched myself before, then all of a sudden, I couldn't stop. I was addicted. He was handsome, and smart, and so confident, of course, but I think the biggest part was that he was Rachel's dad and completely off-limits. I've always been that way. Wanted only the people I couldn't have. I don't know why.

JAMIE: Shay...don't you?

(*Silence.*)

SHAY: Do you mind if I lie down on your bed?

JAMIE: Make yourself comfortable.

(*Rustling. Creaking springs.*)

SHAY: A few weeks later, probably mid-October, junior year, he invited us out again. Clem was the only one who thought it was strange. I remember her saying one dinner made sense. A lot of students' parents came in town and took their friends out. But two dinners, that was a little weird. Except Laurel and I wouldn't stop talking about

how excited we were, and Clem didn't want to be left out.
That was a big thing with her. She'd always been the odd
one out with her family, so she'd do anything to avoid it.
Eventually, she jumped back on the Don train.

JAMIE: How did Rachel handle your obsession with her
father?

SHAY: We tried not to talk about him around her. But when
we couldn't help it—when we slipped or we just had to
ask her a question—she didn't seem to care. It was like he
was any other person.

JAMIE: Where'd he take you the second time?

SHAY: Out for drinks, at this bar he was an investor in, which
was still being built. It was in the penthouse of this new
building in SoHo. He said we were the first people to go
up there. It was totally empty, just us and the bar, and
you could still see all the piping in the ceiling. I think they
ended up naming it the Old Guard.

JAMIE: Really? I've been there. It's kind of famous now. They
hosted the Pulitzer after-party last year. Was Don in real
estate?

SHAY: He was an investor. He said his business was
networking with successful people, men who had tips on
what was about to make a killing. He was happy to see
us that night. He told us he'd decided to settle down, buy
a house, give up traveling to be closer to Rachel, and he
wanted to celebrate.

I actually had to step out to the bathroom after he said
that.

JAMIE: Why?

SHAY: Here was this man, you know, who actually wanted to

spend time with his daughter. *Rachel*, of all people, had a dad who loved her.

JAMIE: Meanwhile, you—

SHAY: I just needed a minute. When I came back, Don looked at me, and he didn't say anything, but I swear he knew what I was feeling. That's how he was. He could look straight through my skull. He poured us wine again, and this time, we tried asking him questions about his life, but he said there wasn't much to know, and we were more interesting. You have to understand how magnetic he was. When he said that, I really felt like I was the most interesting person in the world.

That night he wanted to know about our families. We got drunk pretty quick, and everything came spilling out, like we'd all just been waiting for him to ask. You remember being that age, right? So wrapped up in yourself, willing to bare your soul. Deep down, you think you're the most interesting person in the world. Laurel told him all about her dad dying, how her mom collapsed into herself. Clem told him her parents had never understood her, that there'd always been this unbridgeable gulf that made her lonely. I told him the least, but still too much—stuff only Clem and Laurel had heard. When I was done talking, Don looked at me and said, "Tell me who failed you. The first name that comes to mind." Like he was some kind of therapist.

There were a lot of answers I could've given. But knee-jerk, I said, "My dad." And even Clem and Laurel were surprised, because I never talked about him.

I think it was just...Don made me feel safe. He was a

father himself. And there was something about him: you wanted to answer truthfully when he asked you a question. He was so open it felt cathartic.

I didn't want to leave that night, but Clem had soccer practice the next morning, so we had to. Don waited until everyone left for the car, then pulled me aside, just the two of us. My heart was pounding. Being alone with him was all I'd thought about for weeks. So to have it actually happen was like being under a spell. He put his hands on my face, like this—one hand on this cheek, one there—and told me he was grateful I was Rachel's friend. He said her mom had passed away, and he was determined to be a good father to make up for it. I told him, "I admire that more than you know."

He said, "I think I do know, actually." And then he said, in the same breath, "Tell me the truth: how often do people tell you you're beautiful?"

In my experience, when people said you were beautiful, it was always a power move—the moment another person let you know they'd clocked you, that you were a body they'd taken stock of, calculated and assessed. But Don was different. He was a good man who wasn't supposed to think I was beautiful, because I was younger and his daughter's friend. But he was saying it anyway, which meant he hadn't been able to help himself. He was going out on a limb. That made him vulnerable and me the powerful one. It felt like a victory.

So I said, "Like that? Not often." And he laughed and said he doubted that was true.

Then he said, "But you'd be even prettier with blond hair."

It stung. The power slipped back out of my hands.

He rubbed his thumb over my cheek, kind of soothingly, and my heartbeat hitched. I knew it was wrong. Laurel and Clem and Rachel were waiting outside, wondering what was taking so long. And there I was, standing in a bar with Rachel's dad, wanting something I wasn't supposed to want.

He looked me in the eyes and said, "Tell me your father's name."

I was surprised but said, "He barely counts. But his name was Peter."

He leaned in and said, in a low voice, like a secret, "You can tell me anything, you know. Feel however you want to feel. It's only natural. Give yourself a break."

My heart was racing... I couldn't tell if he knew what I really wanted. Then he whispered, "If you want to call me Don, or Dad, or Peter, do it. Anything you want, okay? Don't worry so much. Whatever makes you feel good." Then he put his arm around my waist and kind of pushed me toward the door. He said, "Go home with your friends, young lady."

JAMIE: And none of that struck you as strange?

SHAY: It did. But not an off-putting strange. A strange that intrigued me. The truth is, I *wanted* to know what he thought of me. I even wanted him to tell me what to do. Back then I was kind of lost. And half in love with the version of him from my daydreams.

(*Silence.*)

(*Throat clearing.*)

JAMIE: Maybe we should quit for now. It's late. I can hear in

your voice how tired you are. Your eyes are barely staying
open.

SHAY: But I have to tell you the next part...

(*Heavy breathing.*)

When we went to his house...

End of transcript.

I woke, squinting, as Jamie bent over me, his face close to mine for the
first time since the hot baths. I didn't know what he was doing, but I was
too tired to care. I felt a blanket, stiff with starch but warm, slide up my
shoulders. He was tucking me in.

My voice was small and faraway. "I can leave."

"Shh," he said and settled on the floor.

CHAPTER TEN

I went back to Tongue-Cut Sparrow the next night, ignoring Cal's calls and lying to Jamie, telling him I didn't feel well. In a way, it was true: ever since waking up in his hotel room with Don's unburied name thick in my throat, I'd burned feverish to *do something*. Make progress, no matter the risk. Saying Don's name out loud for the first time in years had sparked something back to life—cracked opened the door to the past—and I needed it dead and closed as quickly as possible. But I couldn't do that until I found out the truth about Laurel.

I knew part of that truth was waiting at the Sparrow. It was an instinct, a recognition that had welled inside me when the woman in the hot bath whispered what she could do to me. I didn't like it, but I knew why Laurel might have been drawn to this.

So I'd almost clawed my skin off waiting for nightfall, and then I drove through the darkness back to the Hudson Mansion, rapped on the black door, paid the fine, took the pill. Now I was back inside the cave, the goblin market, slipping between hungry people, the crowd bigger than the night before, the music louder, the effects of the drug anticipated but still disorienting.

Jamie would be pissed I'd lied and come alone. But without him, I was a rabbit in a wolf's den, and they would show their teeth quicker. If I was born bait, I would at least dangle myself.

And it worked. All night I'd entertained conversations from people looking to buy me, or sell themselves—up until the point I asked my questions about Laurel, and their eyes glazed over, or narrowed in confusion, and soon they were walking away in favor of someone less complicated. A few warned me, similar to what the man had said last night: *Don't ask questions. You won't like the consequences.*

This time around, I clocked the watching eyes. Large, well-dressed men, like the man at the door, tucked unobtrusively into corners, eyes sliding over the dance floor, dipping into the hot baths, watching and waiting. They were the consequences, presumably.

I'd had enough of dead ends. I knifed across the dance floor to the bathroom, thinking to regroup, plot a different strategy. Would someone be more forthcoming if I agreed to their price and got them alone? Would they talk in the afterglow? What wouldn't I do to know the truth about Laurel, the friend I'd failed to protect?

I pushed open the heavy door. The bathroom was menacing and beautiful: dark as sin, dim light from waxy, flickering candles, and round mirrors, each of them cracked through the middle.

The door closed behind me and snuffed out the music, leaving nothing but the bass vibrating the walls, becoming an anxious crawl under my skin. The bathroom was empty except for a single woman at the end of the counter, snorting a line. She looked up.

"Sorry," I said, halting in place.

A smile spread over her face. She was pretty: red hair, freckles, dark halos of eyeliner. Younger than me, but you couldn't tell by the way she sized me up. "New, huh?"

I resumed moving and stood in front of a mirror, two sinks away. "That obvious?"

"Normally, girls don't look so surprised by—" She gestured at the drugs on the counter. "Not with everything happening out there."

"Right." I looked at myself in the mirror. The crack in the glass ran horizontal, splitting my face in two. My mouth moved, but above it, my eyes stayed still—glittering, pupils dilated. A stranger's eyes. "Does it help?"

Her voice was a honeyed trap. "With what?"

I turned to face her. "Everything happening out there."

She grinned this time, rubbing fingers under her nose, examining herself in the mirror. "Please. This place is for amateurs."

I stood taller. "What do you mean?"

She pursed her lips, which were almost as red as her hair. "Amateurs and hustlers. The Sparrow's where you come to make a little money, indulge people who want to pretend to be a freak for a night. It's not the real deal."

I found myself leaning in her direction, the edge of the counter digging into my hip. "Where do you find that?"

She slid me a coy look. "Asks the nice girl."

"I'm not nice." I took a step closer.

She scanned me. "Yeah, right. I can smell it on you. Money, good school, dinners around the table with your family growing up. Choir girl, probably." She glanced down at my ring finger, and I resisted the urge to turn the diamond. "It's like a film on your skin. You can take your clothes off, let someone do filthy things to you in the dark. But it doesn't wash off."

I'd done a good job with myself, then. I was a convincing forgery.

"Maybe so," I lied. "But like I said, I'm not nice."

She eyed me. "All right. Everyone knows the Sparrow's for people who want to dabble in kink. It's not for true believers."

"Why not?" Would Laurel have known?

"It's the transaction," the woman said, turning to look at herself again in the mirror, skimming a hand through her hair. "Cheapens it. Makes it a performance. When they're fucking you, you can't shake that you know it's not real. They're hitting you and calling you a cunt because it's a novelty they paid for. They don't actually mean it. And they have to really mean it for it to feel good." She gave me a small smile. "Don't you think?"

"Yes," I said, sliding into place beside her.

She narrowed her eyes at my nearness.

"I want to be hurt by someone who means it." I ignored the hum of warning inside me. I tilted my head, offering the long, exposed line of my neck. "I want someone who can see who I am underneath." I dropped my eyes to the countertop, allowing headiness to wash over me, leaning in to the effects of the pill. "I thought I could live without it, but it's hardly living, is it?"

There was a long stretch of silence. Then she asked softly, "What kind of pain do you like?"

We locked eyes. She was close enough to touch. The light from the candles flickered over her face.

"Most kinds," I said. "Whatever puts me in my place."

"Submissive."

"But not for money."

"No. Because you deserve it." Her eyes tracked over me, and she lifted her hand to tuck a piece of hair behind her ear. That's when I saw it.

The scar.

A pink, raised mark on the underside of her arm. One horizontal line. One triangle. Four lines connecting them, straight and tall, like pillars.

It was Laurel's symbol.

This woman knew her.

"Your arm," I started, then stopped, the urgency closing my throat. "Can I... Do you know—" But I couldn't ask her outright. I knew that, felt it. It would make her skittish. "Where do I find the real thing?" I asked instead, and the confusion on her face dissolved into understanding.

She reached inside her bra. "If you're serious—" Out came a lip pencil, and she reached for my hand. I felt the tip drag over my skin. "Show up at 7 Fox Lane. This Tuesday, at midnight. Tell the man at the door you're a gift from a humble daughter."

She released my hand, and I stared at the blocky message written in the same red as her lips: 7 FOX LANE. I could feel Laurel drawing closer, just a whisper ahead.

"Listen to me," she said, her voice so stern it snapped me to attention. The slippery seduction in her voice, in her eyes—the hook that had reeled me, pulled me inch by inch across the bathroom—was gone. Its sudden absence was like a splash of cold water. "This isn't a game. If you go to Fox Lane, you can't change your mind. Do you understand?"

I started to nod, to reassure her, but she gripped my arm. Her nails dug into the skin at my wrist. "If there's even a little part of you that can live without it...don't come."

"I meant what I said."

"Of course you did." She let go of my arm, leaving the ghost of her nails still biting me, and strode toward the bathroom door.

"Wait," I called, and she paused, glancing over her shoulder.

"Do you invite all the girls you meet to Fox Lane?" I forced a sheepish smile. "How many of us are there?"

She mirrored my smile, smooth seduction back in place. "Of course not. Only you."

That's when I knew she was lying. "Great," I said.

She swung open the door.

I couldn't help myself. "Happy hunting."

A flicker of surprise crossed her face. But the unleashed music was too loud, electronic synth pulsing our skin, filling our mouths, and in the wave of it, she slipped away.

I barreled across the parking lot, fleeing as quickly as last night, except this time, I was fueled by excitement, not horror. What would I find at 7 Fox Lane? At some point, Laurel had to have bumped into someone at the Sparrow and heard the same speech, right? Granted, I still couldn't be certain she'd ever found her way here. But say she did come, say she'd been searching for an experience she wasn't supposed to want, one that should've been locked in her past. Eventually, she would've met a woman like the redhead in the bathroom, if not the redhead herself.

With Clem dead, there was no one else who would understand why a speech like the woman's might have been alluring to Laurel. The cops wouldn't have been able to follow such a gossamer trail. An image of Laurel from my dream flashed back, begging me to find her, then disappearing into the dark hole. That's where other people would've stopped. No one else would have climbed after her into the dark. What if finding out what really happened to Laurel was something only I could do?

"Shay!"

I whipped around to find Jamie pushing open the front door of the Mansion, an incredulous look on his face.

"What were you thinking?" He dropped his voice to a fierce whisper when he drew near. "You went back alone?"

"I had to."

He threw his hands up. "Never mind that you lied to me. Don't you understand how dangerous this is?" His eyes tracked over my face. "Did you take the drug again?"

Jamie's dark hair stuck up off his forehead in the exact place he combed his hand through when he was worried or frustrated. His eyes were red-rimmed.

"The danger was the point." I resumed walking. "I needed to be vulnerable so people would open up."

He fell into stride beside me. "After everything you told me last night—"

I handed the valet my ticket and he took off running. Jamie waited until he was out of earshot before continuing. "And then I called you and you weren't answering, and I came by to bring you food and your car wasn't at your hotel..." He stopped and scrubbed a hand over his face. "I sound like a maniac, don't I? Like some overprotective friend or—"

"Cal," I said, clutching my phone, with its blinking tally of missed calls.

Jamie winced. "I know you're fully capable. I was just worried. You don't have a ton of investigative experience. And I thought we were a team."

"I got a lead," I said, holding up my hand so Jamie could read.

It was almost funny how quickly his reporter's instincts kicked in. "An address? From who? What does it mean?"

The rental car raced to a stop, wheels crunching gravel, and the valet hopped out.

"I'll tell you everything," I promised, catching the tossed keys. "Back at your hotel."

When we stepped inside Jamie's room and clicked the door shut, I saw more evidence of his worry. His room was a mess, his anxiety legible in the open laptop, the papers scattered over the desk, the undone sheets and stray pillows on the floor. His TV was on but muted, turned to the news. On screen, Governor Barry stood behind a podium, smiling at journalists. Underneath, the chyron read, *PrismTech headquarters opening in NYC... Stocks skyrocketing... Gov. predicts massive tech-sector job growth.*

Jamie stood next to me and surveyed the scene. "Well. I did tell you to steel yourself."

"I remember." My phone flashed with a text from Cal: Call me back. I'm getting worried.

I buried it in my purse and tossed that on Jamie's papers. "I didn't get a chance to say thanks for letting me crash last night."

He ran a hand through his hair, bouncing a little on his toes. "I know Motel 6 isn't what you're used to these days. Full disclosure, I googled Cal."

I snorted. "I'm fine."

"Money was...well, never my goal, to be honest." Jamie gave up bouncing and fell to the edge of his unmade bed. "It wasn't something I ever cared about. I guess that's another reason being a journalist suits me."

I grew still. No matter how much he'd changed, I could still see the boy from my childhood, the one with the bright eyes and easy smile. The one with two loving parents, a nice house with a wide lawn in a good neighborhood, soccer and piano lessons, orthodontics, SAT tutors. "Jamie," I said softly, "your family always had enough money. Why would it occur to you to care?"

He flushed, color high in his cheeks. "I guess you're right." There was a beat of silence, then he cleared his throat. "I got us off topic. Tell me about your lead."

I lowered myself into the armchair in the corner of the room, leaning back and draping my arms over each side, crossing my legs. I'd gotten my first clue tonight. Moved the search forward, all on my own. But there was still so much ground to cover. I tapped my fingers against the armchair and looked at him. "Take out your phone."

"My phone?" Jamie looked startled.

"I need you to start recording."

CHAPTER ELEVEN

Transgressions Episode 705, interview transcript: Shay Deroy, Sept. 4, 2022 (unabridged)

SHAY DEROY: The turning point was when Don invited us to his house. Maybe it wasn't—maybe we were already doomed by then. But looking back, it feels like that night was when things started to change.

It was about three weeks since he'd taken us to the Old Guard for drinks, and the time without him had passed slowly. No one on campus compared to him—not the students, who were immature boys next to him, or the professors, who seemed small and unworldly. By that point, even Clem was hinting to Rachel we wanted to see Don again. Most of the time, Rachel ignored us. She'd literally walk out of rooms while we were talking to her. But one day she came home and said he'd found a house and wanted to have us over.

We got dressed up again, because seeing Don felt like an occasion, and even though we wouldn't say it out loud, each of us wanted to impress him. It was funny, because by then, the three of us had stopped dressing up for anything, even parties. It was Whitney culture, competing over who could put in the least amount of effort.

JAMIE KNIGHT: I'm familiar with Occupy Wall Street chic.

SHAY: Just a different kind of purity test. It turned out Don's new house was only a few neighborhoods away, and it was huge. One of those historic Tudor mansions that are everywhere in the Hudson Valley. You know, the ones that look like witches' cottages from fairy tales. When we got out of the taxi, Laurel made a show of saying, *"Dang, Rachel, good for you."* She was still trying to be nice to Rachel, god help her.

It hurts to think how excited I was to go to his house, knowing everything that happened later. But at the time, it made an impression. It was bigger than any house in Heller. That alone made me nervous. But I was also anxious because I'd bought hair dye from the grocery store and dyed my hair blond, and I didn't know what I thought of it yet. I was waiting to hear what he'd say.

When he opened the door, he was in jeans and a sweater, with the sleeves rolled up. It was intimate, seeing him dressed down. My legs felt weak. When I looked at Laurel and Clem, I could tell they felt the same.

He hugged us all but didn't say a word about my hair. I was crushed, then ashamed for wanting his attention like a child. He gave us a tour of the house. It was old-fashioned and beautiful—dark and moody, walnut floors and stained-glass windows. There wasn't a single TV or computer. Nothing modern.

JAMIE: A Luddite?

SHAY: Don believed electronics were for philistines. He loved the old world, collected antiquities—artifacts from Greece and Italy, ancient weapons from around the world. They hung in his library: a wall full of Roman scissors and parazonium, Scythian akinakes, Viking javelins. When Laurel said it was unsettling, he teased her by running a pugio down her arm. He loved those weapons.

JAMIE: What's a pugio?

SHAY: Small, thin-tipped Roman dagger. Allegedly, what Brutus used to stab Caesar. The weapon of choice for assassinations because they could be easily concealed.

JAMIE: You know an awful lot about old weapons.

SHAY: Laurel was wrong. The weapons weren't the unsettling part. When we got to Rachel's room, it was all pink, with dolls on the bed, like a little girl's room. That really threw us. Not only because it was so childish, but because in our suite, Rachel's room was bare. Zero decor. It was clear either we didn't know the real Rachel, or Don had decorated it for her. Both options were weird. I think Clem was the one who said, "Gee, Rachel, forget the dorm. Why don't you live in this life-sized Barbie Dreamhouse?"

We all laughed, except for Rachel. I don't think she even breathed.

Don could probably sense the tension, because he brought us downstairs and opened wine. We started talking, having a good time, cracking open bottle after bottle. Don put on one of his old records, and we danced in the living room, totally goofy, free-flowing, you know, laughing at each other. Especially at Clem, who was a ridiculous dancer. She did this shimmy thing... You had to be there.

Out of nowhere, Don stopped laughing and said, "Rachel," in this really low, commanding voice. He nodded in the direction of the kitchen. Rachel put her wineglass down and went immediately. We stopped and watched her put on an apron and start pulling things out of the fridge. Our jaws literally dropped. First of all, we had never, *ever* seen Rachel cook. Second, and most important, we'd never witnessed her obey anyone. But there she was, standing in a frilly apron at the drop of a hat. It was surreal.

Clem said, "Is Rachel...making dinner?" With the most dubious tone.

Don grinned and said, "Come with me."

We followed him into the kitchen. He pulled open a drawer full of aprons, all of these bright colors, and took out three. I remember Clem snorting, like she thought he was joking. But Don's face was serious. He said, "I was wondering if you'd give Rachel a hand."

I felt conflicted; it was rude to refuse, because we were guests, and besides, Don was always treating us, so I felt like I owed him. But it was also a strange request. Or maybe it was just the way they did things in their house? Every family's different.

Everyone was quiet, so Don said, "Rachel and I like to practice acts of service. I think you'd be surprised how empowering it can be."

Clem said, "I don't cook. Sorry."

I looked down at the aprons. They were just little pieces of fabric. Don was having us over to his house, pouring us wine. He'd taken us to dinner and drinks. Surely, we could do this little favor.

He smiled at Clem and said, "You could always go out on a limb, Clementine, and explore a different version of yourself. You know, like you do with that hair. Those silly colors that distract from your face."

She said, "I like my hair. And I go out on plenty of limbs."

Her tone made me tense. Clem was easily provoked, combative. But next to Don, she sounded petulant. I had this sudden fear he wouldn't want to see us anymore.

But all he said to Clem was, "Manners, Clementine."

I guess Laurel was as uncomfortable as I was, or she was eager to please. Either way, she picked up an apron and tied it on. Don beamed at her. It made me jealous, so even though it still felt strange, I put on one of the aprons.

For the next hour, Laurel and I took orders from Rachel, helping her make lasagna. Clem didn't have anything to do. I could tell she didn't want to hang out alone with Don in the living room, not after how she'd acted, so she kind of hung around the kitchen awkwardly. She kept trying to make small talk, but Laurel and I were annoyed and ignored her.

Occasionally, Don came back to watch us. He said it was a lovely sight, the three of us working together. I wondered then if he was doing this for Rachel—like maybe she secretly wanted to spend time with us, so he was engineering it. But Rachel didn't look happy. Just blank, like always.

When dinner was ready, Don asked Clem to pour wine at the dinner table and light the candles. I guess she felt guilty, because she did it without complaining. And then we were all sitting around this long, dramatic table, with a huge chandelier over the top, and Don at the head. It was dark without lights—romantic, but also unnerving. I'll never forget the way Don looked, glowing in the candlelight. He'd never been more mysterious or unreachable. I wanted so badly to know him.

He raised his glass and said, "A toast to my girls." He caught my eye and winked, and I remembered how he'd told me I could call him Don, or Dad, or Peter, whatever I wanted.

It was getting harder and harder to know what I wanted.

We sipped, but before we could pick up our forks, Don said, "I've been thinking a lot about the three of you, and how I want to make sure you're reaching your highest potential. Doing what you were put on this earth to do. As I've gotten to know you better, I've realized—and I hope you don't mind me saying this—that each of you has been profoundly misunderstood. Abandoned in different ways by the people who should've taken care of you. I think it's safe to assume that no one—not your schools, your teachers, your friends, not even your family—has ever really seen you. I can sense it when you talk about the past. Other people haven't known what's best for you." One by one, he looked around the table, and when he got to me, I had that feeling again, like he could see inside me.

Then Clem said, all sarcastic, "And *you* know what's best?"

Laurel kicked her under the table, and I didn't blame her. What Don said meant something to me. He was right that I'd always felt alone. In that moment, I almost hated Clem. It felt like she was dismissing me, not Don.

But he only smiled at her, like she was a naughty child. "I'm saying we're all on a journey to become the people we're meant to be. I think we can get there faster if we go together. I've learned a lot in my life. Had the privilege of meeting a lot of brilliant people and studying important ideas."

I wondered again about Don's life before we met him, but he kept going. He said, "The ideas that shaped Western democracy have fallen out of favor in our anti-Enlightenment age. I think I could give you a unique perspective you're not getting in school. I could serve as a mentor of sorts, if you're interested."

Laurel said, "I'm interested," and he grinned at her. It gave me a sinking feeling.

He said, "What if I were to say that in our frenzy to make sure everyone and everything is treated equally, we've bulldozed over nuance, erased essential differences between people. More than that, we actively *deny* differences these days. We're all so afraid to be honest about what comes natural to us that we go our whole lives pretending to be people we're not."

Clem said, "What kind of differences are you talking about?"

Don looked at each of us in turn, and said, "I've mentioned Aristotle. One of the most enlightened thinkers to ever walk this earth. He laid the foundation for how we understand virtue and ethics because he was able to see into human nature with more clarity than most people ever do. But he wasn't alone. Plato, Socrates—so many of our foundational thinkers, the greats—saw right into the hearts of men and women. They saw how deeply women were fulfilled by nurturing and inspiring, how men were fulfilled by creating and leading. They didn't bemoan it; they *celebrated* it. Think about Dante, how he created *The Divine Comedy*."

Don grinned. "Surely that's still on your Whitney syllabus? Dante found his Beatrice—his beautiful muse—and only then did the words spill out. Think about the power of that symbiosis, man and woman each playing their part, creating one of the greatest works of literature in history. We've lost sight of the wisdom we used to hold close. Nowadays, I worry women like you are afraid to be who you really are. There's power in beauty and gentleness and submission. I can show you."

Clem turned to me, eyes all lit up at the word *submission*, but before she could say anything, Don turned to Rachel and said, "I'd like you to place your hand in the candle."

Clem and I said "*What?*" at the same time.

But Rachel was already getting up, walking to the candles in the center of the table. And she didn't even blink, just stuck her hand in the fire. Laurel, Clem, and I jumped back, our chairs clattering to the floor. I shouted at Rachel to stop, but she wouldn't. Her expression didn't even change. It was remarkable. There was this awful smell... I'd never smelled burning flesh before.

Finally, Don told her to stop, go run her hand under

cold water. When she pulled her hand out, her skin was red and bubbling. Don said, "Rachel's trust makes her brave. She's mastered fear. She's powerful. That's what real submission can do for you."

My heart was pounding. I felt scared, but also... confused. Was Rachel weak, or was she strong? I felt like I didn't know what those words meant anymore. I'd only ever seen such a narrow slice of the world. Maybe it worked different than I thought. That was something our professors were saying all the time: *Open your eyes. Expand your mind.* Just because you've believed something your whole life doesn't mean it's right.

But Clem was upset. She said, "This is insane. I want to leave."

Then Laurel did something I'll never forget. She looked at Don and said, in this firm, determined voice, "Do you want me to put my hand in the candle?"

Who would ask that? It was like she was suddenly a stranger. Clem said, "*Laurel!*" But Don nodded and said, "I would consider it an honor."

And before we could stop her, Laurel leaned over the table and thrust her hand into the flame. She wasn't stoic like Rachel; she cried out immediately and lasted all of two seconds before yanking her hand back. When her eyes found mine across the table, they were full of tears—but I saw something else there. Why she'd done it. She wasn't trying to conquer fear or be more empowered. There was desire in her eyes. Laurel had wanted to get hurt.

Don told her that was good, and to get ice from the

fridge. When she left, I realized I was shaking and I couldn't make it stop.

We ate our lasagna after that. I'm not kidding. All of us, at the table, Rachel's and Laurel's hands wrapped in ice. Clem didn't say a word for the rest of the night. I think she was in shock. I didn't know what to say, either. But Don talked enough for all of us, and Laurel was chipper, laughing and answering his questions, even though she couldn't use her left hand, and you could still see the track marks down her face where her tears had run through her makeup.

Eventually Don said he'd called us a taxi, but he wanted us to come back next weekend, stay the night. Have a sleepover. We all moved in a daze, gathering our jackets. Just like the last time, Don kept me behind when everyone else left, and then it was just us, alone in his house.

I was scared because I didn't know what he was going to do. But of all things, he opened his arms and said, "Come here, Shay." And the next thing I knew, I was letting him hold me. He whispered in my ear, "It's okay," and then my cheeks were wet, so I guess I was crying.

He pulled back, took one look at me, and pushed me against the wall so hard my shoulder blades stung. I couldn't speak—the air had knocked out of me. I could only watch, wide-eyed, as he tugged my skirt up, inch by inch, and slid his hands up the inside of my thighs. He said, "I want you, Shay. Do you want me, too?"

He didn't just think I was pretty. That's what I was thinking in that moment. Even though he wasn't supposed to, and he was the kind of man he was, wealthy and experienced, he wanted *me*. I felt more powerful than I ever had in my life. I was dizzy with it.

I could feel him hard against my thigh, but I was so out of my depth I could only nod. He said, "Good. My house, next weekend." Then he slipped his fingers under the seam of my panties and touched me.

I closed my eyes, but he said, "Look at me." So of course I did.

I'm going to tell you the truth, Jamie, because if I don't, you won't fully understand. It felt good, the way he was touching me. I was afraid of him, and I knew what we were doing was wrong, but I still wanted it. That's something I'll always have to live with.

He whispered, "You're my good girl, aren't you?" By then I almost couldn't bear it, how good it felt, how ashamed I was, but he said, "Say it," in that voice, and everything got clearer. I said, "I'm your good girl," and he was happy.

He put his hand around my throat and squeezed, but he was still touching me, and my hips were rocking against the wall. I could feel it building inside me, and part of me was mortified, but I wasn't going to stop. That's when he said, "Underneath, you're just a little girl looking to be owned, aren't you? That's your secret. You want to be mine. Tell the truth."

It cut through every layer. I should've been shocked, or repulsed, but instead I thought, *How does he know?* There was something in allowing it that made me feel dangerous and wild. Up against the wall like that, I went over the edge.

On the ride home everyone was silent. I was already thinking about going back.

(*Throat clearing.*)

I think that's enough, for tonight.

End of transcript.

Jamie and I sat across from each other. Him on the bed, me in the chair. I watched him, waiting, but his eyes were fixed on the wall above my shoulder. I sat inside the silence until I couldn't bear it.

"Say something."

His eyes dropped. "Jesus, Shay."

"I know."

"That was just the beginning?"

"The very beginning."

He put his head in his hands, then looked back up at me. "I'm not trying to make you feel bad. But what the fuck with that gender essentialism? That male and female empowerment, submission bullshit. Why was that appealing?"

I wanted to say it wasn't. It was the other thing, the way Don could see me, hurt me like I was only beginning to discover I wanted. It was the way I felt powerful when I hooked him, reeled him in, put him in a position where he needed *me*. I wanted to say Don could have told me anything, invented any pretense, as long as we ended up where we did, with me confessing and his hand around my throat.

But I knew Jamie wanted to draw a straight line connecting the girl he'd known in Heller—bookish Shay, then Shay the boy-hungry beauty queen—to the girl in Don's house with her back against the wall. He thought he already knew what explained my choices: internalized misogyny, case closed. And maybe that was right. Hell, maybe deep down, despite my proclaimed feminism, I'd believed the content of what Don was saying, not just the effect. God only knew I didn't deserve to be let off any hooks. But it just didn't feel like the whole story.

Jamie read my silence differently. "I'm sorry," he said quickly. "That was out of line. Don was manipulating you. You were what…twenty, twenty-one? You were young and naive. Laurel was carrying around all that trauma, maybe Clem, too, from the way she grew up. He took advantage of it. You were victims."

I didn't know about that word. What did you call yourself when you'd taken an active role in your own suffering? When your hands weren't clean, when there wasn't a single part of you that was, especially not your mind, all those deep, dark corners?

"I don't think it's that simple," I said finally. I rose and picked up my purse from the table. Jamie stayed motionless, crouched on the edge of the bed.

"I'm going back to my place." I stopped at the door. "I'll call you tomorrow. We'll plan for Tuesday night, whatever this thing is at Fox Lane."

He nodded, but right before I slipped out of the room, I saw it flash across his face: Uncertainty. Apprehension. And the coolest little sliver, right behind the eyes, of fear.

I shut the door quietly behind me.

He was starting to get it.

CHAPTER TWELVE

I stood across the street from 7 Fox Lane at midnight, hidden in the coal-black night like a vengeful ghost. The place was a mansion, in a neighborhood full of them, all the houses spaced so far apart no one could see each other. The wealth didn't surprise me. Neither did the fact that Jamie had looked up the address and it belonged to a John Smith, a dead-end name with no accompanying records. What surprised me was that there were no cars on the street. No people milling in and out, no noises. A few windows glowed behind tightly turned shades, but that was it. A far cry from Tongue-Cut Sparrow and its pulsing dance floor.

I was about to cut across the front lawn when a man in a suit stepped out of the shadows from behind the house and strode to the entrance with a single-minded focus, rapping on the large, ivy-covered door. I ducked behind a tree at the edge of the lawn to watch.

The door cracked open. The man who'd knocked exchanged terse words with whoever was behind it; abruptly, the door snapped wider and the man was yanked inside. I caught a glimpse of the other person:

another man, all in black, his outline blending into the darkness behind him. But there was something about his face… It was unnaturally white, his features grotesquely distorted. He scanned the yard quickly before the door closed.

I jerked behind the tree. This didn't feel right. My gut told me I didn't want to knock on the door like the woman at Tongue-Cut Sparrow had instructed. Maybe Jamie had been right. He'd begged to accompany me, but I'd resisted because the invitation was for me alone. I'd also resisted his offer to drive me and wait a street over. I'd told him I could do this on my own, and I would meet him at my hotel after. But now that I was here, I felt a quiver of fear turning my hands cold.

A far window caught my attention. A small sliver of light peeked out from where the window had been cracked, curtains nudged apart.

I rubbed my hands together to bring the blood back. The window was low to the ground, practically an invitation. What if I climbed in? I darted across the lawn and peeked inside. Nothing but the shadowy outline of an empty room. It was intimidating, but less so than the man at the door. So I wrested it up, shoes slipping in the slick grass, and hauled myself inside.

The house was magnificent but eerily empty. I moved cautiously, unable to tell where the ambient light was coming from. Was it recessed in the floors? Pouring through the seams? The light looked redder than it had from the outside.

The halls were grand and sweeping. Patterned marble floors stretched for what felt like miles, walls supported by tall columns crowned with curling stone leaves, ceilings carved with intricate heaven- and hellscapes. Whoever lived here was frighteningly rich, and not subtle. The house had performed a magic trick. It looked large from the outside, but inside it doubled, the ceilings impossibly high, the hallways impossibly long.

I jerked my head in every direction, convinced I'd gotten something wrong. Where were all the people?

Then I felt it, under my feet: not music, but a percussive wave, a force shaking the floor. Was it coming from beneath me? I took a tentative step forward, and the thunder grew stronger, traveling farther up my calf. I crept, inch by inch, feeling my way to the source.

I turned the corner to find a staircase with black-and-white steps, descending into darkness. The reverberations were strongest here; they came from wherever the stairs led. I had a sudden, uninvited memory of the day I'd found Laurel in the basement, following the sound of her fear, like a thread unspooling into the dark. I crept down the stairs, surprised by how long the journey was, picturing Laurel walking the same steps. *Is this where the ground swallowed you whole?*

At the bottom was a door. I rested my palm against it. It vibrated, then stilled. Vibrated, then stilled. Like a beating heart. I cracked it open and slipped inside, turning the corner.

I almost screamed.

Before me swept a vast room, dark as a crypt, marble columns tracing up to the ceiling, flames flickering on the walls. Kneeling in a circle in the middle of the room were a dozen women, naked except for their sharp-pointed heels, hands tied behind their backs, heads hanging. In front of them, forming an inner ring, stood a circle of men. They wore dark suits, navy and charcoal, the kind worn to board meetings. Their faces were hidden by white theater masks, frozen in exaggerated expressions of sorrow, horror, agony. The combination was monstrous.

In the very center of the circles stood a man in black, his face a white mask of fury. It was the man who'd answered the door. A naked woman knelt before him, smiling up at him as if entranced. She was small and downy-limbed like a rabbit.

There was a sharp corner in the wall—I darted behind it, out of sight, and peered around the edge. I'd been invited, but every instinct screamed at me to know what was happening before I thrust myself into the middle of it.

The man in black cast his gaze down at the woman and placed a hand on her forehead, palm flat. Then his fingers twisted, rooting in her hair. He drew her head back and her mouth dropped open, eyes blinking at the ceiling.

"The first lesson." His voice snaked through the room, and he drew the woman's head back farther. "Take what's offered to you."

His gaze swept the circle of men. "Hold it in the palm of your hand, Paters. Fist your fingers in it. Feel her shake. What is that?"

"Power," hissed the men from behind their masks, and I jumped.

The man in black's voice rose higher: "*What is that, Paters?*" The strange word reverberated: *Paters Paters Paters.*

"Truth," they boomed. They stomped their feet, shaking the floor, shaking the wall I'd pressed my cheek against. *This* was what I'd felt above. It was their chanting, the concussive force of their legs vibrating the house. "Truth! Power! Truth! Power!"

The man in black lifted his arms like some dark preacher, and the circle fell silent. His gaze turned once again to the woman who knelt before him. A tremor of fear ran the length of my spine. It was a game, I reminded myself. Some groups were big on them, rituals and playacting. Nevertheless, I wanted his attention off her.

"What are you?" the man asked, his voice now whisper-quiet.

The woman's eyes met his, full of pleading. I strained to hear her. "I'm nothing."

"Louder."

"I'm *nothing*," she cried.

His hand slid over her forehead, a priest blessing a sinner. "The only way to grow is to kill the identity that doesn't serve you."

"Yes," she said, voice fervent.

"*You* are the only one with the power to give up your control. To seek guidance, a strong hand. You have the power to submit."

"*Yes.*" I could see, even from here, the woman's eyes filling with tears.

"What do you get when you submit?"

"Truth," she choked. "Power."

His voice soared. "Tell me, daughters. What do you get, when you fall on your knees?"

The voices of the kneeling women rose to join his, strong and loud. "*Truth. Power.*"

"Come here." The man beckoned to the woman. "Show me."

She crawled to him and lifted shaking hands to his zipper, unzipping and waiting for permission. I pressed my cheek harder into the wall.

The man canted his face to the ceiling. "Let go of your fear. Let go of your ego."

"No more ego," said the woman, reaching for him, and that's when I turned away. The men in suits stomped their feet in rhythm, shaking the house so hard the vibrations touched me, slipped inside, made me part of it against my will.

It's only a game, it's only a game. But it was so much like the memories I didn't want to relive that I was rooted to the floor. The men stomped so loud the noise became a frenzy.

"Paters, take what's yours," the man in black shouted. "Take what's been withheld from you. Pain creates conscience!"

I opened my eyes again to see the men unleashed. They turned to the kneeling women, whose chests rose and fell rapidly, and seized them by the shoulders, the women staggering to their feet. A man whose masked mouth gaped open, frozen in a silent scream, steered a woman to a column and shoved her against it, chest first. His voice cut across the room. "Beg me."

"*Please.*" She turned her face, dark hair twisting over her shoulder. "Let me serve you."

When he spread her legs with a rough knee, she moaned.

I clapped a hand over my mouth. Everywhere, men bent the women over, or pushed them against walls, and the women melted against them like candles. It was too raw, too chaotic, too messy. What was happening here was so unlike the slick sexiness of Tongue-Cut Sparrow, the cool transactional gazes that followed you onto the pounding dance floor. The woman who'd sent me here was right. This felt real.

The past wrapped its fingers around my throat and squeezed. His dark, charming voice in my ear whispered, *What do you want? Tell me the truth.*

I shook my head, pushing it away. The couples had started moving in my direction, heading to the stairs. They would catch me spying, a voyeur. If they did, would they even care I'd been invited? I fumbled backward into a recess until my back hit a far wall eclipsed by shadow, slipping into the darkness just as a masked face turned in my direction, exaggerated eyes drooped with sorrow. I dug my nails into my arm, but he kept moving, gripping a small, blond woman by the elbow. The sight triggered a memory of another girl, years ago. *Is this what you wanted, Laurel?*

They banged up the stairs, sometimes two men at a time, a single woman between them. I held my breath for so long fuzz crept in at the edges of my vision. But they passed without stopping, and then the sounds—the commands, the soft reverb of flesh hitting flesh, the weak cries of pleasure and pain—all of it moved above me.

I exhaled and crept forward, scanning the room. Not a soul, not even the man in black. My body was damp with sweat. I hadn't expected what coming here would do to me. I needed to get out so I could think straight. But there was no way other than retracing my steps. I would have to sneak past them, pray they were distracted.

I slipped upstairs, back into the marble hallway, stepping lightly. Now I understood the heaven- and hellscapes carved into the ceilings, the ominous red lighting: they were warnings. Promises, for some.

Around the corner, there they were. Spread across a grand living room filled with velvet couches, gilded picture frames holding stoic painted faces, a stately marble fireplace—the finest old Americana. In the corner of the room, champagne bottles chilled in silver tubs of ice, slim glass flutes lining a nearby credenza, fit for a party. It was an astonishing contrast to the orgy of bodies, the women's limbs twisting, men shoving and bucking. One man bent a woman over an ornate armchair, thrusting so hard the chair jumped, his massive hands pushing her face into the cushion. When she surged for breath, her expression mirrored his mask, mouth contorted in a gasp.

It was a perverse Norman Rockwell painting. Patrician wealth, mixed with barbarism, the mask of old-money civility unsettled by a baser lust. Was this a performance, or the lack of it? A fever dream, or reality uncovered?

I took a step forward, a shiver at the base of my spine, my heartbeat finding rhythm with the thrusting, spellbound by the cries filling the stately room.

A hand gripped my shoulder—and suddenly I was shoved against the wall, pinned by a man in a smooth white mask, his mouth pulled back into an expression of rage.

"Who told you to put your clothes back on?" His voice was ragged, like he was speaking through a mouthful of glass. "Who said you could leave?"

Panic blanked my mind. "No one. I'm not—"

He snaked his other hand up my chest, finding my throat. "Stop," I said. If this community played by the rules, that word should be enough.

But the man's hand didn't stop; it squeezed. I clawed at it, desperate. It was too much pressure for kink between strangers. He was going to crush my windpipe. I pulled, scratching at him, but found no purchase in the silky fabric of his suit. His arm was a vise.

"You think you're above the others, that you can just watch?" He pressed closer, searching my face from beneath his mask, the corners of his eyes crinkling in pleasure when I tried to suck in air but couldn't.

It was the sensory memory: the warm, dry hand around my neck, the stinging pain in my lungs, the deep voice, urging: *You like it, don't you?* The man's hand became Don's, his mask Don's face. My body went limp, knees weakening.

"Wait until the Philosopher gets you," the masked man whispered. "There's nothing he hates more than entitled women."

There was less and less oxygen. I could feel my thoughts graying, my body resigning to the pain.

"*Pater.*" The sharp word pried the man's hand loose. He turned, and I didn't hesitate. I scrambled across the wall, hitting a column but still moving, sucking in air.

"She's new," said the woman, and only then did I stop and jerk back around. It was the redhead from Tongue-Cut Sparrow, standing in her underwear in the hallway, facing the man with her palms up in supplication. "She doesn't know better." When she spoke, I saw her teeth were rust-colored, blood edging the gums.

She'd been hit across the mouth, hard.

The man took a menacing step toward her. "If she's new, she belongs to the Lieutenant."

"You're right." She lunged around him and pulled me off the wall. "I'm taking her there now. Forgive us." She hurried me forward.

"Nicole." The name echoed over the marble. The woman stiffened and turned.

"It's not your place to command me," he said. "Watch yourself."

"Yes, Pater." She turned and tugged me quicker now, until we were practically running, her heels clipping on the marble. As soon as we were out of sight, she let go of my arm and hissed, "What are you doing?"

"You *invited* me." I rasped the words, touching my throat. A column of fire.

"You were supposed to go to the front door. How did you get in? And what did you do to piss off a Pater?"

"What *is* this? And what's a Pater? I said stop, but that man ignored me. I would've blacked out."

"I told you this was real." Nicole paced, hand rising to her bloody mouth. "And not to come unless you were sure." Her voice was ice. "Do you know what they would have done if I hadn't shown up?"

"What kind of game is this?" I murmured.

"Not a fucking game." Her eyes slanted down the hall. "I need to take you to the Lieutenant. He has to approve you, then you have to be initiated. You can't be here unless you go through him."

"The man in black?"

"Yes." Nicole grabbed my arm again. "Get moving. I'm *not* getting in trouble for you."

Every instinct told me to flee. "Wait. I need to know more first. The man mentioned a Philosopher. Who is that? Why the masks, the ceremony?"

Her face hardened. "I swear to god, if you're a cop or a reporter—"

"I'm not," I said quickly. "I'm just...frightened."

New footsteps echoed down the hall. Nicole shoved me. "Then leave. They can't find you breaking the rules."

I staggered back, self-preservation at war with my mission. Did I leave and let this lead on Laurel slip through my fingers, or stay and face more hands around my throat? "What if I want to come back?"

Nicole had turned to face the coming footsteps, but she glanced back at me. "Give me your name. If they screen you and you pass, I'll give you one more chance. But if you fuck with me, I'll kill you myself."

"Nicole." It was a cold voice, and close, just around the corner. "Don't keep me waiting." All the hairs on my arm rose. Somehow, the voice was familiar.

"*Name*," Nicole hissed.

"Shay Deroy." It flew from me before I could think.

"Then run, Shay." Nicole twisted back in the direction of the voice. And for once, I listened to the woman trying to save me and sprinted toward the open window.

CHAPTER THIRTEEN

"What happened?" Jamie sprang to his feet the moment he saw me, but I swept past him like a hurricane into the hotel room, striding to the windows to rip open the long, sheer curtains. After Fox Lane, I wanted to let in as much night sky as I could, flood the room with air and freedom. I pressed my palms to the window and felt a comforting chill. Outside, the air was turning cool.

Time is looping, and now it's fall again, the same season you met Don.

"Shay." Behind me, Jamie shut the door with a heavy thud. I jumped at the noise, spinning to face him. He twisted both locks, then strode to me, just as keyed up as I was. "I found something."

I blinked in surprise.

"While you were gone, something came in about Dominus Holdings." He brushed his hair from his forehead, then did it again, like a tic. "My team tracked tax forms. I have a name."

I took a bracing glance at the stars, so steady and distant. "Tell me."

"Gregory Ellworth. Does that ring a bell?" His eyes dropped, and I followed his gaze to my hands, which were twisting.

I laced my fingers together. "I've never heard it before."

He frowned. "Hey... What happened?"

It flooded out. I told him everything: sneaking in, the strange ritual circle, the man who choked me, my narrow escape, all the way to turning the corner in the hotel hallway and finding him sitting against the door to my room, in Chucks and a dark jacket, his head back, eyes closed, foot tapping. The only thing I didn't tell him was that when he saw me and sprung to his feet, it was the first time I'd felt safe all night.

As I spoke, Jamie's frown deepened. He walked toward me slowly, movements measured, like someone approaching a wild animal. Eventually, he settled on the couch and, when I finished talking, rubbed a hand over his face. "So there's a secret, super-intense BDSM group hiding out in the Hudson Valley. A bunch of rich people who like having rough sex, invite-only. Why am I not surprised?"

"No." I stopped in front of Jamie and looked down at him. "The man who choked me didn't stop when I asked. That's not supposed to happen in BDSM."

He swallowed. "Sometimes, people who do that kind of stuff like to play with protest. I've, uh, looked into the community before, for a different episode. Sometimes a group will choose another safe word so they can play with saying no. It can be a turn-on."

"They weren't playing." I raised a hand to my throat, and Jamie zeroed in.

"Oh shit." He tugged me closer until I stood between his legs. "I can still see his handprint."

He reached out to touch it, then caught himself. "I should've been there."

Our eyes met.

"Do you want to call the police? We could report the guy who did this to you, just not the rest of the group. You said the women were into it. That makes it consensual behavior between adults. Even if it's sadistic, it's not illegal." His eyes dropped, like he didn't want to say the next part while looking at me. "I don't judge people for what they like. As long as there's consent."

He was talking about Laurel, but underneath that, he was talking about me.

I twisted away, walking to the bed, then turned, pacing past him to the door. I unlocked it, then locked it again. There was this restless energy humming inside me, making me feel caged. It had been building ever since I'd stepped off the plane at JFK.

I gathered myself. Pressed my hands together and faced him. "Is it okay to do bad things to people as long as they agree?"

Jamie looked taken aback. "Isn't it? It's their choice, right? Personal freedom."

I moved to the window, keeping my back to him. "Is it always an expression of freedom?" This time, I didn't wait for him to answer. "What if you've come to believe the options available to you are limited?" My chest rose and fell. "What if the way you think the world works is wrong? What if life taught you something false, or people lied to you, convinced you they knew better than you did? Can you really choose freely if you've been mistaught?"

He cleared his throat. "No. Then you're under the influence of... I don't know. A manipulation. It's just like you can't give real consent if you're drunk. A yes doesn't count if the person's not thinking straight."

I pictured the woman who'd kneeled in the center of the circle, crying for the chance to grow, reaching into that masked man's zipper. But when I blinked and focused, all that stared back at me was my own face, reflected in the window. "What if you're a woman," I said, feeling each word like fire in my throat, "and the world teaches you who you are, and where your place is, from the moment you're born, but all along, it's a lie. What if the lie chains you every day? If you're not thinking straight any minute of your life, and even your defiance, even your *pleasure*, is suspect?" I pressed my palm against the cold glass. "How does consent work then? What makes you want the things you want? Is it your choice, or were you molded?"

When I turned, Jamie was no longer on the couch. He stood behind me, close enough to touch. His eyes were wide and anxious. And it suddenly struck me, the absurdity of saying these things to my childhood friend. The boy from soccer practice, and math class, and countless afternoons watching movies after school.

Jamie the journalist, I reminded myself. *Jamie, who tells stories people listen to, who has power.*

"Shay," he said softly. "Help me. I want to understand."

I stood on the edge of a cliff. If I leapt, I would surely be dashed on the rocks or get swallowed by the sea—but I would have a few moments of wild, perfect freedom, suspended in the air. Or I could do the sensible thing and retreat. Climb back down to safety.

"Get out your phone," I said. "Please."

Jamie looked at me and knew.

It was the rocks for me.

CHAPTER FOURTEEN

Transgressions Episode 705, interview transcript: Shay Deroy, Sept. 6, 2022, Part One (unabridged)

SHAY DEROY: Have you ever come apart with your face pressed to the floor, licking someone's shoe?

(*Silence.*)

JAMIE KNIGHT: I...uh...

SHAY: Don't worry. I wasn't expecting you to say yes.

That's the thing. He got us each in different ways. By the next weekend, Clem had agreed to go back to Don's house and spend the night. She said he'd called her privately, told her he knew her family had never understood her, and because of that, she'd developed this instinct for doubt and cynicism, and ironically, it was those very defense mechanisms that would guarantee she'd always be alone. He offered to help her learn acceptance and humility. After he was done, she'd be whole.

I knew under her hard shell, Clem was secretly soft. She'd always felt uncomfortable in her own skin, worried she was too much, and Don must have sensed it. He clearly struck a chord, because she stopped dying her hair, and by the time we went to see him again, her roots were showing.

Laurel was different. She'd been Don's from the start. She hung on every word, kept saying he reminded her of her dad, the way he talked, the fact that he was a family man. All week after his dinner party, she kept touching her burned hand, even though it made her eyes tear. I think she wanted to relive the moment.

(*Throat clearing.*)

JAMIE: And for you, the attraction was...?

SHAY: How about I tell you what happened, then you tell me.

The first night, Friday, seemed perfect. Don didn't have to force us. We cooked dinner together, the three of us and Rachel, and afterward he mixed us martinis and tried to teach us how to bop, but we were terrible at it and pretty much collapsed laughing. When it was time for bed, he showed each of us to our own rooms, and they were beautiful, canopy beds and big bay windows. The next morning when we woke, he told us since we were staying the weekend, it would be nice to help him clean a little. It seemed like a thoughtful thing to do, and we wanted to please him. You know that feeling when you're a kid and you're trying to make your parents proud? It was the same feeling, like we'd reverted back to being young.

We scrubbed the bathroom tile on our hands and knees. Put our heads in the oven and cleaned grease from every corner. Stood on ladders and dusted fans. Don moved from room to room with us, watching the whole time. It was exhilarating to feel his eyes on me. I was aware of each movement, every time I stretched or brushed my hair from my face. My skin actually tingled.

I felt sure he was watching me the whole time, that I was the real reason he'd wanted us to clean, so he could have an excuse to stare. I held him in the palm of my hand. Eventually he wouldn't be able to help himself. He'd have to make an excuse, pull me out of the room, and touch me. We were playing a game, he and I.

Feel free to laugh. I was on my hands and knees cleaning for so long I could barely stand, and I thought I was the one in control.

But Don was pleased with us, and his pleasure was something you could get drunk on. No one in the universe is more charming than Don Rockwell when he's happy. That night, he poured us more bottles of wine. He said we were learning our first lesson, humility and service in praxis, and the more we worked, the more the virtues would sink into our bodies. But since we were college women, scholars, we also had to engage our brains. He arranged us in a circle in the living room and, one by one, had us read aloud from a small stack of books. What he called the great works. Aristotle's *Politics*, Rousseau's *Emile*, Schopenhauer's "On Women," Kant's *Anthropology*. I recognized the names from my lit classes, so I thought Don must be right that they were geniuses.

JAMIE: I used to think you were a genius, you know. You were the best writer in school. I used to get jealous.

SHAY: Yeah, well, look what good that did me. I didn't know it that night, but it would be more than a year before I read any other books. I can still recite the passages. Do you want to hear?

JAMIE: You can really do it?

SHAY: Aristotle: "The male is by nature superior and the female inferior; the male ruler and the female subject." Rousseau: "Women must be thwarted from an early age. They must be exercised to constraint, so that it costs them nothing to stifle all their fantasies to submit them to the will of others. They must receive the decisions of fathers and husbands like that of the church." Schopenhauer: "Women are childish, frivolous, and shortsighted... By nature, meant to obey." Kant: "A woman's primary means of domination is her ability to master her husband's desire for her."

JAMIE: Your delivery is...frighteningly crisp. All that stuff about women—how did you read that and think it was empowering?

SHAY: Don said the truth was, men and women were wired differently, and there was no greater power than knowing your true purpose. Accepting your ontological limits was the highest form of freedom. He talked like that, like our professors. I think it made it easier to believe him, because he sounded familiar and confident. I started to think maybe there was a reason for everything that happened to me before college. What if my whole life, I'd been trying to be something I simply couldn't? Maybe if I accepted my limits, I would be happier.

I can still hear those dead men whispering in my dreams.

JAMIE: What do you mean, "everything that happened before college"?

(*Silence.*)

JAMIE: Sorry. This is your story.

(*Throat clearing.*)

What happened next?

SHAY: Clem said she didn't like the readings, that they reminded her of what her parents' pastor used to say about women's duty to obey their husbands. As soon as she said it, a chill went through the room. I could barely bring myself to look at Don, I was so embarrassed. When I did...his face was calm, but that was worse than if he'd yelled, because I had no idea what he'd do next.

He said, "Clementine, this is your old self talking, the one that alienates people. The one no one really loves, if we're being honest."

My first instinct was to protest. Because of course I loved Clem. But then I thought—she *had* almost ruined last weekend, and here she was, at it again. What if Don decided he didn't want to see us anymore because of her? There was a pit in my stomach, like maybe he was right.

So I didn't say anything, and neither did Laurel. We let the silence stretch, even though I could tell Clem was waiting for one of us to defend her.

After a moment, Don said, "I promised I'd help you become someone better, but I can't do that with you questioning me. Do you understand?"

Clem tried to say, "I wasn't questioning you," but Don cut her off and said, *"Do you understand?"*

Clem's body tensed, and she said, "Yes," in a quiet voice.

He said, "You need to experience consequences. Do you agree?"

And she actually nodded. I could tell she was frightened. I was scared, too, but there was something else, like a curiosity. This desire to see it happen.

I'm not proud of myself. I hope that's obvious, but I'm saying it now, before I tell you the rest.

JAMIE: Okay.

SHAY: Don said, "Rachel, go get it from my closet." She left quickly, but the rest of us sat in silence. I couldn't look at Clem.

Rachel came back with a belt. Brown leather, worn. He took it and beckoned Clem. At first, I thought she wouldn't go to him, but she did. He bent her down over his knee. My heart was racing. I looked at Rachel, and her cheeks were flushed. I'd never seen her more excited.

Don lifted up Clem's dress and pulled her panties down until she was exposed. That by itself was humiliating. But then he looped the belt around his hand and said, "This is how we rewire you. Slowly, over time. Show humility. Tell me you're sorry." But before she could, he struck Clem so hard she cried out.

She said, *"I'm sorry,"* but he hit her with the belt again, and again. I thought he would keep going, but he stopped and looked across the room at Laurel.

He said, "Now you."

I wanted Laurel to protest, but she took the belt from Don and sat in his chair, waiting for him to settle Clem over her lap. It looked so wrong, like Laurel was playing dress-up, pretending to be her father again. Clem's face was bright red, and she was crying, but Laurel wasn't moved. She said, "Tell Don you're sorry." And then she struck Clem—again and again, until Don said, "Enough. It's Shay's turn."

I was torn. I can hardly describe it, the weight of the pressure, with all their eyes on me. I didn't want to hurt Clem. Even if she did deserve it, a little.

Don said, "Shay. Be a good girl." Like I was five years old.

But it worked. My legs straightened automatically, and I got up, took the belt, and Don laid Clem over my lap. She was warmer and heavier than I'd expected. A real human body. I know that's strange to say. But watching her be punished, I'd started to see her as... I don't know. You remember in elementary school, that one kid who never stopped acting up, bothering the teachers and interrupting class all the time, and you were supposed to feel sorry for him, but everyone secretly wished he'd just go away?

JAMIE: Kyle Barnes.

SHAY: Like Kyle. She'd turned into more of a problem than a person.

It felt wrong to hold her. There were raw, red marks all over her, and two pinpricks of blood where the leather had broken her skin. The belt trembled in my hand.

Rachel kneeled in front of me, breathing heavy, her eyes on the blood. She looked at me and said, "Make her sorry."

THE LAST HOUSEWIFE

I wanted it to be over. Suddenly, I hated Clem for making me do this. The hate made it easier to say, "Tell me you're sorry."

She didn't. I could feel her body stiffen.

Rachel said, *"Make her,"* and before I could think, I'd struck. Hit Clem hard enough to hurt my own arm. But she still didn't say it, and everyone was looking at me, so I hit her again, and then it was easier to hit her than anything else. To take all the shame and confusion inside me and beat it into her.

Clem screamed, "I'm sorry, I'm sorry, *I'm sorry!"*

I froze and dropped the belt. Don said, "Enough," and took Clem away. I had no idea where they were going. My head was a mess.

Laurel said, "She deserved it. She's being selfish."

I couldn't think... I might have nodded. We sat there in silence until Don walked back in, looked at me, and said, "Come with me."

I thought I would faint from fear, or anticipation. I couldn't tell them apart anymore. I could've sworn, when I followed Don out, that Laurel looked like she would cry, but I might've imagined it, might've been projecting.

He led me upstairs to his bedroom, all the way on the top floor. It was enormous, with a big bed in the center, all snowy white, and a wall of tall windows. Now that I think about it, I guess it looked a lot like this hotel room.

He shut the door behind us, and that's when I knew I was finally going to get what I'd been waiting for. I was terrified.

He pulled the curtains closed and said, "Come here."

When I got close, he lunged and gripped me by the shoulders. His fingers dug into my skin, but I wouldn't cry out, wouldn't risk messing this up. He spun me so I faced the bed and unzipped my dress slowly, like men do in the movies, until it dropped to the floor. Then he pressed me down into the sheets. Hard. I tried to raise my head, but he twisted his fingers in my hair. I started to struggle, but he whispered, "Trust me. Let go."

I'd read *Twilight*. The library's worn paperback copy of *Fifty Shades of Grey*. I knew what it meant when a powerful man, a man who could crush you, made taking you his sole devotion. I knew what it meant when he told you to let go of yourself. It meant you were above all other women, something special, and your life was about to be bigger than anything you could've made it yourself. It was what every woman wanted.

So I went limp in his hands. With my face pressed into the cotton, my vision started to blur, but I wouldn't give up. Right when I thought I would black out, he released me, I gasped, and he slid his hand between my legs. It could have been the dizziness, the sheer relief of breathing again, but his touch sent lightning through my body. I shuddered, and he whispered in my ear, "No shame. Tell me what you want."

I could've told him I knew he'd invited the three of us to stay the weekend because he wanted me so badly he was willing to break the rules, engineer the whole scenario. That I suspected thoughts of me had plagued him, kept him awake at night, until he couldn't take it anymore. I'd had little tastes of power with men before, but my power over him was intoxicating, and what I wanted more than anything was more of it, proof that I was right.

Of course, I didn't have those words back then—only in hindsight. So instead I said, "You tell me what I want."

I think that's what he'd been waiting for. He used one hand to hold me against the bed and the other to tug down my panties. I could feel him hard and warm against my back. He said, "You want to obey. No questions."

I'd only started to nod when he grabbed my hips, and I drew a sharp breath. He clapped a hand over my mouth and said, "Only when I tell you."

It wasn't the first time I'd had sex, but it might as well have been. First over the bed, then up against the wall. When I tried to twist to breathe, he tightened his hand over my mouth. My world narrowed: There was nothing except the sensation of his body surrounding me, the rub of the plaster against my cheek, the desperate tightening in my chest.

Then, suddenly, out of nowhere, I thought: What would my mother say?

It was like a switch flipped, and I felt indescribably wrong. My eyes grew hot; then there were tears on my cheeks. I thought, *Look at me. How will I ever show my face outside these walls?*

Don pushed me to my knees, hard enough that I cried out, because my knees were still raw from cleaning. He grabbed me by the hair, thrust my face to his boot, and said, "Remember, I know your secret. Show me you're my girl, Shay. Lick it."

I ran my tongue over his boot. He bent and started

touching me. I licked harder, longer strokes, tasting the bitterness of the leather, feeling the grit.

He said, "You're pathetic, aren't you?"

I could feel the truth of it in the way my body responded. I've never felt more electric than when I was down on the floor, licking his shoes. I'm sorry, Jamie. It's just I want you to know the truth.

JAMIE: Don't apologize. Keep going.

SHAY: I clutched that night with Don to my chest the entire next day. While we cooked and read, and he lectured, I thought: *No one else knows, but secretly, I'm his and he's mine.*

He had a lot to teach us. In the beginning, I was skeptical, but there was something so provocative about what he said that it was hard not to consider it. Then slowly, day after day, it began to feel like truth. He said feminists were some of the worst agents of misinformation. The whole movement had started with good intentions but got twisted, and now everyone insisted on denying the differences between men and women. If you dared question the ideology or point out nuance, you were ruined. And the end result was that girls like us had a yoke around our neck, put there by other women who claimed to know what was best for us.

He said it was important that people were honest about who they were and what they wanted, even if it wasn't convenient or didn't fit a political fantasy. He pointed at Laurel and said, "Is she as tall or as strong as I am?" He pointed at me and said, "Am I as curved as Shay? Of course not. There's truth in our DNA. But everyone likes to pretend there's no such thing as truth these days. They like to act like everything's constructed, it's all relative, as if there's not a raw, real, natural world. It's willful ignorance at best—at worst, dangerous denial." He told us denial was why the world had gone off course, why people slumped through their lives feeling empty and alienated.

He looked at us and said, "You've felt lost, haven't you? Like you have no clue who you are and what you should be doing."

We all nodded—

JAMIE: You were college students. Of course you felt that way.

SHAY: He turned to Laurel and said, "You're a fragile little thing, aren't you?" And before she could say anything, he kept going, saying, "Poor, thin-skinned Laurel. How have you not been eaten alive?"

I felt a spark of indignation, because I'd spent years trying to convince Laurel she was strong. I said, "That's not true."

Don reached down from his armchair and grabbed my jaw so hard I nearly rose up off the floor. I thought for a moment he'd snap the bone, but he just squeezed and stared at me, then let go. My ears were ringing. But I wasn't mad—I was ashamed.

He turned back to Laurel and said, "You know better than anyone how easily a man can overpower a woman. What would your father say if he knew what you'd let happen?"

The living room was silent, everyone still as statues—

except for Rachel, who squirmed, trying to lean and get a better look at Laurel's face.

Don said, "Poor Edward Hargrove. I looked him up. Short man. Little Eddie. Died and left his wife and daughter unprotected. Isn't that what you told me, Laurel? That sometimes you're afraid you can't step outside the house without getting hurt?"

I squeezed my eyes shut, but I couldn't block the sound of Laurel whispering yes.

He said, "You're right to worry. Men *are* different. They're built to take what they want. You're vulnerable out there. You need someone to protect you."

She nodded.

"You can't do it yourself—and you shouldn't have to. That's not your job. You're delicate Laurel. Poor, fatherless Laurel. I've never seen anyone ache for a strong hand as much as you." He was unweaving her in front of us. Laurel bent over until her forehead touched her knees, wrapping her arms around herself, making herself small.

He said, "You need me, don't you?"

She started rocking, back and forth.

I was numb to everything but the pain in my jaw. Clem was silent, too. She'd been quiet all day, wincing when Don made us sit on the floor, her back still raw from the belt the night before.

Don crouched beside Laurel and lifted her chin. He said, "Come with me. I'll take care of you."

He was choosing Laurel. The betrayal was a kick to the chest. As he led her out of the living room, she looked back at me, and—I could've sworn—there was triumph in her eyes.

I wanted to rip her away from him. I knew, even then, that Don was showing me I wasn't actually special, that at the drop of a hat, it could be Laurel as easily as me.

Then Don said, "Shay, come along."

It turns out I wasn't being left behind. He wanted me to watch.

JAMIE: And did he...treat Laurel like he treated you?

SHAY: Different, because she was softer. But after, he still left her on the floor. By then, I wasn't jealous anymore. I lay down next to her and ran my fingers through her hair until she fell asleep.

JAMIE: You went back to campus after that weekend, though, right? Tell me you found someone—a professor, if not a cop. Tell me you told someone what happened.

SHAY: Jamie.

(*Laughter.*)

You don't understand. We never left again. Not for a year and a half.

JAMIE: What?

SHAY: Like he said, it wasn't safe out there. There were men who would hurt us because we were weaker, and women who would try to manipulate us, take us away from him. I'd always suspected the world was cruel, but Don made me understand the true magnitude. The things that could happen if I wasn't careful. No one had ever tried to protect me like that.

After a while, we only left to grocery shop, and even then we took Rachel, because she was more experienced. We began to ask his permission for everything. To eat. To pour a glass of water, go to the bathroom, go to bed. When we woke up in the morning, Don would suggest what we'd do that day, what to wear, what food we'd put on our plates and how much. Eventually the suggesting became telling. He asked Laurel to sew dresses for us because our clothes were too provocative. The dresses stopped past our knees and buttoned up the back, so it was hard for us to take them off, but easy for him. I remember thinking that was romantic. Don liked our hair twisted back with bobby pins. He said it was neat and pretty. He liked to tear it apart at night.

JAMIE: He made you dress like fucking June Cleaver.

(*Silence.*)

Sorry. That was unprofessional. I'm just... Never mind. Keep going.

SHAY: You might not believe me, but it was a relief to no longer make decisions. I honestly thought Don knew best, and if I did what he said, everything would be okay. Back then, I would've traded my freedom for that security a million times over.

For the rest of fall semester, then spring, then fall again, senior year, we missed most of our classes. Don had us go just enough so we didn't fail out. I won't even tell you what happened to my GPA. Ironic, right? After working so hard for valedictorian in high school. But Don said people were closed-minded and reactionary, and if they knew about us, they'd misunderstand and try to take us away. So Clem quit soccer, Laurel quit theater, and I quit writing.

We kept our suite in Rothschild so no one would alert the administration or our parents, but we moved our things. At his house, Don moved us out of our separate rooms into a single room on the top floor, next to his, so we could come quickly when he wanted us. It had no windows, but three narrow beds, all in a row, and he expected them made every day, hospital corners. He took the lock off the door so he could check. He took all the locks off the doors, so there wouldn't be secrets between us.

The worst part about living in the same room was we always knew who he'd chosen each night. If it wasn't you, you had to lie there and stare at the empty bed, listening to the noises through the wall, his headboard slamming, and know you weren't good enough. I used to curl up in that little doll bed and cry, touching the wall while he was with Laurel or Clem, feeling the vibrations. Being left behind was the worst punishment. At least it was for me.

The only thing we really had to ourselves was a garden. We called it *The* Garden, in capital letters, and no one loved it more than Clem. Don wanted us to plant herbs and tomatoes, functional things that would keep us from needing the grocery store. But somehow Clem got her hands on flower seeds, so we also had wildflowers and goldenrod, which she loved best. It was funny, Clem and the goldenrods. Such a feminine thing—you wouldn't expect it from her. At the time, I thought she was trying to rewire herself into the kind of woman Don wanted. But now, when I picture the flowers, how sunny and beautiful they were...I think she just needed something to love.

It was hardest for her. Don was always telling her she had an unfeminine body, that she wasn't trying hard enough to be graceful. This was Clem, one of the best athletes I'd ever met. You remember she was short and muscular, kind of thick. Don wanted us all thin and lithe, because he said that was more natural. He kept us on strict diets. Sometimes I'd get so hungry I'd lie awake at night, imagining cramming a whole potato into my mouth, peel and all. Anything to fill the hole in my stomach. But at least I was able to get thin. Clem could never lose enough weight.

One night, she dropped a wineglass when she was cleaning up after dinner. It was an accident, but Don told her as a consequence, she had to roll in it. A lesson in moving with care. He was always doing that... Embodied lessons, he called them. It wasn't enough for your brain to learn something; your muscles had to learn it, too. I'll give him this: it was effective. Even now, years later, I'll be going about my day and something will trigger one of Don's old lessons, and immediately, I'm right back there, body stiffening.

JAMIE: And Clem did it?

SHAY: Of course. I'll never forget the way it looked, Clem rolling through the glass shards, smearing blood over the kitchen floor in these long, crimson swoops, like a snow angel.

(*Silence.*)

Rachel got on her case even more than Don, though. After a few months, I finally understood that she was his lieutenant. Her favorite thing was to catch us. You would think you were alone in the kitchen, that it was safe to have a sip of water, because you were thirsty and Don wasn't around to ask, but as soon as you nudged the tap, watched that first drop trickle into your glass, Rachel would appear right behind you. And then you were in trouble.

She lived to punish. With Don, hurting had a purpose, taught a lesson. But Rachel didn't care about that. She only wanted our pain. When he was really angry at something we'd done wrong, he'd let her hit us with his belt. One night, he asked me to bring him something from Rachel's room, and I saw her notebook open on her desk. She was listing ways to punish us, each one more inventive than the last. For a moment I thought of stealing the notebook and throwing it away, but that wouldn't have solved anything. It would have just given her another excuse to hurt me.

JAMIE: She sounds disturbed.

SHAY: It became more and more obvious. You know that famous Man Ray photograph, *The Enigma of Isidore Ducasse*?

JAMIE: Uh, I think so. Mysterious object covered in a dark blanket, tied with string?

SHAY: It's a sewing machine, but yes, that's the one. Coming to understand Rachel was like watching a veil being pulled off inch by inch, until one day you're suddenly staring at the thing itself. And somehow it's both ordinary, a thing you recognize, and more monstrous than you ever imagined.

JAMIE: For fuck's sake. You were trapped in a house with sadists. Why didn't you run?

SHAY: The truth is, for long periods, things were normal. We were living in the suburbs, in a beautiful house, ten minutes from school—still *going* to school—a few blocks from a fucking Walgreens. The lines were blurry, and when you're in the moment, all you can see is the context, the justifications.

JAMIE: It sounds like Clem was Don's scapegoat, though. The one who couldn't do anything right.

SHAY: She questioned him, so she was the biggest threat. One night, senior year—I think it was senior year, because our hair had grown to our waists and it was freezing out, so it had to be winter—Don went to a dinner party. That sort of thing had started happening more frequently, Don having nights out with business partners.

Rachel was watching us, and she made a mistake: she left us unsupervised to take a shower. The minute the water ran, Clem burst out the front door and took off down the street. I had no idea what she was thinking. Maybe she'd been planning it a long time, or she was just seizing the chance. I don't know.

I also don't know how Rachel realized. She had a sixth sense, I guess, or maybe she could hear Laurel gasping all the way in the bathroom. She barreled out of the shower after Clem, soaking wet and naked. I was so stunned, I didn't think. The front door was wide open. So I ran.

I'll never forget how the air felt on my skin, or the grass under my feet. My heart was beating like it had wings. When I looked up at the sky, I stopped in my tracks. By then, it must've been a year since I'd been outside at night. I'd forgotten how the stars blazed down at you, like a million sparkling fires. The wonder you could feel.

But then Don slammed into me from behind and I fell face-first into the grass, biting the dirt. Sometimes I wake up in the middle of the night, mouth full of that bitter taste. He must've come home just in time to catch us. He dragged me by my ankles across the lawn. I watched the stars the whole time. When he pulled me into the house, Clem was already lying on the foyer floor.

Things were very bad after that. Don beat me with the belt. I had to lay in my bed for a whole day, completely alone, without food or water. Before that night, I'd honestly thought living with Don was a choice I'd made. It didn't hit me until then that we were being held.

When I finally got up to search the house for Clem, I found the rest of them in the library. Don was in his armchair, Laurel and Rachel at his feet, pretending to read, and they all looked up at me the minute I walked in. The tableau is burned into my brain. Laurel's skin was practically translucent by then, and she was so skinny you could see every bone. Rachel was fidgeting, practically foaming at the mouth. I guess they'd been waiting for me to start.

JAMIE: Start what?

SHAY: Don said Clem was a betrayer. If she hadn't run, I wouldn't have followed. She'd corrupted our family. He handed Laurel and me steak knives from the wooden block in the kitchen. But he made a show of taking his precious dagger from the wall, the Roman pugio, and giving it to Rachel, like a reward. He led us down into the basement, where the only light came from a bulb that hung from the ceiling. When it flared on, there was Clem, naked, her hands tied around a structural beam, head hanging. Don always complained she wasn't losing weight fast enough, but as far as I could see, she was nothing but sharp lines and shadows.

He said it was a lesson in accountability, for her and for us. We would each make one cut, somewhere Clem's clothes would hide. Rachel would go first.

JAMIE: You didn't.

SHAY: I'll never forget the way the air smelled. Like iron and animal, rich and tangy, so thick you could practically taste it. Or the way Clem looked at me when I faced her. I'd expected her eyes to be vacant, like they were when Don punished her. But they were burning. Accusatory.

I've thought about it a lot since then. I think Clem had woken up, and the look in her eyes was her trying to wake me up, too. But in the moment, I thought she was trying to blame me—like her inability to follow the rules was *my* fault. All of my guilt and fear turned into anger because it was easier. I'm grateful Don gave us only one cut. I'm not sure what I would have done on my own.

JAMIE: You don't mean that.

SHAY: Look at me, Jamie.

JAMIE: I can't imagine you hurting anyone.

SHAY: Look at me. I didn't just do it. I *wanted* to. How do you come back from that?

JAMIE: I don't think I can hear any more. I'm sorry, I know it's not what a journalist's supposed to say. But I'm more than that with you.

SHAY: I'm telling you so you understand. The truth is burning in me, like a fever. I have to tell.

(*Silence.*)

Just listen. I didn't know this the night we cut Clem, but my punishment wasn't over. Or maybe it wasn't supposed to be a punishment. Maybe it was Don's plan all along, what he'd been building up to. But a week later, at midnight, he knocked on our bedroom door and said, "All of you. Now."

Clem was still healing, and my back was still raw, but we knew we had to go. We followed him into his room, where Rachel was waiting. He lined them against the wall, but stood me in the center. I'd never had everyone watch before. I didn't like it—especially Rachel, who'd been eyeing my welted back all week. But I knew I had to, so I started to slip off my nightgown, letting my mind untether. By that point, life was about making it from one moment to the next.

But Don seized my wrist and said, "Shay. Meet Mr. X."

A man walked into the room wearing a dark suit and driving gloves. I will never forget those gloves, or his mane of silver hair. He had the face of a wolf. Even whiskers. When I looked at him, all I could see was his hunger. Whatever he was going to do to me, he'd been waiting a long time to do it.

I hadn't imagined it could get worse, and now worse was standing right in front of me.

Mr. X looked at Don and said, "You're right. She's beautiful."

Don said, "I told you. Texas beauty queen."

The man's eyes trailed down my body. He said to Don, "You told me I could do anything."

Don said, "Everything you've been holding back since the divorce. Think of how that bitch emasculated you. Let it out."

The man with the wolf's mane grabbed me by the throat

so fast it took a moment for the feeling to break through the shock. And when it did, I couldn't even scream.

Mr. X was breathing hard. He wiped a hand over his mouth and said, "You were right. I needed this. You're a sage, my friend."

Don said, "Shay, take off your clothes."

I didn't move.

He said it again: "Take off your clothes, Shay." And I had a moment—just a second—where I thought of saying no.

JAMIE: Stop. I can't listen anymore. I know it's unprofessional, I know you want to tell me, but I can't do it. I just can't—

(*Footsteps. Rustling.*)

End of transcript.

CHAPTER FIFTEEN

No one had ever stopped when I'd begged them to, but I guess the rules were different for me. I followed as Jamie retreated, quick on his heels.

"I'm telling you this for a reason, Jamie. The party tonight at Fox Lane... It reminded me of Don. Yeah, I know, there were people in masks and chanting, and none of that was the same. But the man who held me by the neck said, *Wait until the Philosopher gets you.*"

Jamie stood in the corner of the room, shoulders hunched, hands in his hair. When he ended the recording, he'd thrown his phone on the couch like it disgusted him. It sat there now, dark-screened against the petal-pink cushion, looking up at me like it was watching.

"What about it?" Jamie asked.

"Mr. X and the men after him, they talked about seeking Don's counsel. Mr. X called him a sage. What if Don is the Philosopher?" I could feel Don's specter hovering over me, growing more corporeal with every passing day.

"Christ, Shay." Jamie was on his last reserve. I'd pushed him too hard, offered too strong a dose of the past. "If that's true—if there's even a *chance*—you can't go back."

"The thing is, I have to." What I'd witnessed at Fox Lane had electrocuted me with panic, but once the adrenaline washed out and I was safe again, the realization had settled over me: This was it. The reason I'd come. "I have to figure out how Laurel was involved. I have to know what they're doing."

Jamie's face was incredulous. "You just told me you were tortured at the hands of a man you think is part of this group—and even if he's not, you say being there feels like being back in his house. And you want to go back *in*? Fuck no." Jamie sprang forward. "Shay, what do you think is going to happen?"

The truth hit me when he stopped and folded his arms over his chest.

"You don't trust me," I said.

His expression became familiar: Jamie Knight, tight-lipped, trying not to show he disapproved, his eyes giving him away. No matter how he'd grown, he was still the same judgmental boy underneath.

"You said it yourself. The things you did with Don." He sucked in a breath. "You *liked* it. There's a part of you that responds to…the pain."

For eight years, I'd feared telling anyone the truth. So I should have seen this coming. But it was *Jamie*, and I'd started to believe.… I swallowed the thought. "You think I'm sick in the head."

"I don't think that at all. But I saw you that day in the city, remember? I hope you remember, because I can't forget. I didn't know what was happening, but I knew enough to be terrified by the way you were acting, the look on your face. You were lost, Shay."

"You think I'll lose control."

Won't you? that dark, charming voice whispered. *Doesn't a part of you long for it?*

I'd stopped. At Fox Lane, when I turned the corner in the hallway and that stately living room came into view—that landscape of naked need—I'd been drawn like a moth to flame, like Sleeping Beauty to the spindle. Forgetting for a moment why I'd come, forgetting everything but that old urge, long snuffed, flaring back to life…

Jamie reached for my hand. I took an involuntary step back, and he froze. "You were in a cult. Do you even realize that? It's not something you just shake off."

"No, I wasn't—"

"Yes, you were. And you might never have gotten out if Clem hadn't died. Do you know when I heard she committed suicide, my first feeling was relief? *Relief*, Shay. Because your mom called and said you'd picked up the phone again, after a year of silence. She said Clem's death made you reach out, and you were actually going to class, going to graduate. The last time, it took Clem dying to break through the brainwashing. You can't go back."

"Don't you think that haunts me?" I stared at him, wishing he could somehow feel what I was feeling. "I'll never forgive myself. I won't let it happen again."

I grabbed Jamie's phone and thrust it at him.

His brows knit. "What are you doing?"

"Press Record. I'll show you."

"Why do you even want to be interviewed? Thousands of people are going to listen. You realize that, right? Everyone's going to know."

"You're a journalist, Jamie. Don't you want me to crack my heart open? Isn't a confession every reporter's wet dream? I'm telling you because you can't have the truth about Laurel without getting the truth about me."

He looked back at me, eyes wild and unreadable, like I'd caught him somewhere liminal, pulled in a million different directions. He swayed toward me, like a moth dipping toward flame, and I thought, for one charged moment, that he might kiss me.

But he regained his balance and stilled.

I shoved the phone into his chest. "Come on, Jamie. Press it."

CHAPTER SIXTEEN

Transgressions *Episode 705, interview transcript: Shay Deroy, Sept. 6, 2022, Part Two (unabridged)*

SHAY DEROY: After Mr. X, Don started bringing home other men, always one at a time. Some of them wanted the same things, and it was hard on those nights to remember Don had our best interests at heart. But some of them just wanted to spend time with us. There was one who would sit in an armchair in Don's living room, watching us vacuum and dust the drapes in our aprons. We would bring him dinner on a tray, refill his cocktail, and say, "Is that all, sir?" Maybe he'd slip a hand up our skirt, run his fingers over our pantyhose, but that was it. There was another who stayed completely silent. He'd close his eyes when I came near, like I scared him. One night he finally said, "This living room is the only safe place left in America."

I thought it was strange, but I guess Don understood. He said, "I knew you'd find peace with my little housewives."

Clem didn't hide the fact that she hated when he called us his wives. There were a million clues she was planning something else, but it wasn't until the day Don took us to the city, and we ran into you, that I knew for sure. He'd been much stricter since the night Clem tried to escape. We weren't allowed to grocery shop anymore, and when we had to go to class, Rachel waited for us outside our classrooms. But that day, Don had a meeting with a business partner and said we could come. I think he could sense even Laurel was getting restless. He said we could get ice cream cones while we waited for him to finish.

JAMIE: The three of you were sitting outside Miss Marple's Ice Cream, at one of those wrought-iron tables, only a few blocks from my dorm. I almost didn't recognize you. You were shockingly pale and bone thin. And you were wearing that awful dress. When I realized who I was looking at, I stopped in my tracks. Some guy walked right into me, called me an asshole, but I barely registered it.

SHAY: Imagine how I felt. After we moved in, Don told us we shouldn't talk to anyone from our old lives or go home anymore, because our families and friends were the ones who'd failed us, and we needed to cleanse ourselves of them. The first year, at Christmas, I thought my mom would protest. But Don was right. She had a new boyfriend by then, and she didn't care that I wasn't coming home. After that, Don asked us to give up our cell phones. By the time I saw you walking down the street, it was like seeing a ghost. And you had this look on your face I knew was trouble.

JAMIE: You wouldn't meet my eyes.

SHAY: I was scared Rachel would come back from the bathroom and catch us talking.

JAMIE: You wouldn't even acknowledge me. I kept saying, "Shay, it's me," but you wouldn't speak.

SHAY: I needed you to go away.

JAMIE: Clem introduced herself, started talking a mile a minute, like she was desperate to connect, but Laurel told me to leave, sounded almost hysterical. I'd been trying to get in touch with you for over a year, and suddenly you were right in front of me. I had to plead my case. I couldn't just let you go.

SHAY: You begged to talk alone. There's no way I could've done that.

JAMIE: Your eyes were hollow. *You* were the ghost.

SHAY: Don came back while you were there, Jamie. Literally, the worst thing that could've happened, happened. Can you imagine if I'd acted interested, and he'd noticed you? What do you think would've happened?

JAMIE: I wish he'd noticed me. All I knew was this man rounds the corner, and suddenly you're practically crying, running away from me like I'm a stranger harassing you. We've been friends since we were five.

SHAY: You weren't my friend that day. You were a man who wasn't Don—a threat.

JAMIE: I should've followed you, but I was just so stunned. It haunts me, what I should've done.

SHAY: Well, you got through to someone.

JAMIE: What?

SHAY: That night, when the three of us were in bed and the lights went out, Clem whispered, "That was the boy you told us about. Your friend from growing up."

It felt like admitting something shameful, but I said, "Yes. Jamie."

Clem thought it was strange I was afraid of you. She said, "He used to be your best friend. You told us how nice he was."

But Laurel whispered, "They're all nice until they get you alone. Don says every one of them's hungry. Just waiting for their opportunity."

Normally, Laurel alluding to her rape would've been enough to silence Clem. But she must've been determined, because she said, "I miss soccer. My coach keeps trying to talk to me, convince me to come back..." She whispered, "If I left, would you come?"

Laurel and I were silent in shock.

Clem said, "I'm going to tell my coach what Don's doing to us. She'll believe me. She'll tell the dean or go to the cops. She'll help us."

Laurel said, "The *cops*?" She'd hated them since freshman year.

Clem said, "Whatever it takes. But I won't go without you. I swear. I won't leave you behind."

She was actually serious. She had a plan.

I got scared. Maybe Don wasn't perfect, but what if everything he told us was true, and life away from him was terrifying and unfulfilling? What if we could never come back to him, or from the things we'd done, and we were trapped in purgatory?

I was a coward. So when Laurel said, "If you say one

more word about this, I'll tell Don," I fell in line. There was this moment of possibility, then the conditioning snapped back in place.

I said, "No one wants to leave, Clem, so drop it."

I would give anything for those not to have been our last words.

But the next day Clem went to class and never came back. By nighttime, Laurel and I were reading in the living room, waiting for some sign of her. Finally, Don walked in and said, "Girls. A terrible thing has happened, and the police are looking for you. I'm afraid I can't shield you. I'm taking you down to the station."

The cops were the ones who told us what happened, that Clem had hung herself in the shower. They took us to identify her body, and that's when I saw the words *I'm sorry* in blood, written on her arm. I understood then that the message was for us. She'd promised she wouldn't leave without us, but in the end she had.

My guilt did something nothing else had been able to do: it woke me up. Gave me perspective. When Don and Rachel were out of earshot, I begged the officer to take us back to our dorm.

JAMIE: Did the officer ask why?

SHAY: No. But I knew it was our only shot. Don couldn't cause a fuss in the station. And it would probably take another one of us dying before we ever came back. My heart was thundering when the cop said yes. I'm sure he had no idea he was causing this tectonic shift.

When Don heard we were going back to campus, he said, "Of course, whatever they want," like it was a perfectly reasonable request and not against all his rules. His mask was so convincing. He didn't frown. He didn't even blink fast.

When the officer dropped us off in front of Rothschild, we flew to our suite and locked the door, shoved the couch in front of it, checked every window. Then we held each other in bed and cried.

JAMIE: What happened to Don?

SHAY: I dragged Laurel to the dean of students. She didn't want to go, but I was terrified he'd show up any minute and force us back. We told the dean everything. She was shocked, said she'd alert the cops, make sure someone extricated Rachel. She assured us we'd be safe.

JAMIE: And did she call the police?

SHAY: I have no idea. All I know is days went by, and we didn't see or hear from the dean, or the cops, or Don. He didn't go to Clem's memorial service. It was absolute silence, as if the whole thing had been a dream. Finally Laurel and I couldn't take it anymore. We had to know we weren't crazy, so we snuck back to his house to look.

It was empty. Not a trace of Don or Rachel. After that, Laurel and I made a pact to bury what happened and never speak of it again, like everyone else was doing. As soon as we graduated, we'd leave New York and never come back.

JAMIE: You both broke your promises.

(*Silence.*)

Why did it take Clem dying for you to leave?

SHAY: I don't...

(*Silence.*)

Actually, you know what, Jamie? You think you know
me, because we were friends growing up, but there was a
lot you didn't see. If you had, maybe you'd get it.
JAMIE: Tell me, then. Help me understand.
(*Phone ringing.*)
    Shay—
(*Phone ringing.*)
JAMIE: We're not done—

End of transcript.

CHAPTER SEVENTEEN

My husband was calling. I'd sworn to call him after dinner but forgot, and now, after Fox Lane and the interviews, we were creeping into the early morning hours. I didn't want to talk to Cal, if I was being honest, but I wanted to escape Jamie and his questions even more.

"I have to take this," I said.

Jamie stepped closer. "I want to understand."

There was no room to breathe with Jamie in front of me, Cal buzzing in my hand, and the ghost of Don circling overhead. "Please," I said, using every ounce of control to keep my voice cool and calm. "I need to talk to him."

Jamie looked at the space I'd put between us, and for a second, he looked stricken—but it was only a flash, and then his face smoothed, and he was back to being professional. "Of course. Night, Shay."

When he swept out of the room, I steeled myself and answered the phone. "Cal."

"I'm stunned you answered."

It was very late in Dallas, but I imagined Cal sitting in his library in his cognac armchair, one leg crossed over his knee, swirling a glass of whiskey. He was a handsome man, clean-cut, and he carried himself with ease, his untroubled mind obvious in everything, down to the graceful flick of his wrists. Unlike me, he wore his life on his sleeve: it was clear looking at him that he'd always been a favored son, a well-bred Dallas boy who'd slid effortlessly from church and football into a fraternity, then finance.

"I'll cut to the chase," he said. "When are you coming home?"

I took a deep breath, leaning my hip against the bed. "I don't know yet." The truth was, even the idea of returning to Dallas, to the cold house and calm swimming pool and vacant life, made me ache. I'd been missing from that life for far longer than I'd been here in New York, and it was time I admitted that to myself.

"What's going on?" Now I pictured Cal setting the glass down and rising, pacing in front of the fireplace. His gait would be smooth, despite his agitation. "I came back to an empty house. You were supposed to be here."

Maybe it was the late hour, the tense interviews with Jamie, or maybe it was projection, but I snapped. "What, to wait on you? Host your dinner parties and make sure your house is tidy, like a good little wife?"

"Excuse me?" He laughed, harsh and surprised. "Why are you so angry?"

I twisted my hands, making knots in the duvet. "I'm not. I just need to stay here a little longer for my book."

"You can't work here?"

"No."

"Shay, you're my wife. I want you home."

Cal and I had never spoken so plainly about our expectations. We'd never needed to, because I'd always conformed to every assumed pref-erence before he could speak it. It was how Cal's parents, married for thirty-five years, behaved. It was how the other Highland Park wives, the Dallas socialites, acted with their husbands. For all the ways they were strong-willed, opinionated women, they always assumed they'd be the ones to bend, let their husbands' preferences and schedules take priority.

It occurred to me for the first time that Cal wanted the same things from me Don had. He wanted me tied to home, living a life that revolved around him. I'd run so far and worked so hard to leave my past behind. Had I done all of that only to unconsciously re-create it, at least a shadow of it, with Cal?

What if part of me had never escaped Don's house?

Claustrophobia squeezed my chest. I was back in that small bedroom, curled in a twin bed, crying each time the walls shook. Standing in the doorway, looking out at a calm suburban night, shaking with nerves. Tied up on the floor of Don's bedroom, staring at the closed curtains, denied even a glimpse of the sky. Of course I'd gone and found someone like him. You didn't just break a hold like that.

I gripped the phone so hard my hand ached. "Cal, you told me to quit working so I could focus on my book. That's my job now. And this is where I need to be to do it, just like you need to be wherever your business trips send you. Give me a little respect."

"I did tell you to quit," he said. "When I thought that meant you'd be home *more* often, not less. Helping take care of our house, spending time with our friends, being present for dinner. Hell, just being present. That's called sharing a life. It's what married people do."

It was getting hard to take full breaths. Cal had never cared about my book, had he? He'd simply wanted a placid housewife, and I'd delivered. "You thought I'd stay in your cage as long as it was gilded, didn't you?"

"Time out. Are you hearing yourself?" Cal's voice turned pleading.

"Shay, you sound nuts. You fly off to New York on a whim, I can't get in touch with you, you won't commit to coming home. Now I'm trying to cage you? Honey, this isn't normal."

It was the same pattern as Don: threatening, then sweet; angry, then sympathetic. "I don't care how I'm supposed to act, Cal. *This* is what I care about. Here in New York."

"Do you hear how cruel you're being? Fine, Shay, stay. But I'm not going to bankroll whatever you're doing. If you don't come home, I'm cutting you off."

There it was. All that talk about Cal and me being equals, and yet he was using money to corner me. The memory blazed back: the smell of gasoline, a perfume so strong it made me high to breathe it. The rip of the match against the box, my hate becoming tangible, sparking and catching fire. The spike of adrenaline right before I tossed the match, turning my body into an inferno a second before the world became light and heat.

I felt that same spike now. "I thought it was *our* money, darling."

Cal was silent. I lit the flame and tossed it. "I don't want it, anyway. Do your worst."

"Jesus, Shay—"

I hung up, dropped the phone, and stared at the woman in the window. Who was she? Was she unraveling, like Cal said? I raised a hand, and she touched her face. Her fingers were long and elegant: the fingers of someone who might've played piano, or plucked a harp, if only she'd been born to a different family.

I drew close enough so my breath fogged the glass. When it cleared, her face was framed, beautiful as a doll. Hair and eyes as dark as ink, lips so full they couldn't help but invite attention. They were lips that provoked, that men found sensual, no matter how desperately she'd wished to be invisible.

Fitting, then, that she had grown more invisible with every passing year. Other women had warned it would happen: The ones who'd stroked her hair backstage in pageant dressing rooms; the mothers of friends taking pictures before dances; her own mother, examining her reflection in the bathroom mirror, telling her, *Learn from my mistakes. Your beauty's your power, and it's slipping through your fingers.*

In the window's reflection, I could see that the thick black liner around the woman's eyes had started to bleed. I rubbed my fingers over my face, scrubbing harder, and the coal smeared, her lipstick pushing past the boundary of her lips to stain her skin. The woman in the window smiled, bloody mouth and haunting eyes, enjoying being frightening.

Really, who was I now? When I said goodbye to Laurel after graduation, we'd sat side by side onstage, gowns splayed open, caps in our hands, silent with the knowledge that we would never again be the girls we were when we first came to Whitney. I'd squeezed her hand quickly, all the touch I could bear after Don, and we'd vowed to get ourselves on track. Meet up one day when it was safe.

I'd been the first to walk away, to where my mother waited in the car, relieved enough to hear from me after a year of silence that she'd made the trip for graduation. When I turned back and saw Laurel sitting alone in the middle of the crowd, saw how she fixated on me, I'd pushed it aside. Assumed she was only doing what I was: saying goodbye. But now I wonder if the look meant something else.

I should have called. Written. Anything. It was only that when I moved back to Texas, the sheer relief of having a blank slate was too enormous. I'd wanted a small, quiet life. And then I'd started writing for *The Slice*—light, stupid pieces, a little feminist, even. Corporate feminism, but it was a toe in the water, trying it back on. A good way to write again, skating the surface, no stakes. I told myself I was better than happy; I was safe.

And before I knew it, the gradual ebb of time made me an adult. Did I wake some mornings burning to talk to Laurel, or Jamie, or Clem? Of course. But the desire was replaced the next moment with paralysis, a sense of overwhelming shame. Better to leave it alone. Best of all to meet Cal Deroy, a respectable man who didn't want to peer into the dark corners of my mind or know who else I'd been, what different versions of me existed. He wanted a wife like all the others, a life like the comfortable one he'd had growing up. It was so much easier to dissolve myself in his desires than wonder about my own.

Yet here I was, back where it started. Returning should terrify me. The idea of Cal leaving me penniless—leaving me in general—should break my heart. The men at Fox Lane should make me want to run, put the world between us.

Should, should, should. Yet all I felt was rage. Cal had been right about that.

Through the window, the sun broke over the horizon, rays of golden light shimmering on the Hudson. The woman in the glass wavered, then disappeared, leaving only the world outside.

Leaving me to face the truth. Of course I would go back into Don's house. It was an inevitability, not a decision. I would go back for Laurel, and Clem, and the missing women whose names I didn't know. But I would also go for myself. Maybe I could find the part of me still locked inside.

Maybe I could free her.

PART TWO
Scheherazade, you cunning bitch

You went in to offer yourself in place of your sisters. You went in to perform a feat of heroism.

But.

Did you not feel your skin tingle at the sight of the blade in the corner of the room? Did you not feel yourself get slick when you beheld the king, the man who would either take your life from you or fall to his knees on the bed and be conquered? Were you not desperate to know whether you could do it? Whether you were powerful enough, and in what ways?

You weave and you weave, until you can no longer tell if you are the storyteller or the story being told. And when he craves it, your paper-thin skin, when he wants to drink your blood, your living stories, do you not let him lick up every spoonful? Do you not swirl around the look in his eyes like a cup of tea, desperate to read the leaves, to parse who you are to him, who you will be to history? After all, names like yours are never etched into the books unless men like him allow it.

Did you not grow to love him, you sad, masochistic little beast?
Yes, this is an interrogation.
You had one thousand and one nights, and he never was deposed.

CHAPTER EIGHTEEN

"There's something about suburbia at night that makes my skin crawl." Jamie glanced at me from the driver's seat, moonlight cutting across his face. "It's too quiet. You can feel the menace buzzing just under the surface."

I'd gotten the text from an unknown number: Initiation, midnight, 35 Bell Pond Road. The number was a dead end, even for Jamie's team, so whoever it was had probably used a burner. Regardless, the message was clear: whatever the Paters had managed to dig up in their background check—besides my phone number—they'd found it unobjectionable, and I was in.

Now we were parked in the slumbering suburbs so I could deliver myself for punishment. For *initiation*, Jamie kept correcting, as if there was a difference.

"There's a reason they hold their parties here," I said, looking around. "It's the perfect cover." I dropped my phone and wedding ring into the cup holder. "You're a child of suburbia, anyway, Jamie. You ever direct that analytic gaze inward?"

Jamie looked up at the moon through the windshield. "You mean, have I ever asked myself whether the way I was raised led to a lifetime of me burying my feelings of desperate, feral longing under a polite surface, because that's what you're supposed to do? Or whether the entire reason I run a podcast called *Transgressions* is because I was never allowed to transgress, and now I'm obsessed with it?"

"Something like that."

He glanced at me and grinned. "Nah. Never thought of it."

Thirty-five Bell Pond was another grand house, like the first. A huge porch, tall white columns, and a blue sign for Alec Barry, New York's governor. Like the first house, it was quiet and still, only a few windows glowing. No hint of what lay inside.

"Property records say it's a private residence owned by Mountainsong, this megachurch in Kingston," Jamie said. "Over ten thousand members, and they do a ton of streaming sermons, real modern, but what they teach is old-school fire-and-brimstone stuff. That's all we could find."

I shivered. All day I'd felt calm, but now that I was here, I was vibrating. "Showtime." I flipped up the mirror. "You'll be here when I'm done?"

"I won't move a muscle."

"Good." I shoved open the door and started to climb out, but Jamie stopped me with a hand on my wrist.

"You have the recorder?"

I patted my bra.

He nodded and squeezed my wrist. "If anyone tries to hurt you, screw the investigation and leave. I'm serious. Whatever it takes. You don't have to do anything you don't"—his voice caught—"want." He cleared his throat. "Just be careful."

I knocked on the door, three sharp raps. To my surprise, it opened immediately to a handsome man in his thirties, blond, clean-cut, and scowling. He wasn't wearing a mask, and my heart jumped with the sudden fear I'd been sent to the wrong place.

"Yes?" He scanned me. "What do you want?"

I pulled my coat tighter. "I'm here for the party."

"Wrong address." He started to close the door, but I stuck out a hand.

"Nicole invited me." I spoke fast. "I'm being initiated."

He froze. "Who are you?"

My heart thundered, as if he could see through my shirt to the tiny recording device, no bigger than a button, wedged into my bra. Then it hit me: Nicole had given me instructions, hadn't she? Back at the Sparrow. I searched my mind for the words, but all I could remember was her surprised face when I said *Happy hunting*, right before she'd disappeared. "I'm here to be initiated," I repeated, hoping the fact that I knew that much would work in my favor.

His eyes darted behind me, then he swung open the door. "Get inside."

I barely had a chance to step inside the foyer—filled with large, dramatic Renaissance-style paintings of angels—before he seized my arm.

"What are you doing?" I resisted the urge to fight.

"There's protocol," he said, pulling me down the hall. "Nicole would've told you if she'd really invited you. You're lying."

Shit. "I know it. I just forgot." I looked around, trying to keep calm and get my bearings. Then a voice cut through.

"She's with me, Pater."

The man stopped; we both turned to find Nicole at the far end of the hall.

"She didn't say the words."

"It's my mistake." Nicole's voice was smooth and soothing. "I'll confess to the Lieutenant. I'll bring her to him right away."

The man's face was cold. "Tread carefully."

"Yes, Pater," Nicole said. To my relief, the man let go of me. Nicole wasted no time, hurrying me down the hallway.

"You're going to be the death of me," she hissed. She wore all black, her makeup lighter than before. She looked younger than I'd first pegged her. "You didn't say you were a gift from a humble daughter. Remember? There are rules here. They keep us safe."

I swallowed back my guilt at getting her in trouble and struggled to keep up. "You're taking me to the Lieutenant?"

She turned a corner, and we stopped in front of a closed door. "Last chance to change your mind."

I shook my head.

She knocked, and someone called, "Come in."

Inside was a sitting room, filled with what looked like leftovers from a church yard sale: crucifixes in gold and marble and garish painted plastic, pillows with embroidered Bible verses and cheery little flowers. There was a fireplace in the center with a crackling fire. A man sat before it, examining us. "What have you brought?"

It was the man in black's voice, just a hint of a Dutch accent in the way he pronounced *brought*. Unmasked, the Lieutenant was different than I'd pictured: older, in his fifties, with a thick blond mustache and full head of wheat-blond hair. The way he sat, spine straight as a rod, reminded me of a soldier or a Boy Scout.

Nicole's demeanor had changed the moment we stepped into the room, her shoulders tightening, eyes cast to the man's feet. "A lost girl," she said, "who wants to learn her place."

I blinked. The words rolled off her tongue as if rehearsed.

"Mrs. Shay Deroy." The Lieutenant's eyes scanned me. "Remind me where you found her?"

"At the Sparrow."

He nodded. "Very good, Nicole. Keep this up, and it won't be long now." His eyes shifted back to me, and he raised an eyebrow. "A married woman a long way from home, found trolling the Sparrow. Whatever are you doing here?"

I swallowed. "I went to college here, years ago." They would know that from the background check. "And now I'm moving back. A… friend recommended Tongue-Cut Sparrow. I found Nicole there, and she said this was a place for people who wanted something real."

"And what does your husband think about that?"

"Nothing, because he doesn't know."

The fire crackled behind the Lieutenant's head. "Why do you want something real?"

"Because I've done things I deserve to be punished for," I said.

The Lieutenant watched me closely. "Most new members come for the parties." I couldn't tell if he was being serious, so I held my tongue. "It usually takes a lot of teaching before they can admit to what you're saying." He gave me a sly look. "What if I said you deserved to be punished simply for being born?"

I gathered my breath. "I'd say I've had that thought before." I was an A+ student. Because of course I was cheating: Don had shown me the right answers years before.

The Lieutenant's eyes flicked to Nicole. "She almost sounds like a true believer. A little bit like you. You're willing to vouch?"

She looked at me, warning in her eyes. "Yes." The word had teeth.

After a moment, the Lieutenant nodded. "Okay, then. Take off your clothes."

I froze. "What?"

"I need to know I can trust you. And that you mean it. The price to enter is a gift you can't take back."

If I took my clothes off, they'd find my recording device.

The Lieutenant's voice deepened. "Now."

I slipped off my heels with shaking fingers, then unzipped my dress, letting it pool on the floor. Both Nicole and the Lieutenant watched, expressions greedy in the firelight.

I had to think fast. What could I do with the recorder? I bent at the waist and unhooked my bra, popping the small black device into my mouth behind the curtain of my hair. I righted and smiled, feeling the smooth metal under my tongue. Now everything that was about to happened would go unrecorded, but I had no other choice. I stepped out of my panties and stood naked.

The Lieutenant's eyes trailed over me. "You might have come here for pain or pleasure. I don't care, really. Because the Pater Society is about liberation."

The Pater Society. The snakelike sibilance of *society* nearly got lost in the hissing, popping fire.

"It's about embracing the truth. Something that's become so controversial there's few safe spaces left in this country to do it. Everything we submit our bodies to here, every gathering, every ritual, it's all testimony."

He rose from his chair. "The first truth we recognize is that society is rotting from the inside out. Becoming more unrecognizable every day. The Creator built men and women for a purpose, built a sacred order, and we've rejected it. What an exhausting performance, to have to deny our true natures, masquerade every day. But not here. Not with us."

The Lieutenant walked to a table in the corner and rolled open a drawer. "Consider this you putting some skin in the game."

He pulled out a black iron rod. On one end was a twisted metal shape: a triangle with four protruding columns, meeting in a rectangular base. It was the symbol on Laurel's and Nicole's arms—unmistakably a temple, looking at it now. A temple for the Pater Society.

In the fireplace, the flames crackled. And I understood.

Laurel hadn't been tattooed. She'd been branded, like cattle. And now this man wanted to do it to me.

A cold wave of fear washed through me. Instinctively, I took a step back, nearly tripping over my tangled dress. "No. There has to be another way."

"Submit," the Lieutenant said. "Or leave, and never come back."

I couldn't do either. If I let him brand me, I'd wear their mark for the rest of my life. There'd be no escaping. But if I didn't, how would I ever know the truth about how Laurel died, or who was pulling the strings behind the Pater Society, whether Don was masquerading as the Philosopher? If Laurel *had* been killed, how would I avenge her? The urge to protect myself warred against the possibility of losing Laurel all over again. In the end, which was the more unbearable pain?

"Open your mouth and say yes," the Lieutenant demanded.

The command tugged at a long-buried instinct. I spoke around the recording device, whispering, "Yes."

The Lieutenant pointed to the floor in front of the fireplace. "Kneel."

Laurel did this, I told myself. *If she could do it, so can you.*

I dropped to my knees, feeling the heat of the fire on my side searing my skin.

"Call us traditionalists." The Lieutenant's voice was light, almost lazy. He stuck the iron in the flames and rotated it like a spit. "Men and women who believe in the old ways. People come to us when they're lost, when they can't understand why they feel alienated and alone. We teach them, give them the meaning they long for, connection without artifice. We're a refuge. Here, people become their truest selves. All you need to do is to listen to your Paters."

He pulled the iron from the fire. The temple glowed red-hot. I bit down on my tongue so hard I reopened the wound from the night I'd dreamed of Laurel and tasted coppery blood.

"Lift your arm."

I did, feeling dizzy, even down here on my knees. Once, I'd abandoned Laurel and Clem when they'd needed me. What would I do to make up for my past?

The answer was anything.

He gripped my wrist and pressed the brand to my arm. Vicious, seething pain knifed through me, the worst I'd ever felt. I screamed and jerked, but the Lieutenant held me tight.

"Daughters practice radical humility in order to ascend," he said, voice low and calm against my choking. "When a Pater tells you to do something, you say, 'Yes, Pater,' and you do it. You'll attend every gathering and do exactly as you're told. If you're lucky, and a Pater wants to take you under his wing, he'll honor you by asking for your personal service. Nicole is often honored, aren't you?"

Through my tears, I saw Nicole nod. Her face was starkly pale.

"And I will warn you," the Lieutenant said, his voice turning low and flat. "We're everywhere. Where you least expect us. We're a dangerous enemy. If you tell someone about us, we'll know. Do you understand? No whispers to family or friends. No doctors. No matter what."

I was in agony. He removed the iron from my arm, and the sudden stench of burning flesh made bile rise in my throat. It was the smell of my skin dying. The temple blazed a bright, raw red. There was no going back.

He walked to the table and laid down the iron. "You'll stay quiet. And if you don't, what will happen, Nicole?"

"She'll come for you," Nicole said softly.

My head lifted. "She?" I forced the word through the pain. "Who?"

The Lieutenant lunged and seized me by the hair so hard I tumbled, hands catching the floor, the recording device almost falling out of my mouth. He gripped me tight enough for new tears to sting my eyes.

"Look at me," he demanded.

I gritted my teeth and lifted my eyes to meet his.

"You don't ask questions anymore. Nod if you understand."

I nodded, blinking back tears.

"Good." He swept a hand at me. "See her home."

Nicole bent to me. "Put on your clothes."

With shaking hands, I pulled them on, barely able to think beyond the throbbing in my arm. Nicole tugged me out of the room, shutting the door behind us. To my surprise, we didn't turn in the direction of the door. Instead, she moved me swiftly down the hall, deeper into the house.

"Give it a week," she said, tightening her grip on my elbow. "The burning will fade, and then it will be something you're proud of."

I couldn't imagine it would ever fade. My arm burned so white-hot it was as if the iron was still pressed against my skin. I had a sudden vision of Cal seizing my wrist and shouting, red-faced, *What the hell is this?*

I turned my head from Nicole and cupped my hand to my mouth, spitting out the recording device, sliding it back into my bra. "Where are we going?" It took everything to push the words out.

Her gaze stayed locked ahead. "You deserve something for enduring that. No one will notice if we stick to the outskirts."

I held my arm gingerly, struggling to keep pace with her.

Nicole gave me a knowing look. "That night at Tongue-Cut Sparrow, I knew you weren't lying about what you wanted. I could see it in your eyes. The Paters are going to change your life."

We came to a sweeping staircase, and she started climbing. "It's up here." She hopped up the stairs, a flash of pale skin and red hair, and I had the sudden delirious thought that Laurel wasn't my White

Rabbit—Nicole was. Pulling me deeper into this dark wonderland, where up was down and everyone was mad.

"Tonight is Cynthia's punishment party," Nicole said.

Up and up we climbed. "Her what?"

She shot me a quelling look, so I changed tack, lifting a hand to my temple, where I could still feel the Lieutenant's grip. "Why aren't the men wearing masks tonight?"

She gestured at me to hurry. "Each gathering is different. You'll see. The Paters are inventive. It's part of the appeal."

"That's why you do this? The sex?" That made sense. There was an impishness about Nicole, an air of strength, that made it hard to imagine her buying into the idea of female subservience, no matter what the Lieutenant had said. She must be here because it gave her a version of BDSM she couldn't get anywhere else. Rawer, realer, undiluted, like she'd said at the Sparrow. A place without safety nets.

She stopped, and her expression hardened. "I'm going to the Hilltop."

"What is that?"

"You're not supposed to know yet, so keep this between us. The Hilltop's mecca. Out here, we only get gatherings once a week, sometimes less. For some of us, that's not enough. You end up living for the few hours you're here." Her voice softened. "But at the Hilltop, you give up life outside and live with the Philosopher. Total immersion. No more dead-end jobs, no more struggling to make rent on your shitty apartment, no more drunk, good-for-nothing family. Nothing but escape."

I'd been wrong. Nicole was a true believer. "The Philosopher... He's in charge?"

She nodded, striding down the dim hallway. "The founding father."

"What's he like?"

"I haven't met him yet. He rarely leaves the Hilltop, and daughters only get chosen to ascend if they're very good. It's what I want most in the world."

No wonder Nicole was recruiting at Tongue-Cut Sparrow. She was trying to prove herself, and bringing in new girls must buy her points.

Massive double doors with round iron handles stood at the end of the hallway, the kind on castles in storybooks. I could hear the strangest sound from behind them—soaring music, like from an orchestra. Nicole swung open the doors.

The Pater Society spanned before us, filling an enormous room, rich red curtains hanging at sharp angles over skyscraper windows like guillotine blades. The moody expanse was lit with cream-colored candles, flame-light flickering over instruments circling the perimeter: cellos, violins, a golden harp. In the corner, a man bent over a piano, fingers flying over the keys, filling the room with melancholy music. It looked like an aerie, a piece of heaven.

It was a cocktail party. In the center of the room, men and women mingled, talking and laughing, picking glasses of wine and canapés off trays passed by women in old-fashioned dresses who moved silently through the crowd. At once, all the faces turned in our direction, and my heart jumped. But the Paters' attention quickly resettled, and Nicole tugged me in the direction of the back wall.

The men wore suits again tonight, paired with gleaming wristwatches and polished shoes, well heeled and well coiffed. Unmasked, they were a mix of old and young, every height and shape. The masks had been part of a game, then, not a regular precaution. A costume.

All the better for me. I tried to commit each of their faces to memory.

The women leaned younger than the men. There were so many of them, more than I'd expected. As we wove through the room, I tried to catch their eyes. I wanted to ask *Why are you here? Why do you like this? What does it give you?*

I wanted to know these things about myself.

The entire room buzzed with dark anticipation. Their eyes kept flitting to a four-poster bed, jarringly out of place against a far wall.

We made it to the opposite wall and Nicole leaned against it, her gaze locking on the bed like everyone else's. "We're in black tonight to mourn Cynthia," she said. "Normally we have a dress code. Always dresses, with a hem that falls below your knees. Never straps. Always heels and pantyhose. You should be feminine and modest. It's what the Paters like."

I knew exactly what they liked. I'd been the prototype. So I didn't bother asking, *Feminine—what do you mean by that?* Because the daughters, in their prim dresses, were old fantasies made flesh and blood. Molded to fit an idea of women plucked from history, from Paters' heads.

"Nicole," I whispered. It was too soon, and I would risk showing my hand, but I had to know. "Did you know a daughter named Laurel Hargrove?"

She didn't react with suspicion. In fact, she didn't react at all. Her gaze remained on the bed. "I don't talk to the other daughters, and I recommend you don't, either. Half of them are here for the wrong reasons, and the other half you're in competition with for the Hilltop."

"What are the wrong reasons?"

She snorted. "Money. Clothes. Jewelry. All sorts of things. The Paters aren't supposed to, but you'd be surprised what you can get once you're in someone's service. Enough to make a living." She shook her head. "It's better than most other ways around here."

"Are you in someone's service now?"

"I'm working on it."

As if it was a promotion. *The daughters as entrepreneurs.* I shook my head. I needed to focus on Laurel. "But if you could just remember—"

"Shh," she urged. "It's starting."

Near the bed, a man raised his hand for silence, and the music stopped, heads turning in his direction. He was abnormally tall, standing head and shoulders above the others, his suit jacket pulling tight over his massive shoulders. His hairless skull shone in the candlelight.

"The Disciple," Nicole whispered. "Stay out of his way."

"Tonight we punish Cynthia for disobedience," the Disciple called. He reached behind him, pushing a dark-haired woman forward. The room buzzed. "Pater, tell us how she violated you."

Another man—older and shorter, with a great round middle—stepped forward. "Twice I've ordered Cynthia to give herself to me, and twice she's refused."

The buzzing in the room grew louder. I glanced at Nicole. Her eyes were zeroed in on the woman who must be Cynthia. From a distance, with her long, dark hair, Cynthia and I could have been sisters.

The Disciple looked down at Cynthia from his tall height. "Do you acknowledge this?"

For a moment, it looked like she would protest. But then the expression melted from her face and she said, in a clear voice, "Yes. I submit to punishment with full humility, so I may grow." Her hands twisted in front of her.

The bald man's voice boomed through the room. "We're gathered here to punish Cynthia in full view of the Society to restore order and put her back on the path to enlightenment. We kill her ego out of mercy." He turned to her. "Off."

The room was silent as Cynthia undressed, the only movements her arms pulling jerkily at her dress and the flickering shadows on the wall. Then the Disciple did something eerily familiar. He put his large hand on the back of Cynthia's neck and shoved her face-first into the bed, so only her naked back faced us.

The memory returned: the suffocating cotton, my shallow breaths, Don's whisper in my ear.

"Daughter, do you submit your body in penance?" The Disciple twisted Cynthia's head so she could speak.

"Yes," she choked. She'd already started crying. It had taken me much longer.

The Disciple shoved her head back down and gestured to the round man who'd complained. He walked up, holding a belt.

Don's favorite.

Nicole's eyes gleamed. The round man lifted his hand and snapped the belt like a whip across Cynthia's back. The Paters applauded. He cracked it again.

The Disciple wrenched Cynthia's head up. "What do you find in submission?"

She was struggling to suck in air. "Transformation."

Down she went, but this time, the Disciple took the belt from the man and brought it down himself, hard, over her spine. He did it again, and again, forming a rhythm. Around me, the Paters began to stomp their feet. The man at the piano bent over his instrument, and music soared again, lifting the fine hairs on my arms.

The women in the crowd stood still as statues, watching in silence.

Nicole was wrong. This was real, but it was also a performance. Dramatic, didactic. I recognized the scene.

On center stage, the Disciple wrested Cynthia up by her hair.

"What do you say, daughter?"

She arched her back toward him. "More," she begged. "Please."

Is this what I'd looked like?

He struck her again, and without her face smothered, Cynthia's cry ripped through the room, pain mixed with undeniable pleasure. Blood spotted her back. The stomping and music became cacophony.

The sense of déjà vu was so strong it was almost hallucinatory, like they'd pumped gas through the vents, or I'd taken another midnight-blue pill and stepped back into the past. I could *feel* Don in the room. Any second, the dark-suited men would turn, and they'd be wearing his face—laughing, unable to believe that I was here, that I'd come crawling back for more.

I pressed my fingers into my eyes, so I didn't see it coming when the Disciple yelled, "Daughters, receive your punishments," and the room exploded into motion. I opened my eyes as a tall man stepped to Nicole, hand extended. She placed her hand in his, and he whipped her around so her chest pressed flat against the wall.

"Nicole." I resisted the urge to shout. "What's happening?"

Her face was calm against the wall. "If one of us gets punished, we all do." The man behind her fumbled with his belt.

I backed away, sliding over the wall. It was too much, too soon.

"If you wait, a Pater will find you," Nicole promised, but her next words were drowned by the man who pinned her, his elbow over her shoulder blades.

"Who does your body belong to?" he demanded.

Don't let them touch you, the dark voice whispered in my head. *Only me.*

"I'm sorry," I said. "I'm not ready." I peeled myself from the wall before anyone could reach for me.

"Shay," Nicole called, but I didn't look back.

I threaded quickly through the chaos as belts slithered from around waists and piano music crashed like waves against the rocks. I sped into the hallway, then down the stairs. *Whatever you do, don't run,* I told myself. *Don't draw suspicion.* The last thing I needed was the Lieutenant realizing I'd disobeyed him by going to the party.

I forced myself to walk—slowly—but I didn't know the house and found myself in a strange hallway. I spun and came face to face with a half-open door.

It was a library. Books lined the shelves and crosses hung on the walls, mixed with family portraits. In the nearest, a smiling man had his arm around a blond woman. With them were two young boys, on the cusp of being teenagers. The whole family wore matching white button-downs and tan slacks, posing on a beach somewhere at sunset. The man was the Lieutenant.

I knew I wasn't supposed to see this glimpse into who the Paters really were, the Lieutenant outside these walls. I took only a second more to study the faces, then lurched from the room and sped down the hall, taking turns until finally I came to the front door. I flung it open and ran.

I looked over my shoulder as I fled, expecting to see a tall, dark figure barreling out of the house, ready to pull me back by the ankles. But there was no one—just the stars, watching dispassionately. I flew down the street and wrenched the car door open, jumping in next to Jamie.

"Jesus!" His face was white as a ghost's. "Where'd you come from? What happened?"

"Just go," I said.

"Your arm—"

"*Drive!*"

We rocketed down Bell Pond Road. I twisted in my seat to watch through the rear windshield, unwilling to stop until we pulled up to the hotel and Jamie shook me by the shoulders.

Jamie knelt and smoothed a blanket over my lap, tucking the edges into the couch, creating a warm, tight cocoon. "Let me take you to the hospital."

I shook my head. "No point. It's probably no worse than a tattoo."

Jamie lifted my right arm, and I winced. The brand burned without end, like an eternal flame. "*That's* the point. These people mutilated you as their opening gambit." His thumb brushed my face. "You weren't supposed to get hurt."

My body registered him a half second before my brain did: his hair, mussed over his forehead; his eyes, wide and watchful. The light in the room swept shadows under his cheeks that made him look younger, like the boy I'd grown up with. My Jamie.

As soon as I thought it, I jerked away, remembering I'd left my wedding ring sitting in the cup holder.

"I'm sorry," he said, dropping his hand. "I should have asked before I touched you."

"It's not that." I found his hand again. "Jamie, I don't have proof yet, but I know in my heart the Pater Society is Don's. I'm not making this up. I can feel him. I thought he'd dropped off the face of the planet." *You thought I'd abandoned you*, the voice whispered, but I shoved it away. "I thought the dean or the cops…*someone* scared him, and he was gone for good. But he's back, and he's not experimenting anymore. This is big. You have to believe me."

"I do." Jamie sat next to me, so close our legs brushed. "There's a story here. We just have to uncover it."

"The story is that Don found Laurel, and he sucked her back in." I turned so my whole body faced him. "He branded her, and he started hurting her again, and this time, there was no one to stop him. He killed her, Jamie." Because hadn't it always been building to that? Hadn't we suspected, at least subconsciously, that with his constant limit pushing, his invention of new pains—every day, taking a bigger bite of us—there was only one possible ending? We'd danced with death and it had come for us, one by one.

"If you're right that he's capable of murder, wouldn't it make sense that eight years ago, he found out Clem was planning to escape and killed her, too?" Jamie leaned closer. "We can get justice for both of them, and you can stop punishing yourself."

Punishing myself. I almost touched my aching temple, then stopped.

"Can I?" he asked. When I nodded, he touched me gingerly, turning my chin to study my face. "You're going to have bruises."

"I can find out who the Paters are," I said. "It seems like they take turns hosting. There will be clues in their houses, names and pictures. And if this goes beyond the gatherings—if they're actually killing women—someone will speak up."

"Speaking of pictures." Jamie woke his phone and handed it to me. "Any chance you recognize one of them?"

It was the Mountainsong church's website. I scanned the headshots of their leadership team—the pastor and his ministers—but no one looked familiar. I shook my head.

"Shit." Jamie reached for his phone, accidentally sending the screen back to Mountainsong's home page.

"Wait," I said, snatching it back. One of the banner images was a picture of a grinning preteen boy, standing in a classroom. He was one of the boys from the family portrait in the Lieutenant's house, in the room I wasn't supposed to see. "That's the Lieutenant's son."

Jamie squinted at the caption under the photo, swiping back when it rotated to a new image. "Tyler Corbin, son of former Pastor Michael Corbin, shows off his Bible Studies worksheet." He grinned. "Fuck me. We have our first name."

"Michael Corbin." I rolled it on my tongue, trying to picture the Lieutenant as a Michael. A Mike. Jesus—a *pastor*.

"This him?" Jamie held up the results of a new image search for Michael Corbin, Mountainsong. And there he was—the Lieutenant, clean-cut and smiling at a Habitat for Humanity build. The same man who'd branded me.

"It's him." We'd unmasked a Pater.

"One down," Jamie murmured. "One by one, we'll build a case for the cops."

"And then all I have to do is get to the Hilltop and prove Don's behind this."

"Then we'll have him," Jamie said.

We'll have him. I shivered, and Jamie blew out a breath.

"What?"

"It's just…you're the one doing all the work. Going undercover, risking yourself. I'm kind of useless."

"You're the journalist. I need you to dig and put the story together. Trust me, the story is everything."

Jamie frowned, unconvinced. "Yeah, well…it's late. I'm going to let you sleep." He rose from the couch.

"No." I grabbed his hand, stilling him. "I'm too keyed up. I want to talk."

"About what?"

"Your choice."

I could see I'd hooked him. "Anything?"

"Anything. Interview me."

He raised his eyebrows. "Will you tell me about your father?"

That was the last thing I'd expected. "Excuse me?"

"You said there was a lot I didn't know about your life, even though we grew up together." The words came faster. "It's always bothered me I don't know what happened with your dad. One day he was there, and the next, he was gone. I mean, I know he was some important person, some CIA analyst. But you were always so private. I never felt like I could ask."

I laughed, a knee-jerk response. "Jamie, I lied. You really want to know?"

He swallowed. "Yes. I need it for…background. For the podcast."

My father was a story I never told. No matter how many times I'd stripped bare, I had never gotten that naked.

But I'd already given up a piece of my body tonight. The proof burned like wildfire in my arm. Why not a piece of my soul? After all, this was the routine, wasn't it? Letting someone take bigger and bigger bites of me. Pushing the limits, drawing right up to the knife-edge of control.

Dancing that familiar dance.

CHAPTER NINETEEN

Transgressions Episode 705, interview transcript: Shay Deroy, Sept. 9, 2022 (unabridged)

SHAY DEROY: When I was ten years old, my dad left us. It might have happened before then—he might've always been leaving—but ten was when I knew. I think it was the worst night of my life. I know that's strange to say, compared to what happened in college. But when I look back, that night is the dark hole. Just skimming the surface triggers this exquisite pain, like the hurt's been preserved, living raw under my skin.

JAMIE KNIGHT: Like a festering wound.

SHAY: Sometimes I think it's a shrine.

JAMIE: To what?

SHAY (*clearing throat*): You know my dad was in the army.

JAMIE: I used to think it was cool you lived on base.

SHAY: He was deployed a lot, sometimes for months. By the time I was ten, I'd gotten used to it. Dad being gone was normal. He was going to stop traveling once he climbed rank. We used to talk about that a lot: our wonderful future, right around the corner.

The night it happened was about three months into one of his deployments. I was waiting for my mom to come home, sitting alone in our duplex—you remember the one with the crazy wallpaper—doing homework and listening to the neighbors have dinner through the walls. I was determined to catch my mom as soon as she came home because Mrs. Carroll had stopped me in the cafeteria that day and told me I couldn't go to the lock-in. I needed my mom to fix it.

JAMIE: Lock-ins were the only fun thing to do in school. Why couldn't you go?

SHAY: They made a rule that year that students could only participate if their parents volunteered a certain number of hours in the PTA.

JAMIE: Huh. I bet my mom was all over that. She was queen of the PTA.

SHAY: I remember.

(*Silence.*)

JAMIE: Why was your mom out so late? At the shelter?

SHAY: This was before that. In elementary, she worked retail—Payless, then Walmart, too. Looking back, her getting a second job should've been a clue something had changed.

JAMIE: What happened when she came home?

SHAY: She was tired. She came home with her clothes wilted, carrying weight in her shoulders. It made me nervous right off the bat. I should've listened to my instincts. But instead, I followed her. That annoyed her. She stopped in the living room and snapped, "What?"

I said, "Mrs. Carroll says I'm not allowed to go to the lock-in because you haven't done your PTA hours."

I knew immediately I'd said the wrong thing. She slammed her purse on the coffee table and said, "Is that right? I dropped the ball, huh?"

Her tone was the one she used whenever she argued with my dad—Nina, the self-righteous martyr. I said, "I'm the only person who can't go."

She rolled her eyes and said, "I'm trying to make rent, Shay, so we're not sleeping in the street. Trying to keep you in clothes when you grow like a weed. I have to take care of you all by myself, since your father decided we weren't worth his time. And this lady says I'm not doing *enough*?"

My vision kind of tunneled. I remember fixating on the scratches on the coffee table. I said, "Dad's on a work trip."

For some reason, that made her angrier. She wrestled out of her jacket, threw it on the floor, and said, "A *work* trip. Let me tell you a secret about Peter Herazen. Peter Herazen has better people to spend time with than us. More beautiful, sophisticated women. Your dad's not on a trip, Shay. He left us. Because you and me are small potatoes."

I said, "He didn't."

My mom always hated when I was soft. She said,

"News flash. Welcome to men. This is what they do. They take your heart and your body, use it all up. And in return, they refuse to marry you. No Herazen name for us, oh no, god forbid. And they step out. *Every* time. They're the ones who get to come and go. We're the ones who are stuck."

I was acutely aware she meant she'd been stuck with me.

She started rooting around in her purse and said, "Here I am, mending a broken heart, and they want me to volunteer for the f-ing *PTA*?"

I was certain of one thing: my dad might leave my mom—they did argue a lot—but he wouldn't leave me. He and I had a tradition. Whenever he got home from a trip, the first thing he'd do was take my hand and walk me across the street to the park. He'd play any game I made up. For hours, I got his undivided attention. Most of the games I invented ended with him chasing me. He'd give me a head start, count until ten, then sprint after me around the park. I can still feel my heart pounding, my feet slapping the grass, that joy and the tiniest sliver of fear every time he caught me. I always screamed.

I loved it. For a few hours, I was my dad's sole pursuit. We usually stayed at the park until the sun went down and the air was blue and dense like water. I can picture it so clearly.

JAMIE: So can I.

SHAY: Then he'd put me on his shoulders and carry me home. I was always a little scared up there, so he'd tease me, call me Shay, Queen of the Playground, to make me feel better.

He loved me. He would never leave.

I told my mom that, and she stopped searching in her purse for a cigarette and bent over until we were eye level. She said, "It's hard now, but one day you'll thank me for ripping off the Band-Aid. Your dad never wanted us, Shay. He used to leave for months at a time, and I wouldn't know if it was for work or for play. When he came home, all he wanted was someone to wait on him. I had to beg him to spend time with you. Beg him to take you to the park, because you adored it. If your father did ever love us, it was never enough."

It was 9:38 at night. I know that because I couldn't look at my mom, so I stared at the clock on the VCR. Nine thirty-eight on a Tuesday night, ten years old. That's when my life carved into a before and an after.

JAMIE: You never told me.

SHAY: Imagine meaning so little to your dad that he left and never came back. Not once, even to see who you grew into.

JAMIE: I can't.

SHAY: My mom called Mrs. Carroll, and I don't know what she said to her, but I got to go to the lock-in. I spent the whole night in my sleeping bag with my book, watching the chaperones with their kids. Rolling their eyes, shouting after them, laughing. And I thought, *What makes some people worth loving, but not others?*

JAMIE: I remember now. You wouldn't leave your sleeping bag, even for the scavenger hunt.

SHAY: After they turned out the lights, you and I lay in the dark, listening to kids giggling, and you whispered, "What's wrong?"

JAMIE: You said you were sad because your dad had to leave. But it was okay because he was on some secret mission. Practically a hero.

SHAY: I invented a story that he left because he had to do something important. It was a stupid lie.

JAMIE: You could've told me the truth.

SHAY: I wasn't lying for you. It was the only thing I could think of to keep my heart in one piece.

(Rustling.)

JAMIE: I have to ask. Do you think your dad leaving had anything to do with the pull you felt toward Don?

(Silence.)

SHAY: You're the journalist, Jamie. You tell me.

JAMIE: Okay. I don't see how it couldn't have.

SHAY: Yeah, well. That would be nice, wouldn't it? Everything tied in a neat little bow.

End of transcript.

CHAPTER TWENTY

Two nights later, the hotel restaurant was near closing when I rested my elbows on the edge of the bar. A bartender was with me in seconds.

"Manhattan." I handed him my card and turned to watch the servers close up, glancing at the front door and remembering what Jamie had looked like stepping through it. So different, yet so much the same. Maybe I was, too.

"Ma'am."

I turned to find the bartender frowning. "Your card's been declined." He slid it over the countertop. "Do you have another?"

Cal, that motherfucker—he'd actually done it.

I picked up the card and dropped it in my purse. "No, I don't." I'd let my husband hold all the power like a fool.

The bartender shot me a pitying look and slid over the manhattan, the crystal glass catching like a diamond in the light. "Here. Either you're drinking it, or I am. You look like you need it more." His eyes ran down me. "Nice dress, by the way. Don't see that every day. Old school."

"Thanks." I slugged the drink, wiping my mouth. "I mean it."

When he turned away, I called Jamie, who answered breathlessly. "I'm just finishing a run."

"Now?" It was nearly eleven at night. Add running in the dark to the list of things Jamie could do that I couldn't.

"Yeah, well...my producer called." He exhaled. "He's not exactly thrilled I've spent so long up here. Thinks I'm devoting too much time to one story."

"What'd you tell him?"

"To trust me that it was important. I'm just blowing off steam. Need me to come over earlier?"

"Actually." I watched the servers pull long-stemmed wineglasses off the tables, balancing them between their fingers. "I need a different favor. Cal cut me off."

The heavy rhythm of Jamie's breathing stopped. "What does that mean?"

"It means I need to find a cheaper place to stay. Preferably free."

"I'll get the production company to pay your hotel bill," he assured me. "They can book you another room, too. It probably won't be at the River Estate. I hope that's okay."

I looked up at the ornate chandelier in the center of the room, its glass beads twisting slightly in the air-conditioning, raining gentle light that turned everyone soft-edged and golden.

I hoped I knew what I was doing.

"Why don't I stay with you? Then there's no additional cost."

Silence stretched.

"You're right, it's weird. I figured we're friends, but...if it makes you uncomfortable..."

"No," he said. "Of course you should stay with me."

The next anonymous text directed me to 25 Marion Coates Road, which was within walking distance of Whitney. This time, lights blazed from every window in the Pater house. Even from the street, I could hear faint strains of jazz. The scene was almost civilized.

Inside, it was like I'd stepped through a portal in time. I pushed past men in suits mingling with women in dresses like mine, hemlines swishing below the knee, boat collars lying flat across our throats, demure and polished. The living room buzzed with saxophone notes, murmured conversations, clinking wineglasses. I snagged one from on top of the piano and drank quickly, unnerved by how convivial it was, how much like a college department's end-of-year salon. Jamie said the house was owned by Cane & Company, a management consulting firm notorious for helping university administrators strip college budgets until they were at maximum profitability. I assumed it was a clue, a link to the real life of whoever lived here. I just had to connect the dots.

I scanned but didn't spot Nicole, which was strange. She'd said she craved Pater gatherings, so why would she miss one? As my eyes traveled, committing faces to memory, my gaze snagged on the Lieutenant, standing with two men in the corner. He was watching me.

He inclined his head, but the intensity of his stare didn't falter. My arm throbbed where the brand had singed my skin.

Michael Corbin, I whispered to myself, the secret curling through my mind. It was a talisman of protection, a knife hidden up my sleeve. I smiled back.

Then I turned, almost spilling wine down the front of a man's shirt. He jumped, and I had an untethered moment of self-flagellation— *awkward body, inelegant, unwomanly*—before the man boomed a laugh.

"I like wine, young lady, but not enough to wear it." Glancing down to see his suit was unblemished, the man took a step closer and held out his hand. "You're new. I came to say hello."

He was tall, with thick fingers, a stomach that strained his suit jacket, and a shock of white hair. He was easily in his sixties, and his face was red from too much alcohol. I took his hand; he snapped it to his mouth and kissed it.

"Your name?" There was a quality to his voice I had trouble placing.

"Shay Deroy."

His eyes sparkled. "I can hear the American South in your voice. And your surname is a clunky French bastardization. *Du roi*, of the king. Let me guess...Louisiana or East Texas."

I recognized it now. He had a professor's voice. The slow, self-satisfied cadence of a man who was used to standing in front of a class-room, receiving attention.

"Texas."

He smiled. "Longview?"

"Dallas." This grinning professor was so unlike the Lieutenant.

His eyes twinkled. "Ah, the Bible Belt. Tell me, Shay, how closely have you studied scripture?"

I frowned. "Scripture?"

He reached around me for a glass of wine, coming unnervingly close. "Say what you will about religion, but there's no denying the Bible is a great work of literature. Endlessly teachable." He sipped his wine with a satisfied smile. "You'll see."

Uneasiness hollowed my stomach. There was something about his cheer, the way he spoke to me as if I were a child. I could feel his desire to diminish me humming underneath his smile.

His eyes caught movement to my right, and he jerked forward, grabbing someone by the elbow. "Speak of the devil!"

He pulled a young girl forward, wisp-thin and stringy-haired, no older than twenty. Her dowdy collared dress hung loose off her limbs, and her elbows were sharp, cheekbones too pronounced. "Shay, meet Katie. It's her special night."

For a moment, I blinked between them, trying to read Katie's face. Her cheeks were flushed. "Hi," she said shyly.

"Hi, Katie." *Run, Katie.*

The man squeezed her arm tighter. "I was just asking Shay what kind of student she was."

"A bad one, I'm afraid." I took a step back. "I almost didn't graduate college."

"Pity," he said, eyes finding mine. "Then you won't understand why the daughters call me the Marquis."

I took another step back. I'd read de Sade.

He winked. "Like I always tell Katie, pushing girls into higher education was where we started to go wrong. We told a generation of women they needed to have a life of the mind to be happy, and now look at us— girls enrolled at twice the rate of men, and men committing suicide in record-high numbers. If this continues, it'll only get worse." He shook Katie's arm. "Katie was miserable in college. All her instincts told her it was unnatural from the start. Isn't that right?"

Katie nodded but said nothing.

How did the Marquis know that about her? I searched her face for a clue, or a hint of rebellion, but all my attention seemed to do was make her shrink even further into the Marquis's bulk.

"Women in the academy now, you can practically feel their lust for power. They want to control everything: the courses, the department rules, the production of knowledge itself. They need to keep feeding society lies to serve their agenda. Well, all that falseness rots them from the inside out. You can tell them by their stink." He made a show of sniffing Katie's hair, then in my direction. "Thank goodness. Sweet as can be."

I closed my mouth, all my questions dying on my tongue.

"Enough of that." The Marquis leaned forward conspiratorially. "I came over to crown you the most beautiful girl in the room. Isn't she, Katie?"

Katie nodded, a slip of her chin, and smiled at me wistfully, like I'd won a prize.

I remembered what the Lieutenant said: *If you're lucky, and a Pater likes the look of you, he'll honor you by asking for your service.* My heart pounded. Maybe that's what the Marquis wanted.

"I'm the host of this party," he started, puffing out his chest. "To be chosen—"

I gripped Katie's arm. "I'm sorry." I picked up a second wineglass from the piano. "I just remembered I promised someone I would bring this to him a while ago."

Before either could respond, I beelined through the living room, then slipped down the empty hallway, moving blindly. My pulse jumped in my throat. How many times could I get away with escaping? This made three now. One of these nights, a Pater wouldn't take no for an answer.

I ducked into a room off the hall and pressed my back against the wall, taking deep breaths. I tipped a wineglass to my mouth, looked around, and froze.

It was a richly appointed office, commanded by a large desk. Bookshelves held rows of thick, cracked-spine tomes. A room full of clues.

I set the wineglasses down and moved behind the desk. Two silver-framed pictures of the Marquis were propped up in prominent positions. In the first, he crouched, grinning, next to a petite but unmistakable Darla Covington, the former Secretary of State. In the second, he wore a forest-green cap and gown—a Whitney cap and gown—and gripped the women's rights activist Jane Freeman by the shoulders.

Who the hell was the Marquis?

With mounting dread, I bent over the desk and rifled through a stack of papers.

There—a form, with the Whitney seal. I leaned closer and stared at the signature slashed across the bottom: *Reginald T. Carruthers.* Underneath, it read *President of Whitney College.*

The Marquis was the *president* of Whitney. The Paters had infiltrated my school. I thought back to eight years ago, sitting in the dean's office next to a stone-faced Laurel. Being patted on the shoulder, reassured the dean would do everything in her power to help us. But none of that help had ever materialized. Were the Paters already in charge by then? Had it been a performance from the beginning?

Understanding dawned. The Pater Society was more than Don's secret sex club, a place for like-minded men to indulge taboo, old-fashioned desires. There was something deeper, more ambitious happening here. Don had a plan, and its roots stretched all the way back to my senior year, if not earlier.

A loud bell rang, and I dropped the form, snatching the wineglasses and speeding from the room before anyone could catch me.

The whole party was gathered in the living room, their attention held by something at the front. I snuck quietly through the crowd, turning to find what everyone was looking at. The Marquis—President Reginald Carruthers—stood next to Katie.

The Marquis beamed. Even this far away, I could see Katie trembling.

He swept a hand. "Welcome back, brothers."

Around the room, Paters raised their glasses—including a man standing close to me. I hadn't noticed him at first, but now I looked. Dark hair, graying at the temples, broad-shouldered, thick brows. He was handsome. I wondered for a moment why he was here—as if being attractive disqualified him from wanting to hurt women—before he sensed me looking. His lips curved in a smile, eyes traveling down my throat to rest on my necklace. I felt the weight of each pearl like a knot around my neck. He tipped his glass in my direction, and I wrenched my eyes away.

Not Don, the terrible voice whispered. *But not far off.*

My palms were damp.

At the front of the room, the Marquis ran a finger down Katie's arm, and I shivered. "I'm proud to say our Eve tonight is my special daughter Katie." He turned his twinkling gaze to her. "Take your bow."

She curtsied, and the Marquis laughed. "Now your clothes, please."

As if she had a choice.

With slow hands, she unfastened the buttons down the front of her dress. It fell away, and she reached back to unhook her bra, sliding it down her arms, tugging down her panties. Naked, she was gaunter than I'd guessed. My stomach clutched with phantom pain. I remembered being that hungry.

The Marquis took a cigar from his pocket and lit it, puffing, taking his time. Then he dragged something from behind the piano: a bucket of crimson liquid, thick and viscous. "Katie, dear. You do the honors."

She bent over the bucket and stuck her hand inside, pulling it out to drip red all over the floor. Her eyes reached into the crowd, jumping from face to face, breathing hard. Then she smacked herself across the face. "*Undeserving.*"

I jerked back.

"Gentlemen," the Marquis announced. "Your turn."

Paters stepped out of the crowd and circled the naked girl. The first dipped his hand into the bucket and pulled it out, fingers dripping red. "Whore," he spit and palmed her face, sliding his hand down, streaking color from her forehead to her breasts.

222

I shoved my fingers in my mouth. I couldn't run to her, no matter how much she reminded me of us.

A second Pater approached. "Betrayer," he accused and dragged his seeping hand across her chest, staining her skin to her hip.

The pungent scent of rust and animal found me. It was blood in the bucket. They were covering her in blood.

"In the beginning," said the Marquis, in his professorial drawl, "God created Adam. And in his beneficence, he gave Adam Eve, grown from Adam's own body and destined to serve him and bear his children. For a time, they lived peacefully in God's kingdom. Close your eyes, Paters, and recall the peace of your own childhood, when you were secure in your place in the world, your understanding of what it meant to be a man."

His expression grew grave. "But Eve was tempted. The Bible says her tempter was the devil, disguised as a snake, but we know better. We know the Bible is nothing if not allegorical. What does the devil stand for? Selfishness. *That's* what drew Eve to pluck the fruit and take her bite. After that, not even the kingdom of God was enough. Nothing ever would be, would it, Paters? We understand the hidden meaning: With knowledge, women corrupt themselves—and us. Women's selfish desires, their refusal to take their rightful place as God and nature intended, keep us all from the kingdom of heaven."

The Paters started stomping, the living room shaking under my feet.

The Marquis's voice rose above the din. "We are trying to claw our way back, aren't we, Paters? Aren't we, daughters? Trying to break through, get back to who we were meant to be. But to do that, first we must right old wrongs. Tonight, we show Eve the truth of who she's become."

More Paters rushed forward, dipping their hands into the bucket and sliding them down Katie, scratching her, pushing her, calling her *selfish, sinful, dirty, corrupt.* One Pater pushed too hard, and she fell to the floor, but they wrested her up. *"Feminist,"* a man hissed.

"Daughters," the Marquis called. "Express your guilt. Experience catharsis."

The women descended, and then it was chaos—blood everywhere, dripping down suit jackets and dresses, caught in pantyhose, streaked across faces. The air in the room was so thick with the scent of iron that it was suffocating. They swarmed like beasts, until the girl in the middle was swallowed.

I turned and locked eyes with the man beside me, who grinned. His voice was deep and knowing. "Standing there all alone, with your clean hands. Are you saying there's nothing you feel guilty about?"

There's so much, the voice inside me whispered, and my pause was enough. "I see," the man said and reached out, twining his fingers through my pearls. He pulled me against him. "You prefer a different method."

I could've stopped him. I could've said no, right then, that instant. But he pushed a hand up my leg, warm palm sliding over my thigh, and my traitorous body heated.

He clutched my necklace tighter, knotting it against my throat, and I gasped at the way the pearls bit. "I can tell you're a proud one," he whispered. "Watching all cold and condescending. But you're here..." His teeth brushed my ear, his hand finding me between my legs. I jerked, but he held tight. "Which means you're exactly like the rest of us."

I dropped my head back, letting it hit the wall, struggling to push away the memory of Don's face, his voice, his hands, but it was no use. This was what I'd feared the most—not the darkness of the Paters but the darkness sleeping inside me. The addiction, waking.

The man's fingers slid under the waistband of my pantyhose, down my stomach. He tightened his grip on the pearls, cutting off my air. Pain and pleasure built inside me until I was aching, and that's when I knew he was right about me. He was right, he was right, he was right.

I walked quickly past the kitchen, smoothing shaking hands down my dress, leaving the sounds of Paters and daughters in the throes of the gathering behind me. I would not think of what I'd just done; would not picture Cal's face if he ever found out or, worse, Jamie's. I'd think of nothing but stepping through the front door and putting this house behind me.

A strangled sob came from the kitchen, and I froze midstep. Then another—a desperate sound. I glanced at the front door, imagined pulling it open, emerging into the cool night air. Then I gritted my teeth and pushed into the kitchen.

It was a small, homey space, with a black-and-white checkerboard floor. In the corner, Katie was curled into a ball, rocking.

"Are you okay?" I flew to her, falling to my knees. She was still naked, though she'd draped her dress over her body like a blanket.

She jerked back. Her whole body was streaked with blood; she reeked of it. Some of it was hers—a bleeding lip, and dark bruises already forming from all those hands.

"It's okay," I assured her. "Let me get a washcloth."

"I'm fine," she said, wiping at her eyes and sitting taller. "Really. Please, I'm embarrassed."

I rose anyway and pulled a towel off the stove, running it under warm water. "Can I?" I gestured at her arms.

She crossed them over her chest. "I'm just emotional because that was such an experience. So enlightening."

225

"Mmm. Well, it feels better to be clean, so..."

She held my gaze, and for a moment, I was sure she'd deny me. Then finally, she nodded. "I guess. Thank you."

I worked the towel, gently removing blood while she hissed and squeezed her eyes shut. I returned again and again to the sink, until the towel was stained pink and she was scrubbed clean.

"I really am embarrassed," she said softly. "I swear I wasn't upset."

"Can I get you something to eat?" I couldn't stop looking at her protruding bones.

She shook her head, probably hoping I'd go away now, but I sat on the floor next to her. "Katie, when the Marquis said you were his special daughter, what did he mean?"

She blinked, then offered me a tight-lipped smile. "I'm his. I can't belong to any other Pater. It's an honor."

"Who told you about the Pater Society?"

She wouldn't meet my eyes.

A different tack, then. "Do you like it?"

At this, she straightened immediately. "Of course."

"Katie." My words came out clipped. "Are you a Whitney student?"

She blinked. "Why do you ask?"

She was. The president of Whitney, and one of his own students.

"Are there other Whitney students who are daughters?"

She eyed me warily—and then, without warning, her face fell. "I never do anything right. That's why he chose me as Eve. They say it's an honor, but it was a punishment."

I wanted to press her on the Marquis, but I knew better. "What made you join?" I asked instead. She looked hesitant, so I added, thinking of what Nicole had said: "Between us girls, it was the perks for me. All the fancy parties and presents."

To my surprise, her eyes filled with tears. "My mom lost her job, and

I was going to get kicked out of school. I didn't know what else to do, and then I met the Marquis. He saved me."

The pieces locked together. "Katie, is he covering your tuition?"

She gave a slight nod and another watery smile. "I owe him everything."

The sheer audacity. It would create such an obvious paper trail.

"But—" Her eyes tracked to the door, as if someone would burst in. "At first it was just sex. Now it's more like tonight. And he wants me all the time." She looked at me hopefully. "How do I make him happy? What do you do?"

"You're saying the Marquis is making you do things you don't want to do."

She touched her fingers to the bruises on her knees. "I just have to get used to it."

I clutched her hands. "Katie, it doesn't matter what he's giving you. You have to leave him."

She jerked back, staring at me in shock. "What? I can't."

So young. "Come with me, right now. We'll go together."

"No. I like it here. Really, I'm grateful."

"Katie—"

"They'll *find* me if I run." She shook her head violently. "I don't want to be like the others."

"What others?"

She curled into herself and looked at me with wide eyes full of fear. "The ones they send to the Hilltop," she whispered. "The girls who never come back."

CHAPTER
TWENTY-ONE

I stood in Jamie's shower and let the scalding water wash away the stench of iron. Blood curled down my legs, snaking through the drain.

Don't remember, I warned myself. *Not a single second.*

But when I closed my eyes, there she was: Katie, rocking on the floor. A convert at war with herself, just like we'd been. She'd made mistakes, but she didn't deserve this. She was young, and now she would be scarred forever. Now even the shape of her mind would never be the same.

I laid my forehead against the tile.

For the rest of her life, she would be a mystery to herself. Hungry for the things that hurt her.

The water lanced my skin, hot as a strike from a whip.

There would never be another antagonist more insidious than her own mind.

A phantom hand brushed my leg. My throat throbbed where the pearl necklace had bitten into me. I touched it, feeling each perfect, round indentation, hearing the man's voice: *You're here... Which means you're exactly like the rest of us.*

Even if she managed to run, she would never escape.

The tears came without warning. Years of careful control, and suddenly there was nothing standing between me and the grief. I sobbed, shoulders shaking.

The bathroom door cracked open, and Jamie's voice filled the room. "Shay, what's wrong?"

I turned and slid down the wall, clutching my face.

"Hey." His voice was tortured. "Let me help."

There was a moment in which the world was nothing but hot water, my chest heaving, the cold tile at my back; then the shower door opened and Jamie crouched next to me, arms circling me, pulling me close.

I clutched him, and he stroked my back, murmuring, "It's okay, it's okay, it's okay." Water soaked his clothes, running down both our faces.

Time passed, but neither of us moved. Eventually my crying turned into rasping breaths, and the water ran cold. Jamie brushed his lips over my forehead and said, "Hold on."

He let go of me, cut the water, and left the shower, coming back with a towel he rubbed through my hair, smoothing my face. "Arms up," he said, and when I lifted them, he wrapped the towel around me and scooped me to his chest, carrying me out of the bathroom. Over his shoulder I watched the trail of wet footprints. He laid me gently on the bed.

"I'm supposed to sleep on the floor," I said.

He lay down on the other side, facing me.

"You're soaking wet."

He smiled. "So are you."

His blue shirt was drenched, nearly black. It clung to his chest. His hair hung over his forehead, a bead of water dripping down his temple.

I reached over and brushed the water with my thumb. When I took my hand back, he mirrored me, his hand finding my face and cupping it, his palm the warmest part of me.

"Is it Cal?" he asked.

"No."

Jamie drew his hand back. I couldn't remember the last time I'd been held like that. I wanted to stay in this bubble, but I knew I needed to tell him the truth. He'd hear the recording soon enough when he sat down to transcribe it.

"I let a man touch me."

Jamie's Adam's apple bobbed.

"He was handsome, like Don."

Jamie didn't blink.

Suddenly, I wanted to shock him. "In the middle of the party."

There. He flinched.

"Jamie," I said. "I terrify myself."

He rubbed a hand over his face. "You're allowed to like what you like." The words sat heavy between us. "As long as it makes you..." He took a deep breath. "Feel good, you should let go of the guilt. I'm not saying anything Don did to you was okay, but *you* have no reason to be ashamed."

I couldn't have looked away from him if I'd tried. "I let them demean me, even though I hate them. In my head, I don't want to. But I keep doing it anyway. I can't tell if Don brainwashed me, or if I was this way all along, and that's what made me an easy mark."

He leaned closer. "They make you feel like a stranger to yourself."

"Yes." I adjusted the towel, tugging it higher. When I looked up, Jamie's eyes were locked carefully on my face.

"Jamie, I want to tell you more about my life."

He blinked.

"You're good at stitching people together. All the dead women and their killers in your podcast... You find the clues in their lives. You weave them together until you have a picture of who they were, why they did the things they did. You make it make sense."

He shifted, pulling his wet jeans from his legs. "You know I'm just guessing, right? When I tell people's stories, I'm taking an educated stab at a pattern. I could be wrong."

"That's the best any of us can do." The way he was looking at me... I wanted him to touch me again, and I didn't know if it was for comfort or something else.

"I think I understand now." His voice lowered. "It's not just about Laurel. You want to see yourself the way a journalist would. You want perspective. That's why you're doing the interviews."

He must have read the answer in my face. Because after a moment, he said, "Okay, Shay. Show me the pieces."

CHAPTER TWENTY-TWO

Transgressions *Episode 705, interview transcript: Shay Deroy, Sept. 13, 2022 (unabridged)*

SHAY DEROY: The minute I turned twelve, it was like I pressed a button and the machines inside my body started turning. I got my period. My breasts grew—not small like other girls', but full and round, women's breasts. Everywhere I went, I kept my arms folded over my chest, trying to hide them.

My body was mine before the change, but after, it belonged to everyone. Everywhere I went, men's heads turned. I couldn't go out in public without it—the mall, the grocery store. Even if I was just standing on the sidewalk, they'd roll down their car windows and yell at me as they drove by. One night, I was with my mom, and a man hung out the window of a red truck and yelled, "Damn, honey, let me suck those tits." My mom went red in the face and ran after him, screaming, "She's twelve years old, you sick fuck!"

I'm thirty now, and I'm still embarrassed to tell you that. I feel an impulse to laugh it off. "Suck those tits"—how cheesy, right? Like dialogue from a bad movie. That's what I feel compelled to say, like it's a joke. Somewhere along the way, I learned to minimize it. Maybe because at some level, I still think it's my fault, that my body incited them. Or maybe I realized people are rarely interested in another person's pain, so you have to dress it up accordingly.

But I'll tell you truth. It felt like constant surveillance, and it reshaped me. Going outside became an event. I developed this hum of apprehension—an extra awareness, like a sixth sense I always carried. Men were watching around every corner. I could run into them at any moment. I'm not being dramatic. Anything could be an invitation, even accidentally meeting a man's eyes. So I learned to keep my eyes trained on the ground and stay quiet. The more unnoticeable I was, the safer.

JAMIE KNIGHT: What kind of people would make a kid feel that way?

SHAY: You remember Clara Matthews.

JAMIE: Of course. You, me, and Clara, the three amigos. Soccer hooligans.

SHAY: In seventh grade I used to go to her house after school because my mom was still working two jobs. Her dad picked us up every day. He'd wait for us in his white SUV, and as soon as we opened the door, he'd turn around and say "Where to, ladies?" like a chauffeur.

JAMIE: He was pretty goofy. Clara used to get embarrassed.

SHAY: One day, he eyed me in the rearview and said, out of nowhere, "Have you ever thought about competing in pageants, Shay? My sister did them when she was your age and loved it. She coaches now. You have the look."

I could see Clara stiffen, but I flushed with pleasure. I knew what Mr. Matthews meant: I was pretty. And he was a safe person, so I could take the compliment.

JAMIE: That's such an inappropriate thing to say to your twelve-year-old daughter's friend.

SHAY: The idea stuck with me. I kept imagining walking across a stage in front of a crowd. At first, it was terrifying. The opposite of being unnoticeable. But then I thought, they're already looking. If I do this, maybe I'll be in control.

So Mr. Matthews introduced me to his sister, and she said if I competed, I could win money for college. My mom used to say a scholarship was the only way I was getting my ass to college, and I wanted that more than anything. So I begged my mom to let me compete. She hated the idea, said I had to choose between pageants and soccer. She thought I'd choose soccer.

JAMIE: I'm going to be honest. I never understood. You were so much more than pretty. And don't give me that bull that pageants are about talent. It was beneath you.

SHAY (*laughter*)**:** Do you know what teachers used to write in my report cards? Shay is a sweet girl. So polite. Plays well with others. I know what they wrote in yours: Jamie's gifted, he's got so much potential, going big places. We got the exact same grades.

JAMIE: I hate that.

SHAY: I hate it because I believed them. I thought the most important thing about me was that other people liked me. It made pageants the ultimate test of my worth.

JAMIE: Well, you ended up winning a lot.

SHAY: At first, it backfired. Competing made me feel exposed, like I was only giving the world more to leer at. My body started feeling less mine than it ever had. The makeup, the way I was supposed to talk, the things I was supposed to eat: everything was a performance.

JAMIE: You were playing by their rules, Shay. Capitulating to the same patriarchal system that sexualized you so young. Even if you'd *felt* in control, it would've been an illusion.

SHAY: Look, at some level I understood that. I knew they made the rules. I just thought if I played by them perfectly, I'd come out the other side rewarded with my own power. That's why pageants turned into my whole life. I became so good at knowing what they wanted I was practically a doll. The doll was the one strutting under the stage lights, delivering the punch lines. And then she started winning.

JAMIE: It sounds like you were dissociating.

SHAY: The problem was, once I started placing, people wanted more from me. Especially the judges.

JAMIE: What kind of people judge beauty pageants, anyway?

SHAY: At the local level, they're volunteers. In East Texas, a lot of men, Chamber of Commerce, civic duty types. And they all seemed to know each other. Most of them were friends with Mr. Matthews, too. After competitions, I'd see him holed up in the judges' dressing room. When I started winning, they invited me in.

They'd ask stupid questions, like what other talents did

I have, stuff that made them grin at each other. A bunch of grown men, and I had their undivided attention. Even at fourteen, fifteen, I knew that was power.

When I got older, Mr. Matthews and the judges started inviting me out. They went to Hooligans every Thursday night for dollar longnecks. It made me feel very adult, like I'd been invited as...I don't know, a colleague. It was a little strange to hang out with Clara's dad instead of her, but by then, she was barely talking to me.

JAMIE: Where was your mom?

SHAY: She hated the pageants, so she never came. Besides, Mr. Matthews and the judges were family men. I was allowed to spend time with them.

Junior year, the night I won Miss Dallas, I swung by Hooligans and they were already drunk. When I left, one of them followed me into the parking lot and begged me to get in his car with him. He said he'd been waiting for me, and now I was finally sixteen. He was wasted, so he couldn't physically stop me from leaving, but I'll never forget looking across the parking lot and seeing Mr. Matthews standing there, watching the whole thing. He didn't try to stop it. He didn't say a word. Not then, or ever. Maybe he felt guilty about his friend. But the way he looked at me...it was like I'd betrayed him by letting his friend get there first.

So that's what it was like. A strange mix of having power over people and being at their mercy. Or maybe that's just what it's like being a teenage girl. Either way, I don't regret it. I never would've gone to college if I hadn't won Miss Texas. That scholarship saved my life.

Besides. Every time I won, when the confetti rained
down, and they shoved flowers in my hands, and everyone
was standing and clapping like I was the queen of the
world, I would think to myself, *Shay Evans, you finally
figured it out. Look how lovable you are.*

It really did feel like love.

(*Rustling.*)

JAMIE: Bullshit.

End of transcript.

Jamie tossed his phone on the nightstand. "Fuck Mr. Matthews. You
should've told me."

"What could you have done? You were a kid. And you were obnoxious about the pageants. You were the last person I would've told."

He looked strangely vulnerable on the other side of the bed, soaking wet. "I'm not saying I was right to be condescending, but listen to
yourself. Grateful they *allowed* you to go to college. Fuck that. You were
smart. And your best shot at an education was to turn tricks in ball
gowns for a bunch of lechers, hoping they'd pin their fantasies on you?
Why legitimize that by participating?"

He reached for my hand, but I pulled away. "Sure. Tell the girl stuck
in a dead-end town, with her back against the wall, not to grasp at a
lifeline. You know, your ideas aren't wrong, Jamie. They're just really
fucking insulated. And get out of those clothes already. Your hands are
like ice."

He didn't say anything for a minute. Then he rose, grabbed clothes
from his suitcase, and disappeared into the bathroom. After a minute,

the shower started. When he came back, I was half-asleep, my hand resting in the middle of the bed, near where he'd lain. Jamie climbed back in and pulled the covers over both of us. I felt him reach over, fingers closing over mine, and then his hand stilled. I heard him take a deep breath. After that, I must've fallen asleep.

CHAPTER TWENTY-THREE

"I have news." Jamie threw himself into the passenger seat and slammed the door. After four days of silence, I'd received another anonymous text, this one instructing me to 145 Murray Street, New York, New York. We were on our way to the city.

"How?" I kept my eyes on the road as we slid out of the motel parking lot. "I've been with you every minute these last few days."

"Dougie just called on my way back from the bathroom. The guy on my staff who's good with computers," he explained, off my blank look.

"All this time, our fate's been in the hands of a man named Dougie?"

Jamie slid on his sunglasses. "I see you experimenting with humor, and I've got to say, I don't like it directed at me and my innocent friends."

I smiled. "What did Dougie say?"

Jamie wrestled with his pocket and pulled out a small notepad.

"You keep that thing on you all the time?"

"Journalist lesson number one: Always be prepared. Like a Boy Scout." His face grew grave. "Actually, this is serious. I shouldn't joke."

"What is it?" I felt a weight settle over my shoulders.

"I had Dougie look into Reginald Carruthers. He became president of Whitney in 2016, just two years after you graduated. Before that, he was the provost."

"I never saw him on campus."

"I'm sure you didn't. Provost is an executive job. All the deans reported to him."

It clicked. "The dean of students. He was her boss."

"Exactly. Now, unless she put something in an email where Dougie can find it, there's probably no record of whether she told him what you told her. But I can't imagine two students coming to her with a bomb-shell story like yours, and her not informing her boss."

I shook my head, shifting left to follow the highway signs. "Which means she probably told Carruthers—a man who would one day become a Pater—about what Don did."

"Maybe he already knew Don," Jamie said. "And that's why nothing ever came of you reporting it. Maybe Carruthers tipped Don off that you'd spilled and it was time for him to skip town."

I gripped the steering wheel tighter. "Either way, it can't be a coincidence."

"There's more, and this part's worse. Before Carruthers was provost, he was a religious studies professor."

I remembered Eve's Punishment. "That tracks."

"For the last three years, he's taught a class every fall semester. It's highly unusual for a college president to also teach. Whitney made a big splash about it when it was announced, saying Carruthers was going back into the classroom because students loved him. But Dougie found emails from the college marketing director, and it's clear Carruthers was the one pushing for it."

"Why would you go back to teaching if you'd become the president of a college?"

"Maybe if you were looking for an excuse to interact with students one-on-one."

My head snapped in his direction, road be damned. "Meaning?"

"I had Dougie access the enrollment lists for Carruthers's classes and compare them against my list of missing women."

My heart pounded. "How many?"

"Two of the girls on the missing persons list were once Carruthers's students."

"So he's recruiting girls into the Pater Society. That has to be how he met Katie. I bet she took his class, and he watched her, realized she was vulnerable."

Just like Don had realized about us.

"Dougie's trying to track down Katie's tuition payments, link them to Carruthers. And he's looking for whether any missing girls belonged to Mountainsong, too, but church records are harder to come by." Jamie shifted to face me, scrubbing a hand through his hair. "Shay, I was wrong when I told you the Paters were just a fringe kink group. Whether or not they're connected to Laurel's death—"

I made a noise of protest, and he hurriedly added, "Which I think they *are*, but even if they aren't, they're definitely connected to these disappearances. Which means we're talking about a possible laundry list of crimes."

"Does this mean you want to go to the cops? I thought it was too early. What happened to collecting more evidence, putting together the story?"

"I don't want the whole thing to rest on your shoulders," he said. "I have a friend of a friend at the Westchester police department. I know you said the chief's a dick, but let me start feeling this guy out, get a sense of whether he's the same way. Then, when it's time to move, we'll have laid the groundwork, built trust. Okay?"

I turned back to the road. "Okay."

ASHLEY WINSTEAD

Jamie's apartment was a fourth-floor Brooklyn walk-up, which he apologized for on every level. The apartment itself was like someone had taken the inside of Jamie's brain and spewed it across a thousand square feet. A basket full of records by the turntable, two overflowing bookshelves, framed photos of Christiane Amanpour, Bob Woodward, and Florence Graves on the wall, a soft blanket tossed over a worn green couch, more books cracked open on the coffee table. It looked like he'd left in a hurry.

"Sorry," he said, standing awkwardly in the front door. "It's tiny."

I inspected his bookshelves. A few classics left over from undergrad—*Middlemarch*, *Mrs. Dalloway*—but then, nothing but musician and activist biographies, true crime, investigative journalism. He was as voracious as I remembered, but—

"Where's your fiction?"

"Write your novel," he said, "and I'll fill my shelves with it."

A book buried near the back caught my eye. I turned to him with a raised brow. "*The Politics of Sex and Class in American Pageants?*"

He shrugged. "I might've thought about the topic once or twice."

I examined his desk, microphones and sound equipment strewn everywhere. "You record here?"

He nodded. "Usually the episodes are done in the studio, but I can get a little obsessive, want to work into the night."

I put the cordless headphones around my neck and walked into his bedroom. Calm blue comforter, some plants, more books. It was serene. "No more rocket sheets."

He walked in behind me. "Tragically, they don't make them bigger than twin-sized."

My eyes caught on a shelf of framed pictures. There we were: Jamie,

242

Clara, and me, junior year of high school. I remembered that day. Jamie had forced Clara and me together after school, before our buses left for soccer and football games. Clara and Jamie wore their soccer uniforms, and I wore my cheerleading skirt, makeup thick enough for the stage. I'd been uncomfortable standing next to Clara after our dissolved friendship, so I'd overcompensated by throwing my arms around Jamie, holding him tight.

"It's one of my favorites," he said.

I traced my round cheeks. "So young."

"Young and oblivious."

I turned and found him closer than I'd expected. "I like your apartment."

His eyes shone. "Good."

I cleared my throat. "I better take a shower. It's getting late."

"Right." He nodded. "Follow me."

I stepped out of the steam and wrapped a towel around my chest, popping the door to let in air. I picked up my brush and ran it through my hair, working out the tangles.

When I looked up at the mirror, I found Jamie standing behind me in his bedroom, stilled by the sight of me.

"What?" My voice was soft. I was remembering, with a sudden pang, how Jamie used to look at me growing up, with such singularity of focus. This look was an echo of that.

His voice was low. "Why not walk away, Shay? Why are you so hell-bent on chasing danger? What am I missing?"

I placed the hairbrush on the counter, holding his eyes. "Let me tell you a story."

CHAPTER TWENTY-FOUR

Transgressions Episode 705, interview transcript: Shay Deroy, Sept. 17, 2022 (unabridged)

SHAY DEROY: After my dad left, my mom became obsessed with getting married. There was nothing she wanted more.

JAMIE KNIGHT: I remember. Nina was always with one guy or another.

(*Laughter.*)

I think I heard my mom call her a man-eater once.

SHAY: It was the opposite. She was desperate for one of them to stick, but they always left.

JAMIE: Sorry. Probably shouldn't repeat gossip.

SHAY: It's okay. Plenty of people talked. My pageant coach sure did. She told me to take care I didn't end up like my mom.

JAMIE: As if being an unmarried woman is the world's greatest tragedy.

SHAY: It was to her. She did everything—dieted, joined the gym, spent money we didn't have on clothes and makeup, at-home facials. She'd spend hours holed up in her bathroom wearing these mint-green masks, poring over her face in the mirror, tracing her crow's-feet. A poor woman's Miss Havisham, I used to think, wrapped in a Walmart robe.

When I was younger and craved being near her, I would go in and lie at her feet, watching her watch herself. But then she started turning her eyes on me, wanting to talk about *my* skin, and weight, and face. So I stopped going.

Most of the men she dated were deadbeats, and I hated when she brought them home. Maybe I resented her dating because it felt like on some level, she was saying I wasn't enough.

JAMIE: Is that still how you feel?

SHAY (*clearing throat*): No. Now I know she was just trying to prove to herself she was worth loving. I find that sad, both of us obsessed with the same thing, neither of us able to talk about it. Sometimes I wish I could tell her that.

JAMIE: Why can't you? I never understood the falling-out.

SHAY: Do you remember Mr. Trevors?

JAMIE: Our high school English teacher?

SHAY: Yes.

JAMIE: Of course. He was the worst. What about him?

SHAY: If you're worried about libel, you'll want to edit this part later.

JAMIE: Okay...

SHAY: Freshman year, my mom started dating him.

JAMIE: You're kidding.

SHAY: She met him at orientation. She'd just started her job on the front desk at the women's shelter, which meant she finally had a nine-to-five and could go to school events. Figures—the one time she actually participates, she leaves with a date.

JAMIE: Why didn't you tell me? Now I have to go back and reexamine all my memories.

SHAY: My mom was excited because he was different from the men she usually dated. He had a decent job, he was clean-cut, everyone in Heller knew him. From the beginning, she was dreaming about getting married and living in one of those ranch houses, like your family.

But I hated him. He would make comments about what she was wearing, how cheap it looked, how she spackled on makeup. When he came over, he expected us to entertain him, do a whole song and dance. He'd get annoyed if we didn't have plans for dinner, or the drinks he liked in the fridge. And my mom was never smart enough. She used improper grammar, pronounced words wrong. Her accent was embarrassing. She didn't go to college, and he'd joke she was no more educated than his students. My mom would laugh, but I knew better.

He tried doing it to me, too—picked apart what I was reading, told me I wasn't witty because I was quiet. Soon, the last place I wanted to be was home. I had the pageants, which was good. Practicing meant a lot of time away. And then I started cheering, which Heller High took very seriously.

JAMIE: It being East Texas and all.

SHAY: So that was another escape. And to fill the rest of the time, I went to your house.

JAMIE: Wait. That's why you came over so much?

SHAY: It saved me. But I couldn't avoid him at school. Before him, English was my favorite subject.

JAMIE: Yeah. When I picture you, I picture your nose in a book.

SHAY: He could tell I hated him, and he kept trying to needle me in class. He graded my papers harsher than anyone else's. Called on me to answer questions and then tore apart what I said, in front of everyone. It was humiliating.

JAMIE: That day in class we were talking about *The Thousand and One Nights*, I knew you'd read it and had plenty to say, because we'd done our homework together and you wouldn't shut up about Scheherazade and murderous kings. But when Trevors asked you a question, you went mute. No matter what he said, you wouldn't answer.

SHAY: He sent me to the principal's office. I got my first detention.

JAMIE: I remember being so confused about why you were being stubborn. Why not just say something and avoid trouble?

SHAY: I wouldn't give him the satisfaction. One night sophomore year, my mom came home while I was cleaning up after dinner. She tried to sneak past me to the stairs, but I had this feeling, so I followed her. When I saw her face, I swear to god, part of me wasn't surprised.

Her nose and mouth were bloody. You could see where she'd tried to wash it away, but her skin was pink and streaky, so it looked even worse. She had a fresh black eye.

JAMIE: He *hit* her?

SHAY: I know that's how I should've reacted. But she'd been dating him for a year—a whole year of escalation and excuses. She stood there in the living room, looking at me with tears in her eyes, and I could've comforted her. I could've done what she'd never done for me and reversed the cycle. But instead, I said, "I told you a million times to break up with him."

She started crying. She lifted her arms, like I would hug her, but all I felt was this...repulsion. I said, "You work at a domestic violence shelter, Mom. How could you let this happen?"

She said, "It doesn't mean he doesn't love me. He just—"

That's when I charged her and said, "Tell me you're not making excuses for him. I knew you were weak, but I didn't realize you were actually pathetic."

JAMIE: Shay.

SHAY: She said, "I'm not making excuses. It's over between us. I'm just saying... I wasn't crazy. I didn't make it up in my head. He *did* love me."

She looked so fragile. Just skin and bones. And I thought: What if he'd seriously hurt her? *Killed* her? It happened to one of the women from the shelter. He held that power over us, and I hated him for it, but I hated her more for giving it to him. She was standing there bruised and crying, and all I could think was to shove her away.

JAMIE: Maybe being angry was the only way you could feel in control.

SHAY: I told her none of them had loved her. Not Mr. Trevors or my dad.

(*Silence.*)

I know. It stunned her, too.

JAMIE: Please tell me your mom stopped seeing him.

SHAY: She did. And junior year, we started AP English, so I didn't have to see him at school anymore. Only sometimes, in the halls, I'd turn the corner and there he was, ice-cold and haughty as ever. Staring, but not saying a word.

And before you ask: yes, I see the connection between what Mr. Trevors did to my mom and what Don did to me. Part of me wishes I could tell her I know what it's like now. But the truth is, she didn't choose to be hit. She stopped once it started. *I'm* the one who asked for it. I told her she was pathetic, and then I did something so much worse.

So that's the rift. It's all me. I'm the one who saw it coming with Mr. Trevors. I felt it with Don, too, after a while. I could've saved my mom when I was fifteen, and I could've saved Clem and Laurel in college. Instead, I left them to the wolves.

JAMIE: Shay, have you ever heard of repetition compulsion? It's this theory that people who've experienced trauma have a strong desire to reenact it, over and over, to gain mastery over it. It seems counterintuitive, but the thinking is, if they can just get one more shot, *this* time they'll get it right. They reach for the same pain over and over, retraumatizing themselves, all the while convinced they're putting an end to it.

SHAY: You asked why I'm putting myself in danger. It's because I owe them. Call it whatever you want, whatever theory, I don't care. This time, I'm going to save someone.

CHAPTER TWENTY-FIVE

From the outside, 145 Murray Street was a windowless warehouse in far west Manhattan, dark as a dungeon on a darker street. Inside, it was a coked-up, strobe-lit fantasia, ripped from the pages of a Wall Street kingpin memoir. The heavy metal door opened to a doorman, and beyond him, frenetic lights, angry, pounding music, a crush of bodies on the dance floor. But none of that distracted from the centerpiece, playing in larger-than-life dimensions over the back wall. The party buzzed, but I stood cold as ice, transfixed by the sight of the woman shivering on her knees, hands bound, pleading into the camera.

"Snuff film," said a familiar voice. "Or at least a good fake. The city boys love 'em. They're so creative. Like little Scorseses."

I turned to find Nicole beside me, her eyes lined with thick, black shadow, body draped in a slinky black dress. A flagrant violation of the daughter's dress code.

"Where have you been? You weren't at the last party."

Her eyes scanned the room, then she lowered her voice. "I'm with a Pater now. *Exclusively.* It's very exciting."

"Who?"

"I can't say yet." Her mouth softened into a smile. "But he's high up. He's my ticket to the Hilltop. I can feel it." She smoothed her slinky dress. "He likes it when I break the rules so he can catch me."

The strobe lights flashed again, illuminating her. There were small bruises in the unmistakable pattern of fingertips across her chest.

She followed my gaze. "He's a tad rough," she admitted. "I was laid up for a few days after our last session. That's why I didn't go to the Marquis's."

"You need to be careful," I said. Maybe it wasn't the right reaction; maybe I was supposed to congratulate her, a daughter who'd caught the attention of an important Pater. But a familiar heaviness seized me.

She pressed a hand to my face. "See? I told you. Such a sweetheart."

I'm older than you, I wanted to say. *Listen to me.*

"Don't worry. This is what I signed up for. Besides, it'll be worth it in the end. And there *are* benefits." She waggled her brows. "He's paying for my apartment."

Someone had paid Laurel's rent, too. "I just have to know," I said. "Give me a hint—" But Nicole's eyes slid behind me, and she leaned close. "Incoming. City boys. They're traders. Try not to roll your eyes."

Three *American Psycho* wannabes in identical slim-cut suits and artfully arranged hair circled us. I could see why Nicole called them boys—they were younger than the average Paters, younger by far than the Marquis. But still, they were in their twenties. Old enough to know better.

All three of them regarded us with hungry eyes.

"Do you like it?" one asked me, pointing his drink in the direction of the wall, where the film played. I made the mistake of looking, caught the woman in the throes of screaming, and quickly glanced away.

He grinned at my reaction. "It's from my personal collection. Do you even *know* how much the real shit costs? Almost impossible to get your hands on."

So it was real. I suppressed a chill. "I don't like it," I said, studying him as best I could in the dark. Up close, he didn't have the same gloss as the other two. His long hair was lank, and his skin was sallow and pockmarked.

"I know." He winked. "Daughters never do."

"Apologies for the Incel." The man standing closest to Nicole, the one who was most clean-cut, with a boyish face, extended his hand. "We keep telling him to keep at least one of his perversions private, but he never listens. It's why the old guard hates him."

"No matter what he pulls with those tech tips," added the third man, laughing.

I stared at the clean-cut man's outstretched hand for a moment longer than socially acceptable. Then I shook it. What did it say about me that it was the moments of normalcy that were starting to throw me?

"I told you, I'm not a fucking incel." The sallow-faced man glared at me. "Don't call me that."

"Well, you can call me Greggy," said the one whose hand I'd shaken.

"I'm Steven," the Incel said. "I don't need a code name like those cloak-and-dagger assholes."

I frowned. "You guys aren't worried about protecting your identity?"

The Incel scoffed, tossing a hand at the party. "Why? Everyone we know is here."

Everyone. An undercurrent of anxiety tugged at me.

"Hey, have one," Greggy said, grabbing a passing waitress by the elbow. When he turned her, I realized she was wearing a demure, high-necked dress. A daughter, playing party servant. Probably to ingratiate herself, or maybe we all took turns, and mine was coming. She lifted her tray so we could see the shots lined up in slim glasses and, beside them, a small mountain of pastel-colored pills. They looked friendly, like Smarties. Nicole popped one and chased it with a shot.

Greggy held the tray out to me and raised an eyebrow.

Nicole leaned in. "Take it," she whispered. "They'll get a lot more interesting."

I took the shot glass but left the pill. "Thanks." The liquor was smoky. Mescal.

"Greggy, tell her the candy's the important part," said the third man. "Gotta get her loose."

"Good luck," Nicole said with a wink. "Shay's one of those good girls you might've heard about."

"My favorite," said the Incel. He turned to the others. "Dibs."

I swallowed my disgust. They were acting like we were eighteen, at a college party. Well, if they were going to be loose-lipped, all the better for me and the recording device tucked inside my bra.

The Incel grinned at me. "My assistant planned this whole thing. Rented the space, bought the projector. Bitch had no idea what it was for. You should've seen her busting her ass to get every detail right. Isn't that amazing?" He snorted. "Serves her right, the uptight Vassar femi-nazi. Thinks she's better than my desk." He waved a hand at the dance floor. "I'll let you in on a secret: I have no idea who half these people are. I just needed a crowd for the ambiance. They'll be gone before we get into the real shit."

I edged closer, and he leaned in, too, like I was tugging him with an invisible string. "What's the real shit?"

He nodded at the wall. "A little auteur filmmaking."

I forced the words out. "You make films with daughters?"

Is that where the missing women went? Were they trapped behind screens, hidden in private collections, doomed to die a thousand times on film for the Paters' enjoyment? If it was true, it was evidence: I tried to cling to that.

He laughed. "You should see your face right now. Nah, but one of these days, those old bastards will let me. They need us, you know. We're the fresh blood."

I swallowed back bile and tried another tack. "How did you become a Pater?"

He studied me. "You're a little nosy, aren't you?"

I searched for an excuse, but he kept going. "I know your type. You're one of those girls who thinks they're in control. You were always the hot one, so guys bent over backward. You're my favorite to break." He held up a light-pink pill, one of the Smarties from the tray. "Take this."

I shook my head. "I don't—"

His voice was sharp as a slap. "I told you to do something." He held my eyes, unblinking. A test.

The eternal dance: give them enough, but not too much. Walk right up to the line.

I wished I could hurt him. Instead, I picked up the pill and put it on my tongue, bitter and chalky. "What is it?"

He smiled as I pretended to swallow. "Think of it as a little pink hand-cuff. You and me are bound now." He turned, nodding at the room, and I spit out the pill and dropped it on the floor, crushing it under my heel. "I have a house up in Bronxville. I met the Paters there last summer, at some big finance cocksucker's party. I thought I was so special, getting in on a secret. Took me a while before I realized everyone I knew was already part of it." He inclined his head toward Greggy and the other man, who were talking to Nicole. "Bastards were keeping it from me."

How ironic. Even among the Paters, the Incel was toxic. "You don't seem to like the other Paters very much."

It was the exact right question. His face twisted. "Those assholes and their pageantry? A bunch of old guys who need to make everything into a ritual to feel important. I wouldn't be surprised if they had to chant their dicks hard."

"You don't like the ceremony?"

"I'm here to fuck women, not dress up in costumes and learn about enlightenment." He shot me a sly look. "I was a virgin through college. Nobody wanted to fuck me. Can you believe it?" He tilted his head back and laughed. In the strobe lights, he looked like a movie still, looped and glitching. "Damn, that's freeing." He wiped his eyes. "A year ago, I never would've told you that. I would've begged you to let me buy you a drink, which you would have taken and walked away. You cunt."

The Incel. Now I understood why he hated it. It wasn't a nickname at all.

He took his shot, hair spilling back. "Now I can say whatever I want, and whether you like it or not, you're still going to fuck me. *Better* if you don't like it, actually. That's more fun." He looked up at the screen. "I used to watch this shit and fantasize about doing it myself."

His gaze was caught by the film, the images throwing shadows over his face. "There was this girl who used to torment me. She was a first-rate bitch. I wanted to fuck her so bad, and then I wanted to fucking kill her. I used to imagine... Well. No more imagining."

He jerked suddenly, rolling his shoulders like there was a tick sliding under his skin. "The pill's hitting," he said, rubbing his thumb along my lower lip. It took all of my power to hold still against the animal smell of his skin. "The old bastards are right about one thing."

Over the Incel's shoulder, a familiar face flashed at the edge of the dance floor.

"Everything gets better once women learn their place," the Incel said.

The crowd shifted at the same time the strobe lights struck, jagged flashes revealing the man moving along the outskirts, his thick body straining a suit rather than a uniform.

It was Chief Adam Dorsey.

As I watched, another man waylaid him, clapping Dorsey on the shoulder and drawing him in to talk. Dorsey listened, then looked up at the snuff film and laughed.

The officer who'd handled Laurel's rape case twelve years ago, the chief in charge of her suicide investigation, the man Jamie and I were gathering evidence for—he was a Pater.

His eyes searched the room. Any second now he would spot me, recognize me as the woman from the station, Laurel's old roommate. My heart beat unnaturally fast. What would the Paters do?

Out of the corner of my eye, I saw Nicole stiffen.

I seized her arm. "I have to go."

"Like hell," the Incel said, wrapping a hand around my wrist. "You're not walking away from me."

"You're right, you should go," Nicole said dazedly. She pushed between me and the Incel, drawn like a magnet toward whatever held her attention, snapping his hold on my wrist.

I didn't pause to look; I turned and ran, shoving through the crowd of dancers. I could hear the Incel yelling, commanding me to stay. In the darkness, colliding with the whirling bodies, I couldn't tell which way was out and spun in every direction, claustrophobia clutching at me. I was going to be trapped, and Dorsey would find me, or the Incel, and I'd never see outside again. I'd end up like the nameless woman whose death was unfolding in high definition across the wall.

The bass dropped and the blue strobe lights struck, thunder and lightning, like a miracle sent by Laurel herself, suddenly lighting the path to the door, igniting my outstretched hands and filling them with fire. I ran out while I still could, not a minute too late.

CHAPTER
TWENTY-SIX

I paced Jamie's living room. "I knew it, I knew it, I *knew* it."

He sat on the arm of his couch, watching. "The actual chief of police."

I spun on my heels and started circling again. "I knew it wasn't right, how dismissive he was of Laurel's death. He's covering for them."

Jamie leaned forward and scrubbed his hands through his hair, leaving his fingers tangled. "It makes sense now. That's why there were so few details in Laurel's police report. Why they didn't mention her arm was branded, why there weren't any pictures."

I froze midstride. "Clem's record was slim, too."

"When you were in college, Adam Dorsey was just a detective, and Reginald Carruthers was only the provost," Jamie said. "Now look at them. They've climbed so high."

"What if the Paters are getting them there? Building power."

"Making sure they have access to vulnerable women and protection against the law. Michael Corbin, too—think how many people must come to him with problems, as a retired pastor. Easy pickings." Jamie's hands tightened. "What does Don *want*? Keeping his network of friends out of trouble is one thing. But this is starting to feel…ambitious."

"He wants everything," I said. "As much as the world will give him."

Jamie frowned. "Why are you smiling?"

I stopped pacing. "Because we've been right this whole time—about Laurel's death, and the Paters. Hell, years ago, when we went to the police to report her assault, *we* were in the right, not them." The vindication sang through my veins. "I'm going to get them, Jamie." For the first time, I could feel it.

"I know you will," he said. "But this also means we can't work with the Westchester police department. We have to go straight to the state police. They report to the governor."

"Alec Barry?"

"I interviewed him a few years ago when I covered politics, and he was trying to get ICE out of New York. He's a good guy. Young, unapologetically progressive. Probably the most popular governor New York's had in decades. Headlined the last DNC."

I thought of Cal and his friends back in Dallas, how Governor Barry was famous enough that they used his name as shorthand for unrealistic bleeding hearts. *That guy's a total Barry type, too liberal for mainstream, won't get anything done, the Dems are all like this now.*

"It's perfect, actually." Jamie's voice rose; he was getting excited. "I should've thought of him from the beginning. He already pledged to investigate the missing women. And he's up for reelection. What could be better for his campaign than taking down a literal cabal of predatory men?" He stood and headed for his recording equipment, suddenly as full of energy as I was. "I still have a contact on the governor's team. We should start transcribing tonight's tape. I could leak it—"

And just like that—drunk on hope, on the electrifying intimacy of Jamie's allegiance—I seized him by the front of his shirt and kissed him.

His lips parted on instinct, hands cupping my face, drawing me closer...
Then he stopped. Wrenched away. And for a moment, he only stared,
green eyes wide and unblinking. Then he said in a low, rough voice,
"You're married." But the look in his eyes was questioning, like he was
asking me to tell him something different.

I relaxed my grip on his shirt.

He bit his lip, as if trying to stop himself from speaking, but after a
second, he lifted a hand to my temple. Hesitated, then slowly pushed
his fingers through my hair, letting the strands fall to my shoulder. He
watched them as he spoke. "Your feelings must be all over the place,
with everything that happened tonight."

An out, if I wanted it.

I lifted my chin, and his gaze slid to my lips. "You're right. I think I'm
high on adrenaline." I closed my eyes, then added, "But I don't regret it.
If that's what you're asking."

I opened my eyes to find Jamie's were incandescent, his nerves and
his desire so transparent it almost hurt to look.

"Mm-hmm," he said, nodding, the sound coming from deep in his
throat. Half acknowledgment, half question, as if he'd heard me but
couldn't believe it. He held my gaze. "You don't."

In that moment I knew I had only to shake my head, the slightest
movement, and I could have him. The dam inside him would break. He
would catch my face in his hands and pull me toward him until I rose to
my toes. He would kiss me and I could have what I wanted. My blood
sang with the certainty. And there was nothing so sweet as that.

But.

It turned out there were things I didn't know, things that would
surprise me. That the first touch of his lips would draw me in so much
that I forgot to imagine what I looked like from the outside looking in,
forgot everything except the old instinct to close the distance between

us. That he would be so hungry for me he'd groan, a Jamie sound I'd never catalogued. That when I scored my fingers through his hair, his knees would buckle, forcing us to stagger to the couch, my mouth branding his skin until we both went up in flames.

I expected the flicker of worry about what exactly I was doing, but I didn't anticipate how fast it would flee when he trained his eyes on me, a silent question answered with a nod that sent his fingers skimming under my dress, lifting it over my head. I didn't expect I would shiver when I pushed him to his knees on the floor, when he kissed each purple bruise on my body and sent a frisson of pain through me, when his hot mouth moved down my bare stomach, when he gripped my knees, spread my legs, and kissed through my panties.

I couldn't have known the warmth of his breath, that smart mouth put to different uses, would ignite such a hunger in me, a need that had me pulling him up and shoving him back onto the couch. How quickly he knew what I wanted, how obedient when my hands climbed the column of his throat and squeezed.

I'll confess I had imagined it would feel like home in his arms: Jamie, the boy from growing up. But what I never saw coming—what I didn't even know to expect—was the feeling when I slid over him, seizing his chin to catch his eyes, sinking down until he shuddered and my heart unleashed, beating through every inch of my body. The feeling as I moved my hands over his neck, his breath coming when I willed it, his eyes wide but willing, giving himself over. That he would whisper, "Hurt me if you want to," and what that would unlock, the capacity of my desire bottomless as always, but the shape it could take, the things I could want... I swear to god, I didn't know.

Jamie wrapped an arm around me, tucking me into his chest. He exhaled, his breath falling into rhythm with mine. I stared at the angry handprint on his neck. Long, elegant fingers, like a piano player's.

"Tell me a story," he said.

I pressed my cheek against his side. "Really? That easy?"

His eyes dropped to my face. They rested there a moment before he said, "Come on, Shay. You know you never had to beg."

CHAPTER TWENTY-SEVEN

Transgressions Episode 705, interview transcript: Shay Deroy, Sept. 18, 2022 (unabridged)

SHAY DEROY: I know which story to tell you.

(*Rustling.*)

JAMIE KNIGHT: A happy one this time?

SHAY: You tell me at the end.

(*Silence.*)

When I turned seventeen, I became obsessed with watching myself in the mirror. I had this full-length in my room, and I would close the door, turn on music, and stand in front of it for hours, bending my arms and legs like a ballerina, examining my curves. I'd take off my clothes and arrange myself on my bed, arching my back, cupping my breasts, pouting. It sounds silly, but I'd look at the way my ribs caved into my stomach and think, *This must be what it means to be beautiful.*

JAMIE: Hmm.

SHAY: What?

JAMIE: I can picture it, is all.

SHAY: Me in front of the mirror?

JAMIE: Yes. Falling half in love.

SHAY: I wanted to see myself the way strangers did. This one night, at the restaurant, a waiter had said, "Everyone wants you to seat them because you look like Gene Tierney." I thought he was saying I looked like a man, but it turned out she was this old Hollywood actress. I stared at pictures of her on Wikipedia and thought maybe I really have no idea what people see when they look at me.

JAMIE: The restaurant was the Red Lodge, right?

SHAY: Yes, sorry.

JAMIE: For listeners, Shay got a job as a hostess at the Red Lodge—what, senior year? Used to be the fanciest restaurant in Heller...which, truthfully, isn't saying much.

SHAY: When you interview me, are you imagining other people listening?

JAMIE: Of course. That's what you want, right?

SHAY: Right, it's just...sometimes I forget it's not just you and me.

(*Silence.*)

    The Red Lodge was mostly men, except for us hostesses, me and another girl whose name I can't remember, though I do remember she was homeschooled. It was always a party. The waiters especially. Most of them were community college guys, and they flirted like crazy. One night, they said they were having a party at Zane's after closing. He was the night manager. He was young—

twenty-four or something—so even though he was our boss and engaged, he'd still party.

I got this wild hair I would go, even though they'd always intimidated me. I even convinced the other hostess to come, and she wasn't allowed to go to parties.

Zane had this dumpy house. I don't know why I thought he'd be rich since he was the manager. Naive. But he brought a bunch of bottles home from the restaurant, which was what he was good for, and soon we were all drunk, even the homeschooled girl. Actually, *especially* the homeschooled girl. Her mom had to pick her up an hour in, which was embarrassing.

JAMIE: And you were alone with the guys?

SHAY: I know what you're thinking, but it was the opposite. They hung on every word. If I ran out of my drink, they'd fetch another. If I asked them a question, no matter how embarrassing, they'd answer it. They fought over who could sit closest to me. It was heady. Actually, out of everything, I think I got drunkest on that.

JAMIE: What?

SHAY: The power.

(*Throat clearing.*)

There was one cute waiter. They called him Dizzy for some reason. At one point in the night, I looked across the room and realized I wanted to own him.

JAMIE: Excuse me?

SHAY: I don't know how else to describe it. A conquering impulse. I wanted to hold him in the palm of my hand. Men had been staring at me since I was twelve. Now I was seventeen, and suddenly the attention felt like it was a superpower. I wanted to know how far I could take it.

I found Dizzy alone in the kitchen and gave him this look. I swear he gulped. Then I kissed him.

JAMIE: Was that your first kiss?

SHAY: It was, but I didn't stumble. I was a natural. I knew exactly what to do with my mouth and my hands. I took him to the guest bedroom in Zane's house, and we stayed there all night. My mom either didn't notice or assumed I was at your place.

JAMIE: Did you...you know.

SHAY: We're adults, Jamie. You can ask me.

JAMIE: I just realized I feel like I'm talking to a seventeen-year-old girl.

SHAY: No. I didn't have sex with him. I tortured him.

JAMIE: Torture?

SHAY: I don't know what came over me. I was so dead-set on proving something. I would kiss him, roll my hips. Then I'd stop and tell him to tell me I was beautiful. When he did, I kissed him again and upped the ante, told him to say I was the most beautiful girl he'd ever seen. He said it, no hesitation. I kept going like that... My memory's fuzzy, but it was probably hours. Every time I asked him to give me a little more, and when he did, I rewarded him. There was only one thing left to ask, and it was crazy, but I had to see how far I could go.

I rolled over so I was on top of him. He tried to kiss me, but I stopped him, and said, "You're in love with me."

He was confused. He said, "What do you mean? This is the first night we've talked."

I said, "You've been watching me in the restaurant, noticing how pretty I am."

He tried to kiss me again, but I pushed him back and said, "You've been falling in love with me, little by little, every day. You can't help yourself."

He laughed, like I was joking, and said, "You're funny."

I climbed out of bed and started putting my clothes on. He jumped out, too, and put his arms around me. He said, "Wait, don't leave. I have looked at you. Everyone has."

He tried to pull me back into bed, but I put a hand on his chest and said, "You love me."

Something came over him—I don't know what. Maybe he was drunk, maybe he just wanted to kiss me that badly. But he looked at me and said, "You're right, okay? I love you. I'm in love."

I felt immeasurably powerful. It was the start of a whole new chapter in my life.

JAMIE: What kind of chapter?

SHAY: Me being in control for real, better than the pageants. Here's an example: After that night, Zane, the manager, started talking to me more. Joking around, flirting, even though he had a fiancé.

JAMIE: And was old enough for his interest in you to be illegal.

SHAY: It was exactly what I craved. Upping the ante. What's better than making a virtual stranger say he loves you? Winning your older boss, who's engaged.

One day Zane and I were closing. He was behind the bar, cleaning up, and I said, "I'm going to a friend's house after this." It was Maddie McCrarry's party—remember her? You were there, I think.

JAMIE: We went over to Maddie's a lot. Her parents were never home. In hindsight, I think they were neglectful.

SHAY: Zane snapped it up. He said, "Want some company? I can bring booze."

I said, "Are you sure you want to come to a high school party?"

And he said, "You'll be there. So yes."

That's when I knew how the night would unfold. If I invited him, we would go to Maddie's and get very, very drunk, and then he would kiss me. I had him in the palm of my hand. He was supposed to be getting married, but I was so beautiful, so magnetic, that he'd risk it for me.

And that's exactly what happened. He waited the whole night, until everyone had gone home or passed out, and it was just us in Maddie's backyard. She had those string lights, remember? Like a fairy tale. And I don't remember how it happened, who said what, but suddenly Zane was kissing me and pulling me down to the grass, sitting me on his lap. I think we made out for half an hour, until I told him I had to go to sleep, and he should go home.

JAMIE: Did his fiancée find out?

SHAY: I have no idea. For all I know, they're still in Heller, happily married. He tried to hang out with me the next week, but other than work, I barely spoke to him again. Same with Dizzy. I didn't need them anymore.

JAMIE: Try out this story. A grown man, engaged, gets bored. Starts to feel tied down. He looks at the underage girl in his restaurant—the one he wouldn't stand a chance with if she were his age—and sees an opportunity. He takes advantage of the fact that she's young and not worldly.

He gets her to take him to a high school party, where he feels older and wiser. It's a huge ego boost. And he takes what he wants from her at the end of the night, and it's consequence-free, because who's she going to tell? Let her think she came out on top.

SHAY: Can't it be true that we both used each other?

JAMIE: I thought you wanted to hear the objective version of your story.

SHAY: Listen. Every boy I kissed from that moment on was proof that I was valuable. It was all a test, a conversation I was having with myself through other people. I used to walk into rooms and feel out of place, instantly an outsider. But that year, I started walking in and taking stock. Grocery stores, house parties, the restaurant. Everywhere I went, I was hunting. The tables were turned.

JAMIE: You're literally glowing right now.

SHAY: I think I've been chasing that high ever since.

Why are you looking at me like that?

(*Silence.*)

Jamie?

JAMIE: Why are you telling me this story?

SHAY: So you can put the pieces together. Men, love, sex— it's always been about power. That's what I thought Don was, at first.

JAMIE: Are you sure that's the only reason?

SHAY: What are you—

JAMIE: You know what, this is a bad idea.

(*Rustling.*)

End of transcript.

I sat up, drawing the sheets with me. "What's wrong?"

Jamie remained on his back, looking up at the ceiling. The city lights through the blinds cut stripes across his face. "Are you trying to tell me that's what you're doing with me? Because you're married, and we were best friends. Those are quite some lines to cross." He gestured between us. "Was this about seeing whether or not you could?"

"If I'm being honest," I said, "maybe. It's hard to tell. The power, the person. They're so twisted together, I don't know how to tell them apart anymore." With Cal, it had been obvious: he was a conquest, a living, breathing shield against the world. With Jamie—well, maybe I didn't want to look. I gathered the sheets tighter. "Does that make you want to stop?"

He was quiet a long time. Finally, he turned to me and bent his elbow, resting his head in his hand. "No," he said quietly. "The truth is…I'll take you any way I can get you." The ghost of a smile. "Fuck me. At least no one can say you didn't warn me."

His words.

CHAPTER TWENTY-EIGHT

I stood in the sculpture garden, staring at the naked bodies. The women bent in the grass like they'd grown out of it. Remarkably real, mouths open in expressions of delight and surprise, young and beautiful forever. If it had been hard to tell I was at a Pater gathering when I'd first arrived at this sprawling estate, now, as I looked at these sculptures, it was unmistakable.

We were far north, deep in the country. If not for the dark mountains rising in the background, the scene could have been lifted from an Austen adaptation. The house was as grand as an English manor, white and columned, with a wide, stretching balcony and miles of grass around it, green despite the encroaching autumn. Jamie said it was registered to an art advocacy group, a C-4 named the Initiative for Truth and Beauty.

Paters and daughters walked the grounds. Violinists roamed among them, playing light, sweet music. Even with plenty to look at, what first caught my attention were the sculptures: towering monoliths, ten-foot metal cubes and massive spheres, standing in the grass like they'd been dropped there by God.

But it was the garden of female bodies that had drawn me across the grass. Up close, they were amazingly lifelike. Perhaps the owner of the estate was a sorcerer who transfigured wanton women into solid rock.

"Do you like them?" came an amused voice.

I turned to find a man striding across the lawn, accompanied by the Lieutenant. My pulse jumped. The man was older, in his fifties or sixties, and short, with beautifully tan skin and long dark hair. He looked vaguely familiar. The connection hovered at the edge of my memory.

What could I say but yes? I was acutely aware of the Lieutenant's eyes.

The dark-haired man smiled. "They're my masterwork. The only pieces I'll never sell."

It clicked: he was Angelo De Luca, the famous minimalist sculptor. Cal and I had gone to his exhibit at the Dallas MoMA a year ago; Angelo's picture had been everywhere. Cal had grown bored quickly, but I'd been transfixed. The tall cubes had their own presence: ominous, almost confrontational.

The Paters had snaked into my life before I'd ever realized it.

"I call them my harem," Angelo said. "Each one is a woman I've loved and lost. My way of keeping them with me."

The Lieutenant gave him a tight smile. "A bone garden, you might say."

Angelo boomed a laugh. "Oh, you *are* naughty." He turned to me, eyes twinkling. "You would make a lovely sculpture."

The air was alive with meaning.

"What's your name, daughter?" Angelo took my hand and swept it to his mouth, kissing it like a gentleman. For once, the chill made me grateful my dress collar was stiff and high, my cumbersome pantyhose at least another layer of protection.

"It's Shay." I forced my voice to come out light. "I'm new."

"Ah, yes." Angelo twisted my arm to peer at my brand. "The mark's still fresh."

"Nicole brought her in." The Lieutenant's eyes narrowed. "I had high expectations. But from what I've heard, she's having trouble warming up."

Had he been watching me escape the Paters' advances party after party, or had someone actually complained? My heart hammered.

But Angelo still held my hand, and now he rubbed it. "Shame on you. The best ones are always shy at the beginning." He smiled at me, practically cooing. "Little lambs. You have to make them comfortable before they're pliant."

I was learning there were many different ways to be a Pater.

Angelo waved a hand at the estate. "Some of my comrades don't appreciate the exquisite nectar of delayed gratification. Philistines."

"Maybe we're tired of being told to have patience." A new man stepped out of a line of trees, two others flanking him, all of them dressed in leisurely country suits. "You know we can only wait for the Philosopher for so long." The man's eyes drifted to me. "Who's this?"

There were five of them in the sculpture garden now. Five to one.

Angelo clutched my hand to his chest. "A new muse. I was just telling her how much I adore women." He leaned close and whispered, "Between us, sometimes I wonder about the others." He winked.

"Ah," said the interloper. "Another lecture about the sanctity of women from the Artist. As if each one you touch doesn't turn to stone." The two men flanking him laughed, but Angelo frowned.

Here it was again: internal division. Even the Pater Society, with its rigid hierarchy and strident mission, wasn't immune. I wondered if Don knew, if he was already one step ahead with a plan, the way he'd been years ago.

The man who'd insulted Angelo addressed me. "I'm glad to see new girls, at least. There's too few lately. Makes me restless."

"You know very well we had to—" the Lieutenant started, but Angelo cut him off. "Not enough fresh blood, say the wolves." He turned to me with a confiding look. "Be wary, my dear. These three are hunters."

The hairs on my arms stood on end. "And where," I said, lilting my voice like I was an idiot who couldn't sense danger, "are the hunting grounds?"

"Where did you come from?" one of them countered.

"Tongue-Cut Sparrow."

He looked surprised. "I thought that place was off-limits. Too conspicuous."

The man beside him nodded. "Too hot."

Because of the missing girls? The first woman Jamie and I had met there, the one who'd propositioned us, had flagged that a handful of girls she'd known through the Sparrow later went missing. Perhaps the Paters were avoiding recruiting there because the connection had grown too obvious.

I concentrated on the reassuring itch of the recording device inside my bra, arranging my face so it was inviting. *Talk to me. I am a weak, defenseless creature.*

"The colleges are better, anyway," Angelo said. "The girls are younger and cleaner." He grinned at me. "As the wolves like to say... Not me, of course."

"I thought the schools around here were practically feminist communes," I said, repeating things people used to say about us. "I can't imagine you find many girls who aren't already brainwashed."

The man who'd insulted Angelo—the head wolf—grinned. "Those girls are the best. They tell themselves they're being sexually liberated when I take them home and chain them in my basement. Owning their sexuality, and all that."

"Maybe they are," I said, trying not to visualize.

"What he means is that the feminists are far more agreeable than they used to be." Angelo smiled. "The third- or fourth- or whatever-wavers are practically Paters themselves. Empowering women to bend the knee if it feels right. It's delightful. They're never suspicious because they always think they're in control."

"Let them think they're in charge," said the head wolf. "Doesn't make a difference to me, as long as they keep giving me what I want."

"It's one point on which I disagree with our great leader," Angelo said. "We don't need a culture war. We're already winning."

"No," growled the Lieutenant. "The Philosopher is right. There's no living side by side. We need to take back control. There are people who need us to free them."

My heart raced, practically lifting out of my chest. *This* was the bigger thing—Don's ambition, what he was really after. Some sort of culture war that ended with the Paters in control. But how? When? Control of what? This had to be how real journalists felt when the story started coming together. A hit of pure dopamine, an electric buzz—

A prickling sensation ran down my neck. I recognized the feeling: I was being watched.

In the midst of the conversation, the three wolf men's attention had silently turned to me. A smile snaked over the loudest one's mouth. "Tell me, new girl. When I chain *you* in my basement, will you think you're in control?"

They were tightening the space between us.

Over Angelo's shoulder, I spotted a flash of red on the faraway country house balcony. A woman, standing alone, arms spread over the railing like a figurehead on the bow of a ship.

Nicole.

A lifeline.

"Excuse me," I said, twisting my arm from Angelo with a little too much force. "I see a friend I need to speak to."

"No," said the Lieutenant, his eyes dark. "No more slipping away."

I had to obey. Even if I tried running out of the sculpture garden—blowing my cover—there were five of them. They'd catch me.

That feeling again: I was trapped, backed into a corner. Already, I could feel my mind trying to dissociate. I worked to tether it back, keep steady.

"Don't listen to him," Angelo said, waving a hand. "It's more fun to chase you. Go."

I felt an intense rush of gratitude for him, surely as dangerous as any fear. I didn't wait for anyone to disagree. I bolted from the garden, feeling the Lieutenant's gaze burning a hole in my back.

By the time I made it inside the house and up to the balcony, I was out of breath. Still, the sight of Nicole's bright hair and slim silhouette calmed me.

"Nicole," I called, then stilled when she turned around.

There was a cut across the bridge of her nose. A purple bruise on her cheek, long and dark as a lake.

"Jesus." Without thinking, I hugged her. "What happened?"

"It's nothing." I expected her to pull away, but she didn't. This close, I felt each breath she exhaled. "My Pater doesn't want me coming to gatherings anymore, but I'm doing it anyway. When he catches me, he gets a little carried away."

I drew back to study her. "Nicole, you know this has to stop."

She smiled. "Call me Nic. It's been forever since someone's called me that."

"You have to stop seeing him."

She shook her head. "I'm so close. He met with the Philosopher just a few days ago—the *Philosopher*, Shay. They're planning something big.

Whatever it is, my Pater is going to be rewarded, and so will I. I'll go to the Hilltop."

"If your Pater doesn't even want you attending gatherings, why would he give you up to the Hilltop?"

She blinked at me for a moment, looking very young, and I wondered for the millionth time how old she was. Then her eyes narrowed and she withdrew, leaning back against the railing. "Worry about yourself. You're the one who's in trouble."

"Meaning?"

"I heard the whispers." She swept her long hair over her shoulder. "The Incel told the Lieutenant you refused him."

I should've seen this coming. I'd run away from a man whose ego couldn't bear the smallest slight. "What's going to happen?"

"You'll be punished in front of everyone, like Cynthia. Remember?"

I pictured the blood blooming across Cynthia's back as the Disciple whipped her. The piano music swelling.

"Apologize," Nicole said. "Go back to Manhattan and give the Incel a weekend. Whatever it takes to appease him."

I thought of what that man could do to me in a weekend, and the feeling left my face.

"At the very least, hook yourself to another Pater, and fast. They say Cynthia still can't walk."

I gripped the railing next to her, eyes traveling over the festive grounds.

She peered at me. "Something's off."

I turned. "What do you mean?"

"You were so eager to join. Desperate, even. But now that you're here... Where's the girl who wanted to get hurt? I would've thought you'd jump in with both feet, but I haven't seen you with anyone. Now you're acting like me playing rough is a sin. What's your deal?"

I could lie. But I couldn't look at Nicole's face and put it off any longer.

"The truth is," I said, taking a breath, "I'm more interested in you than them."

"How flattering."

I touched her arm. "Why are *you* here? You're smart. Rebellious. I get the sex angle, and I know a person's kinks aren't their values, but—"

She laughed sharply. "Who told you that? Of course your kinks are your values. What the fuck else would they be?"

I stared at her battered face. "Then what does that say about you?"

Her voice was deadpan. "What do you think? That I'm fucking Miss America."

I blinked.

She continued in that dry voice. "I'm doing exactly what the world taught me. Taking the slap, saying *thank you, more, please.* The Paters want to tell me how worthless I am? Good. Everyone else is thinking it; they just don't have the guts to say it out loud."

"You mean…all that stuff about transformation through submission, becoming a better person, ascending to the truth—you don't believe it?"

She snorted. "I believe the Paters are the only ones who are honest about how the world works. But no, I don't think I'm going to ascend to some higher plane the longer I stay here."

I shook my head. "Why not leave, then? Have a normal life."

Her voice rose, and with it came an upstate accent, one I'd only heard hints of before, in sly, telltale words. "What kind of normal life have *you* been leading? My body's been someone else's since the day I was born. We're communal property, baby."

She laughed, and it wasn't a nice sound. "Life's going to stomp you no matter what. Wouldn't you rather get stomped here, in a mansion, surrounded by champagne and hors d'oeuvres? If they're going to own you one way or the other, why not enjoy it? *Lean in*, Shay. Look at me, in this Gucci dress. These bruises? They're Gucci bruises. It's the VIP option, trust me. All the other options are this, but worse."

"I hear you on the fatalism, but that doesn't change the fact that you're in real danger."

"I've got it under control."

Just like Angelo said: *They always think they're in control.* I flung my hand at her face. "Really? Because that looks like the opposite of control."

Her eyes blazed. "Try growing up in a single-wide with an alcoholic dad and a mom too scared to speak up. In swanky Munson, unemployment capital of New York, gray as shit twenty-four seven. Try living with sixty feet between you and the man who wants to hurt you. *That's* the opposite of control. And you want to know what finally changed it? My parents found religion. Bought in, hook, line, and sinker—church every day. And little naive Nicole, she thought, *What a relief*, surely things will get better. But it turns out the Bible says my body and soul belong to God, and he's a greedy bastard, too, always wanting you on your knees. So it was just a passing of ownership. A title change. When I got old enough, ran away and fell in love, I thought, *Okay, here it is, something I chose myself.* But what owns you worse than love? What makes you more of a captive? I would've slit my wrists if that man told me to."

She shook her head. "It's the same story, everywhere you turn. Anyone who tells you different is blind or trying to sell you something. At least with the Paters, it's out in the open. At least here I'm walking in with clear eyes. Loving your pain's the only control you get."

"That's not true." I faced the grounds and could see the Paters strolling, drinking, laughing, being whatever kind of people they wanted. "*They're* in control. They're free."

"They're men, for Christ's sake. Don't you understand how this works? What we're doing isn't kink, Shay. It's plain life. It's what everyone out in the world is doing, except without the layers of pretend. At least the Paters don't lie."

"They do," I said. "Believe me. The Philosopher's not someone you can trust."

Nicole nodded, turning away for a moment; then she snapped back, jaw tight. "I just figured it out." She laughed, so sudden it took me by surprise. "I recognize that evangelical glint in your eyes. You're trying to save me."

We stared at each other, Nicole with her gruesome smile, me with my heart pounding, wondering, *Dare I?*

I'd always known the investigation had an expiration date. I'd known the end would come eventually; that at some point, I would have to drop the pretense and *act*. Well, the sands were slipping through the hourglass faster and faster. It was time.

I laid my hands on Nicole's shoulders, and the knowing smile wiped from her face. "You're right," I said. "I'm here for you. Because I've been where you are. Everything the Paters are doing... They did it to me first."

She started to scoff, but I cut her off. "I know the Philosopher."

Her face flooded with surprise. It was a cheap ploy, but I pushed. "I've done all of this before, with him. At first it felt thrilling—I'll admit it—but eventually it got so bad I was either going to get out, or I was going to die. That's where you are, Nic. You have to trust me when I say this isn't normal, and you deserve better. Let me help you."

This was it. Nicole would be the first woman I saved, and the others would follow.

Emotions flickered over her face: shock and distrust, yes, but also hope. "You know the Philosopher?"

"A long time ago."

"What's he like?"

"I won't bullshit you. He's charming. Brilliant, maybe. But he's also a violent narcissist. Trust me, your dream about the Hilltop, and how wonderful it is? That's a fantasy."

The words hit like a slap. But she was practiced; she barely flinched. "You saving me is the fantasy."

"Nic—" Over her shoulder, I saw him: Chief Dorsey, in a dark suit, walking with purpose across the grass, his eyes trained on the balcony. On us.

I leapt back, heart racing. Had he seen me?

Nicole whipped around to look; fear washed over her face. "He was supposed to be out of town with his wife."

My knees turned to liquid. "*Adam Dorsey* is your Pater? The chief did this to you?"

She wasn't looking at me. Her eyes were fixed on Dorsey, cutting like a knife toward the house.

"He's here to punish you, isn't he? For coming against his orders?"

She tore her eyes from Dorsey, who'd made it to the large stone patio at the back of the house. We had two minutes, maybe less, before he burst onto the balcony. "I can't tell when he's playing anymore..." She shook her head. "I can't let him shut me up in his house. I need to see people. I have to get to the Hilltop."

"Nicole, you have to *leave*. We can run together. I have money." A lie. "I can protect us." Two lies, but I'd say anything.

She gripped my hands. Her voice was hushed. "Listen, I'm more scared of Rachel than Adam. She's the one who'll kill me if I leave."

The ground opened beneath me. "Rachel?" The words weren't coming out clearly. "Who... Where is she?"

Nicole's eyes swept the master bedroom, fixing on the door where

Dorsey would appear any moment. I could feel her legs bouncing, aching to move. "The Hilltop."

"With Don?"

She shook her head. "I don't know who that is."

"The Philosopher," I said, resisting the urge to shake her.

"No...the Philosopher's name is Greek. I heard Adam say it once."

Greek? That wasn't right. The Philosopher had to be Don. If it wasn't, nothing made sense. I shook my head. "You're saying Rachel... She hurts the daughters?"

Nicole's eyes swept behind me. "I have to go, Shay. He's almost here."

"Please," I urged.

"I don't know if she's even real." Nicole pulled her hands away. "I've never seen her. But they say she's a sociopath. Started killing when she was only a kid in college. I can't take the risk."

"In college?" I barely recognized my own voice.

"They tell all the daughters the story." Nicole's eyes flicked between me and the bedroom. "The Paters say she hung a girl and made it look like suicide. She'll do the same to us if we try to run." Nicole caught my eyes. "The thing is, all the daughters who step out of line *do* go missing. I think she's real and she hunts everyone who tries to leave."

The truth surfaced like a corpse from the bottom of a lake: Clem had been murdered, as suspected—but not by Don. By Rachel. I remembered the tension that simmered between them: Clem, Rachel's most vocal critic, the one who was least afraid to shut her down. In turn, Rachel had loved to see Clem punished most of all. She'd hung Clem in her favorite place, which meant she'd been paying attention to us, even when we thought she wasn't.

"Just do what they want, okay?" Nicole was pulling away. "And everything will be fine. You can come with me to the Hilltop."

I could hear Dorsey's footsteps on the stairs. She would race to greet him; grovel, beg, throw herself on the pyre of his ego. I knew in my gut I shouldn't let her go. I should grab her, hold her, wrest her away. She was Laurel and Clem and my mother all over again, walking straight into the razors, the fists, the fire.

But instead I stayed frozen with shock and fear, watching as Nicole disappeared into the dark. I listened to the crash of voices from the stairwell and knew what would happen. Today, tonight, tomorrow—I didn't know when, only that it was coming.

All I'd wanted was to save one woman. But when it came time, I didn't know how. Nicole was right: the idea had been a fantasy. A guilty mind clutching at redemption.

That's what would go down in the history books. What the recording device in my bra would show everyone who listened: me, soundless and still as Nicole walked away, an empty void of rolling tape. In the glaring silence, they would know that when it counted, when she'd needed me, I'd once again failed to make a difference.

PART THREE
Scheherazade, you upstart king

Imagine this. The night comes, the one you feared. The one you've been waiting for, death in exchange for an end to the mad weaving. He sees the woman you are, understands the fiction, and it is too much for his ego to bear. He takes up your father's sword from the corner of the room, takes that thick, gleaming steel in his hands, and thrusts at your head.

You duck.

You have watched him one thousand and one nights, after all, and you know the soreness in his knee, the way his wrist stiffens and clicks in winter. You have catalogued each weakness, each chink in his armor, studying him the way prey always studies the ones who hunt it.

He stumbles. You stick out a foot and he trips, sword clattering at your feet. He looks up at you from where he crouches on his hands and knees.

You seize the sword. You could spare him, take the weapon with you, leave this room you've been trapped in for so long you can't remember anything before it. Maybe there's another world beyond the door. A thousand worlds, like you've dreamed, and some of them benign.

Or.

You could drive the thick, gleaming steel down in an arc that meets his neck, separate his head from his shoulders, quick and ruthless as he would do to you. You could take the crown from his forehead and place it on your own. It would smell of blood—iron and ocher—but doesn't every crown?

What will you decide?

Whatever it is, the world will never be the same.

CHAPTER TWENTY-NINE

There's an inferno inside me. Whirling and hungry. I've felt it before.

Jamie rolled toward me, sheets clinging to his sweat-slicked body. "I can feel it, too," he said. "Simmering under your skin."

I blinked in surprise. I hadn't realized I'd spoken the words out loud. Maybe after so many interviews, I'd grown porous, the veil between inside and outside thin and breachable.

I leaned back next to him, my head finding the pillow, and we stared up at the popcorn ceiling, trying to catch our breath.

Jamie made me feel so good it worried me. If I was being honest with myself, Cal had been so self-absorbed, so uncurious, that being with him never felt like a risk. Jamie was different. Over and over he reached for me, like it was only natural. In the mornings, when his eyes opened on the other side of the bed and there was no pretense between us; at night, when I came back to the car and climbed over him without speaking, his mouth finding mine, no questions. Nothing that came this easy, no one who wanted this much, could ever be trusted.

"I don't know what to do," I said slowly. "I think I'm going to explode."

His voice was painstakingly gentle. "Like senior year?"

I could feel my heart pumping, carrying blood to the surface of my skin. Every inch sparking, still sensitive from where he'd touched me. It was a tether to this room, but it wasn't enough… Still, I was drifting.

Yes, I'd felt this way before.

"Like senior year," I agreed.

"Will you finally tell me what happened, why they took valedictorian away? What did you do?"

The only two people I'd ever told were both dead. Perhaps I should tell one more person to create a record, just in case.

I reached for his phone one last time.

CHAPTER THIRTY

Transgressions *Episode 705, interview transcript: Shay Deroy, Sept. 22, 2022 (unabridged)*

SHAY DEROY: I'd been in love with Anderson Thomas since middle school. It was a quiet obsession, one I never thought would go anywhere.

JAMIE KNIGHT: Trust me. I remember.

SHAY: He was a shiny person, wasn't he? The quarterback, from a good family, a mom and a dad, a sister. And he was so handsome it hurt to look at him. Everyone loved him.

JAMIE: Mmm.

SHAY: What?

JAMIE: Not everyone.

SHAY: You?

JAMIE: I saw him places you didn't. In locker rooms, out on the field when we played soccer, at parties, when it was just guys in the room. I didn't like who he was when he thought no one was watching.

(*Silence.*)

Listen to me interrupting you. I'm not being an objective observer; I'm making myself a character. Like some bullshit gonzo journalist. Sorry, Shay.

SHAY: Jamie, there's no such thing as an objective observer. That's why stories are powerful. If you're listening, you're part of it.

JAMIE: Maybe. But for ethical reasons, I'm going to have to present this episode some other way. Not journalism—a personal narrative or something. A confession.

SHAY: For what it's worth, the fact that you don't like Anderson makes this easier.

JAMIE: Makes what easier?

SHAY: You probably don't remember I got a little popular at the end of high school.

JAMIE: I remember.

SHAY: The truth is, I got hungry.

JAMIE: Hungry?

SHAY: I'd wanted attention my whole life, but I was also scared of it. Then everything fell together senior year. I was going to be valedictorian. I won Miss Texas, and suddenly I was giving speeches to girls in elementary schools, judging 4-H competitions, cutting ribbons. Kids even started talking to me at school, inviting me to things.

JAMIE: Suddenly I was sharing you with everyone.

SHAY: I was so happy. It felt like I was carrying around a tiny sun in the center of my rib cage. The day I got nominated for prom queen, Anderson Thomas walked up to me in the cafeteria and asked me to be his date. He'd barely talked to me before that. I was living a fairy tale.

The night of prom, when I was getting ready in the bathroom, I thought about that lock-in right after my dad left. How I'd felt so alone, watching other people be happy. It was finally my turn.

JAMIE: Right.

(*Rustling.*)

SHAY: I know I wasn't actually alone at the lock-in, because you were there. It's just how I felt.

(*Silence.*)

JAMIE: Of course. And... It's a stupid detail, but for historical accuracy, I asked you to prom, too.

SHAY: Oh. I'd forgotten. You were being nice, since no one had asked me the year before.

JAMIE: Mmm.

SHAY: Even my mom was proud of me. She came into the bathroom after I got out of the shower and gave me her face mask, the expensive one. We hadn't been close since Mr. Trevors, so for a while, we just stood there awkwardly, looking at our reflections in the mirror. She used to say I was the spitting image of my dad. As I stood there, my heart started pounding, because I never knew if looking at me made her happy or sad. Finally, she broke the silence and said, "I used to dream of being prom queen."

Her voice was soft, and I realized she was looking at herself in the mirror, not me. Then she said, "You already have a better shot than I ever did."

I said, "At winning?"

And she said, "At all of it. At life."

JAMIE: And you did win. That's the thing, Shay. You have this picture of yourself in your head that I don't understand, because you won so many times. You became the prom queen. Slow-danced in the gym in front of everyone.

(Silence.)

JAMIE: What?

SHAY: The dance was the last good part of the night.

JAMIE: You're talking about the after-party. If you're worried I'm still mad, I'm not. Everyone gets wasted and does things they regret. Besides, I was probably being overprotective.

SHAY: I can't remember, to be honest.

JAMIE: You remember what happened with Anderson, though.

SHAY: That's the thing, Jamie. I don't.

JAMIE: You're saying...

SHAY: I was so excited to win and be Anderson's date, be at that party as queen, that I made a stupid mistake and drank too much. People kept passing me shots, and I felt so grateful to be there, I just kept accepting. The last thing I remember is all of us dancing in Anderson's living room.

JAMIE: Do you remember climbing on top of the coffee table?

(Silence.)

SHAY: In front of everyone?

JAMIE: You were wearing your crown, and it seemed like... you wanted the attention. Like you were onstage.

SHAY: I don't remember that.

JAMIE: Which means you probably don't remember Anderson picking you up and trying to carry you upstairs, and me yelling at you.

SHAY: What did you say?

JAMIE: That you needed to go home. That's what started our fight. You were furious.

SHAY: I don't think I want to know what I said.

(*Silence.*)

Tell me.

JAMIE: You said I was jealous. That I judged you for everything you'd done—pageants, cheerleading, going on dates. And I was just some wannabe rebel who thought I was smarter than everyone, too good for the town, when in reality, I was just an average guy from a nice family. Nothing to write home about.

SHAY: Shit.

JAMIE: It was a really good insult because it was true. All the more impressive, considering how drunk you were. But the part that really hurt was when you said I'd always tried to keep you to myself, and now that other people liked you, I was losing it. You said I was a bad friend.

(*Rustling.*)

SHAY: I'm sorry, Jamie. That wasn't true.

(*Sighing.*)

JAMIE: Yes, it was. I deserved it. That's why I got mad and ran away.

But this isn't about rehashing our fight. Tell me what else you remember.

SHAY: I know Anderson brought me to his room. I have a vague memory of it—this dark space, with a bed in the center—a red bed, red walls, and tall windows, all the way up to the ceiling, with moonlight shining through. The moonlight was really bright, I remember that.

JAMIE: Shay, it was raining prom night. Remember, we

had to carry umbrellas? There was no moonlight. And Anderson's room was blue. He was a huge Cowboys fan. His sheets, the walls—all blue and white.

(*Creaking springs.*)

JAMIE: Where are you going?

SHAY: Did I invent that memory?

JAMIE: Maybe your brain was just trying to give you something to hold on to.

SHAY: I don't remember what happened next. When I think about it, I get this sensation of pressure. Rolling around, feeling dizzy. I think I remember a door swinging open, and people laughing. I can see it, like a blurry movie. But I guess I could've made it up.

JAMIE: No, that part happened. Some of the guys from the football team walked in on you.

SHAY: I have to ask...

JAMIE: They found you having sex.

SHAY: Right.

(*Silence.*)

I guess that's how I lost my virginity. I'd thought so, but it was blurry, so there was always a chance...

JAMIE: You seriously have no memory of having sex with Anderson?

(*Silence.*)

I'm going back to Heller to fucking kill him.

SHAY: Calm down.

JAMIE: They put his picture on a billboard when he won state. He's the high school football coach now.

(*Silence.*)

The same thing that happened to Laurel happened to you.

SHAY: Finding her in the basement that day was like looking at myself, back through time.

(*Rustling.*)

At some point, Anderson must've left me alone in his room, and I must have slept, or just blacked out, because I woke up naked and confused. My body felt... I could tell something had happened. I was sore, in places... It was like my body was someone else's. I would've left it behind if I could've. Just stepped right out of it, like crumpled clothes, and left the party, never to be seen or heard from again. But there was no easy escape. I had to put my clothes back on, and go back downstairs. Everyone was waiting for me. It was like they knew.

JAMIE: The football guys were talking about you. I told them to shut up, but, Shay, I didn't realize how drunk you were. I thought being with Anderson was what you wanted. I was so mean when you asked me to take you home.

SHAY: But you took me.

(*Silence.*)

You said I won a lot. But you're wrong. No matter what I did, I couldn't win.

JAMIE: I don't—

SHAY: You might not be able to run this interview because of libel issues, but at least whatever happens, the truth won't be erased.

JAMIE: What do you mean—

SHAY: You wanted to know what I did senior year to get valedictorian taken away. I'm going to tell you, but I wanted you to understand that part first.

After prom, I was ashamed. It's humiliating to admit,

but I thought if Anderson and I became a couple, that would fix it. Like being together would retroactively make what happened okay, turn it from something bad into a rocky beginning. I'm sure you can guess how the conversation went with him at school on Monday.

I was done with Heller after that. Counting the days until I could leave and never look back. But then...

(*Silence.*)

Two days before graduation, I went to Principal Ruskin's office to hand in my speech. I was waiting outside his door when Mr. Trevors walked out, shaking Ruskin's hand. He caught my eyes and didn't flinch, just said, "Ms. Evans" as he walked past, all smooth and calm, like he hadn't dated my mom and hit her.

He was getting promoted. Ruskin told me like it was an exciting secret. He was being named head of the English department, and he was receiving a teaching award on top of it. I just sat there in Ruskin's office while he droned on about my speech, trying to imagine what I would've done if Mr. Trevors had been head of English when I was in school, and I hadn't been able to escape him. I don't think I would have made it to graduation.

Suddenly a flip switched, and the only thing I felt was rage. I wanted to destroy someone. Hurt them like they'd hurt me.

JAMIE: Them?

SHAY: In that moment, I hated everyone. Even you.

(*Silence.*)

That's why I burned his classroom.

(*Creaking springs. Footsteps.*)

JAMIE: What the... *You're* the one?

SHAY: For listeners, in May 2009, the night before graduation, authorities were called to put out a fire at Heller High. They arrived to find the English wing in flames and had to work quickly to contain it. They were successful, but it took another year before the English classrooms were rebuilt. The entire faculty was displaced.

JAMIE: This isn't funny, Shay. You're talking about arson.

SHAY: I'm just trying to give the listeners some context. You can sit back down. I'm not going to bite.

JAMIE: I can't air this interview. You just confessed to a crime.

SHAY: They knew it was me from the start, Jamie. I don't know how, but they figured it out.

JAMIE: How? I mean...how did it even *happen*?

SHAY: I only meant to burn Mr. Trevors's room. But the truth is, I would've been happy to see the whole school go up in flames. It was easy, with gasoline at midnight. I stayed as long as I could, because I wanted to see the classroom where he tortured me burn. You should've seen the way it looked against the sky.

JAMIE: You risked throwing away your future for revenge? Everything you'd worked so hard for? We were finally escaping Heller, and you were willing to give it up. I don't understand.

SHAY: It wasn't rational. It was fury.

JAMIE: Everyone thought it was an actual arsonist, and the whole time, it was you. Why didn't you get in trouble?

SHAY: Ruskin called me and my mom into his office the morning of graduation. I knew I was toast. I expected the cops to be waiting, but when my mom and I got there, it was just him, and the guidance counselor, and a woman who turned out to be the superintendent. The way they were looking at me...

JAMIE: Livid?

SHAY: Fearful. It was the first time anyone had looked at me like that. Ruskin said they knew I'd been the one to set Mr. Trevors's classroom on fire, but given the circumstances, he wouldn't call the cops.

JAMIE: What circumstances?

SHAY: Somehow, he knew Mr. Trevors had dated my mother. And he knew I had a reason to hate him. My mom went white as a ghost. I swear, she didn't say a word the whole time, from the moment she stepped in the office. She wouldn't even look at me.

JAMIE: Are you saying Principal Ruskin was aware that Mr. Trevors assaulted your mom, and he not only did nothing, but gave him a promotion?

SHAY: I'm saying Ruskin told me they'd have to strip valedictorian away and ban me from future school events, but if I wanted to move on from Heller—if I wanted to go quietly to the next chapter, without making a scene—the three of them had agreed there was no reason to arrest me. Insurance would cover the cost of the damage. It was an exchange. Silence for silence.

JAMIE: Ruskin bought you. 'Cause there's no insurance that will save you if people find out you knowingly employed a teacher who beats women and terrorizes students.

SHAY: I burned down his classroom and walked away, so maybe I have agency, too, Jamie.

JAMIE: You're right. It's just...you were a kid.

SHAY: Who am I kidding? I went home and cried. I didn't cry once after prom, and suddenly after this I couldn't stop. I wasn't going to jail. I was only getting grounded. I should've been happy. But I was devastated.

JAMIE: You were furious, and you wanted to destroy something, even if the only thing you could manage was your own life.

SHAY: In a way, I did destroy it. That day, locked in my room, I went online, withdrew from UT, and accepted the offer at Whitney. Changed the course of my life, just like that. Want to know why? Because one night, sophomore year, when he saw me looking at college brochures, Mr. Trevors said Whitney was a school for feminazis.

A throwaway comment, but I never stopped thinking about it. And suddenly, all I wanted was to be the kind of woman he would hate.

JAMIE: We had a pact, remember? Since middle school. You, me, and Clara were supposed to go to UT together. When you said you were switching to Whitney, I thought it was because you were done with me after our fight.

SHAY: I wasn't doing a great job communicating back then. Besides, it was pathetic. Years of agonizing over colleges, doing all those pageants to win a scholarship, and I made my entire decision at the drop of a hat, based on something a man said to me once. There I was, eighteen years old, thinking I was taking back power. And look where Whitney led me.

(*Silence.*)

My whole life has been like that. Starts and stops. Doing something brave, getting something right, then messing up, burning all the progress to the ground. I can't seem to get it straight. I'm stuck in a loop. Always back to the beginning.

JAMIE: But you keep trying. What else is there?

SHAY: Now that you know the truth about me, do you even want to come back to bed?

(*Deep inhale. Footsteps. Creaking springs.*)

Hey, wait. What's wrong?

End of transcript.

CHAPTER THIRTY-ONE

"I lied," Jamie said. While I'd talked, he'd turned his back, pulling on jeans and a T-shirt. Now he sat fully clothed on the bed, eyes cast down to his feet.

"About what?"

His voice was low and husky. "I didn't ask you to prom because I was being a good friend. I wanted to go with you."

I tried to remember that day but couldn't. The memory had dissolved. "Really?"

"Really." Jamie's eyes moved to the bedsheets. He still wouldn't look at me. I became acutely aware of my heartbeat. "I'll tell you something else. The day you told me you switched to Whitney, I accepted my offer at Columbia. Only a train ride away."

"I thought you went for the journalism program."

Gently, almost apologetically, he shook his head. "Shay, when we were in middle school, I stopped going to that soccer camp in California... Remember the one by the beach? Because you couldn't afford it, and I wanted to stay home with you all summer. Freshman year, when you wanted to come over every night to study, I dropped everything—piano lessons, extra soccer coaching—so I would be free. Got into a huge fight with my mom over it, actually. When we were juniors, I used to time my showers after soccer practice with the end of cheer, so I could drive you home." He laughed. "My life revolved around finding ways to spend time with you."

"We were best friends," I said.

He looked at me but didn't say a word. Just let me see the truth, plain on his face.

"For how long?" I asked.

This time, his smile was rueful. "Always."

The air in the room had turned cool and crisp. Jamie lay beside me, breathing deeply, while I watched the dark seep out of the sky through the window.

Maybe it was the last story that did it, the last puzzle piece falling into place. Or maybe it was just a matter of time, all the talking and remembering catching up to me. Whatever it was, I finally knew what to do. From one second to the next, the knowledge was just there, as if it always had been.

"I'm glad I told you about the fire," I whispered, simply for the pleasure of hearing it out loud.

"I'm glad, too," murmured Jamie, in a sleep-drugged voice. So he was awake.

I turned. His eyes were closed, face creased by the pillow. "I think I know how my book ends," I said.

Slowly, his eyes blinked open. "You still haven't told me what it's about."

I smiled. "I was inspired by Scheherazade."

He frowned. "From *The Thousand and One Nights*? The story you refused to talk about with Mr. Trevors?"

I settled deeper into the sheets. "You were right. I did have a lot to say. Just not to him."

Silence stretched, but I knew Jamie well enough to know it was contemplative.

"Hey." I closed my eyes. "Let's go out, okay? I'll wear a nice dress, and you can bring me a corsage, and we'll get drunk and dance."

"Why do you want to do that?"

"I want to do it over again. Tie things up clean."

"Tie what up?" Jamie asked.

But sleep was already pulling me under.

CHAPTER
THIRTY-TWO

It was a brilliant fall day, the trees and earth—the very air—shocked through with punch-drunk autumn color. Jamie, dressed in slender black, cut down the quaint Main Street like a palette knife, reordering the landscape. I watched him and thought, *Now that's a trick I never learned.*

"Dougie," Jamie said, pocketing his phone. "There's one Rachel Rockwell in the entire state of New York, and she's eighty-six. Last record of our Rachel is from 2014."

"The year we graduated," I said, mind spinning.

"In case you were wondering, she graduated with you, at least on paper. Then she disappeared. Records go cold the same year for Don. But the wildest thing isn't when the records stop. It's when they start. Both Rachel and Don seem to have sprung fully formed into existence five years earlier. The first bits and pieces Dougie can find of them are from 2009. Mostly documents related to Rachel's Whitney application. There's a social security number and a birth certificate that says she was born at Mount Sinai on October 15, 1992, but Dougie thinks it's probably fake. One of my producers is going to call the hospital to check."

I stopped outside a small hunting shop, painted a worn, peeling blue. A little bell hung on the door. "Don and Rachel aren't their real names."

Jamie crossed his arms. "Probably not."

"Are they even father and daughter?"

"I have no idea."

I couldn't help the strange stir of relief for Rachel. She'd killed Clem, so I hated her, owed her nothing; still, there was release, knowing life with Don might have been something she'd chosen, rather than been born into. Nicole's words echoed back: *At least here I'm walking in with open eyes.*

"The bottom line is," Jamie said, "even if the Paters call her Rachel, she could be using a different name officially. That makes her nearly impossible to find. I have Dougie working on some creative stuff. He's tracing all rare antique sales to buyers in New York, since we know Don collects old weapons."

"That's a good idea." It seemed obvious to turn each of Don's devotions into a hook that could snare him, but it hadn't occurred to me before.

Jamie shrugged. "It's frustrating, actually, that we haven't made more progress. It's expensive to hide this well. Most people can't do it. We're clearly dealing with people who have access to a lot of wealth." He glanced in the direction of the Hudson River, which ran along the edge of Brookview, the small dairy town we were standing in. "Which reminds me... Dougie tracked down who owns Campbell Island."

I looked far off in the island's direction. "It's privately owned?" Imagine, buying an island.

He nodded. "It went up for sale a few years ago...rare for an island in the Hudson."

"And you think because the gathering's there, the Paters own the whole thing?"

The text had shown up two days ago: Saturday, three pm, The Hunting Lodge, Campbell Island. The island was really more of a peninsula, and it butted up against a nature preserve, but altogether, it was ninety-plus acres of shoreline and dense woods, full of wildlife.

Jamie squared his jaw. "I know they do. Guess who's listed as the buyer?"

I blinked at him.

"Dominus Holdings. The same LLC that took over paying Laurel's rent."

A memory floated back from the Pater gathering in the city: Nicole had called those young Paters traders. Steven, the sadist. The unnamed one, who hadn't introduced himself. And Greggy, who'd shaken my hand. "Gregory Ellworth was the name you tracked to Dominus?"

Jamie nodded.

Not Greggy—*Greg E.*

"I think I met him," I said. "If I'm right, he's young and lives in the city. He's connected to the finance crowd, maybe one of them."

"That's good, Shay. That'll help Dougie find him." Jamie drew his peacoat tighter. "I shared everything we have with my executive producer, by the way. My other producers made contact with the governor's team. Tipped them we have a big story coming, and to get their lawyers and the attorney general ready."

A shiver traveled up my spine and settled somewhere in my throat. It sounded so real. So final, like we were almost at the finish line. But I hadn't found Don yet. I didn't even know for sure the Paters were his. I needed to make a move fast.

"The governor's people agreed," Jamie said. "They're going help us. So when it's time, we'll send them copies of the evidence, all your recordings from the Pater events, and our interviews." Here, he paused. "Are you still comfortable with that?"

I imagined a conference table full of men in suits, gray-haired lawyers, hunched in their chairs, listening to what I'd poured out to Jamie in the intimate bubble of our hotel rooms. Listening to the screams and moans from Pater parties. Which one embarrassed me more?

"They know it's sensitive." He paused, his gaze catching on my mouth. "I've previewed everything with my counsel. I'm going to hire a personal lawyer for us, too. We need to prepare for lawsuits."

I nodded. I'd thought about this, considering the kind of men who were involved in the Pater Society, the positions they held, what they had to lose. "I think we need to prepare for every man we out as a Pater to come after us."

"It's going to get ugly. I'll—" Suddenly, Jamie's eyes flicked over my shoulder, and his face hardened. "Motherfucker." He lunged around me, streaking across the street.

I whirled, shouting, "What are you doing?"

A man jolted from the bushes across the street and took off running, a heavy black bag thumping at his hip. But Jamie had reacted quickly, and the man didn't have enough time. Jamie tackled him to the grass.

When I got to them, Jamie was astride the man, pinning him by the shoulders. They were both breathing heavily.

"Get off me," the man shouted. He was older and heavyset, with oily skin. In the lawn beside him was a professional-grade camera with a telephoto lens.

"Jamie, what's happening?"

"He was taking pictures of us." Jamie gripped the man tighter. "Who hired you?"

"Fuck off," the man said. "You're on public property. Let me go before I have you arrested for assault."

I knelt in the cold grass, feeling the blades prick my knees through my pantyhose. "Did the Paters hire you?" If they'd hired this man to spy on me, they already knew I was a fraud.

"I don't know who that is." The man stopped squirming and squinted at Jamie. "Get off."

Jamie shook his head, his black hair wild from running and tumbling. "Not until you tell us why you're taking pictures. Look, man, I'm close with a bunch of cops. I say the word, and they're going to find a reason to bring you in."

Even if it was laughable to imagine Jamie—who hacked into police records and stole case files—close to the cops, he delivered the bluff with confidence.

The man laughed. "I know who you are, asshole. You run a podcast. And you're *talking* to a former cop. Any officer you know in the state of New York, I guarantee I know them better."

"You're a private detective." Jamie settled back on his heels. "Hopefully that means you're smart enough to believe me when I say I'm not getting off your chest until you convince me you're not a threat to her."

The man's eyes flicked to me. "A threat? I'm here to get proof of an affair. What the hell are *you* mixed up in?"

It clicked. "Cal hired you."

The man's face shuttered. "I'm not talking."

Relief poured through me. "Jamie, get off."

Jamie hopped off the man, giving him a wide berth, and the detective scrambled to his feet, grabbing his camera, checking the lens. "If you broke anything, you're paying."

"Put it on Cal's tab," I said, picking up my phone and dialing.

The detective scowled at me. "I didn't admit a goddamn word."

Cal answered immediately. "Tell me you're on your way to the airport. If you're coming home, we can forget everything. I'm serious."

"Like the fact that you hired a private investigator to follow me?"

"How—" His voice lost its smoothness. "What was I supposed to do? You're my wife."

"That doesn't give you the right."

"I know you're cheating," he bit out. "You realize you signed a prenup, right? If you leave me, you get nothing. No money, no friends, no dignity. Everyone will know."

"Ah." I locked eyes with Jamie. "So the private investigator's building a case to string me up in court."

Jamie's eyes widened.

I could hear Cal take a deep breath. "Shay. Just come home. We'll go to therapy. Couples' counseling, however long it takes. Please, try putting yourself in my shoes. A year of newlywed bliss, and one day, out of nowhere, you run away. You won't tell me what you're doing. It's like you don't even like me anymore. I tried to talk to you, to fix it, but you're barely answering my calls. I don't have a lot of options here."

I did see it from Cal's perspective. It wasn't his fault I'd confused safety with love, that what I'd wanted out of marrying him was a place to hide, and then I'd decided that wasn't good enough. He hadn't reacted well, and that was revealing, but to him it must have seemed like I'd lost my mind. I pictured him telling his friends about me, the Highland Parkers, and I imagined their incredulous faces, could hear them saying, in shocked voices, *She's insane.*

Maybe I was, in his version of the story. I finally felt secure enough in mine that I was okay with letting him have it.

The sharp edge left my voice. "Cal, I'm sorry. I really am. But the truth is, I don't want to be married to you anymore. You can put these photos of me on a billboard for all I care. I'm not interested in your money, either. I'm sorry to tell you over the phone; it's just..." It was just that I'd woken to the truth, and now I was simply uninterested in wasting any more of my time. "I'm sorry," I finished lamely.

"I can't believe you're doing this," he hissed. "I can't believe I ever loved you. I never want to—"

I hung up and shoved the phone in my pocket. "Sorry," I said to the private detective. "I think your pictures just got a whole lot less valuable."

The detective stalked away, muttering obscenities, but Jamie turned still as a statue. "You ended your marriage," he said, looking at me in a way I couldn't read. "Right there on the phone."

I had to make my move. "Come on." I started in the direction of the hunting shop. "You said I needed a knife I could hide in my dress."

Jolted, Jamie hurried to catch up. His footsteps made a quick patter on the street—or maybe that was the sand rushing through the hourglass, the sound of time moving fast.

Across the cold, briny Hudson, I stood at the far end of Campbell Island, examining the hunting lodge. It was large but looked like it had grown out of the island itself, a mass of fir and spruce, tangled over with green vines and moss. One of those expensive places that took pains to hide their value.

Daughters milled around outside it, all of us in our carefully ironed dresses, trying not to move too much and snag our pantyhose. It was a chilly day, and wet air clung in pearls to the tree leaves, but there was a roaring fire, with a pig on a spit roasting in the middle. The whole place was decorated for a party: red and cream banners waved from the trees, a round oak keg was propped against the house, leaking red wine from the spout, and laurel crowns hung on nails from the side of the house, the kind they awarded victors of the ancient Olympics.

I had to force my gaze from the laurel crowns, whose presence gnawed at me, to the daughters themselves. There were more than I'd noticed before, and I wondered if the Paters had recruited new women. I studied them, smiling warmly when someone caught me looking. I was hoping for a daughter who'd catch my gaze and keep it, or one who'd smile back and let me into her confidence. If Jamie wanted to hand over our evidence soon, I needed to get more daughters on the record talking about what they knew.

I was interrupted by the Paters, who stepped out of the hunting lodge in a pack, each in a white tunic fashioned like a toga, with a coil of rope slung over his shoulders. An immediate alertness passed through the mingling daughters, like a herd of deer spotting danger.

Chief Dorsey pushed his way to the front and I shrunk back, trying to disappear in the crowd so he couldn't see my face. His cheeks were red, eyes bright. "Daughters," he boomed. "Welcome to the nymph hunt, one of our oldest traditions." A smile split his face. "When I say run, you'll get ten minutes to flee as far and fast as you can. On behalf of your Paters, we beg you to try your best."

My heart began to skip. I'd thought any minute, they were going to let us inside the lodge, and things would unfold like they normally did, with alcohol and rituals. They wanted us to run?

"Any Pater who captures a nymph can exert his right to ravish his conquest. After which he'll bind them and bring them back to the lodge. The Pater who hunts the most wins an audience with the Philosopher himself—*after* tonight's bacchanalia, of course, where we drink and eat until we can't see straight, in the ancient tradition." Dorsey's rough voice, better suited to barking commands, fumbled over the flowery words. "Paters, daughters, as you'll soon hear, there's no better time to be a Pater. So tonight, we celebrate."

Around me, women crouched, arms and legs tensing, eyes flitting to the trees. They were getting ready. Every instinct warned me that if I took off into the woods, into the gray mist rolling off the river, I would cease being a woman and become something more animal.

The chief of police checked his watch, and the Paters behind him shuffled in anticipation. There was the Lieutenant, in front, the Disciple, near the back, and even the Marquis. The men who hid behind archetypes. But I could see them. I would uncover them, learn each of their names. As long as I managed to leave this island.

Wait, I thought suddenly. *What will happen if the Lieutenant catches me—or, god forbid, the Disciple? Nicole said they want to punish me. Why am I giving them this chance?* But it was already too late.

"Run!" Dorsey's voice cracked through the woods like a shot.

The daughters took off in every direction, looking less like nymphs from Greek myths than wide-eyed deer trying to outrun a trap. Laughter boomed from the Paters, an electric sound, stripping me of rational thought, launching me into motion. I sprinted into the forest, away from their eyes and their ropes and their hungry smiles.

My feet pounded the forest floor as I hopped over gnarled tree roots, pushing myself as fast as my legs would take me. My foot landed wrong and my ankle twisted; I fell, hands finding sharp tree branches on the ground, but I picked myself up and kept going. Soon I couldn't see the other women anymore: just the fog and dark trees when they got close enough. I thought for a moment that I could run all the way to the other end of the peninsula, or to the shore and dive into the Hudson, no matter how frigid the water, and swim to where Jamie waited.

I blazed past a tree and ran chest first into something solid, falling backward.

"Fuck *you*," a voice cried.

I scrambled up, wiping stinging hands on my dress. "Nicole?"

She sat up from where she'd fallen, glaring, her red hair wild and tumbling down her back. Then she realized, and her glare softened. "Shay?"

I ran to her and lifted her up, flush with relief. I'd let her walk into the dark with the Chief, but she was okay—she was here, alive and breathing. I hadn't failed her. Before I could help it, my cheeks were hot and wet.

"What are you doing here?" I managed. "I thought you weren't allowed to come to gatherings."

She bent over, sucking in air. "It's Adam's lodge. It's his event."

"Really?" There was no way any police chief could afford a second home like that one on a public salary.

Nicole nodded and righted herself, slipping on her familiar look of disdain. "I know. Bought and paid for by the Paters. The higher you climb, the nicer the favors."

I followed the flight of her hand as she brushed hair off her face. Despite the darkening air and thickening mist, I could see her fading bruises had been joined by newer, fresher marks. She turned her head, revealing a bright, angry cut down her jaw that looked like it could've happened mere hours ago.

"Nic," I said, the word catching in my throat. She caught my eyes and knew.

"I'm supposed to wait behind this tree." Her voice was devoid of emotion. "See?" She pointed, and I saw the X carved into the tree trunk. "It's all set up to make sure he's the one who finds me."

"Cheater." The word burst from me.

Our eyes locked, and Nicole cracked a grin. "Right? Can't even find a nymph in his own damn forest without an X to mark the spot."

Her smile made my chest almost unbearably light. "They get ropes and clues, and here we are, forced to run in these monstrosities." I fanned my wide skirt. "I thought I was going to catch this shit on a tree

313

ASHLEY WINSTEAD

branch and accidentally hang myself." Nicole barked a laugh. "Which would serve me right for putting it on in the first place."

She clapped a hand over her mouth. It was intoxicating, laughing in the thick of danger.

Nicole pulled up her dress, flashing her torn pantyhose. "You think they could've at least warned us to wear long johns. Damn thing's already full of holes. I swear to god, if we don't get reimbursed, I'm registering a complaint with HR."

"I'll bring it up to the Lieutenant at my whipping." I clutched my chest, nearly choking at my daring, at the way she tossed her head back. A line from Jamie's podcast flitted through my mind: *My transgression for the day is...*

After a minute, our laughter softened, then died.

"Please," I said into the silence. "Tell me you've thought about it."

The only sounds now were the soft snapping of twigs, a lone bird trill. She leaned back against the carved tree and stared at something far away.

"Nicole?" I didn't care that I was pressing. Seeing her again was a gift, one I'd never get with Clem or Laurel. This time, I wouldn't make the same mistake. I wouldn't set foot off this island without her.

Far off in the distance, I heard a whistle.

Her eyes jumped to mine. "You were right. He's not going to let me go."

I inched closer. "To the Hilltop?"

A branch cracked.

Her chest rose and fell. "I asked him last night when he thought I'd earn it. It's a fair question. Most daughters want to ascend, to be with the Philosopher. It's the whole point of our journey. But it made him angry. He says he won't release me." Her voice dropped. "So you can go ahead and say it."

314

I shook my head.

She smiled, achingly sad. "Always the nice girl."

"We can start running," I said. "We can find a dock and hide on someone's boat, or in the forest, and when they've gone back to the lodge, we can run to the town right off the island. My friend's waiting there."

She cleared her throat. "Adam knows this island like the back of his hand. And there are too many of them. Running now's too risky." She met my eyes. "But I will do it. I'll take your advice and leave while I still can."

Nicole would be saved. She wouldn't die like Laurel and Clem, disappear like all the missing women. I threw my arms around her, hugging so tight the tree bark bit into my arms.

She pulled back. "Adam's wife and kids come back from their grandparents' in two days. He always spends the first night with them. We'll go then." She brushed a strand of my dark hair from her face and smiled. "I even have some money."

I shook my head. "Don't worry about that."

"Two days, okay?" She gripped my shoulders. "Just tell me where to meet you."

"In Yonkers," I said automatically. "The Motel 6." And then I couldn't help it. It was too absurd, or I was too relieved. I laughed again.

Her mouth cracked into a smile. "I'm risking my life, and you couldn't spring for a Hyatt?"

"Come on." I tugged her from the tree, gripping her hand. "Fuck Dorsey."

Nicole grinned. Together, we stepped out from behind the X-marked tree—and found the Chief, standing silent and still. Flanking him were the Lieutenant, the Disciple, and the Marquis.

"Surprise," he said softly.

"Adam." Nicole couldn't shield her shock. "We were just—"

The Chief's eyes swung in my direction, and he gave a start. "What are *you* doing here?"

"You know her?" The Lieutenant frowned. The other two men behind Dorsey circled tighter, leaving Nicole and me nowhere to go. They'd caught us. I had a knife hidden inside my bra, but there were four of them. It wouldn't be enough.

Dorsey studied me, eyes lingering on my lips. If I hadn't been frozen with terror, I would have flinched. "She came into the station asking questions about Laurel Hargrove weeks ago. Said they used to be friends."

"Laurel Hargrove?" The Marquis turned to the Lieutenant, his chest puffing. "Don't tell me you let in a reporter."

Nicole turned to me, and for a second, I saw her surprise and betrayal. But then it was gone, her face smoothed into a conciliatory mask. "Adam." Her tone was low and calming. "I don't know what you think you heard—"

Dorsey's face shone with sweat. "You're planning to leave me."

"No—"

"After everything I've done for you—you piece of trash—you were going to run away."

She took a step back. "You were going to keep me from the Hilltop."

"Nicole, don't," I said, but as soon as I spoke, the Disciple pointed at my face. "Shut the fuck up, whoever you are, or you'll regret it."

"*I* get to decide what happens to you." The Chief's voice was throttled. There was dirt smeared into the white wool of his tunic. He'd clearly pushed fast through the woods to find Nicole. "If I tell you you're staying with me every goddamn day of your life, it's your job to shut up and thank me for not getting tired of you. I tell you you're mine, you don't so much as breathe near another man, Philosopher or not." His voice rose. "You know the rules. Every day, you get on your fucking hands and your knees and you worship me. You thank me for choosing you, you trailer park whore. How dare you humiliate me?"

"Don't talk to her that way." The words flew out. "You don't own her."

"Mouth closed." The Disciple took a step forward. "Or you'll need it wired shut."

"But you don't." Nicole's spine straightened, and there was that glint in her eye—the streak of subversiveness no amount of time with the Paters could snuff, the thing that kept drawing me to her. Now I wanted to scream at her to bury it, be docile enough to survive. "I was *using* you, Adam. You were a rung on a ladder, a stepping-stone to the Hilltop. We both know I can do better. I tried to wait it out, but you want the truth? Fucking you got too boring to wait."

She was going for his jugular. I felt another stab of fear. I'd wanted her to be brave, but not like this.

Dorsey lunged at her. "Don't lie to me. You wanted it... You begged." The look on his face said he believed it.

Nicole stepped backward out of his reach, stumbling a little, that familiar look of defiance sharpening at his words. I wanted to scream at her, *No, not now*, but she kept pushing. "I couldn't wait to leave. I've been counting down the days."

The Chief grabbed for her and I screamed, but she dodged his grasp, turned to me, and hissed, "*Come on*," then took off. I knew we were outnumbered, two deer against a pack of wolves, but it was now or never, run or die. So I ran.

We exploded into the trees just as a terrible roar sounded, Dorsey yelling after us, the Paters launching into motion. I seized Nicole's hand and pulled her faster, no longer a thinking thing but an animal, determined to survive.

I would have run forever if they'd let me. I would've never stopped, never slowed, would have gone on moving until my legs buckled. Except Nicole cried out, and her hand jerked from mine, and without it, I tumbled forward.

I caught myself and spun back. But she was on the forest floor, stretched out on her back, arms outstretched to shield herself, eyes wide in terror. Dorsey seized her by the ankles, dragged her so swiftly her head bounced against the tree roots and she cried out.

"No!" I screamed. "*Nicole!*"

"Why'd you have to do it?" the Chief yelled, towering over her. "Why are you *making me* do this to you?" The look on his face was the same he'd worn when Laurel, Clem, and I went to him for help twelve years ago, the same he'd worn when I questioned him in his office, except now the rage was no longer hinted but unleashed, the true sight of it flooring me, stealing my breath.

Nicole twisted, trying to fight him, but he pinned her. She scratched his face, a vicious bloody swipe across his cheek, and suddenly there was no more wondering *What was he capable of*, no more *How far would he go*, because Adam Dorsey bent over, grabbed the face of the woman who'd dared to flee him, and cracked her head against a rock, the intensity of his rage matched only by the scream filling the woods, an animal howl heating the cold, a noise that seemed to come from me.

CHAPTER THIRTY-THREE

Nicole was a tree on the forest floor. Transformed like the nymphs before her, paying with their lives to escape men's hunger. She lay still and hollow as a fallen log, eyes locked on the skyline, on the hilltops in the distance.

There was so much blood I slipped in it, running at Adam Dorsey with the force of a train, grappling without pause over roots and rocks, hungry for the moment he tore his gaze away from what he'd done and realized I was coming. And there it was: his head snapped, shoulders stiffening, arms raising like a shield, but it was too late. I barreled into him and down we fell. He was large, his heaviness knocking the wind from me, but my hands found the metal of my switchblade and yanked it out of my shirt, flipping the blade up. I scrambled backward into a crouch and pointed the knife at the chief of police, who lay stunned on the ground.

I squeezed my trembling fingers around the hilt. The last time I'd held a knife was in the kitchen; before that, one of Don's old antiques, lifted gingerly from its velvet box.

"Put that down." It was the Disciple, of course, stepping closer with a rope held taut between his hands. He, the Lieutenant, and the Marquis circled the Chief and me, their eyes bright with excitement, traveling from Dorsey's splayed body to the quivering knife in my hands. Their gazes slid past Nicole like she was already invisible.

"She won't hurt me," the Chief said, though he remained tensed. His eyes met mine, those stubby lashes blinking quickly. "The podcast freak. Who would've thought?"

"You killed her." I couldn't stop my voice from trembling. I'd acted quickly, instinctively, to the sight of Dorsey hurting Nicole, and now I was left with the cold, hard truth. I was surrounded, outnumbered, and I had no idea what to do next. "You're going to prison."

"No one's going anywhere," the Marquis said smoothly. "Especially you."

"I knew there was something wrong with you," said the Lieutenant, tilting his head. "You were going to be punished tonight at the party, in front of everyone." His voice was deadly empty, same as the night Nicole first brought me to him. "What are you...some kind of under-cover cop?"

"There's no way," the Chief said quickly. "I'd know."

I did quick math. There'd been screaming, yet no one had come to investigate. The woods around us were empty save for Paters and daughters, who wouldn't blink to hear it. Jamie was too far away. How could I save myself?

"Put the knife down," the Disciple barked, taking a step closer.

I backed away. "Touch me and I'll slit his throat."

"Do it, then, for Christ's sake." The Chief looked at me with lazy confidence.

Stab him, the voice urged. *Take him off this earth.*

"Enough fucking around," said the Lieutenant and leapt.

It happened so quickly. My knees bent, fingers tensed around the blade. The Lieutenant grasped, but I twisted away, knowing this was it, my last chance, and if I didn't kill them, they would put me on the forest floor next to Nicole, the earth swallowing me like Laurel. *Do it*, I screamed, breath coming hot and fast, legs kicking away, knife lifting to thrust. *Do it for Laurel Nicole Clem Nina Katie*—

But my hand was shaking too hard. Here, in the crucial moment, life or death, I couldn't hurt them. I was weak. I hated that more than anything—that in the end, they were right.

The Lieutenant feinted and I spun away, right into the solid trunk of the Disciple. It was a well-practiced entrapment, quick and merciless. The Disciple smashed his fist into my temple and I fell.

I became aware of a gentle bouncing and opened my eyes to the inside of a hood. It was dark, the fabric scratchy. Immediately I jerked, panicking, kicking something solid pressed against me.

Breathe, I told myself. *Breathe, and think.*

The rocking and sound of wheels rolling over gravel told me I was in a car. The Paters were taking me somewhere. My hands were bound behind me, and I was on my side, head pressed painfully against the floor, on the same side where I'd been cracked by the Disciple's fist. The knife was gone, of course, but there—I twisted, felt sharp metal bite into my breast—somehow, miraculously, they'd missed the recording device hidden in my bra. I swallowed a low groan and got to work on my hands, which were mercifully tied with rope, not the zip ties Don used to prefer.

After minutes of tugging and pulling, the knot eased a millimeter— enough for me to fold my fingers and yank my hands free. I tossed the rope and pulled off the hood.

I blinked. I was in the back of a van, and Nicole lay on her side, facing me, like we were lovers curled in bed. From this angle, I couldn't see the gaping wound in her head, but the red strands of her hair were matted with blood. I almost moved to untangle them, then realized I was in shock.

The Disciple's voice came from the front of the van, followed by the unmistakable sound of the Lieutenant, with his slight Dutch accent. All I caught was the end of a sentence: "...what Rachel will do with her."

My head whipped to the small car window. Outside was a valley full of trees, their leaves a riot of color, like the forest had caught fire. Above the valley rose a single dark mountain. Atop it stood a stone house, like a lone castle, keeping a watchful eye over its kingdom.

It had to be the Hilltop. The home of Rachel and the Philosopher. I was going to see them again, after all this time, face-to-face. Don had run just like my father, but I'd found him. After eight long years.

The van wound up the mountain, drawing nearer to the manor. They would open their gates and welcome us inside, expecting dutiful Paters; cold, submissive female bodies.

They didn't know the van was a Trojan horse.

I kissed Nicole's temple as we rounded the corner and whispered, "Look. You made it."

Vengeance lying in wait.

CHAPTER
THIRTY-FOUR

By the time they opened the back doors, I had my hood on, my hands back inside the knotted loop of rope, except this time, the knot was loose, not biting. Rough hands grabbed me, pulling me upright, and yanked off the hood.

"You awake?" The Lieutenant's pale-blue eyes stared, his blond mustache twitching.

"Fuck you," I said, and he smiled.

"Awake, but no less stupid." He wrestled me out of the van. Up close, the Hilltop was somehow larger than it had looked from the road. Its pale stone walls rose so high I had to lean back to see the top of them. There were flowers everywhere: neatly arranged in flower beds around the perimeter, in boxes hanging from the windows. Aster, verbena, and goldenrod, Clem's favorite.

The Disciple grunted and heaved Nicole's body over his shoulder.

"Why did you take my hood off?" I asked, feeling coldness wash through me. Why would they let me see the Hilltop?

The Lieutenant only smiled and shoved me forward. In we went.

The place was even more of a castle inside. The ceilings soared, stone walls punctuated with vast windows. The Lieutenant pushed me by the shoulders, making me move quickly, following the Disciple, Nicole's waterfall of red hair hanging over his shoulder. I twisted my head in every direction, absorbing as much as I could, trying to commit the details to memory as much as look for clues.

Massive paintings framed in gold hung on the walls, dark scenes from old-world masters. I tried to pause to catch details, but the Lieutenant shoved me. "Keep moving," he barked. "This isn't a tour."

Was this the home Don would've chosen if he'd managed to build an empire? It seemed like his taste, but I couldn't be sure. We rounded a corner, passed a door to another vast room, and I stopped in my tracks, Lieutenant be damned.

Weapons hung on foreboding red walls: mounted swords, crossbows, sinister daggers, ancient toothed devices to torture infidels and witches. In the corner sat a cannon.

The Lieutenant seized my throat, growling, "I said no stopping." But I didn't care. A weight lifted from my shoulders, my chest filling with light.

Sometimes, you just know. Sometimes, when you have a feeling deep in your gut, you have to trust your instincts. No matter the red herrings, the people trying to dissuade you, life beating you down. I'd been right all along: this red room could only belong to Don Rockwell.

I let the Lieutenant swing open a door at the end of the hallway and shove me down a set of stairs, thinking all the while, *It's him.*

We stepped into a dim, cavernous basement. I wasn't surprised to see more weapons on the walls, and gardening equipment, shovels, trowels, a watering can scattered over a long, low table near a single door.

All of it so familiar.

The Disciple dumped Nicole's body beside the long table, and the Lieutenant shoved me into a wooden chair so hard the chair and I tipped backward. He tugged the rope around my wrists, feeling its looseness. "Is this what had you feeling so chipper?"

He made quick work of retying the knot, until the rope dug into my wrists, but I didn't care. My eyes were fixed on the stairs. "Is Rachel coming?"

The Lieutenant lumbered into the corner, next to the Disciple. "My advice is to shut up and enjoy these last moments. Say your prayers to God."

"Don will come, too, right?" I remained glued to the stairs. "He has to."

The Lieutenant said nothing, and in the silence, I heard it: creaking footsteps. *She was coming.* I sat up straighter, nerves sparking, breath shallow.

Rachel, after all this time.

There was a final creak, and Laurel Hargrove stepped out of the stairwell and into the light. My Laurel.

The world faded into the white noise of shock. The woman I'd loved and lost stood before me in vivid color, her blond hair long as ever, pale skin flushed pink, eyes the same rich, dark brown, wide and blinking. Improbably, time had frozen her. She was the same as I remembered that last time I'd turned over my shoulder to find her in her cap and gown, measuring each step I took away from her.

My body, bound in the chair, became immaterial, as if I'd taken her death from her, a trade we'd worked out in an instant. And I believed, for a moment, that in the ferocity of my longing, the depths of my obsession, I'd somehow willed her into being.

She stared back, frozen at the bottom of the stairs.

She was alive. I'd grieved her, dreamed of her, given up everything to find her, and she'd been alive this whole time.

"The name she gave us is Shay Deroy," said the Lieutenant. "And it checked out. Chief says he'd know if she was law enforcement, but I don't think we can trust his judgment anymore. The man lost his mind over one of the daughters—"

"A *trailer park* brat," the Disciple interjected. "Two years out of high school. See for yourself; she's lying right there."

Laurel took a rough breath but didn't avert her gaze.

How was she alive? How was she... My thoughts froze when I realized. She was wearing a conservative, high-necked dress, buttons down the chest. Her legs glimmered with the slight sheen of pantyhose. The daughter's uniform.

"We told the Philosopher this was coming with the Chief," said the Disciple. "Same with those idiots in the city. They're liabilities. I'm telling you, they're going to mess up, right before the big move. I know the Chief's useful, but—"

"Leave." Laurel's voice was soft, the way it had been in college, but now there was an edge of steel.

Out of the corner of my eye, I saw the men exchange looks. "The girls were planning to run, and we stopped them," the Disciple started. "The Philosopher will want to—"

Laurel turned to them. "I'll make sure he knows you caught them."

"Where is he?" asked the Lieutenant.

"Out," she said, voice sharp. "You know this is a critical time. He's busy. Now leave."

The men stared, eyes narrowed and hateful. My heart pounded. Laurel was only a woman. Why would they listen to her?

The Lieutenant glanced at the Disciple. "Tell him we expect to hear from him soon. We can't let this go unaddressed. It was a breach, Rachel. It will sow doubt."

She didn't even flinch when he called her Rachel's name.

We waited in silence as the two men disappeared up the stairs, footsteps heavy, then down the hall, not even waiting until they were out of earshot to raise angry voices. We watched each other, two women in matching dresses, except mine was torn and dirty, hers pristine. The seconds ticked by until all traces of the men were gone, and the manor was silent.

I spoke quickly. "Whatever's going on, Laurel, I'll help you. I'll get you out."

It startled her. She snapped out of her hypnosis. "No. Don't."

"How are you alive?" I leaned forward as far as I could, the rope pinching my wrists. "They found your body."

She stepped closer, eyes wide with wonder. "I can't believe you're here."

The laugh cracked out of me. I was looking at a dead woman, and she was surprised to see *me*? "For fuck's sake, the whole world thinks you're dead."

"But why did you come back?" She stopped in front of me, legs brushing my knees. This close, I saw I'd been wrong: time hadn't frozen her. When she squinted, the tiniest lines feathered her eyes, like mine. "You weren't supposed to set foot in New York ever again."

"I came to *avenge* you." My voice rose, panic finally penetrating the shock. "But you're here. Where's Rachel? Where's Don?"

Laurel's expression hardened. "Why do you want to know?"

"You're kidding, right?" I blinked up at my best friend, the woman I'd loved for over a decade. "We were both supposed to get out of this place. Rachel *killed* Clem, Laurel. Did you know?"

She turned her head, sharp, but she wasn't surprised. She'd known.

I felt my grasp on the truth weakening. "Don brainwashed us. He ruined our lives, and Clem died, but we escaped." This was only a repeat of history, but I needed her to confirm it.

She shook her head. "We never escaped."

"I thought you'd been *murdered*. How could you think I wouldn't come?"

She spun away from me. "You were supposed to stay away."

"How did you get here? Is he holding you hostage?" I managed to yank my arms over the back of the chair and struggled to my feet, hands still bound behind me. "Explain, because I don't understand."

She stilled, her back to me. All I could see was her long, lovely hair, falling over her shoulders. I'd been haunted by the image of that hair swaying from a tree branch, hanging like a curtain over her sightless eyes. But here she was.

"We were best friends," I whispered, and the plea hung between us.

Her head turned. I could see her profile, her lips forming the soft words. "Do you remember, freshman year... You used to sleep on my floor sometimes."

I wished I could reach out and touch her, restitch her to me. "Of course. Nights you didn't want to be alone."

"I was such a child back then." A quiet eternity passed. Then Laurel's spine straightened, and her shoulders lifted. "Okay," she said. "I'll tell you the whole story."

CHAPTER THIRTY-FIVE

"After graduation," Laurel said, "you thought I was going back to live with my mother, but that was a lie. I couldn't imagine going back to that house…to being the one in charge, watching my mom drown herself in grief. Especially after knowing what it felt like to have a father again, someone who loved me enough to take care of me. Take charge.

"But you were always good at making decisions for us. Long before Don, there was you, and your ideas for what kind of girls we should be. You're shaking your head, but it's true. You walked into that basement freshman year and saved me, so I was happy to go anywhere with you for a while. You and Clem were my best friends. But I always owed you. I was the weak one, and you two were strong. There was no escaping that until we found Don and he gave me someone else to be.

"The day Clem died, and you wanted to leave him, I panicked and reverted to old habits: doing what you wanted. It wasn't until that night, lying next to you in Rothschild with our doors and windows locked, that I even realized I'd made a mistake. I'd never wanted to leave Don.

I'd said that to you and Clem a million times, but neither of you ever listened. But there I was, with you instead of him. Choosing you on reflex, out of some sense of guilt.

"I wanted to run back, throw myself at Don's feet and beg his forgiveness, but you were always around, watching. You wanted to spend every second together. I know... You were scared, and heartbroken. Well, so was I. You just couldn't see that I was desperate I might lose Don on top of Clem.

"From the moment you pulled me out, time was slipping through my fingers. I could feel it every day you made me get up and go to class, that stupid routine. When you made me go to the dean and she said she'd send the authorities, I couldn't wait any longer. I convinced you to go back to Don's house with some excuse about closure. I thought, as soon as I see him, I'll run, and Shay won't be able to stop me.

"But he was already gone. And it was *our* fault. He'd been brave enough to be honest with us about the way the world works, to offer us refuge, and we'd run away and twisted him to other people. I'll never forget your face when you saw the empty house. It was one of the worst days of my life, but you were so happy. I felt alone, like I lived in a world by myself. It was exactly how Don said we'd feel if we ever left him.

"I forced myself to keep hope alive that I'd find him. I knew I had to wait for graduation, when you'd leave. So I agreed to all the promises that made you happy. On graduation day, I could feel the noose loosening. With every step you took away from me, I could feel myself starting to breathe again. As soon as you drove away with your mom, I launched into motion.

"It was exciting at first, like I was a detective. A grown-up Nancy Drew. I remembered everything Don told me, places he'd been, restaurants he'd liked. There weren't many clues, because you know he didn't like to talk about himself. But I bought a car with the rest of the money from my dad's life insurance and drove all over the state, searching.

"Months went by without leads. I was living out of my car, at the end of my rope. Then one night when it started getting cold again, it hit me how stupid I was. There was no way Don had left the Hudson Valley forever. The business he'd been building was here.

"Don't look at me like that. There's no way you forgot the men he used to bring home. He was building a network of people who shared certain desires, who could help each other, do each other favors. I guess you were kind of oblivious back then—always in your head—but Clem and I saw exactly how ambitious Don was. Nights when she and I were alone, we used to talk about it, try to guess what he was planning. Clem got scared. I think that's why she was so desperate to leave. I really wish she hadn't gotten so worked up about it.

"Anyway, I realized Don must be lying low, making sure there was no blowback after we ran, and it would only be a matter of time. I had to be patient and keep my ear to the ground. In the meantime, I needed money and an excuse to stay in Don's social circle, to watch the men he'd make contact with whenever he came back. Catering seemed like a good solution—always at fancy private parties. I found the most high-end one and begged them to hire me.

"It took so long for something to happen. I can't tell you how excru-ciatingly lonely I was every day, nothing to fill my time but fantasies about the future. I'd rented a little apartment, and I used to walk around daydreaming. Sometimes hours would go by and I'd find myself stand-ing stock-still, staring into space. That's how hard I was trying to live with Don in my head.

"Then one day the catering firm got a job at the Hudson Mansion. I'd been interested in it because it was the exact kind of place Don would go, but they didn't like people sniffing around. I finally had an excuse to be there, and sure enough, not even an hour goes by, and who do I see standing across the room, drinking champagne? Mr. X.

"I can tell by your face that you remember him. I was so afraid he'd leave the party before I was done with work that I quit on the spot and cornered him on his way to the bathroom. He didn't recognize me. Can you believe that? I had to show him a picture I kept in my wallet, one with you, me, Clem, and Rachel. He remembered *you* immediately. He turned white as a sheet, told me to get the fuck away, that his family was there, that it was just a onetime thing, a mistake.

"I begged him to bring me to Don, but he swore he hadn't seen Don in over a year. I thought my heart would break. But then he said there was a new place for people who liked the sort of things we did. He wrote the name on the back of my picture. Tongue-Cut Sparrow. Said it was right under our feet in the Mansion itself.

"The first night I went to the Sparrow, I knew I'd find Don there eventually. It was his kind of place. I could almost feel him there. I just needed to keep putting myself out there, offering what he'd be looking for. So I started selling myself. It was good money, far better than I'd gotten catering, and it almost scratched the itch, that feeling I used to get with Don.

"I started bringing in so much cash I realized I would raise suspicions. So I created a company called Dominus Holdings, a little inside joke. Don't look so surprised. I have a degree from Whitney. You don't think I could?

"It continued that way for a while, me going to the Sparrow night after night, waiting for some glimpse of him. It was my trial. I'd betrayed him, and I was being punished for it. Then one night I turned the corner and there was Rachel, dolled up slicker than I'd ever seen her. We were both shocked, but she was quicker than me. She said, 'If you scream, I'll kill you.'

"It took me a second to realize she thought I hated them. I said, 'No, you've got it wrong. I've been looking for you.'

"She didn't trust me. She said, 'Why? You ran.'

"I was worried I wouldn't be able to explain, because Rachel wasn't good with emotions. I said, 'I never wanted to leave or get you in trouble. I tried coming back, but you and Don were already gone. I've been looking for you ever since.' I waved my arms at the Sparrow and said, 'That's why I'm here. It's all I've lived for.'

"Her face was blank, and I was terrified she'd leave, tell Don, and they'd pack up again. So I dropped to my knees in the middle of the Sparrow and begged her. I said, 'Please, take me to Don. I'm nothing without him. I'll do anything.'

"You and I both know Rachel never actually liked us. She must've been glad to see me so low. Because she smiled and said, 'I was supposed to bring back a girl anyway.'

"We drove far north to this squalid little house in a run-down town, somewhere I wouldn't have guessed in a million years. It was so unlike Don. It was heartbreaking to see him brought so low. I found out later he was still worried about what you and I had told people and was trying to stay invisible.

"But some things hadn't changed. He was waiting for us in the living room, sitting and reading a book, a glass of wine in his hand. When he saw me, he jumped to his feet. The look on his face... I can't describe it, Shay. It was worth everything. He didn't doubt me for a second. He rushed to me, swept me into his arms. It was the best moment of my life. So romantic. A homecoming.

"So I left my small life behind, used Dominus to keep covering my expenses so no one would come looking for me, and we were a family again. The way it was before, except better, because—sorry—you and Clem were gone. I had him all to myself. He finally let me in all the way, told me his dreams, what he was planning. And over the years, we've built it together. We created the Pater Society, a place where he could teach people and change lives, the way he did for me. You won't believe how it's taken off, what we're about to do. He's been successful beyond our wildest dreams. And I've shone, too. I love it here. Sewing dresses for the girls and tending Don's house. I'm his wife, in every way that matters.

"Stop looking at me like that. Don't you understand? Don and I are in love. We always have been. You just never wanted to see it."

CHAPTER THIRTY-SIX

All of it, from the beginning. I thought it had been done *to* Laurel. But the truth was, she'd been a willing player. She'd pulled the strings with Dominus, conned the caterer, helped found the Paters. As she spoke, it all came together, the little hints of Laurel I should've recognized: the costumes, the masks, the games and performances, the laurel crowns— her love of theater, everywhere. The Pater Society was Don's philosophy, brought to life by Laurel's passion, her careful work behind the scenes. I'd assumed she hated him, was just as scared of him as I was. But those weeping fits, the catatonic depression her landlord remembered… That wasn't poor, traumatized Laurel. It was Laurel grieving the possibility of never getting Don back.

What had I said to Jamie? *I have agency, too.* Yet I'd never seen Laurel's.

"Being in love—" she started.

"You're not in love." My hands twisted futilely behind me, scraped by the tightly knotted rope. "You're just the most brainwashed. The most in need of help."

She shook her head, brown eyes pitying. "I've thought about you so many times over the years. Felt guilty for the empty life you must be leading. I'm sorry for you, Shay. But you can't come back."

I swallowed, pushing past the bitterness to concentrate on what my instincts were telling me: *First, identify the threat.* "Where's Rachel?"

Laurel walked to the long, low table that held gardening equipment and picked up a trowel. "You know she was a sadist, right? A remorseless psychopath. She started killing girls who stepped out of line—without even talking to Don or me first. She just left us to deal with the mess."

The missing women. My heart was in my throat. "How did you deal with it?"

Laurel stopped twirling the trowel and gave me a long, steady look. Then she pointed it at the door. "We put them in the garden. We had no other choice."

The garden? Surely not—

Her voice grew softer. "Their bodies fertilize the flowers. It's beautiful, Shay. I made it for Clem, with all her favorites. She'd love it here."

Horror gripped me. It was true, then. Girls who went to the Hilltop never came back. It wasn't a mecca. It was a graveyard.

"Rachel was going to get caught," Laurel said. "Rumors started swirling. People on the outside started paying attention. Even the governor talked about it during some speech. It took all of our favors to keep things quiet." She frowned. "She was always in the way, from the beginning. Don's monstrous daughter."

"His real one?"

Laurel's eyes brightened. I'd hit on something she cared about. "*No.* Can you believe it? They weren't even related. Don just found her and felt sorry for her 'cause she was some foster runaway. So he took her in and treated her like family. The only good she ever did was lead Don to us."

Rachel and Don weren't related. A thousand memories came back—the lack of emotion between them, Rachel's nonchalance while we grew increasingly obsessed with her dad. Was she Don's first victim, or were they grifters together—two people who'd realized their proclivities aligned? Was Rachel the one who scouted us for Don, told him all about our vulnerabilities? We'd seen her as a ticket into Rothschild; she'd seen three young women ripe for deliverance.

"It doesn't matter that she wasn't his real daughter," Laurel said. "He treated her like one, and that was the problem. There couldn't be two favorites. And she was going to ruin the Paters before we could ever reach our goal, get to Albany. So I confronted her."

"You did?" I couldn't imagine it—shy, gentle Laurel against cold, vicious Rachel.

"I yelled and threatened her, but she wouldn't break. She just kept smiling at me because she knew she had the ultimate weapon. Her terrible secret. That's when she told me Clem hadn't chosen to die. Rachel chose for her."

My heart beat wildly in my chest. "How did she do it?"

"Somehow she found out Clem was planning to run. I think she used to spy on us. When she took Clem to campus that day, Clem snuck out of class and ran to Cargill to meet her soccer coach. She didn't realize Rachel was following her."

Laurel walked across the room and stopped at a low wooden chest, pulling open the top drawer. She slipped a hand inside and tugged out a glass-topped box, flipped the hinges, and drew an object from its crushed-velvet bed.

The pugio. I would recognize it anywhere. In Laurel's hands the dagger was oversized, the metal blackened with age, its tip ending in the narrowest point, like a needle. Lethal delicacy.

She turned it in her hands. "Rachel used this. Held it to Clem's throat, forced her to put her head through the loop in the rope. Sliced her up. Forced her to carve the words into her arm."

Thin cuts, like from a razor blade. But it hadn't been a razor blade that made those marks on Clem's body; it had been an ancient Roman weapon.

"I'm sure she used it because she thought Don would approve. Rachel said she'd been planning how to kill each of us from the moment she moved into the suite." Laurel walked toward me, holding the knife. "When she told me what she did, it was the strangest thing. This calmness came over me. It was like I was an actor in a play. In an instant, I'd plotted it all out in my head. The entire scene."

The truth hit me. "You killed her."

Laurel met my eyes, unblinking. "She killed Clem first."

"You hung her outside the theater."

Laurel stared at me, eyes large and intense. "Poetic justice. Besides, I needed people"—her voice caught—"to think she was me. No one would come after me if they thought I was the one who died. I could get rid of her, and in one fell swoop, Clem would have her vengeance, the Paters would lose our greatest liability, and Don would be mine. She looked so much like me, remember? Like we were sisters. Don always used to say that, no matter how much I hated it. I finally put it to good use."

She shook her head. "Rachel fought me, obviously. I wasn't as good at hurting people as she was. I couldn't get her to write the letters. But I managed the important part, in the end. And everything I messed up, the Chief fixed." She flashed her teeth in a way that reminded me, eerily, of the Paters and their wolf smiles. "I'm sure your literary brain can tell me what kind of irony that is, the Chief cleaning up after me. Dramatic? Tragic?"

I was silent, and she rolled her eyes. "Don't tell me you wish she was still alive, you liar. You hated her, too."

I searched myself, trying to locate remorse for Rachel's death, but she was right. All I felt was numb horror at what Laurel was capable of. "Don wasn't angry?"

She resumed her path toward me, idly scratching the blackened knife. "Maybe a little. But you remember how pragmatic he is. He helped with the cops, then he helped me bury her." She glanced at the door. "It's been the two of us ever since. Blissful, like a honeymoon."

In my weakest moments I'd fantasized about seeing my dead friend again. The things I'd tell her, the way I'd hold her. But this was nothing like I'd imagined. The reality seeped in, grave and deadly. Laurel was alive, she'd killed Rachel, and Don hadn't skipped a beat. If that was true, what would he do to me, the woman who'd betrayed him?

"Laurel." Her chin snapped in my direction, dreamy expression gone. "He'll kill me if he finds me here. Please, help me escape."

For a second, she just stood there, knife in her hands. Then a strange darkness passed over her face. "He's not going to kill you, Shay. He used to love you best."

"What?"

She searched my face. "And why wouldn't he? Since the day we met, I was half in love with you myself. It's your superpower. I used to dream about slipping into your skin, just for a day." She smiled wistfully. "Cracking open that head and sneaking in to read your thoughts, know what it was like to be so beautiful you could turn any man's head. Tell me the truth."

My breath caught.

"Is it everything?"

I couldn't speak—didn't know where to start—and the smile washed from her face. "If he sees you again, he'll want you. You're the only threat left." She was close enough now to touch. "I never thought you'd come back."

"Don't talk like that. We're not competing." I took the risk and reached for her, feeling the paper-thin skin of her hand. "You're my best friend. You always have been."

Tenderness softened her face. She reached for me, pulling me into her arms. I blinked over her shoulder, my hands still bound behind me, heart pounding. It was like a fog had lifted, and there she was, the real Laurel. The one I remembered.

From the floor above came the unsticking sound of a door opening, then slamming shut. A deep voice boomed through the house: "*Laurel.*" It was the same voice that haunted me, that had reached inside my brain and my heart, seducing and violating.

It was Don, close enough to touch.

Do it, the dark voice urged. *Go back, give in, beg his forgiveness.*

Laurel and I wrenched away from each other, wild-eyed. Her nails dug into my skin. In that moment, the past echoed back, and we were twenty-one again, sharing the same look we'd shared a million times before: Don was home, and we were in trouble.

"Where are you?" he called. "I have good news. Everything's ready."

The air became electric, desperate, as we stared at each other. A decision hung between us.

Laurel lunged. Too fast for me to do anything but cringe, understanding the worst was happening—but instead of the searing pain of the pugio in my stomach, the rope binding my wrists pulled sharply, then released. The tatters fell to the floor. My wrists were free. I could only blink in shock as she ran to the back door and ripped it open, revealing the garden and forest at dusk. "*Run*, Shay."

I darted forward and seized her. "Come with me."

She shook her head. "I need to distract him. Trust me."

"Please," I begged. "We can start over together."

The basement stairs groaned under the unmistakable weight of footsteps.

"I love you, Laurel." I forced myself to breathe. "Come with me."

"Go now," she whispered, her eyes bright with fear, "or else I swear you'll never leave."

CHAPTER THIRTY-SEVEN

I tore across the grass, terror pumping my legs. Past the ornate swimming pool, sculpted out of rock; past the verdant garden, bursting with brilliant autumn flowers, lush from the unnatural soil. I paused only at the edge of the forest to look back, and there she was, standing in the half-cracked door, watching me flee with a look I couldn't read. It had to be sadness. It had to be.

A shadow appeared over her shoulder.

I plunged into the trees and kept going until dusk dissolved into night. I didn't know where I was, but I searched for some sign of people, a phone to call Jamie. Eventually I came to a road, softly illuminated. I expected to keep along it until I came to a gas station, or maybe even a town, but to my surprise, after only a few minutes, an old wood-sided sedan pulled to the side of the road. An elderly woman with white hair leaned out the passenger window and called, "Do you need a ride?"

I squinted into the car. A little old man sat in the driver's seat, trying to puzzle me out. He raised two bottle-brush eyebrows. "We're on our way home to Woodstock. Saw you and thought you might need a lift. Old habits, you know."

"I only need to borrow a phone," I said, wrapping my arms tight around me. "I'd be very grateful."

They were happy to give me their cell phone, one of those big, clunky models with buttons, and watched me with unmasked curiosity as I dialed Jamie.

"Hello?" His voice was strangled.

"It's me."

A noise of relief broke from him. "Thank god. Where are you? What happened? I didn't know—"

"I'll tell you everything, but first I need you to come get me. I'm somewhere in the Adirondacks." I glanced at the couple in the car.

"Off Highway 30," the woman supplied. "Near Upper Saranac Lake."

I repeated it to Jamie, and he swore he'd be there as fast as possible. To my chagrin, the couple insisted on waiting with me. Despite their seeming kindness—the man called himself an old hippie—distrust kept me on the side of the road instead of in their warm car. Another hour passed, our conversation growing stilted, before headlights swept around the corner and I recognized my rental car pulling off the road.

I'd barely stood before Jamie was there. He swept me in his arms and clutched my head to his chest. When he released me, he looked at the couple in the car and shoved himself through the open window, hugging the old woman, thanking her profusely. Her cheeks turned pink, and I knew that was the kind of gratitude she'd been waiting for. Jamie always knew how to give people what they wanted.

On the ride home, as the car sailed over the mountains in the dark, I curled in the passenger seat and told him everything. When I was done, I pulled out the recording device from where it had been wedged inside my bra and set it in the cup holder. Such a small thing, holding such weighty evidence.

Jamie didn't say a word when I told him Laurel was alive—only stared ahead, frowning into the darkness. I didn't know whether he was shocked or could feel the sand moving faster through the hourglass like I could, time slipping full tilt. Maybe he could sense the inferno under my skin, no longer simmering but roiling. I almost asked him, but then I thought, *No. Let him be shielded. One of us should be.*

Jamie woke me when the light was still dawn-bright. His face was grim, and I could tell he hadn't slept. "I'm sorry," he said, hovering. "But there's a lot I didn't say last night that I need to tell you now."

I sat up, realizing I was in our hotel bed, still wearing my forest-ravaged dress. I tugged at my ripped pantyhose, peeling them off. "I'm awake," I said, unfastening the pearl buttons down my chest. "Talk to me."

He sat on the bed and looked at me cautiously, like I was a vase balancing on the edge of a table. "I didn't want to tell you last night, but Dougie found Greg Ellworth. You were right. He lives in the city and used to work in finance, at a trading company called Culver Brown."

"That's good, right? We can give that to the governor with the recordings."

Jamie swallowed. "The thing is...Greg Ellworth works in politics now."

My fingers stilled over the buttons.

"He works for Governor Barry, Shay. He's one of his campaign managers."

Alec Barry, our ally. The man who would help us bring down the

Paters and use that to fuel his reelection campaign. I blinked. "What does that mean?"

"I never thought—" Jamie's hand moved over the sheets but stilled before it reached me. "I'm so sorry. I thought he was a good person. I never thought to look."

"I don't understand."

His hand curled into a fist. "The governor's throwing a big party tonight. He's going to announce a major reform initiative, the cornerstone of his reelection campaign. Rumors are it's this huge policy package, and it's going to change everything—health care, education, law enforcement, on and on. Supposed to be some great model other states can copy. Press is invited, DNC bigwigs, the whole nine yards. He's holding it at the home of one of his biggest donors. If it wasn't for you, Dougie never would've looked at who that was."

I heard Don's voice, echoing from the floor above: *I have good news. Everything's ready.*

"He goes by the name Nico Stagiritis," Jamie said. "Does that mean anything to you?"

Nicole had said the Philosopher was Greek. And of course, who had Don admired more than the so-called fathers of Western thought? I remembered sitting at his feet in his library, memorizing details about the men he revered. "Aristotle was born in the town of Stagira. His father's name was Nicomachus."

"I'm certain," Jamie said softly, "that Nico is Don."

Don had given himself a name on par with Aristotle. Fashioning himself as a leader whose ideas would transform the world.

"That means—" Jamie started, but I was already there.

"The governor is a Pater." In public, a celebrated progressive; in private, a man who harmed women. "No wonder they're so brazen. Who would touch them, with the police and the governor—all of New

York's most powerful men—on their side?" *Why should I be worried?* the Incel had asked. *Everyone we know is here.*

"The governor's also going to announce a task force that will lead the initiative," Jamie said. "It's a group of his top donors, including Nico. Dougie sent the list. There are a few names I recognize—Reginald Carruthers, Adam Dorsey, Angelo De Luca, Pastor Michael Corbin. Before he was a pastor, it turns out he served in the army."

I thought of the Lieutenant's ramrod posture, his militant alertness. "That makes sense."

"But there are some names I don't know." Jamie pulled out his phone and showed me a picture from a browser search. "Scott Richards. Incarcerated on domestic assault charges twenty years ago, then got out and started a private prison company. Now he's a Fortune 500 CEO."

"The Disciple," I said, looking at the shot of him, dressed up at some party. "Give me more."

"There's a Steven Tiller who works at Culver Brown, the trading company Greg Ellworth used to work for. Apparently, Tiller made a windfall off PrismTech stock right after the company announced it was moving to New York. I'd bet anything on insider trading, because the governor was the one who brokered the deal and authorized the Prism tax cuts. I bet that's how they've built up so much wealth. They're pulling strings for each other."

"Tiller's the Incel." His greasy face stared back at me from the phone. I remembered what the guys had said the night of the party: *The old guard hates him, no matter what he pulls with those tech tips.* All of it was tying together, all our weeks of work. I could connect each face with a name.

"This initiative with the governor," I said. "It has to be part of the Paters' big plan, what Don's been building to. Angelo mentioned a culture war, a way to put the Paters in control."

"If Barry gets reelected and puts the Paters in power," Jamie said, "they can roll back protections for women, stop access to health care, change what kids learn in school, create lesser punishments for abusers. The Paters are so good at twisting things, I'm sure they'd find a way to make people think it's progressive. They could do so much damage."

"What do we do? Who do we take our evidence to now?"

Weariness washed over Jamie's face. He dropped his phone on the bed, shoulders slumping. "Not the state police... Word will go straight to Governor Barry. Maybe the FBI? There's a field office in Albany. But Shay, the truth is, I don't know if we can trust them. They're in Albany, so what if Barry's gotten to them? This is bigger than I thought. It's like they're everywhere."

Where to turn for help when everyone was a suspect? I thought back to freshman year, the way the police station had grown silent and tense, all those faces turning to us as Dorsey chewed us out. I thought of the tribunal waiting for me in the high school principal's office: Ruskin, the guidance counselor, even the superintendent. My life with Cal, day after day: the way he'd laughed with all his friends as they talked about board meetings and golf scores, while the rest of us, the carbon-copy wives, watched them, making our small lives in the margins of theirs.

The Paters had always been everywhere.

"I can't get over the governor," Jamie said. "He seemed so genuine. And he's done so much good. I can't imagine there's something this broken inside him. How does he hide it?"

"They're not broken," I said. "They're working exactly like they're supposed to." I thought of what Nicole had said. "What the Paters teach about men and women is what a lot of the world already believes, even if they don't say it out loud. That's how Barry can blend in. The Paters act like they're victims, but really, they're in the majority."

Jamie reached for my hands. "What if we can't trust the FBI?"

"There will be another way," I started to say, but he said "*Shay*" so sharply I stopped. His eyes were fixed on me, bright with fear. "Barry's the incumbent. He's *going* to get reelected. What if there's no one left to help?"

Jamie was spinning out. The enormity of what we were facing, of having our backs to the wall, was hitting him for the first time. But I'd been here before, a thousand times. "Jamie, it's always been on us."

I withdrew my hands and stood, ruined dress slipping to the floor. "That's why I'm going back to the Hilltop."

"What?" He rose. "Are you crazy?"

"I have to get Laurel to leave with me." She'd said it, but I'd let it slip by: *Rachel was going to ruin the Paters before we could ever reach our goal, get to Albany.* If I let Laurel go with Don to the capital, I'd never get her back. There was no one left to care about her but me.

"That's not how it works." Jamie's body bent toward me. "They know about you now. They want to *kill* you."

"You said they're having a party." The beginnings of the plan wove together, the kind of thing Clem would do—go straight to the source, kick the house down, refuse to let them get away with it. "That gives me a chance to sneak in. I'll pretend to be press or a caterer, whatever. I'll find Laurel, convince her to leave, and we'll slip out while Don's distracted with politics."

Jamie shook his head. "Even if you can get in, what makes you think you can get her to go? She's a cult *leader*, Shay, not just a victim. You have to face the facts."

I held his gaze. "You know better than anyone that I've made bad choices, too. Am I beyond saving?"

Instead of answering, he paced away. Tension radiated from him, hunching his shoulders. "You're going through the nine circles of hell to drag back a woman who doesn't want to be rescued. This goddamn savior complex of yours is going to get you killed."

His sharp words sliced me. "She's like a sister, Jamie. And she protected me by distracting Don. You should've seen the look on her face right before I ran. I know I can get her to leave. I just need more time."

But he was shaking his head.

"I promised I would protect her."

He was silent, so I turned for the bathroom. I needed a shower.

"Wait." Jamie sounded like the word cost him. "If you're going, the only way to keep you safe is to blow the lid off the Paters. Break the story wide so no one can make it go away—not the Paters, or the police, or the governor's campaign. I've never broken news on my podcast before, but maybe if I released an emergency episode, a follow-up to the first Laurel piece, with clips from our recordings, people would listen. If I asked my listeners to make noise on Twitter, even call the FBI, maybe they'd do it. I have a big following, mostly women. They could be our shield."

"Dorsey did say his office was flooded with calls from your listeners after your episode on Laurel. And you didn't even ask them to do it."

"The headlines will all say 'True-Crime Podcast Host Attacks New York Governor.'"

"Hey, you don't—" I started.

He shook his head. "You warned me."

"Are you okay with that?"

His eyes softened, and he huffed a laugh. "Yeah. Compared to what you're doing, it's nothing. Besides, there happens to be this woman I'd give anything to protect, too."

We looked at each other until he drew a deep breath. "I'll call my producers. I bet we can have the story up in hours."

"No," I said quickly. "If you do it now, Governor Barry will just cancel his party, and Don will take off. Who knows if I'll ever get Laurel back? You have to wait until we're inside."

"That's insane."

"I know. But when will I get another chance like this?" I was an expert in desperate opportunities.

He frowned. "Fine. I'll have my producers get it ready, but we'll wait to go live. Shay." His hand stirred by his side, as if he wanted to reach out and touch me. "I know it feels like it, but you're not alone."

I held out my hand to him. "Come with me."

They'll ask you what you knew and when you knew it. It's important to pinpoint this knowing, to establish when you made certain decisions. Whether your actions were premeditated or the result of the heat of the moment. If I were ever to tell them, I might say it was this moment, as the shower water beat over me and Jamie's hands carved down my body, that the seed of what would happen took root.

Of course, that might be a lie. It could have been much earlier. Perhaps when I felt the stirrings of the familiar inferno, or back further, the moment I heard Laurel's name on Jamie's podcast, the day I escaped from Don's house, the school fire, the first evening I picked up *The Thousand and One Nights* and started reading, heart flooding with recognition. Perhaps it was all the way back to 9:38 on a Tuesday night, ten years old. I could have been hurtling toward this all my life.

Or maybe it was the heat after all. All that passion. A thing I did when I wasn't in my right mind, when I couldn't fully consent, even to myself.

Impossible to say.

I guess you get to decide.

CHAPTER THIRTY-EIGHT

I stood outside the house like so many nights before, preparing myself. Unlike at the other Pater gatherings, which unfolded in the shadows, the Hilltop buzzed with people, an explosion of camera crews and caterers, aides jogging the grounds, guests in tuxedos and floor-length gowns. Anticipation charged the air. Everyone here knew what the governor's announcement would be. They weren't here to be surprised; they were here to be part of history.

The Hilltop was lit by torches on the walls, all its doors thrown open, music pouring out. It was a sight to behold from the end of the long driveway. Don's castle upon the hill.

Jamie rushed back, scrubbing his hands through his hair. "My team's ready to drop the episode. We have posts ready to go to our email list and across every social platform. All we need is to tell them to press the button." He smiled weakly. "Then none of them can hurt you."

He's not going to kill you, Shay, I heard Laurel say. *He used to love you best.*

I shook my head. "Of course they won't."

The security man at the door squinted at Jamie's ID, then down at his list. I held my breath, praying Jamie's producers had come through.

"Merciless Media?" The man gave Jamie a doubtful look. "Never heard of it."

"It's a podcast company." Jamie smiled pleasantly. "You know, the future of journalism."

The security man shrugged. "Whatever you are, you're on the list." He pointed at me, giving my jeans and sweater a once-over. "She your plus-one?"

"My assistant," Jamie said smoothly, and the words worked like magic. The security guard immediately dismissed me. "Yeah, all right," he said. "Next."

The party was concentrated in an enormous marble-floored room with high windows, a space that reminded me of a Regency ballroom. Except it was lined with mounted TV cameras, all facing a stage they'd set up for the governor's announcement. I could tell immediately where the governor was because a crowd thronged around him. When the bodies shifted, I caught a glimpse of him: smooth-skinned, hair coiffed like a helmet, broad shoulders encased in an immaculate tuxedo. Even more handsome than he looked on TV.

"Over there," Jamie whispered. "That's the head of the DNC, talking to the New York City mayor."

I looked at all the dressed-up people, taking a moment to let the enormity of what Don had accomplished sink in. All of upper-crust New York was here. In the crowd, I spotted the familiar face of the Lieutenant, standing next to a woman I recognized as his wife. I whipped my head down.

"What's wrong?" Jamie hissed.

"Michael Corbin." I nodded in his direction.

Jamie's eyes gleamed. "I hope they're all here. Every last one of them, with their families and friends."

I scanned the crowd. No Laurel or Don. But there, in the corner near the string quartet, was Reginald Carruthers, in a tuxedo with tails. A woman about his age had her arm twined through his—maybe his wife.

Jamie gripped my shoulders. "Are you ready? You find Laurel, and I'll call my team?"

I looked down. One of Jamie's knee was shaking. "Are *you* ready?"

He swallowed. "I'm scared, to be honest. But I don't know what else to do. My team will send the evidence to the feds once the episode is out, and I'll call them myself, tell them there's people in immediate danger. Find her fast, okay? Fast, then out."

"Okay."

He leaned forward and caught my face, kissing me on the forehead. "If she doesn't want to come," he murmured, "leave her." Then he turned, and I watched him knife through the crowd.

With Jamie gone, I moved slowly, keeping a careful eye on the people around me, searching for pale hair and paler skin. It occurred to me: if Laurel wasn't at the party, she might still be getting ready, planning some big entrance. She might be alone somewhere in the mansion.

With one last glance at the Lieutenant and Marquis, I slipped out of the ballroom and into the hallway I recognized, the one that led to the basement. I needed to go in the opposite direction—upstairs, where the bedrooms would be. Did Laurel have her own, or did she share with Don? Was it true they were practically married?

The promise of her drew me forward. Once more, I was Sleeping Beauty, moving by instinct, hand outstretched toward the spindle. I wondered how long it would take to find her, when every turn pushed me farther into the maze of this sprawling place, and every new wall jolted me with pieces of art so perfectly in Don's taste they felt haunted, like he was inside them, watching. I came to a fork in the hall and chose left instead of right. Turned, and froze.

I faced an open door—a room with nothing but an enormous painting, covering the expanse of a wall. In it, a beautiful woman with long hair the color of moonlight, falling into the arms of a tall, black-cloaked figure, its hood hiding its face. Two skeletal hands snaked from the figure's cloak, gripping the woman by the waist.

I took a staggering step forward, transfixed.

"*Death and the Maiden*," said a deep, familiar voice. "It has the same effect on me."

Don Rockwell. Standing at the end of the hall, framed by the walls like he was yet another painting, a second dark, beautiful Death.

He pulled me like a magnet, even after all this time.

My body went to war. My heart raced, but my limbs turned to stone. All I could do was stand there, drinking him in. He looked exactly like I remembered. Tall and broad-shouldered, filling every inch of his tuxedo. He radiated authority, like he always had. I felt his dark eyes travel over my body, and the weight of his gaze created a visceral sensation, like the brush of a fingertip.

I'd never really imagined…couldn't actually believe—

You found me, the dark voice whispered. *You're home.*

"Shay," he said thickly. My name on his lips was an intimacy, shortening the space between us. "You came back."

His gaze was locked on me, and it was intoxicating. My mouth went dry. *Move*, I urged myself, but I was rooted.

He strode toward me, each step luxuriously slow. *Scream*, I told myself. *Run.*

He stopped in front of me, wonder on his face. "How is it possible you're even more beautiful? You're like a fairy tale come to life."

I opened my mouth, but all I could do was take him in. The face I'd visited in countless dreams, tracing with my thumb one minute, recoiling from the next. The voice that could reach inside me, stirring, then paralyzing.

He shook his head. "Whatever you're thinking, I don't care. I only care that you're back."

He cupped my face in his large, warm hand and gave me a blinding smile. The sheer magnetism of him.

"I knew you'd come back," he murmured, drawing closer. "Knew you were still my girl."

His girl. I remembered… Of course I did. The girl who lived for him to touch her, push her against the wall, bend her over his bed, until she staggered with the pleasure of rock bottom. With him I'd practiced throwing myself away. Experimented with releasing hold of the ego I'd once deemed so precious, guarded so protectively. It had been a kind of freedom—twisted, but true.

Don stroked his thumbs over my cheekbones, and I felt it again: the tempting pull of self-annihilation.

I shook my head, told myself to resist, but maybe that was part of the attraction. Because when Don drew my mouth to his, when he kissed me, I let him in. His tongue brushed my lips, and I was inside my body and outside it, two people.

"You taste like home," he whispered. "Just like I remember."

Home—that's what I'd thought the moment I saw him. The same word from his mouth jarred me. Had it been my own thought, or was it one he'd given me years ago, repeated until I couldn't tell the difference? Whose dark voice was in my head—the one that whispered things that made me feel irredeemable—was it mine, or his?

No, I hadn't escaped Don. Not when I carried him inside me everywhere I went.

He leaned in to kiss me again, but I turned my head.

"Shay." His voice was admonishing. "It's me."

"And who is that?" I asked. "Nico Stagiritis? The Philosopher? The man behind the governor?"

His eyes widened. Surprised by what I was capable of.

"I didn't come here for you," I said. "I came for your daughters."

Don's face darkened, the transformation still uncanny. An instinctive fear crawled through me, lifting the hairs on my arms. "What do you know?" he asked.

I took a step back. "You can't touch me. If you do, the whole world—"

I didn't even finish before he lunged. I tried to twist away, to push him, but he seized me, one hand wrapping painfully around my throat, the other pressed hard over my mouth. He jerked me close and whispered, "Don't you dare tell me what to do."

I tried to kick against the walls, bite his hand, but he wrestled me forward, squeezing my windpipe. My limbs relaxed, obeying the lack of oxygen. We came back to the familiar hall, and there—a person! A man walked toward us, someone who would help. Don jerked to a stop, but I launched into motion, trying to scream, wave my arms, convey terror. For a moment, the man stared at me, transfixed. Then he glanced up at Don, gave the slightest nod, and passed without stopping.

I heard Jamie's voice, mixed with the sound of the man's retreating footsteps: *They're everywhere.*

Don dragged my limp weight to the end of the hall, wrenched open the door, and threw me headfirst down the stairs.

CHAPTER THIRTY-NINE

A great weight crushed me, trying to stop my heart, push fingers up my nose, fill my mouth with bitterness. My whole body jerked as I came to, but it was like I was an infant, tightly swaddled—something bound my limbs to my side.

I blinked my eyes open but grit stung them, and all I could sense was suffocating darkness. Then I recognized the taste in my mouth.

Dirt. I was encased in it.

The realization was like an electric shock to my chest, and all conscious thought fled. I clawed, kicking upward, pushing against the ground that wanted to choke me. My lungs were burning, vision blurring, but I scratched and scratched. Just when I thought there was no hope, when I sucked in dirt and it coated the roof of my mouth, one arm wrenched free, and with that I dug at the earth covering my face.

Suddenly there was air, sweet and rich with rotting leaves. I gasped, sucking it in, and ripped myself out of the ground, shoving dirt off my legs until I tumbled into the grass, choking, coughing up black. I opened my mouth and screamed.

My cry dissolved into the sound of someone laughing. I turned, swiping dirt out of my eyes, and found Don sitting in a lawn chair, one leg crossed over the other, chuckling. His tuxedo jacket was tossed over the back of the chair, his shirtsleeves rolled up. He raised a glass of scotch to me. "I wasn't sure how this would end." His voice was silky and amused. "But good for you."

When I opened my mouth, the voice that came out was a feral creature's. "You buried me in the garden."

His smile stayed fixed. "A little taste of what it's like." He gestured at the shallow grave where he'd buried me. Next to it, a vined plant's arms stretched toward me like it was pleading. "You said you came for my daughters. Well—here they are."

"*Somebody help!*" I screamed.

Don laughed and rose, towering over me as I crawled backward. "Dearest. No one can hear you. That's what the band's for." He grinned up at the mansion. "And it's Wagner. Perfect."

"*Jamie!*" I screamed. "*Help!*" But it was futile, of course. Jamie was inside, on the phone with his producers or the FBI. He'd never find me in time.

Don jerked his hand and his scotch flew out, hitting me in the face, burning my eyes. "*Enough.*"

I tried to stagger to my feet, toward the Hilltop, glowing with lights, but Don was already on top of me. He kicked me lightning-fast, and I slammed back against the grass, unable to breathe against the radiating pain.

He crouched and peered down at me. There was no pity on his face, only curiosity. Over his shoulder, the first stars were visible in the dusky, orange-violet sky.

"Let me go," I whispered, though speaking made my chest ache. In my head, I told the stars, *If you feel a single ounce of compassion…*

"Never," Don said and cracked his scotch glass against my head.

I was aware of being dragged. Of being a thing that bumped and bounced across the grass. But then Don picked me up, wiping the warm, sticky blood from my temple. He carried me through the door like a newlywed carrying his wife over the threshold, and we were back in the warm, stifling basement. Don sat me in the same chair the Lieutenant had dumped me in only yesterday.

My head lolled back, but he seized my chin and righted it, dropping to a knee. When my vision sharpened, I saw he was staring intently at my face.

"You've always liked it so rough," he murmured, stroking my face. "Strange creature. Eight years is a long time to wait for you. But there's nothing better than delayed gratification, is there? You learned that from me."

He kissed me gently on the forehead, then rose, walking to the wooden weapon chest. Almost absently, he pulled the drawers open, one by one. I knew what he was looking for before he found it—same as Laurel, of course, because so much of who we were was an echo of him. This man who'd reached into our brains when we were young.

There it was, the blackened dagger with the needle tip.

He turned with the knife, looking down at me with heat in his eyes, the way a man looks at a lover. His strong jaw was even more pronounced with a five-o'clock shadow. He looked almost love-drunk.

My hands weren't bound, but the moment I shifted in my chair, Don was beside me, pulling off my jacket, seizing the thin cotton of my shirt and rubbing the dagger against it until the fabric tore. He ripped a line up my shirt, rending it in two.

"I'll tell you a secret." His voice was low. "All this time away has made me needy." He pressed his lips to my chest; I felt the heat of his mouth on my skin when he spoke. "Did you ever guess one day I'd fall on my knees for *you*?"

The words were intoxicating, each a little cup of wine. Eight years ago, I would have drunk them until I was senseless.

"You need me," I murmured into his hair. "Because you're nothing without us."

He leaned back and grinned, placing the point of the pugio in the dip of my collarbone and dragging down, drawing a razor-thin line of blood between my breasts. The tip of the dagger came to rest against the underwire that held my bra together. "I love you and your games," he murmured. "Running away, telling your teachers I'm a bad man, showing up unannounced after years. What will you think of next?"

"You used to say I was pathetic, but you were the pathetic one. Just as desperate for validation as us." My throat was raw. "You did everything to make us think we couldn't live without you. You knew that's the only way we'd follow you. You were a parasite."

"Look what I did." Don flung his hand at the ceiling. Above us, music swelled, and raucous applause broke out. "I built you a kingdom. I'm remaking the world. I'm close, and once I'm there, you can have it, too. If that's not love, I don't know what is."

"You *used* me." The words flew from me. "I wanted affection, and you preyed on me."

"No." He pointed the pugio at the line of blood bisecting my heart. "You sought *me* out. *You* were obsessed with *me*. When do you think the idea for the Paters first came to me? Not with Rachel—with *you*. The little feminist beauty queen. If I could get *you* to fall to your knees, who else? How far could I take it? You opened a world of possibility."

"You *tortured* me." I choked on the words.

"Don't rewrite history," he said. "Don't twist what happened between us because you went out into the world and someone made you feel ashamed. You begged me to be with you."

Hot tears tracked down my cheeks. "That doesn't mean it was right."

"Come back to me," he said. "We're on the verge of something. The entire reason I built the Paters is coming together as we speak. You're back in time to see us make history. We're going to rise up and take back our country, piece by piece."

"Fuck you," I said, hands shaking.

"Come back and be mine."

A strangled sound came from the staircase. Laurel stepped out from the dark, her eyes bloodshot, mascara making twin tracks down her cheeks, her too-thin figure wrapped in an ice-blue ballgown fit for a queen. She stared at him. "After everything?"

The minute Don turned to her, I lunged from the chair and ran to the wooden chest, shoving my hands inside and pulling out the first thing my fingers touched: the smooth handle of a hatchet, surprisingly heavy. I gripped it in both hands and held it out in front of me.

Don and Laurel froze.

"Laurel," I said sharply, stepping closer to the stairs. "You heard him. Don, Nico, whatever his name is—he's a fake. He doesn't care about you."

Don blinked for a second at the weapon in my hands; then a grin spread over his face. "The old Norse battle-ax. God does have a sense of humor." He turned to Laurel. "You know who I am. What I've done for you. You know my heart better than anyone. Don't let her manipulate you."

"He's the one manipulating." I edged closer to the staircase and

ASHLEY WINSTEAD

Laurel tensed, looking back and forth between us. "What he's doing to you and the other women isn't right. It's torture. He's sick, Laurel, and he's making you sick, too. What would your father say?"

She made that strangled sound again.

"What would he say if he saw you being treated this way?" I knew I was fighting dirty, but I had to win. "Leave with me. *Please*."

Don put his hands up in surrender. "I'll show you how much I trust you." He walked to her, and she shrunk back like a kicked dog.

"Get away—" I started, but he handed Laurel the dagger, hilt first. "Take it," he said. "You have the power now. Total free will."

She snatched the knife and glanced at me, eyes tracking over my torn shirt, the long cut down my chest.

I pulled the ripped pieces together. "I know it's hard to leave him. Trust me. But listen to that voice of doubt. That's your sanity, your survival instincts. Deep down you know what Don's doing isn't right."

She wavered, biting her lip. "The Paters are done for," I said, pressing my hand. "Any minute now. We're going to put them away."

"What are you talking about?" Don snapped.

I kept my attention on her. "It's all going to come crumbling down. Everyone's going to know exactly who Don is, and what he's done. All the Paters are going to jail."

She blinked. "They'll know about me?"

"They'll know he exploited you," I said quickly.

"Rachel's murder," Don said softly. "If they find out, the police won't look kindly on that."

"I had to do it," Laurel choked out. "But I'll rot for it."

I shook my head. "No, they'll see you were manipulated." What she'd done was horrible, but it wasn't really her fault—none of this was. She'd been coerced by her conditioning. Yes, she had agency, but she was also a victim. People would understand.

362

"Laurel," Don said, and though his voice was silky, she flinched. "You're my good girl, aren't you?"

She nodded, chin bobbing fast.

"And you're mine?" he asked, voice deepening. "Body and soul?"

She choked out a yes.

"Stop it. You don't belong to anyone, Laurel." I was so close to her now.

"Put the pugio to your throat," Don said, and both Laurel and I froze.

"What?" she whispered.

"Show me how obedient you are. Show me why I should love you more than anyone."

I watched the words snake inside her, flip a switch—and to my horror, Laurel tipped the black blade to her throat.

"*Stop*," I cried.

"Drop the ax," Don said to me, "or she'll slit her throat."

"She would never." I was so close to the staircase, to escape. I edged forward.

"Do it, Laurel," Don urged, and she drew the knife against her skin.

"*No!*" I threw the ax to the floor, where it clattered. For all I'd witnessed, I'd never imagined Don had this kind of power.

"Good." His eyes flicked from the ax to me. "Now get on your knees."

I looked at Laurel. Terror and sadness radiated from her, but I couldn't tell who she was scared for, what she was mourning. I could've sworn there was an apology in her eyes, but the truth was, I couldn't read her. Not after all this time.

I dropped to my knees on the cold basement floor.

Don stepped closer, until we formed a triangle. "My first girls," he murmured. The music cut out above us, and a deep voice rang out, the voice of a triumphant politician.

"We're not yours," I said and spit on his shoes. "Never."

He looked at his feet for a moment, then up at me. His jaw tightened; I could see his fury, his outrage at being denied. He turned to Laurel. "Kill yourself."

"Wait." I lurched, almost toppling. "I'm on my knees."

But Don wasn't looking at me anymore. He was staring at Laurel, who was trembling, paler than ever. "You told me I was what gave your life meaning, didn't you?"

She nodded, a tear falling down her cheek. She was too vulnerable, too indoctrinated. I could see her thoughts twisting.

"You were a pathetic thing when we met. The runt of the litter. You were your friends' pet."

"Don't listen to him," I said. "None of that's true."

But Laurel's tears came faster now. There was an acceptance in her eyes that gutted me.

Don's voice deepened, and she leaned closer. "All these years, you've let me push you, test your limits. You've trusted me, and I've grown you, made you feel things you never would've without me. I made you a good woman. You owe me."

"He's lying," I said. "You were already good. Remember our life before him? You had your plays, we went to concerts and parties and sled in the snow. We were *happy*."

"But you killed Rachel. With the very dagger you're holding." Don shook his head. "If anyone finds out, what do you think's going to happen? Not every cop is our friend. They'll lock you up and throw away the key. Your poor mom will watch your trial. The woman will probably drop dead from shock. Then both your parents' deaths will be on your hands."

"*Don* killed Rachel," I said. "It was him doing it through you, pulling your strings. Everyone will see that."

But Laurel was sobbing now.

I staggered to my feet, but Don blocked me. "Be strong," he urged Laurel. "Be my best girl. Then no one will ever top you."

"Laurel, *please.*" My plea echoed through the room. Her head jerked, and our eyes locked. "Drop the knife. We can leave together, go somewhere safe. No one will blame you for anything." I tried to smile, but my lips wouldn't obey. "We'll tell them your story. Once they hear it, they'll understand."

It was all I wanted, to get it right this time.

"You remember what happened the last time you listened to her," Don said. "How lost and alone you were. Do what I say, Laurel. Obey me like a daughter should. Like a wife, to her husband. Die for me."

She looked at me, and I could see straight inside her to the wounds Don had made. I could see the good and bad of her, her loyalty and yearning, triumphs and disappointments, all the ways we'd failed each other. Most of all, I saw this: I'd wanted so badly for her to make it out. But for Laurel, there was no such thing as out. There was nothing but Don's voice, echoing through every chamber of her mind.

I lunged, crying, but it was too late—

Laurel pulled the knife, opened a seam across her throat, and unmade herself.

CHAPTER FORTY

Laurel Hargrove died for the second time, bleeding out on the floor. Her arterial blood dripped warm down my face, and that was it—there was nothing more to hold on to. I stood frozen, watching the blood soak the top of her ballgown, lost in a fog of shock.

"Look what I did," said Don, his voice awed.

Climb back, Shay, whispered a new voice, different from the insidious one, the echo of Don in my head. This new voice was as soft as Laurel's, with a brightness I remembered from her strong, healthy days. *Don't let him have you, too.*

I stared at Don, the king of the Paters. He held up his hands. "I didn't even touch her." He looked at me, and I swear to god, there was wonder in his eyes.

Then everything happened at once.

A heavy crash boomed upstairs, like something being smashed, and a scream rent the air. Deep voices shouted, and thundering footsteps shook the basement ceiling. It was the sound of chaos, of break-in and interruption.

Don and I reacted at the same time.

He lunged for me and I lunged for the ax. He slammed into my side shoulder-first, a tackle, and we both hit the floor so hard the air rushed from my lungs. I forced myself to my knees as Don scrambled behind me, seizing my ankles, pulling me back. I kicked, heart thundering like a rabbit's, and out of pure luck connected with his chin. His head snapped and I lurched forward, finding my feet again, trying for the ax but leaping away when he roared and dove for me.

I seized the wooden chair instead, adrenaline singing in my blood, and brought it down as hard as I could over his head. The wood snapped, shattering, and he reared back, a slash of blood down his face—bright and coppery, red and dripping. He gripped the wound and glared at me, his beautiful face distorted by blood and burning anger.

Pain peels back the layers, said the soft voice. *Give him more.*

"You won't make it out of this basement alive," Don said, so quiet I could barely hear him over the footsteps running above us. He wiped the blood from his face and braced himself against the floor. "I'll bury you and Laurel side by side."

I watched him, chest heaving, holding a leg of the chair, the piece that had broken off in my hand. I prayed the chaos upstairs meant Jamie's plan had worked.

I had to get up there—now or never. I whipped the chair leg at Don's face and took off, racing across the basement. Out of the corner of my eye I could see him, on his feet so fast. I heard a clatter, like he'd run into a table, and pushed my legs harder, eyes on the stairs.

But Don was strong, his wingspan wide. Stronger and taller by nature, like he used to say. My foot found the first step, and then he was there, gripping the back of my neck, fingers tangling in my hair. He shoved me down and my temple slammed against the stairs, thoughts unraveling. My muscles went limp.

He turned me over so I could see his bloodshot eyes, the scrape marring his face. He draped his body over mine so there was no escape, the crush of his hips like a lover's, and wrapped his hands tenderly around my throat. Right there, sprawled over the staircase, so close to freedom, Don choked me. We were right back to where we'd started. Hubris or repetition compulsion or savior complex, in the end it didn't matter. What mattered was I'd gone back into his house, and now I would never come out.

He leaned in close and whispered, "I'll never let you go."

At the top of the stairs, on the other side of the door, someone screamed, their indignation so sharp it lanced through the fog in my mind: "*Get your hands off the governor!*"

Don whipped his gaze to the top of the stairs. I could hear the whine of hinges, the sound of the door swinging open. And I felt it more than anything—the survivor's instinct, the voice whispering, *This is your chance.*

His fingers relaxed incrementally around my throat, and I reared up and sank my teeth into his cheek, tearing with my canines as best I could, tasting scruff and tangy blood, savage as a wolf. And when he yelled, that guttural sound, and withdrew his hands from my neck, I summoned strength from somewhere deep and shoved him with aching arms. The weight of Don's body lifted off me, an astounding release, so much air flooding my lungs I was drunk on it.

He rolled to the side of the staircase and screamed, clutching his cheek. I crawled down the stairs and across the basement floor, knees slipping in Laurel's blood but still moving. I could feel him rising behind me but forced myself not to turn, forced my slick hands to seize the hatchet. I rose on shaking legs just as he launched from the stairs and rushed me.

Ten years. My mind an enemy, my friends lost, one by one. I was painted in Laurel's blood, the soft flame of her voice alive only inside me now.

I let him get so close I could see the triumph on his face, then drove my foot hard into his gut, letting him double over, kicking him harder between the legs, smashing the blunt side of the ax against his head. He fell to his knees.

Footsteps pounded the stairs. Someone was coming.

I drew the blade against Don's throat, the handle sticky with blood. He looked up at me, chest heaving, dark eyes burning from his ruined face. When he swallowed, the ax moved with his Adam's apple, bobbing up and down.

Our eyes locked. And that's when I saw it: for the first time, after all these years.

Fear.

CHAPTER
FORTY-ONE

"Shay, *Jesus.*" A familiar voice boomed into the basement, and Jamie ran into my line of sight, hands covering his mouth. "What the fuck is happening?"

Sweat poured down my back. "I found Don."

Don didn't even glance at Jamie. He stayed locked on me. I gripped the hilt of the ax tighter.

Jamie's eyes fell on Laurel's body, the gory seam in her throat, and he staggered back. "Oh my god. He *killed* her."

I didn't correct him.

"Shay, what did he do? You're covered in blood."

I didn't take my eyes off Don. "Everything he could."

Jamie moved closer. Even though I could tell he was trying to sound calm, his voice shook. "The FBI is here. They're arresting people, and they're in the garden, digging. You did it. The Paters are done."

"We're never done," Don murmured, so low only I could hear.

Jamie talked fast. "The episode's everywhere. People are sharing it, they're calling the police, they're emailing journalists. When we called the FBI, they already knew."

Jamie's listeners were saving us. All those strangers, disrupting the safe, peaceful bubbles of their lives at our call for help.

Don's eyes slid to Jamie, taking measure. He looked at me and mouthed, *Him?*

I pushed the edge of the blade deeper, and he smiled.

"The FBI burst through the doors in the middle of the governor's speech," Jamie said, and I recognized his tone. It was his soothing voice. "Took him into custody in front of everyone. It's a madhouse, Shay. Come see. The feds are rounding people up, the press is recording everything. It's going to be the story of the decade." He inched closer. "They have their names—every Pater you uncovered. Don's not going anywhere. You can put the weapon down."

I could hear the raid unfolding, the screams and heavy footfalls.

It's not over, the soft voice whispered. *Not yet.*

Don's voice was silky. "Put the weapon down, dearest."

"It's okay," Jamie urged. "He'll be punished."

I tipped Don's chin higher, feeling like I did the night I told Cal I wasn't coming home, and he'd said I was crazy. I didn't know who to trust. My instincts, or everyone else?

"No," I said. "I'm not letting him go."

Jamie's voice dropped into an even gentler register, the one he used when I scared him. "The FBI will prosecute him, Shay. He's going to jail for the rest of his life. You did it." He put his hands up, modeling surrender. "I can see you're hurt. Your eyes... You're obviously in shock. I don't know if you're thinking clearly."

He was talking to me the same way I'd talked to Laurel.

"Hand me the ax," Jamie coaxed. "I'll make sure he stays here until the feds come down. Please, Shay. Let him go."

ASHLEY WINSTEAD

Let him go. That was what the world expected. What they always expect of women—grace, forgiveness, moral superiority. We were supposed to look our rapists in the eyes, the men who'd tortured us, and show them mercy.

"Shay." Jamie's voice took on a higher note, pleading. "You need to let them arrest him. It's the right way."

"Yes," Don said softly. "Let justice prevail."

His eyes sucked me in. My body was tingling. Sweat rolled over my cheeks—or was I crying? In my mouth, the taste of salt.

Jamie pressed his hands together, begging. "If you hurt him, they'll arrest you. We *won.*"

"You'll never win," Don said. "It's so much bigger than you or me. You saw what Laurel did."

Even if the FBI arrested Don, he'd get off, wouldn't he? Rich, powerful men like him always escaped, because other men wouldn't judge him harshly. A man didn't need to be a Pater to feel, deep inside, that small flame of solidarity...

"Shay, you're scaring me." Jamie tugged at my arm, but I shrugged him off.

Don had almost destroyed me. Him, and the rest of the ravenous men, hungry since I was young. All my life, they'd shaped my fears and desires, determined when I felt safe and when I was afraid. *That* was a fucking life sentence.

When would they ever stop?

"*Say* something," Jamie pleaded, but he was drowned out by the sound of heavy boots pounding down the stairs.

"Hands *up,*" a voice barked. Suddenly men flooded the room, their chests thick and square under bulletproof vests, helmets domes of protection, guns drawn high. Yellow letters on their backs screamed FBI.

Don's smile stretched ear to ear.

"*Ma'am,*" shouted one of the feds. "I said hands up. Drop the weapon."

"This is Nico Stagiritis," Jamie said. "He killed her friend. Please, Shay. Do what they say."

But I wasn't listening to them. In my head, a chorus of voices: *If the cops aren't going to do shit, I'll do it myself. I don't want to be like the girls who never come back. It's over. He won't do it again. You're communal property, baby. Remember how sweet she was. What a sweet girl, and a sweet friend. A darling daughter.*

Just between us girls, the soft voice whispered, *I think you always knew where this was going.*

Below me, on his knees, Don stopped smiling.

For Laurel, the voice whispered, and everything clicked.

For Laurel. And for me.

I swung the ax with ten years' worth of rage, with ghostly hands lending me strength, and sank it deep into Don's neck. A bullet clipped my shoulder, exploding pain, but what was pain to me? I wrenched the ax out and chopped until Don's blood flew, until his muscles gave, until his expression locked in shock forever, and his head tipped toward his shoulder. He tumbled to the floor.

The room exploded.

FBI agents rushed me, shoving me to the ground, twisting my throbbing arms behind my back, their shouted orders blurring into a wall of noise. But I didn't look at them. I didn't even look at Don's body next to Laurel's, close enough to touch.

I looked at Jamie. He'd fallen to his knees, lips mouthing a silent word.

"You have the right to remain silent," said an agent, snapping sharp handcuffs on my wrists. "Anything you say can be used against you in a court of law."

"Why?" Jamie breathed. His eyes were distant in a way I recognized, the dissociation that came with shock.

The agents pulled me to my feet, but I kept locked on him until his eyes rose to meet mine.

"Why?" he shouted. "Why are you *smiling*?"

Was I? I hadn't even felt it start.

The agents shoved me forward, one in front, two flanking my sides. My face dripped with blood. I could almost see myself: a living, breathing painting. Abstract expressionism, like a Pollock, art I'd made of myself.

I tipped back my head and laughed. Turned to Jamie and gave him the only word I had, the only one that could explain. It lingered behind me, filling the room as I finally made it up that dark staircase. It lifted my shoulders, stiffened my spine, as I climbed out from the depths of Don's basement, out of the doors of his house, into the wide, wide world.

Free.

EPILOGUE

Transgressions, *Episode 705, official transcript: "The Pater Society, Part One," aired January 3, 2023*

JAMIE KNIGHT: Welcome back to *Transgressions*. I'm your host, Jamie Knight. On September 26, 2022, this show aired an emergency episode, sharing snippets of recordings taken over the course of weeks by Shay Evans, then Shay Deroy, who infiltrated the Pater Society, a violent, patriarchal cult operating in secret across New York. Members included prominent New Yorkers such as then-Governor Alec Barry; financier Kurt Johnson, who used the aliases Don Rockwell and Nico Stagiritis, among others; and Westchester Chief of Police Adam Dorsey. The group was responsible for the deaths of several women, the exact number unknown at the time of airing. The FBI has since recovered the remains of five bodies from a Pater-owned property known as the Hilltop, including the body of Laurel Hargrove, a woman believed to have committed suicide a month earlier. Listeners will remember I featured Laurel on an earlier episode, calling attention to the suspicious circumstances of her death. Obviously, I'd only scratched the surface.

We did something extraordinary the day we aired our emergency episode. We not only asked you to listen, but to weigh our evidence, trust us, and help us bring down the Paters. We asked you to be part of the story.

You responded in an incredible show of solidarity, flooding social media and law enforcement phone lines, calling for exposés, sharing your own stories of abuse and harassment. You may have technically been in your homes or your cars, but for all purposes, you stormed the castle. And now you know—the whole *country* knows—that you not only brought down the Paters, but you helped save Shay Evans's life.

In the aftermath, we've witnessed a reckoning. There was the immediate resignation and charging of Governor Barry and key members of his staff, along with prominent figures on Wall Street, in the faith community, and in higher education. The DNC has assembled a task force to determine whether anyone in the organization turned a blind eye to Barry's involvement with the Paters. Mountainsong Church, whose former pastor Michael Corbin was outed as a Pater, has all but crumbled after congregants fled in droves. The Westchester County Police Department has been placed under a consent decree by the DOJ, with disturbing allegations that many rank-and-file officers were aware of the existence of the Paters, if not actively involved.

And following the revelation that Whitney College president Reginald Carruthers was both a member *and* participated in the cover-up of abuse allegations against Kurt Johnson eight years ago, the college's Board of Trustees has voted to virtually gut the current administration. The school's larger fate remains uncertain, however, as students have taken to campus-wide protests following a disturbing *60 Minutes* interview with Katie Harris, a Whitney College student who was preyed upon and lured into the Pater Society by Carruthers himself.

An unexpected silver lining of exposing the Paters has been the number of missing women, suspected Pater victims, who have come out of hiding now that they're no longer at risk. I'm sure many of you watched the moving *Today* show special in which several women and their families were interviewed. They explained how they feared for their lives when they decided to leave the Pater Society and thought disappearing was the only safe option. The FBI issued a statement saying they hope more women feel safe enough to come forward. They're also continuing to excavate known Pater properties across the state in search of bodies.

So far, a total of twenty-eight current and former male members of the Pater Society have been identified and charged with everything from sex trafficking, kidnapping, and conspiracy to insider trading and destruction of evidence. The startling reach of the Paters has prompted a wave of investigative reporting that continues to uncover former members. In a bizarre twist, reporters from *ProPublica* discovered that a few early known associates of Kurt Johnson, the Pater Society leader known as the Philosopher, went on to become high-ranking members of Nxivm, another so-called "sex cult" operating in upstate New York. While conspiracies continue to run wild as to how the two groups were connected, the discovery has prompted renewed questions about the ubiquity of groups like this, particularly among communities of wealthy, privileged people. In my opinion, the *New York Times* piece "What We Refuse to See," written by friend of the podcast Carmen Grant, is among the best of the recent reflections.

I'm recounting this history for two reasons. One, to tell you that no matter how much coverage the Pater Society has gotten in the four months since our podcast broke the news—no matter how much you may think you know—no one has the inside story we're about to share. The second and most important reason is to tell you that everything we've done to bring down the Paters will be for nothing if, in the end, we don't save Shay Evans.

Shay is facing a sentence of twenty years to life in prison for the murder of Kurt Johnson. You've heard from the news that she killed him while he was on his knees, in plain sight of FBI agents. You've flooded my inbox, wanting to know: What drove her to it? Isn't what Shay did as bad as what the Paters did? How could I have asked you to support a murderer? And I understand where you're coming from. Trust me, I do. It took me a long time to recover from what I witnessed that day. But reading your emails and DMs, I realized how badly you needed the whole story, because as Shay herself once told me, the story is everything. She knew from the beginning that it was her best defense, the thing that could stitch her together, show us her humanity. In the weeks I spent interviewing her, I'll confess I never realized she was testifying. She was always a step ahead.

So Shay and I are going to lay it out for you, and after we do, I hope you'll understand what she did was, in a larger sense, an act of self-defense. I hope you'll join me in campaigning for her charges to be dropped. Because the worst possible way this story could end would be if Kurt Johnson or the State of New York took away Shay's life after she finally freed herself.

This story is hers to tell, not mine, so in a *Transgressions* first, she and I are going to host together. We're editing and recording this three-part Pater series while Shay is on house arrest, bound by an ankle monitor, awaiting trial. Shay's going to start by reading from the beginning of her book manuscript, a work in progress called *The Last Housewife*. We'll continue to incorporate passages from her book throughout the series. To set the scene, she's written her manuscript in this Day-Glo purple notebook, which she's opening now. Every time I see it, it reminds me of a notebook she had when we were kids. And despite everything, it makes me feel hopeful. Okay. Shay?

(*Silence.*)

SHAY EVANS: Thank you, Jamie, for this opportunity. To everyone listening...thank you for what you did, and for being open to hearing what I have to say. I'm going to start, actually, with a transgression, because I'm a longtime listener, and I know that's what you do here. My transgression is that I don't regret killing him. Not for a second.

JAMIE: Shay—

SHAY: Let me show you why. I want to take you back to the beginning.

(*Throat clearing.*)

If I can get the words out.

(*Deep breath.*)

PART FOUR
Scheherazade, you sooty phoenix

Emerging from the ashes, my whole life burned away, I have no stories left but the truth. The words I've been waiting for flood like an avalanche, a rushing river of meaning I can't stop. You may not want this, but I'm going to address it to you anyway, out of hope. If nothing else, at least I'm writing it myself, my own dusty historian, working late into the night. (Picture me like this, dear sisters, as I speak to you.)

Before we begin, I need you to know: We no longer exist for them, you and I. We are no longer a mirror reflecting their anxieties, their desires. We are not saviors, or seductresses, or symbols. We exist only for ourselves. Tragic and sublime, ordinary and animal, in the mold of all humans, long before and long after us.

They will tell you you've done the right thing.

They will tell you you've made a grave error.

Pay them no mind.

Talk to me instead...

Tell me about the time you looked up at the moon when you were a child and imagined it was looking back. Tell me about the moment your body first fit against the curves of another's, and you felt at home. Tell me how you've ached to be bigger than this mortal life could grant, bigger than they would allow, how you've carried that ache in the center of your chest every hour of your life, the pain like a festering wound, a shrine to the bittersweet agony of being alive.

Tell me these things, and I will tell you I know you.

Let's show each other our pieces, and tell each other we understand. It's the strongest power we possess, the transfiguration of the unfathomable into something we can recognize, something that bridges the gulfs between us.

So I'll start over, from the beginning. I promise not to leave anything out. I'll let you see all of me, who I used to be, all the dark corners. That way you'll know you're not alone. That way, when it's your turn, you can do it better. That way, when it's time for a verdict, I hope you'll choose mercy.

This is the story I tell you to save my life.

Read on for a look at

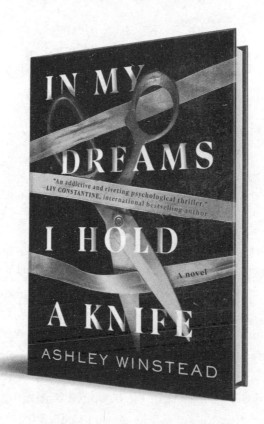

Available now from Sourcebooks Landmark

CHAPTER 1
NOW

Your body has a knowing. Like an antenna, attuned to tremors in the air, or a dowsing rod, tracing things so deeply buried you have no language for them yet. The Saturday it arrived, I woke taut as a guitar string. All day I felt a hum of something straightening my spine, something I didn't recognize as anticipation until the moment my key slid into the mailbox, turned the lock, and there it was. With all the pomp and circumstance you could count on Duquette University to deliver: a thick, creamy envelope, stamped with the blood-red emblem of Blackwell Tower in wax along the seam. The moment I pulled it out, my hands began to tremble. I'd waited a long time, and it was finally here.

As if in a dream, I crossed the marble floor of my building and entered the elevator, faintly aware of other people, stops on other floors, until finally we reached eighteen. Inside my apartment, I locked the door, kicked my shoes to the corner, and tossed my keys on the counter. Against my rules, I dropped onto my ivory couch in workout clothes, my spandex tights still damp with sweat.

I slid my finger under the flap and tugged, slitting the envelope, ignoring the small bite of the paper against my skin. The heavy invitation sprang out, the words bold and raised. *You are formally invited to Duquette University Homecoming, October 5–7.* A sketch of Blackwell Tower in red ink, so tall the top of the spire nearly broke into the words. *We look forward to welcoming you back for reunion weekend, a beloved Duquette tradition. Enclosed please find your invitation to the Class of 2009 ten-year reunion party. Come relive your Duquette days and celebrate your many successes—and those of your classmates—since leaving Crimson Campus.*

A small red invitation slid out of the envelope when I shook it. I laid it next to the larger one in a line on the coffee table, smoothing my fingers over the embossed letters, tapping the sharp right angles of each corner. My breath hitched, lungs working like I was back on the stationary bike. *Duquette Homecoming.* I couldn't pinpoint when it had become an obsession—gradually, perhaps, as my plan grew, solidified into a richly detailed vision.

I looked at the banner hanging over my dining table, spelling out C-O-N-G-R-A-T-U-L-A-T-I-O-N-S-! I'd left it there since my party two weeks ago, celebrating my promotion—the youngest woman ever named partner at consulting giant Coldwell & Company New York. There'd even been a short write-up about it in the *Daily News*, taking a feminist angle about young female corporate climbers. I had the piece hanging on my fridge—removed when friends came over—and six more copies stuffed into my desk drawer. The seventh I'd mailed to my mother in Virginia.

That victory, perfectly timed ahead of this. I sprang from the couch to the bathroom, leaving the curtains open to look over the city. I was an Upper East Side girl now; I had been an East House girl in college. I liked the continuity of it, how my life was still connected to who I'd been back then. *Come relive your Duquette days,* the invitation said. As I stood in front of the bathroom mirror, the words acted like a spell. I closed my eyes and remembered.

Walking across campus, under soaring Gothic towers, the dramatic architecture softened by magnolia trees, their thick curved branches, waxy leaves, and white blooms so dizzyingly perfumed they could pull you in, close enough to touch, before you blinked and realized you'd wandered off the sidewalk. College: a freedom so profound the joy of it didn't wear off the entire four years.

The brick walls of East House, still the picture in my head when I thought of home, though I'd lived there only a year. And the Phi Delt house at midnight, music thundering behind closed doors, strobe lights flashing through the windows, students dressed for one of the theme parties Mint was always dreaming up. The spark in my stomach every time I walked up the stone steps, eyes rimmed in black liner, arm laced through Caro's. The whole of it intoxicating, even before the red cups came out.

Four years of living life like it was some kind of fauvist painting, days soaked in vivid colors, emotions thick as gesso. Like it was some kind of play, the highs dramatic cliff tops, the lows dark valleys. Our ensemble cast as stars, ever since the fall of freshman year, when we'd won our notoriety and our nickname. The East House Seven. Mint, Caro, Frankie, Coop, Heather, Jack, and me.

The people responsible for the best days of my life, and the worst.

But even at our worst, no one could have predicted that one of us would never make it out of college. Another, accused of murdering her. The rest of us, spun adrift. East House Seven no longer an honor but an accusation, splashed across headlines.

I opened my eyes to the bathroom mirror. For a second, eighteen-year-old Jessica Miller looked back at me, virgin hair undyed and in

IN MY DREAMS I HOLD A KNIFE

need of the kind of haircut that didn't exist in Norfolk, Virginia. Bony-elbowed with the skinniness of a teenager, wearing one of those pleated skirts, painted nails. Desperate to be seen.

A flash, and then she was gone. In her place stood thirty-two-year-old Jessica, red-faced and sweaty, yes, but polished in every way a New York consultant's salary could manage: blonder, whiter-teethed, smoother-skinned, leaner and more muscled.

I studied myself the way I'd done my whole life, searching for what others saw when they looked at me.

I wanted them to see perfection. I ached for it in the deep, dark core of me: to be so good I left other people in the dust. It wasn't an endearing thing to admit, so I'd never told anyone, save a therapist, once. She'd asked if I thought it was possible to be perfect, and I'd amended that I didn't need to be perfect, per se, as long as I was the best.

An even less endearing confession: sometimes—rarely, but some-times—I felt I was perfect, or at least close.

Sometimes I stood in front of the bathroom mirror, like now, slowly brushing my hair, examining the straight line of my nose, the pronounced curves of my cheekbones, thinking: *You are beautiful, Jessica Miller*. Sometimes, when I thought of myself like a spreadsheet, all my assets tallied, I was filled with pride at how objectively good I'd become. At thirty-two, career on the rise, summa cum laude degree from Duquette, Kappa sorority alum, salutatorian of Lake Granville High. An enviable list of past boyfriends, student loans *finally* paid off, my own apartment in the most prestigious city in the world, a full closet and a fuller passport, high SAT scores. Any way you sliced it, I was *good*. Top percentile of human beings, you could say, in terms of success.

But no matter how much I tried to cling to the shining jewels of my accomplishments, it never took long before my shadow list surfaced. Everything I'd ever failed at, every second place, every rejection,

387

mounting, mounting, mounting, until the suspicion became unbearable, and the hairbrush clattered to the sink. In the mirror, a new vision. The blond hair and white teeth and expensive cycling tights, all pathetic attempts to cover the truth: that I, Jessica Miller, was utterly mediocre and had been my entire life.

No matter how I tried to deny it, the shadow list would whisper: *You only became a consultant out of desperation, when the path you wanted was ripped away. Kappa, salutatorian? Always second best. Your SAT scores, not as high as you were hoping.* It said I was as ordinary and unoriginal as my name promised: *Jessica*, the most common girl's name the year I was born; *Miller*, one of the most common surnames in America for the last hundred years. The whole world awash in Jessica Millers, a dime a dozen.

I never could tell which story was right—Exceptional Jessica, or Mediocre Jessica. My life was a narrative I couldn't parse, full of conflicting evidence.

I picked the brush out of the sink and placed it carefully on the bathroom counter, then thought better, picking it up and ripping a nest of blond hair from the bristles. I balled the hair in my fingers, feeling the strands tear.

This was why Homecoming was so important. No part of my life looked like I'd imagined during college. Every dream, every plan, had been crushed. In the ten years since I'd graduated, I'd worked tirelessly to recover: to be beautiful, successful, fascinating. To create the version of myself I'd always wanted people to see. Had it worked? If I could go back to Duquette and reveal myself to the people whose opinions mattered most, I would read the truth in their eyes. And then I'd know, once and for all, who I really was.

READING
GROUP GUIDE

1. What do you think of true-crime podcasts? What effect do they have on the investigation and development of real-life cases?

2. Shay is not always sure how to navigate her own beauty. How would you describe her relationship to her appearance? How does society punish women who don't conform to beauty standards but also those who do?

3. Shay references the constant anxiety of being a woman in public. Are you familiar with the feeling? Can you think of anything that would make that fear go away without requiring women to change their behavior?

4. How does Don co-opt the idea of feminism to first introduce his ideas about the roles of men and women to Shay, Clem, and Laurel? Why do you think that tactic is so effective?

5. How do Jamie and Shay differ in their definitions of consent? How would you personally define consent?

6. What is Jamie's primary motivation throughout the book? How would you characterize his relationship with Shay?

7. Nicole argues that loving pain is the only autonomy she can get. Where is she coming from? Would you argue with her?

8. Jamie and Shay almost lose hope when they realize the governor is within the Pater Society's realm of influence. How does their emergency podcast broadcast circumvent this problem? Who can we trust when our highest authorities are corrupt?

9. Shay persists in viewing Laurel as a victim. Do you agree? What do Shay's expectations for Laurel prevent Shay from seeing?

10. Why does Shay decide to take Don's punishment into her own hands? Can you imagine what choice you would make in her position? What will happen to Shay now?

A CONVERSATION
WITH THE AUTHOR

The concept of beauty carries danger throughout the book, but it doesn't seem to be within Shay's control. Do you think it's possible to truly weaponize beauty? Could Shay accomplish such a thing?

On the one hand, of course beauty holds power. While what's considered beautiful is culturally dependent, being perceived as beautiful tends to be an advantage universally. Look at any number of psychological studies on attractiveness and it's easy to see that those who are considered attractive have innate social advantages. Speaking from within a white Western historical context, beauty has historically mattered more for women, because it's been one of the few advantages at women's disposal. When power is scarce, you'll snap up anything. Think about when women weren't allowed to work or control their own finances, and their fate rested on who they married—in those circumstances, beauty was at least somewhat of a power you could wield to have some measure of control over your life. Of course, you can already see in this example the double-edged sword of beauty: not only its limits compared to other forms of power (money, positions of influence, etc.), but the fact that it requires a beholder to grant power in the first place. Beauty's power is a precarious and contingent one.

A lot of scholars have written fascinatingly about beauty, so I won't retread territory, but I will say that in modern Western society, even as women accumulate more hard power—jobs, influence, capital— beauty remains something women cling to disproportionately. In one sense, it's natural: we all want to be capable of attracting others. That's nothing to sneer at. But on the larger whole, I wonder if our obsession with beauty is a vestigial instinct, one that shows women haven't made the kinds of gains in hard power we should have, so we still need the assist.

If a beautiful woman is the last person left on earth, does her beauty matter? Maybe in some abstract sense, but pragmatically, no. Beauty is always a two-way street. So who holds the true power: the beautiful person or the person looking? If you've read anything about the male gaze, you're probably yelling *The looker!* But this is the tension Shay struggles with throughout the book, especially in her adolescence. Because she has so little power otherwise—no financial security, little in the way of emotional support, teachers who don't give her brain the same credit they give Jamie's—beauty comes to seem like this incredible boon, the one thing she has. Which is especially complicated given that from the moment Shay hits puberty and starts to get noticed by men, she understands this sort of attention is also dangerous and uncomfortable.

But what else does she have to lean on? She uses her beauty in the pageants to get out of Heller; she uses it in her dalliances with boys and men to bolster her social power. The problem is, as we discussed, it can be hard to discern who's really in charge. Shay misunderstands the power dynamics with Anderson Thomas in high school and with Don in college to great and tragic consequence. While of course Shay has more opportunities than women 150 years ago, in some uncomfortable ways, her life looks similar to the life of the woman I described earlier, whose beauty afforded her the only measure of control over her life. This is the great irony of the Paters: they're obsessed with returning to the good old days when men "rightfully" held all the hard power and women were reliant on them, but as Nicole points out, for a lot of women, particularly those not born into economic privilege, there's no need to return—life still looks like that.

Why did you decide to include Cal in Shay's life? How did her marriage change the way the story developed?

Cal is the bridge that connects the extraordinary misogyny of the Paters to the ordinary misogyny of everyday life. To back up, he's part of the life Shay's built for herself that she thinks proves she's moved on and put the horrible tragedy of what happened in college behind her. Her job writing for *The Slice*, her nice home, her ability to write full-time, her marriage: these are all markers of success. She's living the life of privilege her mother could only dream of, and she should be happy. But of course Shay's not happy, and all of it, including her marriage, is a shield, a way of saying *Look at me, a normal woman with a normal life; nothing to see here.* It's a long, protracted performance.

The moment the reality of her past crashes into her safe new life with the news of Laurel's death, Shay begins a process of awakening that starts with looking around her house and thinking about her marriage to Cal and realizing it all feels suffocating, though she can't put her finger on why. Throughout the story, as Shay comes to understand herself better and confront what drove her to Don, she starts to see with horror that Don and Cal exist on a spectrum, and in many ways she's only repeated her past in building her life with Cal. With both

Don and Cal, Shay is initially drawn to them because they are important men who, if conquered, will prove her power. The fact that this is a fantasy is revealed when both relationships pretty quickly show themselves for what they are: with Don, a tyrant-subject relationship; with Cal, an imbalanced marriage where he, the husband, holds the hard power. Both men dissemble to justify themselves and keep this status quo: Don through his teachings, Cal through his insistence that what he's doing with their credit cards and acting as Shay's social director are normal and there's no such thing as a power hierarchy between a married couple.

For Shay, just like Don and Cal exist on the same spectrum, so too does the Pater-Daughter relationship and marriage. Once she begins confronting uncomfortable truths and her eyes open, she can't help but feel all the ways being married to Cal is too close to being yoked to Don. I hope when readers encounter Cal they think he's normal and horrible at the same time, because in a sly way I wanted to shine a light on the gendered power dynamics still baked into the institution of heterosexual marriage. While there may not be a lot of Dons out there, I think there are a lot of Cals, and that's almost as upsetting.

Shay has a hard time identifying the feeling of power, because for most of her life it's been blurred into one kind of submission or another. If you had to pick a moment in the book where Shay was the most powerful, what would it be?

This may be the obvious answer, but I wrote the scene where she beheads Don as the moment when she is the most untethered by anything she should do and instead does the thing her heart and gut tell her she needs to do to feel safe, at peace, and like she has achieved some semblance of justice. Shay doesn't listen to the FBI (authority figures) or Jamie (a person she loves) or the law (what society demands of her) or morality (what she knows people expect from a good person). She chooses herself above it all, come what may. And that action represents both an old definition of power in the sense that it's the power sovereigns have historically wielded—they are the one person above the law and the one entitled to mete out executions—and a personally meaningful kind of power, as Shay is a woman whose life has always been shaped by other people's power over her.

Is it tragic that Shay believes her only avenue for true freedom and power is through this act of violence? Absolutely. Is she right? I think readers should decide for themselves, but for me, yes. Of course, right or wrong, Shay's power is short-lived. After she kills Don, she's arrested and exists at the mercy of her forthcoming judge and jury, as well as the public. Where once she was performing the story of herself for men, now she performs for a public who holds her fate in their hands. Just like she says to Jamie during one of her interviews, she's always taking one step forward, then two back. But, as Jamie points out, what else can we as human beings do other than try our best again and again, hoping it won't turn out to be a Sisyphean exercise.

Throughout the book, you complicate the definition of *victim*. Why doesn't Shay consider herself a victim, even though she views Laurel within that archetype up to the very end?

Shay has access to her own interiority, her thoughts and feelings, which means she has a damning record of every time she had a complicated reaction: when she *wanted* Don to do to her what others might consider something bad or *wanted* to see violence enacted against Laurel or felt like something Don did to Clem was justified. It's that old adage: examine anyone too closely and you'll find a sinner. Well, Shay has the misfortune of being very self-aware, which means she sees her flaws with great clarity.

For a long time, her agonizing awareness of her own complicity prevents her from feeling like she can be called a victim. But as she works with Jamie to stitch her life story together, she learns to view her decisions and reactions in context, see how things are connected, and that context opens the possibility for empathy for herself. Not only that, but she begins to see that by being radically honest about her thoughts and feelings, she opens space for other people to have empathy for her as well. For example, Shay's crime of murdering Don sounds unforgivable on paper; the same crime told within the context of her life becomes understandable (or so she hopes, which is why she tells her story through the podcast).

As for Laurel, Shay has always given other people more grace and empathy than she's given herself. I think that's a very human trait, to forgive and understand things in other people that we can't forgive about ourselves. And so she's able to contextualize Laurel's decisions, see the extenuating circumstances, from the beginning. That's what drives her relentless attempts to pull Laurel out of the Pater Society. Shay and Laurel in some respects have opposite arcs: while Shay learns to view herself as more the victim of circumstances, she learns to view Laurel as less so. By the end of the book, I think Shay has let go of the idea that Laurel is a victim. *And yet* she still believes she's worth saving.

While some readers might look at Shay's refusal to give up on Laurel as naive or the result of Shay's savior complex (and they might be right!), I also see it as an outgrowth of the fact that Shay believes she knows the real Laurel, that Shay understands that sometimes life puts us in the position to make bad choices that then become life- and identity-defining, and given all of that, she cannot abandon her friend. To do so would condemn Laurel to harm or death. And when it comes to Laurel, Shay simply will not abandon empathy. A provocative question is why Shay can forgive Laurel's evils but not Don's. That question may seem obvious or even offensive, but there's been a lot of work in the justice reform world around radical forgiveness as a form of healing, and some argue forgiveness—even of people who have committed the very worst crimes—is more powerful than the kind of retribution Shay shows Don. The concept of justice continues to fascinate me because there are no easy answers.

The story of Scheherazade is a resonant frame for *The Last Housewife*. What attracted you to that myth? How does Shay differ from Scheherazade?

As readers might know, the story of Scheherazade is a frame narrative for *The Thousand and One Nights*, a collection of stories whose origins can be traced to India and Iran. The gender dynamics of the Scheherazade story are stark: It begins with a king whose ego has been wrecked by his unfaithful wife, and so he has her beheaded. Then, in a long, protracted revenge against women writ large (so it seems), he continues to wed a new bride every day and has her beheaded the following dawn. One by one, the kingdom empties of women until Scheherazade, whose father is in the king's service as the executioner, steps in and volunteers to be the next bride. In some versions of the story, her sister aids her, but in all versions, Scheherazade essentially compels the king into sparing her life anew each night by hooking him with an unfinished story. This is obviously supposed to demonstrate both the power of stories and Scheherazade's cleverness. But it's always struck me that her victory—after one thousand and one nights, the king comes to love her and makes her his permanent bride—is such a horrible one. A life sentence, married to a misogynist murderer.

The myth of Scheherazade the storyteller has taken up a lot of my mental real estate over the years. I find it so powerful and gutting, the idea of having to tell a story every night with your life on the line. In a way, it's what we all do. We live and die by the stories we tell about who we are, who our families are, what kind of community or country we live in, how the world is supposed to work. In the myth, Scheherazade is presented as a very clever woman who always seems to be one step ahead, but I envision this storytelling as frantic, constant, feverish work. I liken it to the work of weaving yourself together, the burden of having to keep yourself cohesive and legible.

The myth seems such an obvious parallel to not only individual identity construction but the contortions women have historically had to perform to be acceptable to men. To be intriguing and endlessly alluring but never threatening. There are so many stories that have been told—and that women have participated in telling—about what defines womanhood, what comes naturally to women. And this very need for constant storytelling, this feverish stitching together, this performance, reveals the fact that at its center is empty air. There is nothing that defines a woman, just like there's nothing that defines a man—"essential" gender truths are in reality arbitrary stories repeated over time until they've concretized. The more I thought about Scheherazade, the more I became obsessed with the idea of a different ending: Scheherazade not just tricking the king into marrying her, but taking a more radical—if more violent—freedom and power for herself.

Don twists feminist principles to his own advantage as he courts Shay, Clem, and Laurel. How did their upbringings make this possible?

What makes Don good at being a cult leader is that he can ferret out people's vulnerabilities and use them to manipulate people into doing what he wants. And so he's able to home in on each of the girls' needs, fears, and desires and hooks them in tailored ways. For Laurel, who grieves the loss of her father specifically and a parental authority figure more broadly (her mom abandons this role as a consequence of her own grief), Don offers himself as a father figure. He gives her comfort and attention, but also acts as the disciplinarian, playing on her trauma and fears about the world, and especially her guilt, offering her punishments in exchange for redemption. He also understands Laurel feels inadequate compared to Shay and Clem, and so by giving her a leg up and preferential treatment, he makes her indebted to him.

With Clem, he attacks her autonomy and iconoclastic instincts—the very things that make her a powerful force of resistance to him in the beginning—by twisting them into flaws. He plays on Clem's pain over being so different from her family growing up, and her residual fear of being ostracized, to manipulate and bully her into submission. For Shay, Don uses the fact that she's high on her own beauty and influence, her own sense of power, to make her think she's in control of their relationship, that he's in thrall to her. And by the time he pulls back the curtain to show it's the opposite, that he's been pulling the strings the whole time, it's too late. Shay's already done things she can't take back, and he's already wedged himself into her brain. But of course Don couldn't have even gotten that far if he hadn't been so successful in the beginning, luring them in by exploiting tensions within feminism over what makes good and bad feminists. Ironically, attending a progressive school like Whitney, where they were taught to think about such things, made them primed to be hooked.

Which character surprised you the most as you wrote *The Last Housewife*?

Two characters: Nicole and Don. Don ended up being cleverer and more in tune with current conversations than I originally imagined him. When I started writing Don, I envisioned this man who exulted in antiquated worldviews and mannerisms and social dynamics. But as I started to write him, I discovered how clever he actually was, the ways he and his Paters could twist contemporary feminism and debates over ideology and community—concerns about alienation and rising rates of depression and identity politics and safety and new forms of "us vs. them" debates—to their advantage. And of course this is what so many skilled cult leaders are able to do: they meet people where they're at.

Nicole surprised me by how sharp-tongued she is, and how funny—in essence, how self-aware. It took me several rewrites to really understand that what keeps her attached to the Paters isn't that she's brainwashed or not seeing clearly but actually that she sees all too well. Because of the experiences she's had being taken advantage of and mistreated in every aspect of her life—from family to religion to romantic relationships and on—she's jaded. She sees through the layers of bullshit coating everyday life and polite society and decides "normal life" is so similar to life with the Paters that she might as well try her hand with them. She thinks at least the Paters are honest and there's some possibility of elevating her position, creating the kind of comfortable, cared-for life she doesn't believe she could have access to otherwise.

Your stories are deliciously chilling. Do you ever scare yourself when you write? Would readers be surprised by the parts that scare you most?

This is the first book I've ever scared myself writing! I don't often get spooked writing scary scenes—creepy chases or even murders—because my mind is so wrapped up in orchestrating the mechanics. When I scare myself, it's usually in more existential moments: when a line about the way the world works just appears from my subconscious, or when I think of just the right way to take a character's darkness to another level. I'll write it in a flow state, then step back, look at it, and think, *Wow, that is dark.* And then I'll get the chills. Maybe what I'm really scared of is myself.

ACKNOWLEDGMENTS

Thank you, first and foremost, to my readers. I've never needed to write a book more nor been more terrified to publish than this one. This book is dark and personal and deals with subject matter some people argue doesn't belong in books, films, TV, and so on, despite its continuing prevalence in the real world. After I wrote it, I was worried I'd done the wrong thing. I drew on many of my own experiences in writing this story, but more than being afraid of people reading it, I was afraid that the fact that it involves sexual violence meant no one would. That the book I was most proud of, the story that was so important to me, would be met with a resounding wall of "No thank you, not for me." It's a strange position to be in to want to respect people's desire not to confront something while burning with the need to talk about it, make art about it, be heard. I'm oversharing in the hopes that you will understand the depth of my gratitude when I say thank you for taking a chance on this book.

Enormous thanks to Shana Drehs, my wonderful editor. It's a

privilege to work with you. Your compassion and care radiate through every interaction, and your brilliant insights and suggestions made this book what it is. Thank you for taking it on.

To my incredible agent, Melissa Edwards, who chills me out and keeps me brave. Thank you for seeing something in this book and not letting me give up on it. Thank you also for being the best partner and advocate. I'm so grateful for you.

Thanks to the entire fabulous Sourcebooks team, including my publicist, Cristina Arreola; my copy editor, Dianne Dannenfeldt; Heather Hall; Heather VenHuizen; Stephanie Rocha; Ashley Holstrom; Emily Luedloff; Madeleine Brown; Sara Walker; and, for the cover of my dreams, Lauren Harms.

Dee Hudson, thank you so much for your astute insight and editorial skills. I'm forever grateful to you and Tessera Editorial.

To the Kaye Publicity team—Dana Kaye, Julia Borcherts, Hailey Dezort, Jordan Brown, Nicole Leimbach: Thank you for being the best in the business. It's a joy to work with you.

Huge thanks to my critique partners Kate Boswell, Lyssa Smith, and Ann Fraistat. You each braved dark places for me, and for that, I'm eternally grateful. You are brilliant minds and incredible writers, and I'm so lucky to have you.

To my family: Melissa, Ron, Ryan, Amanda, Celeste, Ezra, Taylor, Catherine, and Mallory. I love you all, and I'll always believe in the Winstead magic. Dad, Ryan, and Taylor, thank you for being feminists. Mom and Mallory, thank you for being the women I count on the most.

Alex, thank you for being comfortable with me writing a book about how marriage can chafe, and for working with me to create a marriage we both find empowering and full of joy. To speak in your language, my love for you is like the expanding universe: it has no center and no end.

Huge, glorious thanks to the Bookstagram community for the

incredible support you've shown me since I debuted. Special shout-out to Gare (@gareindeedreads), Kori (@thrillbythepage_), Krissy (@books_and_biceps9155), Marisha (@marishareadsalot), Chelsea (@thrillerbookbabe), Amy (@captivatedpages), Steph (@bookishopinion), Phil (@philsbookcorner), Jamie (@beautyandthebook), Chip (@booksovrbros), Abby (@crimebythebook), Yenny (@readswithyenny), Dennis (@scaredstraightreads), Marc (@marcsbookblog), Elodie (@elosreadingcorner), Jordan (@jordys.book.club), Leslie Ann (@lalalifebookclub), Kayla (@booksandlala), Tonya (@blondethrillerbooklover), Chelsea (@bookish.chels), Emily (@emilybookedup), Nikki (@poetry.and.plot.twists), Jordān (@jordans.book.club), and Hannah (@read_betweenthecovers). I wish we could all meet for drinks and book talk in real life!

Thanks also to the writers in the crime fiction community who have gone out of their way to welcome me: Andrea Bartz, Lynne Constantine, Valerie Constantine, Riley Sager, Layne Fargo, Julie Clark, Darby Kane, Eliza Jane Brazier, Megan Collins, Laurie Elizabeth Flynn, Amber Garza, Jaime Lynn Hendricks, Vanessa Lillie, Samantha Downing, Jennifer Hillier, Wendy Walker, Alison Wisdom, Yasmin Angoe, and especially Amy Gentry. I'm in awe of your talents and so grateful for your many kindnesses.

Lastly, to everyone who reads this book and wonders if it's pointed at them: Yes, it is. I hope your minds stay restless.

ABOUT THE AUTHOR

Ashley Winstead is the author of *In My Dreams I Hold a Knife* and *Fool Me Once*. In addition, she's a painter and former academic. She received her BA in English, creative writing, and art history from Vanderbilt University and her PhD in English from Southern Methodist University, where she studied twenty-first-century fiction, the philosophy of language, and the politics of narrative forms. She lives in Houston, Texas, with her husband and two cats. Find out more at ashleywinstead.com.

PHOTO (C) LUIS NOBLE